PRAISE FOR *The Ticket Out*

"Helen Knode has written a first mystery that is highly literate, exceptionally action-packed and occasionally harrowing, and (best of all) insightful about films and the people who try to make them."
—*Chicago Tribune*

"This smart novel, packed with an insider's viewpoint on Hollywood and the film industry, is an indictment of the star system and Hollywood's manufacture of "products" rather than "art."... It successfully catapults desire, greed and ambition into murder and gruesome acts of violence." —*USA Today*

"Knode's first novel makes the most of her experience as a former film critic, turning the seemingly lethal ambitions of many L.A. denizens into an actual murderous romp. Ann Whitehead is, you guessed it, a burned-out film critic who discovers a dead screenwriter in her bathtub; sensing a great story, she tries to unravel the mystery in between dodging bullets, her editor, and the cops. Knode's heroine is wholly likable, and the plot zips along with fun Hollywood-insider details." —*Entertainment Weekly*

"Part noir lament, part witty liberal rant, this masterful first novel from Knode—the wife of bestselling crime writer James Ellroy—is fast-paced and complex." —*Book Magazine*

"She offers a juicy portrait of contemporary L.A. in which Hollywood's elite kill one another for script ideas and follow secret passages from MGM to a high-end whorehouse.... Knode's clever, sophisticated plotting packs a punch." —*Publishers Weekly*

"Old Hollywood collides with new Hollywood in Helen Knode's intricate and engaging first novel, *The Ticket Out*, and except for the mythic starlets, none of it is pretty. Which, of course, makes for delicious crime fiction.... Although Knode shares some of the L.A.-noir sensibilities of her husband, James Ellroy, her voice is all her own." —*The Kansas City Star*

THE TICKET OUT

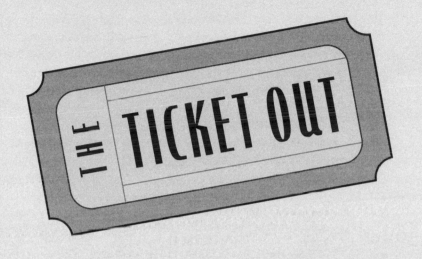

THE TICKET OUT

Helen Knode

A HARVEST BOOK • HARCOURT, INC.

Orlando Austin New York San Diego Toronto London

www.HarcourtBooks.com

*This is a work of fiction. Names, characters, places, organizations,
and events are the products of the author's imagination or are used
fictitiously, and any resemblance to actual persons, living or dead,
events, or locales is entirely coincidental.*

Library of Congress Cataloging-in-Publication Data
Knode, Helen.
The ticket out/Helen Knode — 1st ed.
p.   cm.
ISBN 0-15-100184-7
ISBN 0-15-602905-7 (pbk)
1. Women film critics—Fiction. 2. Motion picture industry—
Fiction. 3. Hollywood (Los Angeles, Calif.)—Fiction.   I. Title.
PS3611.N63 T53 2003
813'.6 dc21   2002007804

Text set in Electra
Designed by Cathy Riggs

Printed in the United States of America
First Harvest edition 2004
K J I H G F E D C B A

To James Ellroy

THE TICKET OUT

CHAPTER
ONE

THE MOVIE lost me way early on. I sighed, uncrossed my legs, and stuck them in the aisle. Mark poked me. He whispered, "Stop it. Sit still."

I said, "If this tuna doesn't end soon, I'm going to shoot myself."

Mark patted my arm. I pictured the gun I kept in a closet at home, and laughed out loud.

Someone said, *"Sssh!"* Two people in the row ahead of us turned around.

I bit my lip and slumped down lower. The theater was packed with journalists. A new Tom Cruise movie was always an event, and the studio had put us in their largest screening room. I picked the major critics out of the crowd and tried to guess what they were thinking. Their faces were blank, of course: their jobs were too political for them to let their real feelings show. But I could guess what the feature writers were thinking. They were worried how much time they'd have with Cruise and how much space they'd get after the photo spread. They had no choice about the movie; they had to be nice. Sometimes I envied them.

I sighed again. Mark reached over and tapped my notebook with his pen. He whispered, "Write."

"Can't I please go?"

Mark pointed at my notebook. I flipped to a new page and looked up at the screen. Tom Cruise was kissing Penelope Cruz on a background of dark bedsheets. He dabbed at her mouth while the camera and music tried to make it sexy.

I stopped myself from laughing again. I'd never bought Cruise as a romantic hero. The film could be set in the nineteenth century or cyberspace; it didn't matter. He was a plastic corporate doll. He made love like a guy who'd answer to CEOs if he mixed his bodily fluid with the costar's.

I shut my notebook and started to get up. Mark looked over. I whispered, "I'll be right back."

He nodded and I walked up the aisle to the lobby. Out in the light I checked the press kit for a running time. The movie still had an hour left. I found an upholstered bench, lay down, and closed my eyes. There was the rest of this screening, then Barry's party tonight. I didn't want to go to his useless party. I wanted to be alone to think.

Something was very wrong with me. I'd been acting unprofessional and I couldn't figure out why. Over the past month I'd missed a deadline and refused to write about the fall season. I just couldn't get enthusiastic about *Harry Potter*—or even a new David Lynch film. It wasn't normal. The summer movies were bad, but low morale was no excuse. There'd been bad periods before and I didn't miss deadlines or fight Mark's assignments. No one had said anything at the paper yet. But there were hints that I might be in trouble.

If I was in trouble, I knew Mark would take my side. I didn't know, though, if Mark could protect me from our boss. Barry's attitude about Hollywood had changed. He'd softened up toward the studios and started to interfere in the film section; he said he wanted our coverage to be more "mainstream." Mark and I were having a hard time believing it. On every other topic, the *L.A. Millennium* was raucously un-mainstream: we couldn't believe that Barry Melling would cave in to Hollywood. We also knew that the pressure to cave was tremendous and that Barry wouldn't be the first or last casualty.

I'd felt the pressure myself when I moved to L.A. I knew that Hollywood was a company town, but I didn't know what that meant for me as a critic. I'd gotten the picture fast. The *Millennium* was a hip local weekly—close to the bottom of the clout barrel by Industry standards. Our opinion might affect the fate of an independent or foreign film, but we couldn't hope to affect the opening weekend of a studio movie. Which meant, among other things, that we weren't on the list for early Tom Cruise previews. Tonight was a total surprise. Barry had exerted himself to arrange this screening. He'd made phone calls and twisted arms and somehow gotten Mark and me in.

Mark didn't know what Barry was planning. He feared what I feared: that Barry wanted Cruise for the cover. We both thought that was impossible. The *Millennium* hardly ever got access to Hollywood stars, and never a star as big as Cruise. But Barry just might swing an interview, and if he did, I might be forced to contribute. I might not be in a position to refuse.

Someone touched my shoulder. I opened my eyes. Mark was standing over me. He said, "It's been fifteen minutes."

I rolled off the bench and followed him back into the theater.

This was the best job I could ever imagine. I loved movies—and all I did was see movies, think about movies, and write about movies. They let me say what I wanted and I earned decent money doing it.

But I opened my notebook, looked up at Tom Cruise, and felt profoundly tired.

BARRY'S PARTY was going full blast by the time I got home. The driveway was blocked with cars, so I left mine down the street and walked back up to the main house. The front door was standing open; voices and light came from the ground-floor windows. People stood around on the lawn, talking.

I lived in the pool house of a mansion in an old section of town called Los Feliz. Los Feliz was one of L.A.'s first movie-money enclaves. It grew up during the silent era, when most of the film companies were based between downtown and Hollywood. The mansion was a huge stucco Spanish with painted tiles and hand-carved wood everywhere. It'd been built by a fruit rancher for his mistress, a Mack Sennett bathing beauty. Now it belonged to a group of investors who rented it out for parties and film shoots. Barry was one of the investors and he'd offered me the pool house in exchange for minor caretaking. I jumped at the chance to live on a movie set in the historic Hollywood Hills. I'd never liked to do anything halfway.

I ducked through the crowd in the foyer looking for Barry. Last week the mansion had been dressed to imitate a Santa Barbara hotel. That film crew was finished and the interior had been stripped again. The walls were blank, the floors were bare, and the big front rooms were empty except for catering tables. There were two bars and a ton of hors d'oeuvres. Barry had put on a spread.

I found him in the telephone alcove at the back of the foyer. He'd just hung up the phone and he was frowning. His clothes were different for the occasion; he was wearing a blue blazer and tan slacks. At the office he wore thongs and a kimono over jeans.

Barry saw me and checked his watch. He said, "You're late. How was the flick?"

I made a face and dropped my briefcase in the corner. "Tom Cruise always has been, and always will be, a human prophylactic."

"I knew you wouldn't like it—I had Mark take you as a test."

Barry pointed at the stool. I sat down. He leaned against the wall and crossed his arms.

Barry Melling owned and ran the *L.A. Millennium*. He was a former hippy radical turned Wall Street investment analyst. In the '80s he took a trip to California and had yet another revelation. He sold his business, moved west, and started the *Millennium* with himself as editor in chief. I'd met him at a party in New York in '96. An intense little man with frizzy red hair had come up to me and started talking about his hot alternative weekly. I'd mentioned movies and we had a long argument. After the argument—which I won—he offered me a job. I'd just gotten in from Paris and was looking for work. It was an incredible stroke of luck.

Barry said, "I've been going over your recent stuff and I have to tell you, I'm not happy."

I leaned out of the alcove and waved at the people. "Aren't you the host here? Can't this wait until tomorrow?"

Barry quoted one of my lines from memory. "'*Bridget Jones's Diary* made me sorry to be female.'"

"Well, it did."

"Listen to yourself, Ann — 'human prophylactic,' 'sorry to be female.' You sound like a bitch. What's happened to your sense of humor?"

I thought about the screening that afternoon. If Mark hadn't been there, I would have run out of the theater for sure.

Barry nudged me with his knee. "What's up?"

I sat there thinking. Barry nudged me again. I said, "I think I need a break, actually. You know that I saw four hundred movies last year? I counted. I've averaged four hundred every year since I started working for you. That's more than a movie a day for five years, and I think I'm just sick of it."

Barry looked down and brushed a crumb off his jacket. He didn't want to hear about a break, I could tell. He said, "You're coming across like you hate movies — our readers have been commenting."

"You mean that your new Hollywood crew complained. I'm rattling the wrong cages."

"I'll remind you that Hollywood is the *Millennium*'s main source of entertainment advertising."

"You don't consider out-call massage 'entertainment'?"

"Ann . . ."

I laughed. "Barry, come on, until recently my mandate was to be tough and iconoclastic. You gave me that mandate yourself, remember? I can't start lying just because you've crashed the movie business."

We blamed the LAPD for Barry's change.

The Rampart scandal broke two years ago, and the *Millennium* beat everyone to the story. This impressed Industry liberals who'd ignored Barry as too low-rent during previous police scandals. The *Millennium* suddenly became a legitimate political tool. Barry was recruited for the district attorney campaign, and the civilian-oversight work that had mushroomed since the Rodney King riots. Now he attended skull sessions with movie stars, and Democratic fund-raisers in Malibu. Now he could get the biggest names in Hollywood on the telephone. He loved the milieu and he loved the action. Mark and I guessed that he wanted in for keeps: that's why he was pushing to make our film coverage more mainstream.

Barry said, "Before you get excited, listen. I want you to do some feature writing because I agree, you need a rest from reviews."

I sat forward. "How about a piece on the Rampart groupies? They hang around at a couple of bars in Elysian Park called—"

Barry shook his head. "What I want is a big profile of Scott Dolgin and his new production company."

I shook *my* head. "No way, you've mentioned Scott Dolgin before. There's no story in someone's unborn dreams—let's wait until he makes a good movie."

"I threw this party to introduce Scott to my Industry connections, and I want you to meet him."

"I'd rather have a month off. You don't have to pay me."

Barry shook his head.

"I could print a retraction for the video release. *'Bridget Jones's Diary*—I laughed! I cried! See it!'"

Barry wasn't going to be moved. He crooked his finger and walked out of the alcove. I sighed, stood up, and followed him. He walked into the dining room and touched a younger guy on the back. The guy turned around.

Barry said, "Scott, this is Ann Whitehead, the writer I've assigned to your piece. Ann, this is Scott Dolgin."

I said, "Hello."

Dolgin smiled and looked past me. He said, "I'm a big fan of yours." His eyes roamed over the crowd.

He was good-looking and probably my age, thirty-two or thirty-three. I remembered what Barry had said about his background. He'd been kicked out of film school and lost some studio jobs before he tried independent producing. His soul patch and Prada suit told me he aspired to the cutting edge. I really hoped he wasn't scum.

Barry said, "Give her your card, Scott. She'll call you tomorrow."

Dolgin handed me a business card. His company was In-Casa Productions; the logo was an old-fashioned California bungalow and the office was in Culver City. Barry patted us both and walked out of the dining room. He headed back to the telephone.

I stuck the card in my pocket and waited for Dolgin to make his pitch. But Dolgin wasn't thinking about me. He was looking around the rooms, taking an inventory of the guests. I looked around, too.

The turnout was high for a weeknight. But the crowd wasn't as glamorous as I'd expected; it wasn't the famous people Barry had met in his anti-LAPD crusade. The famous people must have sent their personal assistants, I decided, or executives from their film companies, or midlevel studio contacts. Whoever they were, they couldn't dial a phone and get Scott Dolgin a producing gig. They could eat and drink for free, and maybe set up a few meetings.

Dolgin finished his survey of the guests. He said, "After you write your article, you should come to work for me. Critics don't create anything, you know. They're parasites —"

He stopped. Something in the foyer had caught his eye.

A tall blond had just walked in the front door. Her looks were striking, and so was her expression. It was the opposite of partylike: it was grim. She slipped past the woman checking invitations and crossed the foyer. She was carrying a beat-up duffel bag over her shoulder. As she scoped out the guests, she opened the hall closet and dumped the bag inside.

Dolgin took off in her direction, pushing through the crowd. The blond saw him coming but her expression didn't change.

Dolgin said something to her. She said something back and walked away. That didn't satisfy Dolgin. He followed her into the living room. Heads turned as she passed; she had that kind of looks. I saw a guy stop Dolgin for a talk. Dolgin didn't want to stop but his career instincts won. He shook the guy's hand and let the blond get away. She disappeared at the far end of the living room.

I realized I was hungry. I walked over to the buffet to see what they had. People stood two deep in front of the tables, and I had to wedge in. The group beside me had just seen a preview of *Training Day*. I served myself a spring roll and listened. They were raving about Denzel Washington's performance. They called him by his first name: "Denzel." Someone asked if his character was based on Ray Perez, the crooked Rampart cop. Someone else had a crooked-cop script in development; they'd seen a working print of the movie months ago. Another person wondered how *Training Day* would do overseas; stories with blacks were a tough sell in foreign markets.

Barry saw me at the buffet and waved from the front hall. He had a new guy with him. I groaned inside, set my plate down, and walked out to them.

Barry said, "Ann, this is Jack Nevenson. Jack works for Len Ziskind at PPA. They're negotiating to sign Scott."

Nevenson and I shook hands. This was interesting. Leonard Ziskind had left CAA to form his own management company. He'd caused a recent stink when he criticized the studios in *Variety*. He'd said that the star system wasn't working anymore, aesthetically or financially.

Barry was waiting for me to talk, so I said, "I'm anxious to see what Ziskind does. He's saying the right things."

Nevenson smoothed his necktie; it had blue-and-white stripes. I knew they were Yale colors because Barry'd gone to Yale. Nevenson said, "Len is surrounding himself with very smart people."

"Do you think smart people make the best artistic decisions?"

Nevenson was instantly offended. He looked at Barry and Barry frowned at me. I wanted to explain what I meant but Barry cut in. He said, "She'll call you about the Scott piece."

He hustled Nevenson away, frowning at me behind Nevenson's back. I shrugged and turned, and saw Mark and Vivian at the bar. They must have just arrived. Mark waved and pointed toward the back of the house. Vivian made the strangling sign at her throat. I laughed and nodded. They picked up their drinks and we snuck around the edge of the crowd. We passed Barry in the back hall. He didn't see us. He was in the alcove again, dialing the telephone.

Back in the library it was quiet and cool. I opened the French doors for a breeze and a view of the swimming pool. I took my shoes off and stretched out on the floor.

Vivian said, "What a bunch of freaks."

I said, "The guest of honor called me a parasite, and I insulted the guest of honor's future manager. I was beginning to think you guys wouldn't show up."

Mark and Vivian were my closest friends at the paper. Vivian was a reporter and Mark was an encyclopedia of world cinema. He and I had a short affair when he was hired to run the film section. The attraction had been more about movies than sex; all his vitality, I discovered, was mental. But he'd taught me lots and we worked well together. I was a better critic because of him.

Vivian picked a spot against the wall and sat down. "It's the new DA. We're hearing rumors he's closing the Rampart investigation, but there's other rumors that he's impaneled a secret grand jury. I feel like I spend my life at city hall."

Mark sat down beside me. He said, "I forgot to tell you—your sister was at the paper today."

I said, "What for?"

"Your father arrived this morning. You're supposed to have dinner later in the week."

I shut my eyes a second. *Father, damn.* My sister had mentioned a business trip, but I hadn't heard anything since and I was praying it wouldn't happen.

Vivian lifted her vodka. "To Barry's freaks. May they stay forever on the Westside."

Mark lifted his beer and drank. I said, "I pitched him on the cop-groupies but he wasn't interested."

Vivian said, "Then he's an idiot because they'd be a fun story. I've been talking to a registered nurse who has the Rampart logo tattooed in four places. Two pairs—think about it."

Vivian lifted her eyebrows. I laughed. Mark said, "Tell Ann what else held you up."

Vivian sighed. "First, I'm late at city hall. Then I get a tip on

Doug Lockwood and go chasing over to Parker Center to check it out. He's back from suspension—excuse me, *leave*—and they've buried him somewhere until things cool off."

Detective Douglas Lockwood was the cop in the Burger King siege. A Latin gangbanger took some people hostage and Lockwood, who was inside the restaurant at the time, shot and killed the kid. It was one of many second-tier police scandals.

Vivian said, "Lockwood's a mystery. He hardly talked to the media and it'd be a coup to get him on record. But I couldn't find out where they put him, and my usual sources are acting pissy. The LAPD's in a state, my god. The rank and file hate Chief Parks, they're drowning in internal audits and short on manpower, they're hamstrung. They can't go backwards, and they can't go forward either. It almost makes you feel sorry for them—almost."

She poked at her ice cubes. Mark squeezed my shoulder. "Have you talked to Barry?"

I nodded. "If you can call it a talk. I resisted and he pretended not to notice."

"And?"

"I'm in a different kind of trouble than I thought. He says my reviews have gotten bitchy, and he's not wrong."

"But you don't like the Scott Dolgin story."

I squinted at him. Mark said, "I know, it's terrible—but I want you to do it anyway."

"What I really need is a break from movies. I'm going in tomorrow and demand a vacation."

Mark pointed his beer bottle at me. "Don't."

"But I'm burned out—I need a rest."

Vivian said, "Don't do it, Ann."

Mark nodded. "This is a bad time to leave the paper. Barry's in a mood, as we know, and I'm concerned because he's always been such a booster of yours, and now he's having problems with your stuff. I think we should do what he wants until he sees that this 'mainstream' idea is nonsense."

I said, "Which is why you're going along with Tom Cruise."

"Which is why I'm going along with Tom Cruise."

A knock at the door interrupted us. We all looked up: it was the grim blond from earlier. She stood in the doorway and she was staring straight at me. She said, "I want to speak to you."

I sat up and patted the floor between me and Mark. The woman shook her head. "I want to speak to you *alone*."

Her manner was very bizarre. I looked at Vivian and Mark for an opinion. They just shrugged, so I got up and walked over to the door.

The woman backed into the hallway, signaling me to follow. Up close her looks were amazing. She was beautiful. She had green eyes, perfect skin, and ash-blond hair twisted up in a messy knot. She might have been an actress, but there was nothing self-conscious or artificial about her. She had a locked-down ferocity that suggested something else.

She said, "You can't give up."

Her voice was low and gravelly; any actress would be thrilled to have that voice. I waited for her to go on.

She jabbed her finger in my chest. "You're ready to give up. But *I* didn't give up, and I won't let *you*."

I stepped back from the finger, noticing other details. Her clothes were too casual for the party: she wore a tight T-shirt and bell-bottom jeans. The hair around her face was damp, and her T-shirt had fresh water spots, like she'd just washed up in the powder room. But there was dirt under her fingernails and I could smell stale sweat.

She said, "*Thelma & Louise* is ten years old this year. Why didn't you write an anniversary article?"

"I—"

She grabbed my arm. "It's the most important movie Hollywood ever made about women! It took a subject no one wants to hear about—female freedom—stuck it in a traditionally male genre, the road movie, and hit big. It proved that the American public is ready for the truth about the condition of women, *if you present it entertainingly!*"

She dug her nails in hard, and the emotion in her eyes was weird. *She* was weird. I pulled my arm free.

She said, "All we have these days is kicking feet and talking vaginas, *Lara Croft—Tomb Raider* or *What Women Want.* But *Thelma & Louise—*"

I cut in on her. "Why don't you do a piece for us? It's a perfect time with Callie Khouri directing *Ya-Ya Sisterhood.* I can introduce you to my editor right now."

"I'm not a critic—I'm a filmmaker. I've just sold a screenplay that starts where *Thelma & Louise* left off."

I smiled. "They hit a trampoline in the Grand Canyon and bounce back alive?"

The woman was beyond humor. She said, "I'll send you a copy of the script when we close with the studio. I'm going to direct it."

I caught a whiff of stale body. I said, "Really? Direct?"

She leaned close and clenched her fist in my face. "*I will beat the System.*"

The body odor got more distinct, then she spun around and ran down the hall. I pinched my nose, waved the smell away, and walked back into the library.

Mark said, "She looks like a Swedish ingénue."

Vivian nodded. "Fabulous collarbones. What's up?"

I rubbed the nail marks on my arm. "Just another unhappy reader. The consensus seems to be that I'm not doing my job."

Mark smiled. I said, "We better get back." Vivian shrugged and finished her drink.

The party was winding down out front. Most of the guests had left and waiters were taking dirty dishes to the kitchen. We split up at the foyer. Mark told me to call him tomorrow, and Vivian went to check the buffet.

Barry and Scott Dolgin stood at the front door saying good-bye to people. Barry had a mentorly arm around Dolgin's shoulder. A petite woman in a black pantsuit was trying to get Dolgin's attention. She pulled at his sleeve while he passed business cards to the people leaving. Barry waved for me to come and talk.

I pretended not to understand. I smiled, waved good night, turned around, and walked out of the foyer. Barry called my name. I ignored him and walked faster.

I hurried down the back hall toward the service stairs. There was a furnished office in the back corner of the mansion; it was for the film companies that rented the place. As I walked past the office, I saw the blond woman again. She was sitting at the desk, flipping through the Rolodex, talking to someone I couldn't see from the hallway.

The blond looked up and saw me walking by. I nodded at her. She didn't acknowledge the nod. She stared through me like we'd never met.

Too nuts, I thought, and kept walking. A few seconds later the blond raised her voice. *"In-Casa Productions is a farce and you know it!"*

I heard that and started to laugh. It would have made a great lead for my Scott Dolgin story.

CHAPTER
TWO

I WOKE UP the next day feeling better than I'd felt in ages. Movies had been getting to me; I didn't realize how badly until I was given a break. No reviews for a while felt like a giant relief.

I threw off the covers and bounced out of bed. The bed was a foldaway couch — the only piece of furniture on the mansion's second floor. I'd stayed there overnight because part of my caretaking duty was to sleep upstairs for parties and check for damage after. I did a fast tour of the main floor. Everything looked good; no one had stolen the vintage fixtures or gouged the woodwork.

I headed to the pool house to fix coffee, clean up, and plan the day. Mark would have to reassign all my screenings. I'd call him first.

I walked out the kitchen door and looked across the backyard. The screen door to the pool house was standing wide open.

The pool house was a miniature copy of the mansion — a stucco box with striped awnings and a tile roof, shaded by old avocado trees. I didn't always lock my door because I didn't think I needed to. The mansion sat on two acres on a quiet street that dead-ended at a steep hill. There were no neighbors to the north or west, and the backyard was enclosed by a ten-foot wall. The pool house sat at the back of the property. It was only accessible from the mansion or the driveway gates, and I kept both locked and alarmed unless the mansion was being used.

I walked around to the pool house. The inside door was open, too. I walked into the front room.

Someone had turned all the lights on, and the radio was playing soft rock. A canvas duffel bag drooped off the daybed. Jeans, a T-shirt, and cotton underpants lay in a pile on the floor. A pair of platform sandals stood next to the pile.

My throat went dry. I crossed to the bathroom, took a deep breath, and looked inside.

It was the blond.

She was naked and stretched faceup in the bathtub. Her head was resting on the back ledge. Her hair was dark where the water had soaked up to her ears. Her eyes were almost shut; a green half-moon showed under one lid, white showed under the other. Her skin had a healthy flush, an effect produced by condensation and the sun on pink porcelain. The bathwater was pink, too, from the porcelain, and diffused blood. Her hands floated palms down on the surface.

I stood in the doorway, shocked to the absolute core. I knew I was seeing what I was seeing but no action or thought would come to me.

I might have stood there forever if my legs hadn't given out. I started to fall. I grabbed the door frame to keep myself up and felt suddenly sick. I staggered forward and threw up in the sink.

I ran cold water and splashed it over my face and neck. When I felt ready, I turned around and looked again.

There were neat vertical lines carved up both her wrists. A knife was sitting at the bottom of the tub. I recognized the handle; it had come from my kitchen drawer.

I saw a blood smear on the tiles beside her ear.

I bent to see closer.

She had a big lump high on her head. Red drops oozed from an abrasion on the lump. The moisture had stopped the blood from drying.

My mind was beginning to work again. She did not do the lump herself. I walked out of the bathroom and out to the backyard. I was moving like a zombie.

I looked around.

The back of the mansion, the swimming pool, the patio, the lounge furniture, the gardens, the garage: everything looked normal. Except the ivy. The wall around the yard was covered with thick old ivy. The ivy by the pool house had been torn away in a strip all the way to the top. The vines were sagging loose.

I took hold of an attached vine, climbed the wall, and looked over. A vacant lot adjoined the backyard. It was packed dirt and covered with scrubby bushes. I looked hard but I couldn't see footprints or anything.

I wedged my hand under a vine and hung there to think.

I was having the stupidest, most dangerous idea. It's the shock, I thought. But the idea wouldn't go away. It was a bad idea—the worst possible idea—but it grew in my imagination until it became very, very important.

I stared down at the pool house. I stared for an age, fighting the idea. But it won in the end.

Los Feliz was LAPD territory. The cops hated the *Millennium* at least as much as we hated them. They would never let me in on this story.

Any way I looked at it, I only had one choice: to let myself in without them knowing it.

Could it be done? Could *I* do it?

I had no experience with that kind of journalism. And I'd have to lie to the cops. Did I have the nerve for it? I'd always been a lousy liar, and this would mean lying on an unknown scale for who knew how long. What happened if I got caught? "Obstruction of justice" and "tampering with evidence" were clichés from a thousand crime movies; they had no reality for me. Did they mean jail? Was I prepared for jail?

I shut my eyes.

Of course I wasn't prepared for jail. I didn't know if I could do this at all. But I knew that I had to try. I had to find the guts to lie, playact, stonewall, obstruct, tamper—to do whatever had to be done.

Because *she* was the Hollywood story I was going to write.

———

ONCE I'D made up my mind, the next part was easy. I gave myself an hour to accomplish everything. One hour would make no difference to her or the cops.

I put on kitchen gloves, dumped out her bag, and hunted around for a wallet. It was in a zippered pocket inside the bag.

I pulled her driver's license out first. Her name was Greta Maria Stenholm. Five feet nine inches, 140 pounds. Green eyes. No corrective lenses needed. Date of birth: August 10, 1970.

I paused over that coincidence: August 10, 1970. Greta Stenholm and I were born on the same date, two years apart. I'd just turned thirty-three; she'd just turned thirty-one.

The address on her license was 7095 Hawthorn Avenue, number 1. Hawthorn was in the center of Hollywood.

I put the license back and went through the rest of her identification. She was carrying expired credit cards from Visa and two department stores. The Visa had a maroon plastic card stuck to the back. I pried the two cards apart. The maroon was a student ID from the academic year 1995–96. Stenholm had been enrolled at the School of Cinema-Television at USC.

SC: one of the best film schools in the country. The best, if you wanted to work in the Industry — and she'd gone there.

I turned the wallet upside down and shook it. Loose change and movie stubs fell out. She didn't have any paper money, and the change added up to $1.68. I shuffled through the various stubs. They were dated August 24 — Friday, four days ago. She'd spent all day and night seeing movies on Hollywood Boulevard. She'd seen *The Princess Diaries* at the El Capitan, *Rat Race* at the Chinese, *Forever Hollywood* at the American Cinematheque, and a double feature of *A.I.: Artificial Intelligence* and *Jurassic Park III*. Her first show was at 9:30 A.M.; her last at 9:05 P.M.

I put everything back in the wallet and stuck the wallet back in the zippered pocket. It was time to take notes.

I switched on the computer and opened a new file. I detailed my actions since I'd seen the open screen door. I described the crime scene, indoors and out, and listed the contents of the dead woman's wallet. All that was done in my own shorthand, the kind

I used to take notes in the dark: "lites, radio — party clos. on floor — her + knife/tub full — ivy down." I typed fast and kept making mistakes because of the gloves. I'd fill in details later. Details like the bathroom smelled of lavender oil, not dead body. Someone had poured half my bottle into the bathwater.

I got up and sorted through the rest of her stuff.

A cosmetic kit. A man's wristwatch. A key ring. A checkbook. A stuffed rabbit. A small envelope. A bulging, scuffed-up Filofax held together by an elastic band.

I went back to the keyboard and typed the list. I starred the items that weren't normal for an overnight bag. I noted that the bag itself was Air Force surplus or an imitation. It had faded black wings stenciled on the side.

Her cosmetic kit contained the bare essentials: toothbrush, toothpaste, comb. She'd worn no makeup at the party, I remembered, and no jewelry except the wristwatch.

The key ring was a cheesy souvenir of the Hollywood sign; it held four door keys and two GM car keys. Her checkbook showed an account at the California National Bank. The last balance entered was thirteen dollars, and she'd written five checks since then. I could only assume that they bounced.

The rabbit was a threadbare child's toy. It had ripped seams, a missing ear, and a very strange dress: a crimson velvet gown, trimmed with gold fur that resembled a lion's mane. The dress looked homemade and newer than the rabbit.

I picked up the envelope and tried the flap. It wasn't sealed. Inside I found a three-by-five color Kodak.

It showed a sinewy old man draped facedown over the lap of a brown-haired woman. His left side was to the camera, and he was naked and tan except for white swimsuit lines on his flank. A dark wig and wraparound sunglasses hid his identity. The brunet was facing the camera with one arm raised to spank him. She looked incredibly bored. She sat at the foot of a bed covered with a dinosaur spread. Large posters lined the wall behind her: *Jurassic Park I* and *II*, *Schindler's List*, *Saving Private Ryan*, *Jurassic Park III*.

I said out loud, "Steven Spielberg."

I slid the picture back in the envelope and picked up the Filo-fax. Flipping to the address book, I started with the As. I read a few names and stopped, surprised.

I skipped forward to the Bs and Cs, the Ls, the Ts—and couldn't believe it. Her book was crammed with big names. It was a *Who's Who* of current Hollywood.

That was too much to type out. I gathered up the Filofax and key ring and ran to the mansion. The downstairs office had an industrial-size copy machine. I only glanced at the chair where I'd last seen her alive. I popped open the Filofax, pulled out a fistful of pages, threw them in the automatic-feed bin, and hit PRINT.

I checked the clock. I'd promised myself one hour: twenty-six minutes were gone.

I ran to the front door and looked outside. Everyone on the block parked in their garage or their driveway. I saw my car at the end of the street. And I saw a powder-blue Impala at the curb two houses down.

The Impala had expired Kansas plates. The passenger window had been smashed, and the glove compartment hung open and empty. Glass pellets were scattered all over the floor. The trunk lock looked like someone tried to force it: the chrome was nicked and dented. I inserted both GM keys, one, two—fast. The second key worked; the trunk clicked open.

It was full of boxes and loose junk. I found movie reference books and a ton of videocassettes. One box was labelled MISC.; an-other, WORK IN PROGRESS; a third, SCREENPLAYS.

I dug through the screenplays. I wanted the *Thelma & Louise* sequel she'd talked about at the party. The scripts were all bound, but they weren't dated, and the titles told me nothing. I needed the whole box. I started to lift it out and realized it wasn't practical. There was no place to hide the box from the cops.

I said, "Damn," slammed the trunk down, and ran back to the house.

The copier had finished the first batch of pages. I grabbed a second batch, tossed it in the bin, and punched the button. While I waited I skimmed through her 2001 appointment calendar. I got a blast of famous names, studio meetings, and Industry hangouts. She never said which studio or with who, she just wrote, "Studio meeting." Barry's party was her last notation. The pages for the week preceding it were blank.

I checked the time and decided to copy the calendar. I pulled the pages out and fed them to the machine. The job took fifteen more minutes, but by the end I had a complete duplicate set of her address and appointment books.

I ran to the pool house, climbed on a chair, and stuffed the xeroxes through the slats of the attic fan. I arranged everything the way I'd found it, tossed my gloves in a drawer, copied the crime-scene notes into a second file, closed both files, grabbed the telephone, and dialed the cops.

An operator answered. "Nine-one-one. State your emergency."

"Yes, I found a woman." I could hear my voice waver.

"What is her condition?"

"She's dead."

"What is your location, ma'am?"

"8918 Nottingham in Los Feliz."

"Is there an apartment number?"

"It's a house."

"What is your name, please?"

"Ann Whitehead."

"We'll have a car there in a few minutes, Mrs. Whitehead."

I hung up and walked to the bathroom door. Greta Stenholm lay in the bathtub—silent, perfect profile, serene.

She had better be worth the risk.

CHAPTER
THREE

Aɴʏʙᴏᴅʏ ʜᴏᴍᴇ? Police! *Anybody home?!*"

Two uniformed cops stood at the driveway gates. The woman cop did the shouting. The male cop had wedged his foot between the bars and was starting to climb over.

I ran to the gates, hit the release latch, and dragged one side open. The cops pushed from their side and crowded through the gap. They were both clean-cut Latins.

The woman cop said, "Are you Ann Whitehead?"

I said, "Yes."

"We rang the front doorbell. Nobody answered."

"The body's back there." I pointed at the pool house.

The cops took off at a jog. I followed after them. They stopped me at the bathroom door, then they went inside. The male cop squatted beside the tub and I braced myself for questions.

The woman cop said, "Did you touch anything?"

I said, "Just the doors when I came in."

The male cop said, "You lived here together?"

"No, I didn't know her. I live here alone."

"All alone?" His tone meant: "In this palace?"

"Some businessmen own the property—I'm the caretaker."

He nodded and pointed me into the front room. I backed away as the two cops came out of the bathroom. I tried to hear what they were whispering. The woman cop caught me and pointed outside.

I walked outside and they escorted me to the back patio. The woman cop pointed at a lounge chair. I sat down.

The male cop said, "How can we reach the owners?"

"They have a lawyer who handles things here." I told him the number from memory.

He nodded. "Where's a telephone?"

I pointed at the portable bar standing nearby. He walked over, found the cordless phone, and punched in a number. Turning his back, he spoke to someone in a low voice. I tried to hear but couldn't.

He finished his call and walked out to the gates to wait. The woman cop stationed herself on a chaise lounge next to me.

I ignored her and focused on the pool house.

My whole body started to shake. At first I thought it was the temperature—I must be cold because the patio was in shade. I leaned sideways, pulled a beach towel off the bar, and wrapped myself up. That didn't help: the shaking only got worse. My teeth started to chatter and I felt sick to my stomach again.

It hit me then. It had taken this long to kick in. The blond was dead—and she'd been murdered—

And it might have been me.

The woman cop was watching. I didn't want to come unglued in front of her. I bit down on the towel and clenched my muscles to stop the shaking. But the shaking wouldn't stop.

THE DETECTIVES took half an hour to arrive. I heard footsteps in the driveway and saw a tall man turn the corner of the house. He wore a suit and tie, and he seemed familiar. At the sight of him the male cop saluted and the woman cop jumped to attention. I realized who the detective was. It was Douglas Lockwood, the cop from the Burger King siege.

I said without thinking, "Jesus, it's you."

He said, "Ann Whitehead?"

I nodded.

"Ann Whitehead, the writer for the *L.A. Millennium*?"

I nodded again, standing up. I stood too fast. I wobbled and had to steady myself against the chair. Lockwood saw it, reached for my elbow, and made me sit back down.

He looked me over for a minute. Bare feet, jeans, wrinkled shirt, uncombed hair—hair, shirt, jeans, feet. When he finished, he pulled a notebook and pen out of his jacket. I remembered that he'd been shot at the siege.

"I hope your newspaper's attitude won't prevent you from co-operating with this investigation."

It was said in a perfectly neutral tone. I took the remark to be rhetorical and didn't answer. He went on, "You live in the pool house, is that correct?"

"I do."

"And this property belongs to businessmen?"

"Yes, they rent it out."

"And you say you don't know the victim."

"There was a party last night. She was one of the guests, but I never formally met her." My throat tightened. That wasn't good: I hadn't even lied to him yet.

"If you live in the pool house, how did she get there? Where were you?"

"I sleep in the main house when there's people—it's part of my caretaking deal."

Lockwood jotted notes in his book. I glanced past him and watched three men walk down the driveway. They stopped beside the garage and set their briefcases on the cement. All three were drinking coffee from take-out cups. One guy yawned; one guy rubbed sleep out of his eyes. One had a greasy paper bag that he started to pass. They all took a doughnut and a napkin and started eating.

Lockwood waved his pen around the backyard. "Was this out-door area used for the party?"

"The guests were inside, but the valets parked cars in the drive-way, and the caterers had access to the kitchen door."

Lockwood studied the layout. The woman cop hadn't left; she

was watching every move—mine and his. Lockwood said, "Officer, would you accompany Miss Whitehead to your car and wait there, please?"

I said, "I'd like to stay here."

Lockwood shook his head and walked off toward the pool house.

The woman cop gripped my arm and marched me up the driveway. I didn't appreciate being handled like that. I tried to shake her off, but she held on tight until we got to her car and she put me in the backseat. Shutting the door, she stationed herself at the curb.

Wire mesh separated the backseat from the front. I sat looking through it.

The street below the house had been blocked off by official cars. I counted two unmarked cars, two black-and-whites including mine, a hearselike station wagon, and an ambulance guarded by a guy in a jumpsuit. One cop stretched yellow tape across the front yard, and one was posted outside the tape. The nearest neighbors stood on their lawn, straining for a look at me.

I ducked down in the seat and started to lay things out.

If this killing was random, I owed my life to Barry and his party. I wouldn't have slept in the mansion otherwise.

But I didn't think it was random. Yes, the house was isolated at the end of the cul-de-sac, and it and the yard were wide open last night. Yes, the victim was gorgeous and vulnerable—a stray psychopath's ideal target, if you considered national statistics or the lessons of late-night cable movies.

The argument against randomness was stronger.

The wounds were too neat, for one thing. A random sex killing would be gorier. And there would probably be an assault or rape. But I saw no signs of a fight, and no sign that she was dragged to the tub from somewhere else. The crime was clean, cold, and intelligent in its simplicity. A blow to the head and slits in each wrist.

The killer didn't want me. I was sure of that now—now that I thought about it and the panic had passed. All the pool house lights were on, Stenholm and I didn't look anything alike, and the bathtub was clearly visible from the door.

He didn't want me: he wanted her. The whole context of the murder was *un*random. The party was Hollywood, she was Hollywood, and her address book was BIG Hollywood: corporate chairmen, studio heads, producers, managers, agents, lawyers, writers, directors, stars. And the Hollywood theme—with a Steven Spielberg subtheme—carried over to the picture of the old man getting spanked. *Jurassic Park* was a Spielberg franchise, and he was connected with all the movies featured in the dinosaur bedroom.

Her appointment calendar was Hollywood, too. She'd had lunches and dinners with Leonard Ziskind of PPA. There were drink dates with Callie Khouri, who wrote *Thelma & Louise*. And there were a string of Sunday brunches with Julia Roberts, Cameron Diaz, Sandra Bullock, and Drew Barrymore. She must have been seeing actors about her screenplay.

The obvious motive for her death was the spanking picture. By all indications she was broke. Broke, and nutty, and overwrought—if her behavior at the party was anything to go by. Maybe she'd blackmailed an old pervert, and the pervert killed her, or had her killed.

But that theory didn't cover it all.

Why would she resort to blackmail? She'd sold her screenplay to a studio. Did the scheme predate the studio deal? Or did the studio fiddle around and delay the payment check?

And, the murder didn't appear premeditated. A prepared killer would bring his own weapon and not leave that picture for the cops to find.

I paused, and thought of her. Greta Maria Stenholm—

Oh, Christ!

I grabbed the wire mesh and sat up. *Wasn't I the number one suspect?*

I'd been so busy, I hadn't stopped to think how this would look to the cops. My place, my knife, a woman my age who worked in movies. They would have to think I did it, or that I knew the person who did.

I burst out laughing.

It was only one more thing to scare me shitless—and I had a

policy about fear. It came from my childhood and went like this: fight fear or else it will rule your life. Fear paralyzed action, and that would wreck all my plans.

THE CAR door opened. The woman cop leaned in and said, "Detective Lockwood will speak with you now."

I climbed out of the backseat and ducked under the yellow tape. Lockwood was waiting for me in the driveway. I followed him around to the back of the house.

He stopped and held out a sheet of paper. "I'd like you to sign this."

"What is it?"

"Permission to search the buildings and grounds."

He handed me a pen. I said, "But I'm not the owner."

"We've spoken to the lawyer. You have control of the premises — that's all we require."

I rested the paper on my knee, signed, and passed it back. Lockwood said, "The garage is empty. Where's your vehicle?"

"Down at the corner of Los Feliz — there was no place to park last night."

He said, "I'd like the keys, please."

I dug them out of my jeans and Lockwood took them. I checked the time on his watch. It was still early, but the sun had risen over the roof and it was getting hot. Some of the cops had removed their jackets and were working in their shirtsleeves. One guy squatted on top of the back wall; he surveyed the vacant lot and made notes on a clipboard. Another guy dusted the pool house door. The sounds of a vacuum cleaner and of splashing water came from inside. A third guy stood by the pool, drawing a diagram of the yard.

Lockwood said, "I want you to walk me through the party and tell me what you saw."

The kitchen door had been propped open for dusting. He motioned me into the house. I led him through the pantry and watched him absorb the scale of the place. The way our steps echoed off the hardwood, it sounded like an empty gymnasium.

Lockwood stopped in the front hall. "Who gave the party?"

"Barry Melling. He's part owner of this place and he runs my newspaper."

Lockwood wrote BARRY MELLING in his notebook.

If he recognized my name, he'd have to recognize Barry's: Barry had written vicious anti-Lockwood editorials. I thought Lockwood might take another deadpan swipe at the paper, but he didn't. He looked around the bare rooms and said, "I see no evidence of a party."

"The caterers cleaned up afterward."

He nodded and asked for a guest list, and the names of the caterers and valet parkers. I said that Barry had made the arrangements. He asked me to describe the party. I told him the purpose, gave him the demographics of the guests, and mentioned the people I'd talked to.

He asked to see Scott Dolgin's business card. I got it out of my shirt and showed it to him. He wrote down Dolgin's address and phone number. Already I was finding this process tedious; I wanted to get to Greta Stenholm.

I said, "She arrived a little after 10 P.M."

Lockwood knew who "she" was. He looked up from writing. "With people or alone?"

"Alone—and she looked like she had the wrong party."

"What do you mean?"

"I mean she didn't fit with the crowd or the tone of the event. These were businesspeople in business attire. She was dressed wrong, she was dirty, and she acted weird. She was also very beautiful."

Lockwood said, "'She was very beautiful.'"

He made it sound too banal. I tried to clarify: "Yes, in an unself-conscious way. She seemed oblivious of herself and to the attention she got."

"Who did she speak to?"

"Only three people that I saw. Scott Dolgin was one, and I couldn't see the other person."

"Who was the third?"

"Me."

Lockwood flipped to a new page and wrote. I described Greta Stenholm's weirdness and related our conversation word for word. When I finished, Lockwood said, "You talked to her about movies?"

I nodded. He said, "Nothing else—just movies?"

I nodded and walked down the back hall to the office. Lockwood followed me. I stopped at the threshold, showed him the perspective, and described the scene: Greta Stenholm sitting at the desk, talking to someone behind the door, thumbing the Rolodex as she talked.

Lockwood walked into the office. "You never asked the woman's name?"

"She didn't give me a chance, and I went to bed before the party was over."

"What time was that?"

"About eleven."

"How did she know the pool house would be unoccupied?"

"I have no idea."

Lockwood pushed the door wide with his pen. On the floor under the door was a blank sheet of paper. It was from the xeroxing; I must have dropped it. I froze as Lockwood bent down and picked it up. He looked at it, then he looked at the Xerox machine. I saw his face change. He turned very carefully... and looked at me.

HE JERKED me around for the next two hours. I wasn't prepared for the way he did it; I'd gotten too used to the average movie.

Movies either overplayed or underplayed. Movie cops cried, crashed cars, and fired shots into crowds of people. Or you had cold cops who showed nothing and became psychotic blanks. What you didn't have was Lockwood. You didn't have a civil servant with a suit and tie, and a total absence of drama. He didn't hate me or even want to know me; I only existed as a problem. If he hated the *Millennium*, or journalists in general, there was no way to tell. As I fended him off, I thought of an older generation of actor. Sterling Hayden and Dana Andrews made good cops. They weren't trying to display their range or express the masculine condition; they just did a job.

Lockwood never mentioned the Xerox machine. He lingered in the back office, repeated his initial questions, and asked new and more oblique ones. He ran me through the party five times and made a note of every discrepancy. He asked me about spatial relations and time frames — endless details about who was standing where and when. I acted out the dead woman's first appearance; I showed how she dumped her bag in the closet and paced off her path through the foyer. I repeated our conversation outside the library, complete with gestures and body language.

I knew what Lockwood was trying to do. He was trying to grind me down with petty mechanics. Because I knew that, I made myself be calm. I didn't get irritated, or worry about the stakes if I cracked. He wasn't going to get to me.

We walked from the back office to the front hall five times — and he never mentioned the Xerox machine. When we were done, and he walked me outside, and the Xerox machine still hadn't been mentioned, I knew what the next strategy was: suspense. He was going to let me stew and see what happened. I already felt wrung out and unnerved, but I told myself I was doing fine. What could he prove without the xeroxes themselves?

A coroner's guy was wheeling Greta Stenholm toward the driveway. She was strapped in and covered with a sheet. I stopped to let the gurney pass. Without planning to, I reached out and touched her. I couldn't feel anything except the starched cotton of the sheet. I saw Lockwood watching, but I didn't care. He would think what he wanted.

A tubby cop in latex gloves waved at us from the pool house. Lockwood walked over to him, and they disappeared inside. I had no orders, so I tagged along and stood in the doorway.

The pool house was really a glorified changing room made livable by a kitchenette. It had hardwood floors, the original fixtures, and came furnished with movie-set leftovers. The cops had turned off the lights and radio, and removed the dead woman's things. But they'd left my clothes closet open and some of my stuff sitting out. The attic fan had not been noticed.

The tubby cop pointed to my word processor. It made a distinct humming noise in the silence. *Damn.* I'd closed the Stenholm files, and in my rush, forgotten to shut off the machine. *DAMN.*

Lockwood and his partner looked at me. I kept my face blank, but I was holding my breath.

Lockwood went to the computer, grabbed the mouse, and opened the hard drive to search my files. He clicked the mouse twice. My crime-scene notes flashed onto the screen. He scrolled through the pages, reading every word. I leaned against the door-jamb and stuck my hands in my jeans.

The tubby cop read over Lockwood's shoulder a minute, then shook his head, went to my closet, and started pawing around in it. I heard him drop things and bang things together. It was loud, pricky behavior, and I knew he was doing it on purpose.

He dragged one of my boxes into the middle of the room. It was a box where I kept old press kits. Press kits and . . .

I was screwed.

Lockwood turned around to see what was going on. The tubby cop reached into the box and pulled out my Colt revolver. He held it up by the tip of the barrel.

Lockwood looked at me. He said, "We have to have a talk, Miss Whitehead. Not here — somewhere else."

"Do I need a lawyer?"

"No, I just want to talk to you."

"Can I make a phone call?"

"Make as many as you like as long as you don't discuss the case with potential witnesses."

I ran to the mansion and called Barry. His lawyer had already notified him about the death. I explained the situation in more detail and said that Douglas Lockwood was one of the detectives.

That's all Barry had to hear: Douglas Lockwood. He was ecstatic. He kept saying, "We can nail that cocksucker! We can nail that cocksucker now!"

He didn't seem to care about the crime, or the trouble I might be in; he only wanted another chance to ream the LAPD. He said that Lockwood needed a *real* reporter and started naming names off the staff. I'd been thinking of Lockwood as an obstacle. Now he occurred to me as material. I interrupted Barry in mid-list.

I told him that the story was mine—Lockwood and the dead woman were *mine*. I only wanted his help if they arrested me.

Barry got mad and said a truly ridiculous thing: "Did *you* kill her?"

I gasped—I couldn't believe it.

"Well, did you, Ann?"

I banged the phone down without answering. He really was out of his mind lately.

And I was so tense, I couldn't even laugh about it. He'd reminded me of something I hadn't thought of in years. In my entire life I'd only dreamed of killing one person. But the fantasy was all rage and heat and splattered gore—not the neat, cold blooded job that someone did on Greta Stenholm.

CHAPTER
FOUR

LOCKWOOD SAID, "Tell me about the gun."

"Why? She was killed with a knife."

"*Your* knife."

We were sitting in a back booth at the House of Pies on Vermont. I'd ordered breakfast to prove I wasn't cowed. Lockwood ordered coffee and asked the waiter not to bother us.

He said, "Tell me about the gun."

"It's part of a set that my grandfather bought to protect himself from Bonnie and Clyde. According to family legend he drove the oil fields of east Texas with one gun strapped to the steering wheel and the other one on the seat beside him. They're both hair-trigger—he had them customized."

"Why does a movie critic need a customized Colt .41?"

I shrugged. "My father gave it to me."

"Why?"

"He thinks L.A. is a dangerous place, and he knows I wouldn't buy a gun myself."

"It's too much weapon for a smaller woman."

"I agree, and besides I don't like handguns—I'm better with shotguns and rifles."

Lockwood stirred his coffee, obviously waiting for an explanation. I said, "I was raised in western Canada. I fired my first .22 when I was ten."

"How did your people end up in Canada?"

"They're in the oil business."

"And now you write about movies in Los Angeles."

I felt myself smile. "Have gun, will travel."

The joke fell flat. I flushed red as Lockwood just looked at me. The official mask was working on my nerves. I said, for something to say, "It took awhile to get used to the Colt."

"Do you mean you target practice?"

I showed him the calluses on the webbing of my thumbs. I always practiced with both hands, like Father taught me.

Lockwood said, "Why wouldn't you purchase your own firearm?"

"Because I don't like them. I've seen what they do."

Lockwood picked up on the phrasing. He said, "'Seen'?"

With my own two eyes, I thought. I didn't ever talk about the family tragedy, but if he really suspected me, he'd check my background and get the story anyway.

I cleared my throat. "Thirteen years ago my mother shot herself in front of all of us. My father was throwing my sister around, and Mother took one of the Colts and threatened to kill herself if he didn't stop. I arrived in time to see the gun go off."

Lockwood sipped his coffee. "What did they rule it?"

"Accidental death."

"Is that accurate?"

"As accurate as any single label could be. I personally think it was murder, suicide, and an accident combined."

"And the Colt we found—"

"—is the Colt that killed her."

"And you practice with it."

"Because it's tricky and I don't want to be afraid of it. Mother hated guns. She refused to come shooting or listen to Father's lectures. If she'd listened, she wouldn't have been so cavalier about a loaded gun with a hair trigger—"

I realized I was babbling. I broke off, and Lockwood let the sentence hang. He said, "You mentioned two guns. Where's the other one?"

"My sister has it."

He got out his notebook and pen. "I'd like to speak to your family."

I gave him my sister's phone number in Venice, and told him that Father was staying at the Biltmore downtown. He asked when Father had arrived in L.A. I told him, yesterday morning. Lockwood wrote notes and drew linking arrows in the margin.

What had Vivian said at the party? Lockwood was a mystery; he'd hardly talked to the media, and it'd be a coup to get him on record.

That's what I remembered from the siege: his stone-faced silence. He hadn't talked at the press conferences I saw, and he'd looked to me like the intellectual version of an unrepentant thug. I wanted to believe it, but seeing him in person, I couldn't tell if that were true. He was smart—but there was no clue about the personality or character behind the brains. He held himself straight, the lines of his face were austere, and he had a stern, self-contained manner.

Lockwood dropped his pen and leaned forward. "How did the victim know the pool house would be empty?"

"I don't know."

"How did she know what you looked like?"

"I don't know."

"Why didn't you ask her to leave the rear office?"

"Because I'm not Barry's bouncer at these parties. I just look after the house, and she wasn't hurting anything."

"What were you doing in the back hall at that point of the party?"

"I told you before."

"Tell me again."

"I was going to bed because I was tired, and I wanted to avoid more conversation with Barry and his movie boys."

Lockwood repeated, "'Movie boys.'" It was the same thing he'd done with "She was very beautiful."

I said, "Critics shouldn't hang around with Industry people. It messes with your objectivity—"

Lockwood wasn't listening; he was off on a different track. "What kinds of parties are held at the house?"

"What do you mean?"

"Who rents the house? For what occasions?"

I gave him a rundown of the activity in the past six months. The people and occasions were so different that there was no short answer.

He said, "Are there ever all-women parties?"

"All *women*?"

I saw right then where he was leading. I said, "You think I'm a dyke, don't you? You think this is some kind of lesbian love-nest killing?"

Lockwood gave me his standard look.

I said, "I'm heterosexual, a fact you can easily check. Just because I called her 'beautiful' doesn't mean I desired her."

"There are other indications."

"Did 'movie boys' sound antimale?"

"The victim wore no makeup, brassiere, or jewelry, and neither do you. Her way of dressing was masculine, like yours. And she owned a man's watch."

I laughed, and for one second didn't feel tense. "Detective, you have quaint notions about the modern woman."

Lockwood closed his notebook. "You made Xerox copies of Miss Stenholm's personal papers, didn't you?"

The question caught me off guard. I hesitated—and knew instantly I'd lost. So I said, "Yes."

"Where are they?"

I was silent.

He said, "Where are they?"

"At the house."

"Where at the house?"

He'd take everything if I didn't make a last stand. I swallowed and said, "You'll have to find them yourself."

THE YELLOW tape had been removed, and the crime-scene technicians were gone. A single patrol car was still parked in the driveway. Two uniformed cops were standing sentry—one at the mansion, one back at the pool house.

The front sentry let us into the mansion. Lockwood asked to see the bedroom where I'd slept the night before. I led him upstairs to show him, and he pulled out a stopwatch. "I'm going to time you from the minute you woke up. Go."

He pressed the stem in. I said, "This isn't necessary."

"Go."

I just stood there. Lockwood clicked off the stopwatch. "Maybe you gave the xeroxes to someone in the vicinity, or maybe you took time to remove other evidence."

I said, "I want Greta Stenholm's story."

Lockwood reset the stopwatch. "I assumed that you did."

"If I give you those copies, my last resource is gone! You'll confiscate them like you confiscated my notes and my gun!"

I was pleading for the piece now. I'd forgotten to worry about obstructing justice, evidence tampering, and jail. But the way Lockwood paused, I thought he was finally going to threaten me.

He said, "Here's how this works. I have no legal way to stop you from conducting your own investigation."

"... You don't?"

He shook his head. "You're a journalist. Because you're a journalist, all I can do is ask for your voluntary cooperation. If you agree, I'll guarantee you first shot at our information once my partner and I put a case together and make an arrest. In exchange for that, you'll do exactly as I say."

It took no time to see the hole in that deal. "If 'cooperation' means sitting around doing nothing, I don't want to cooperate."

"We'd prefer that you do nothing."

"That's not going to happen, so tell me specifically what you *don't* want me to do."

Lockwood ticked off his fingers. "Don't talk to anybody who attended the party in any capacity. Don't talk to anyone whose name you found in the victim's address book or appointment calendar. Don't act on any information or evidence you found among the victim's effects."

"What if I research her background? Won't you talk to the party guests first?"

Lockwood nodded, but it was an effort for him.

"Journalists often do a better job on background than we do. I've had reporters provide critical information that came out of left field as far as our investigation was concerned—"

I smiled and started to say something. He stopped me.

"—but I'd prefer that you didn't. I'll keep you apprised of our progress as long as you don't print anything without my permission."

"I promise not to print anything, but that's all. I can't not act."

He nodded, and it was another effort.

"Then if nothing else, don't bother the Hollywood people. They'll cause trouble if they aren't handled correctly. And I'll need to know where you can be reached."

I said, "What do you mean? You know where I live."

Lockwood gave me a look. "Has it occurred to you that you might have been the intended victim?"

"It did. But all the lights were on, and Stenholm and I aren't twins."

"What if it was dark at the time? Maybe the killer made a mistake, then tried to cover it with the lights and simulated suicide."

I felt a wave of fear—much stronger than anything I'd felt that morning. I sat down on the bed.

I whispered, "But there's no reason to kill me."

"Just tell us where you decide to stay, and don't leave town under any circumstances."

"How can I be a suspect *and* the intended victim?"

Lockwood held up his stopwatch. "When I say go, I want you to show me everything you did from the time you woke up. Go."

He pressed the stem in.

"But—"

"Go."

I leaned over and pretended to get my clothes off the floor. I pretended to put them on, wondering if this was payback for the way the *Millennium* had savaged him. But Lockwood's face told me zero.

CHAPTER
FIVE

I DROVE INTO the office at dinnertime thinking about a cartoon. It was an animated short I saw at a festival once called "Bambi Meets Godzilla." A giant prehistoric claw comes down from the sky and squashes a doe grazing at the bottom of the frame. It lasted less than a minute. *Splat!* The End. And you laughed.

My encounter with Lockwood was just as lopsided. I had braced myself for a hero's resistance and he broke me down so fast, it was pathetic. The Xerox machine, my computer, my family, the Colt: he'd gotten everything there was to get almost. He didn't even give me a chance to struggle; I never saw the claw coming.

But I wasn't squashed flat. He didn't find my copies of Greta Stenholm's Filofax. He hadn't threatened legal action, or warned me in graphic terms not to get involved. I'd expected him to play the prehistoric heavy, and he hadn't. But he did make one mistake. I discovered it after he left. When he erased my notes on the crime scene, he didn't think to look for a backup file. I always put an extra backup file on disk.

So I had the xeroxes, and I still had my notes. All I needed now was Barry's permission to go ahead. I was determined to fight him for it, but I also had to be diplomatic. I remembered what Mark said about Barry's schizy mood—and I remembered our last conversation. It wasn't smart to hang up on him.

Barry's assistant had gone for the night. I knocked on Barry's door and walked in unannounced. He looked up from what he was reading.

"*Where have you been?*"

"I didn't know you were expecting me."

"We have to discuss your piece. Where've you *been?*"

"With Lockwood."

"All this time? What for?"

I sat down on the edge of his desk. "Like you, Lockwood thinks I did it."

"I was kidding, Ann. You can't take a joke anymore."

"I can when it's funny. Have you talked to the cops?"

"Some guy named Smith came by a few hours ago."

"He's Lockwood's partner. What did you say?"

"Tell the pigs as little as possible, that's always been my rule."

"Barry, Jesus, a woman was murdered!"

"And I'm sorry for it, believe me." He pushed a folder across the desk. "I've put together the clips on the Burger King siege."

I leaned my elbow on the folder so he couldn't take it back. I said, "I think your friend Scott Dolgin knew her. I saw him try and talk to her."

"Yes, he told me, but he was just being a good host. As far as we can tell, she crashed the party. She wasn't on my list or Scott's, and nobody I've called knew who she was."

"But she knew about In-Casa Productions. I heard her say it was a farce."

Barry tapped the folder. "I want twelve hundred words on Lockwood by next week. Let's concentrate on that."

He could act like he didn't hear me, but I'd already set the research in motion. I'd called Mark from home and he agreed to call his Industry contacts for information on the former film student Greta Stenholm.

Barry tapped the folder again. I opened it and checked out a handwritten note on top. I recognized Vivian's writing and skimmed a couple of sentences: it was cop-groupie gossip about Douglas Lockwood's love life. Vivian liked the juicy stuff.

I closed the file, smiling. "I thought you wanted an experienced reporter for this assignment."

"I changed my mind. You're already inside his line of defense, and you have an excuse for maintaining contact. No other reporter would get that kind of access—"

The telephone interrupted him. Barry ignored it. It rang three times before I said, "Aren't you going to answer?"

Barry shook his head. "It's been ringing all day—every news organization in town wants to talk to us."

I'd seen reporters on the street when Lockwood drove me to the House of Pies. A lieutenant had been briefing them, but Lockwood's presence caused a bigger stir than the murder. He'd referred all questions back to the lieutenant and refused interviews to the on-camera people. I missed the evening news so I didn't know how the murder, or Lockwood's reappearance, was treated.

The phone stopped ringing. I said, "Doesn't everyone have their hands full with Rampart?"

Barry said, "Rampart's getting old, and she was a foxy blond killed in a rich neighborhood."

"Good thing we have the exclusive."

"You're not doing her."

I leaned toward him. "Scott Dolgin is a typical—"

"You don't know anything about Scott."

"I know that he's not news. *I want Greta Stenholm.*"

Barry took a deep breath and came on with his tone of patronizing omniscience. "Ann. Doug Lockwood is our only concern now. This newspaper's mission, one of them, is to get dirty cops off the streets of L.A. I think we can pressure Lockwood into retirement if we make it a big enough issue."

I forgot to be diplomatic. I thumped the desk with my fist.

"Look, yesterday I realized I was sick of my job. You said yourself that my reviews had gotten bitchy, and I was going to ask you for a break. Now I don't want a break. Now I have an opportunity to write a real blood-and-guts story about Hollywood. I care more about movies than I do about the LAPD—"

Barry broke in. "You've made that clear at editorial meetings."

I thumped the desk again. "Because it's not my fight! I have nothing earth-shattering to add on the subject of police brutality and corruption. I can't imagine Lockwood will talk to me, or what's left to say about dirty cops. But I'm not doing *him* unless you let me do *her*. If I can't do *her*, I'll—"

The phone started to ring. Barry lifted the receiver and dropped it back in its cradle.

I smiled. "—I'll go somewhere else with two stories that any editor will pay money for."

Barry shook his head. I decided it was time for a bluff: I stood up to leave. He grabbed my jacket and pulled me back down. He said, "You're not getting it. She was murdered at *my* party—it's an embarrassment for everyone involved."

"I don't see why. It's not your fault she crashed the gate." I brushed his hand off and picked up the Burger King file.

Barry said, "I don't want the piece."

"Then I'll call an editor I know at the *Times*."

I started to walk out. Behind me, Barry said, "Wait."

I turned around; Barry was tugging at his hair. I stood there and watched him. We'd played brinksmanship before. If Mark was right, and my position with Barry was precarious, I'd find out now.

A minute went by on the wall clock, and another minute. One minute more and Barry nodded. "But do Lockwood first. I want twelve hundred words by next Tuesday."

He waved me out of the office and picked up the telephone. As I shut the door I heard him say, "Scott, it's me."

GRETA STENHOLM had lived a block south of Hollywood Boulevard over by the Chinese Theater.

I made a left off La Brea and cruised for a place to park. The city had renovated the Boulevard, but her street was residential Hollywood in all its eclectic squalor. Front lawns were worn through to dirt and paved over for driveways. A few bungalows survived, squeezed in by dingy apartments in every style from '30s

Spanish to '60s Tiki Village. 7095 Hawthorn was a four-story building with mosquelike minarets. Eroded Moorish carvings framed
the front door and ground-floor windows.

I parked outside and walked up the front stairs. They led to a
lobby lined with mailboxes, and a long dim hall. The mailboxes
were numbered with a black pen. Stenholm's apartment was number 1. I jiggled the lock on her mailbox. It was old and I thought
it might give, but it didn't. The building manager lived in apartment four.

I walked down the hall and rang the buzzer to number four. A
man cracked the door with the chain on. I could only see a bloodshot eye and a patch of three-day beard. I said, "Greta Stenholm—"

He didn't let me finish. "—can go to hell."

"Why do you say that?"

The guy coughed; I smelled cigarettes on his breath. "First, she
gets her apartment broken into, and I gotta replace the doorknob.
Then after I let her slide on rent, she takes advantage of my good
nature and I have to kick her out for delinquency. Then just when
I think I seen the last of her, she's here Saturday stealing change
from my candy machines."

He started to close the door. I stuck my shoe in the crack.
"Wait! When was her apartment broken into?"

"Last winter."

"Was she hurt? Was something stolen?"

He grunted and leaned on the door. I leaned on it from my
side. "When did you evict her?"

"June."

"Where'd she go?"

He said, "Like I give a rat's ass?" He kicked my shoe and
slammed the door shut.

I knocked again, and kept knocking. He turned up his TV to
drown me out. I walked back to apartment number one and
knocked there. I pressed my eye to the old brass peephole. The
glass was funky and I couldn't see inside.

Someone walked into the lobby from the street.

It was a short swarthy man. He wore a Hawaiian shirt untucked over white pants, and loafers with buckles. Before I could move, he walked up and rapped at Stenholm's door. I nearly gagged on the smell of his cologne.

He said, "You Greta Stenholm?"

I tried to ease past him. "Yes, I mean, no—"

He grabbed my arm and pushed me into the utility room. He pinned me to the wall, pulled an envelope out of his waistband, and laid it alongside my cheek. My mind said to kick him, but I couldn't. My legs froze—I froze.

He said, "Take it."

I couldn't lift my arm. He jammed the envelope into my coat pocket. I heard the pocket rip.

"My client says to forget the second part. It isn't doable."

He gave me a shove and let go. That unfroze me. I kicked out and caught his shin. The guy didn't blink: he raised a fist and slugged me right in the face. My head hit the wall, my knees hit the floor, and the room went black.

CHAPTER
SIX

I WAS UNCONSCIOUS for a solid half hour. I'd been punched before, and I took a pretty good one, but I'd never been hit that hard ever. When I came to, I couldn't even sit up. My head spun and I felt hot all over. All I could do was lie there and stare at the brooms.

I felt a lump pressing my hip and remembered the envelope. I reached for it, bit open the flap, and counted the separate bundles. I handled everything as best I could by the edges. It was slow work, lying on my side. I counted twice to make myself believe it.

The envelope contained twenty thousand dollars. The money was still in its original bank wrappers. Twenty thousand-dollar bundles in new hundred-dollar bills.

Twenty thousand bucks in cash.

I managed eventually to stand up. Using the broom rack for support, I stuffed the money in my jeans. My head hurt so bad that my eyes watered. I felt my way out of the utility room, wiping the tears off as I went. How I found the car I couldn't say. How I got home I couldn't say. Los Feliz wasn't far from Hollywood but the trip was a blur. I remembered stopping a couple of times to rest.

Three reporters had staked out the mansion. As I pulled into the drive, they surrounded my car and started asking questions. I told them no comment, go away. They kept at me. I lost my temper and told them to fuck off. The tone turned ugly. One guy threatened to ram my car. I locked the doors and prepared to wait them out. Feeling hot and dizzy, I lay back on the seat and fainted again.

When I woke up at midnight the reporters were gone.

I ROLLED OVER in bed and slowly opened my eyes. I was looking at French doors, a balcony, and bright blue sky. The light hurt. I covered my eyes and tried to think where I was. What did I do after I parked . . .

It came back to me. I was upstairs in the mansion. I had crashed on the foldaway couch when I realized I couldn't face the pool house at night. I'd decided not to sleep there until they caught the killer. Or I stopped feeling weird about living where someone had died — if I ever did.

I uncovered my eyes and checked the time. Early. I wanted more sleep, but I knew I couldn't.

I sat up.

The movement jarred my head. It started to ache. It made my teeth and jaw ache.

I had dumped my clothes beside the bed. Reaching down, I felt around and grabbed the envelope. I smoothed the blankets and emptied the money out in a pile. I arranged the bundles into two rows of ten. Then I rearranged them to make a G and an S.

The money proved two things. It proved that she *did* blackmail someone; it wasn't just a logical leap based on the spanking picture and her empty wallet. And it proved that the blackmail wasn't related to her death. You wouldn't pay her off a day after you'd murdered her.

But I still had questions. Why would she blackmail someone when she'd sold her script? Why didn't the goon in the Hawaiian shirt know what Stenholm looked like? What about the last thing he said? What was the second part that wasn't doable?

I fiddled with the S and reviewed my options.

The money put me in concrete danger — as opposed to my hypothetical danger as the hypothetical victim of an incompetent killer. It was impossible to give it back. How much time did I have before the goon realized he paid the wrong woman? How much time before he identified me and came after me? The police were going to get the envelope, but that wouldn't change anything: the goon would *still* come after me.

I patted a bundle. It seemed like a fortune. Twenty thousand dollars was half a year's salary after taxes. I thought of the Impala with the Kansas plates. What if the research for Stenholm cost money? What if I had to go to the Midwest? I'd lent my sister a lot since she'd moved to L.A.; it had exhausted my savings and I was living from paycheck to paycheck. But I didn't want to ask for expenses in advance. Barry might use it as an excuse to kill the piece.

I thumbed the bills of one bundle. One bundle — make it two, to be safe. That would be two thousand dollars for research. It was more than enough for comfort, but not so much that I couldn't pay it back. I'd think of a way to finesse it with the cops. Lockwood had exposed me as a bad liar, but I'd think of something.

I packed up the money, got dressed, and went out to the pool house.

The pool house felt fine in the daylight. In fact, the only spooky part about walking in there was how unspooky it felt. The place was sunny, the cops had cleaned the bathtub, and I'd straightened up after Lockwood had left. Her death had left no visible trace in my house.

That wasn't true: *I* was a trace. I started to laugh but had to stop. It hurt too much.

I took a long shower, then examined my face in the mirror. The punch had missed my nose and caught me on the left cheekbone. The skin there was greenish yellow and swollen. My left eye hurt, and there was a squishy lump on the back of my head.

I swabbed the lump, spread arnica cream on my cheek, swallowed four aspirin, and went to the kitchen to make coffee. While it was brewing, I stood on a chair and pulled the xeroxes out of the attic. I stuffed the envelope through the slats, poured some coffee, sat down with the telephone, and went to work.

First, I left a message for Lockwood to call me.

Second, I left a message on Vivian's voice mail. I told her about Stenholm's apartment and asked her to ask her cop sources about a burglary last winter.

Third, I called Mark to see what he'd heard from his Industry sources. Something had come up and he'd only made one call. I told him to get cracking. I also asked him to get the guest list for the party from Barry's assistant. He said I would owe him for this, and I said definitely.

I put the phone down and opened Barry's file on the Burger King siege.

I set Vivian's juicy note aside for the end. Underneath it was a shorter note from Barry. He listed the subjects that he wanted Lockwood to comment on. Most of them were common sense, as if Barry didn't trust my basic reporting skills. But one of his suggestions surprised me. He wanted me to ask Lockwood what *really* happened during the siege. I thought we already knew that.

The *L.A. Times* carried the initial story. It was dated Sunday, December 24, 2000.

Off-Duty Officer Slays Gang Member

Juan Pablo Marquez, 25, a gang member with an extensive criminal record, held Christmas shoppers hostage at gunpoint for two hours in an Echo Park Burger King yesterday. The siege ended when off-duty LAPD Detective Douglas Lockwood, 48, shot and killed Marquez. The hostages sustained no serious injuries. Lockwood suffered a minor gunshot wound.

According to eyewitnesses, Marquez, a Pico-Union resident, entered the Burger King fast-food restaurant at 1301 Glendale Blvd. at 1:15 P.M. Saturday. He was wearing an overcoat and carrying an old suitcase. He pulled a weapon, later identified as an AK-47 assault rifle, from under his coat and ordered the customers to lie down. He claimed the suitcase contained a bomb. An employee at the drive-through window told a car customer to alert the police.

An LAPD SWAT team and bomb-disposal unit arrived quickly as LAPD siege experts began negotiating for the release of the some forty hostages.

At 3:15 P.M., two hours into the siege, witnesses heard shots from inside the restaurant. A single gunshot was fired, followed by a burst of automatic-weapon fire, and a second shot. Hostages ran from the restaurant a short time later.

An LAPD spokesperson said Det. Lockwood, a veteran with 24 years on the department, was eating lunch when Marquez entered the restaurant. Marquez appeared disoriented and did not respond to Lockwood's request to surrender. An attempt to disarm Marquez resulted in the gun battle in which Marquez was killed. He died instantly from two wounds to the head and neck. Lockwood sustained a slight injury when a bullet grazed his ribs.

Nineteen people were treated for minor injuries and shock at Hollywood Presbyterian Hospital.

In a written press release, an LAPD spokesperson praised Det. Lockwood for his "cool thinking under fire," saying that "Angelenos have forgotten that its police force risks their lives every day to keep the city safe."

The LAPD is under investigation by local and federal authorities after the Sept. 1999 revelations by ex-officer Rafael A. Perez of corruption in Rampart Division. Perez is currently serving a five-year sentence for stealing cocaine from an LAPD property room.

I turned pages and kept reading. Lockwood was hailed as a hero; Marquez was treated like a lowlife. He was an 18th Street Gang member, and had weapons and drug arrests as a juvenile and adult. It came out that the siege was not gang related: Marquez's longtime girlfriend had left him for another man. She was an employee at the Burger King.

I realized as I read how much I'd forgotten about this particular scandal. Forgotten—or never knew. Christmas was a film critic's busiest season. We had last-minute Oscar contenders, the big family movies, and year-end wrap-ups to write. My Ten-Best list alone took days to decide. I never knew that, in the beginning, media opinion was on Lockwood's side. Given the circumstances and the rules of police procedure, he'd done the right thing.

I came to a brief biography.

He was an L.A. native, born and raised in Torrance. He'd gone to UCLA and law school, and had passed the California bar but never practiced law. He joined the LAPD instead and became a detective fifteen years ago. His wife was a senior deputy DA for Orange County. They had no children.

An old head shot of Lockwood in uniform accompanied the piece. He looked thirty years old, and scary in a buzz haircut.

Then the tide of opinion turned. The *Millennium* helped turn it.

A former hostage claimed that Lockwood shot Marquez as Marquez was preparing to surrender. The media went berserk. Marquez went from lowlife to misguided lover boy. Someone discovered that Lockwood once worked a homicide case in Rampart Division. Suddenly Marquez's criminal record was in doubt; maybe he was another victim of Rampart frame-ups. Calls came for Lockwood's firing. The pun machines cranked into overtime. Headlines read, BURGER CON CARNAGE and PARKS TELLS A WHOPPER. The *Millennium* had said nothing while Lockwood was a hero. Now Barry jumped in with a series of editorials.

Lockwood denied the hostage's allegations; a dozen witnesses backed him up. The *Times* discovered that the former hostage was a felony fugitive and reputed 18th Street Gang member. There were scattered attempts to clear Lockwood's name, but the scandal petered out into messy ambiguities.

Lockwood went on a three-month leave in May. The media read it as a tacit admission of guilt. The leave overlapped with Perez's release from jail; that was construed as an LAPD safety move. A short wire item from late July said that Lockwood spent his leave fishing in Mexico.

The file ended there. I picked up Vivian's note and laughed at her first line: she thanked me for hogging two great stories. The rest was gossip and advice.

"Rumor is rampant that DL came back from Mexico <u>a changed man</u>. My p.d. contacts won't discuss it, and the groupie girls, long on libido but short on insight, can't describe the change. DL is a <u>major</u> groupie heartthrob, especially now that we hear he and his wife are splitsville. By all accounts he was faithful while married ('divine but unfuckable' in the words of one oversexed admirer), unlike your average cop. Now that he might be free, there's a scramble for his favors. <u>Your story is this change</u>. Imagine what DL must have gone through. What is he thinking and feeling since the siege?"

I reread the note, flipped the stack of pages, and started over from the beginning.

I WAS NOT happy with Barry's clip file.

I wasn't happy because it didn't answer the critical questions. What exactly *had* happened inside the Burger King? Was Lockwood guilty or not? If he was a changed man, what did he change from? I knew from Vivian that every cop had a personnel package; it contained citizen complaints, Internal Affairs findings, letters of commendation and support, and ratings reports. The contents were confidential, but the information could be had from friendly sources. What did Lockwood's package contain?

Vivian's note also threw me off. She spent a lot of time around cops and would call a pig a pig. She didn't take that line with Lockwood.

I left a message on her voice mail, then checked the file for recurring bylines and started phoning around.

I found two Lockwood reporters at their desks. They recognized my name and knew about the murder in Los Feliz; they'd even been trying to reach me. But neither of them was willing to talk for free. They would only trade information—if I told them what I knew, they'd tell me what they knew. I said I wasn't trading, and the conversations ended there. I did find out that the cops still hadn't released Greta Stenholm's name. That's the first question the reporters asked: could I confirm the name of the victim?

I got off the phone and played my messages. The light had been blinking since yesterday but I'd been ignoring it.

Most of the calls were from reporters; I erased them as I went. My sister had called twice to tell me about dinner with Father tonight. I checked the clock. I knew I'd have to see him sooner or later, so I decided to show up for dessert.

I went to work annotating the Lockwood file. I was still annotating when a long fax arrived from Mark. I put Lockwood down and skimmed the pages as they came in.

Reading made my head ache, and coffee and aspirin only helped some. It occurred to me to try ice. I made an ice pack, took Mark's fax over to the daybed, and stretched out flat.

It was a relief to switch to Greta Stenholm. I had no personal interest in cops or their lives. Stenholm, I understood immediately.

I held the ice against my cheek and read with one hand.

She was the daughter of rich Kansas ranchers. She discovered movies at college and decided to go to graduate school in film. Her father cut her off because he wanted her to study business; so she borrowed and worked her way through USC. Despite the financial pressures, she became the Class of '96 star. She won the award for best senior film and left school with an agent—Edward Abadi at CAA—and a writing partner, Neil John Phillips. She and Phillips had just graduated when they sold a screwball comedy for big money. Name actors chased the title role, but the script disappeared after a series of rewrites and executive purges.

Stenholm disappeared, too. She did uncredited polishes and

rewrites, and worked odd nonmovie jobs. Phillips, on the other hand, was hot until last year. His screenwriting price had gone up and up until 1998, when he sold an action script for $1.1 million. MGM wanted to launch a retired football star as "the New Stallone." They let the football star fine-tune Phillips's screenplay, and the finished movie was a disaster. It tanked at the box office; the critics trounced it; the studio looked stupid; and Phillips's overpriced script was blamed. But Phillips fought back. He filed lawsuits and took out ads in the trades to defend himself. He wouldn't take his screwing quietly—which upset all the people who did. The Industry blackballed him and he filed for bankruptcy late in 2000.

Unlike the Burger King siege, I remembered this scandal well. The *Millennium* film section had even weighed in on Neil John Phillips's side. It was wild that he and Greta Stenholm were connected. I shuffled through the xeroxed pages. Stenholm had numbers and addresses for Phillips and her agent, Edward Abadi.

I called Mark and told him I'd take it from there. Mark was full of news. The morning *Times* had given the murder a long paragraph in the Metro section; Stenholm wasn't identified and Lockwood got most of the space. Then two plainclothes cops stopped by the paper to interview him and Vivian about the party.

There were also things he hadn't put in the fax.

He said that USC hadn't been much help, but I should pursue a guy named Steve Lampley. Lampley was an Academy librarian and part-time film teacher. He'd followed Stenholm out from Kansas and was trying to make it as a screenwriter; he provided most of the personal facts. Lampley told him that Stenholm spent her spare time at the Academy library. She was there last Thursday: she was the one who defaced the *Hollywood Reporter* piece on the Class of '96.

I flipped through the fax pages to the *Reporter* piece. Stenholm had written "<u>CHANCE!!!</u>" in the margin of the article—right on library property.

Mark said that everyone called Greta Stenholm a "bright girl" or a "bright young woman." It was uncanny how the word *bright* kept coming up, as if by consensus.

He'd also talked to Stenholm's sister-in-law, the wife of her brother in Kansas. The parents were dead and the brother didn't intend to talk to the media. Heavy implication: we are private people, butt out. The brother had just left for L.A. to claim the body. The wife wouldn't give Mark his flight information or hotel.

I asked about the party guest list. Mark said that Barry wasn't around, and Barry's assistant refused to give it to him.

I told Mark to keep all this to himself, hung up, and started on the *Reporter* piece. It was dated May 21, 1996. It reviewed the SC information I already had, and added more.

Stenholm and Phillips shared an agent: Edward Abadi. I drew a fat box with stars around that name. It also listed two more outstanding students: Hamilton Ashburn Jr. from Georgia, and Penny Proft from Brooklyn, New York. I checked Stenholm's address book for an Ashburn or Proft. Neither of the names appeared.

A photograph of Stenholm had run with the piece. It was a picture of her making a movie in the rain. She stood under a canopy, leaning on the tripod of a Panaflex camera. Her hair was tangled, she wore gum boots and a wet poncho, but she looked radiant. She looked like she was queen of the world: she looked like she wanted to sing. I juxtaposed that picture with the woman I met at the party. The change was stunning. Five years — and a million Hollywood miles later.

I read down to the Stenholm section. The writer had given her a lot of play.

She was quoted praising mainstream American movies and defending people's right to escape and forget. She also defended the Industry's right to make movies about males for males, if that's what sold.

The piece ended with a rousing Stenholm speech:

"I want to be the next Steven Spielberg. Spielberg represents the very best of Hollywood with his dazzling technological and cinematic sophistication, and his basic emotions, universal in their humanity. He's had the privilege of maturing onscreen, and now he has the freedom to make whatever films he wants, whether they be light or serious. I aim for a career like his.

"Contrary to what people say, I believe that Hollywood is wide open to any woman who wants to direct commercial movies. But they can do more than domestic drama and romantic comedy. They can be trusted with big budgets and Oscar material. They can make action films, war films, crime films, adventure films, sci-fi films— any type of film. All you have to do is give them the chance."

Stenholm had underlined the last sentence in ink. She'd crossed out "chance" and written "<u>CHANCE!!!</u>" in big letters in the margin. She pressed so hard that her pen ripped through the original page.

I ran a finger over the rip. It was a jagged black line on the fax page.

Stenholm had come back to this article after five years. I understood the impulse. She'd sold her *Thelma & Louise* sequel and wanted to celebrate the victory. But five years had changed her. In 1996 she defended escapist male entertainment. In 2001 she wanted the moviegoing public to know the truth about the condition of women.

The bell rang at the driveway gate.

I looked out the window, ready to hide my papers. But it wasn't Lockwood—it was a woman.

She rang the bell again. I knew I'd seen her some place recently. Then I remembered: the petite woman from Barry's party. She'd worn a black pantsuit and couldn't get Scott Dolgin's attention in the reception line at the end.

I walked outside to see what she wanted. The sunlight made my left eye water. I wiped it on my shirttail and shaded my eyes.

The woman waited for me to get close. When I was, she said, "What happened to you?"

She had a pixie haircut and a pointy freckled face that she powdered white. Her hair and lipstick were the same red. She wore a cutesy summer dress and carried a straw basket for a purse. Her car was cutesy, too, a little two-seat roadster.

I stopped at the gate. "Did you ever talk to Scott Dolgin?"

The remark caught her by surprise. "What? We haven't...No, what do you mean? I never met Scott before the party."

I made a note of that nonanswer. I said, "How can I help you?"

"Let's get out of the sun." She rattled the gate.

"I'd rather stay here."

"You're wigged about the murder, aren't you? You can let me in. I promise I'm not—"

"What do you want?"

She shrugged, reached into her basket, and passed a business card through the bars. Her name was Isabelle Pavich. She worked in development at a company in Studio City.

I put the card in my pocket. She said, "I'm always on the lookout for original stories and I heard through my SC connections that Greta wasn't your average murder victim."

I called up the names from my research. "Let's discuss USC, then. What can you tell me about Edward Abadi, Neil John Phillips, Hamilton Ashburn Jr., and/or Penny Proft?"

She ignored the question and smirked at me. "I heard she was killed in the pool house." She pointed across the patio.

I said, "Get lost."

She grabbed the bars and shook them. "Talk to me, Ann! We can write a treatment together and I'll get us a development deal. Who do the cops think did it?"

I said, "*Get lost.*"

She smacked a bar with her hand and turned to leave. Then she turned back. The movement made her dress puff out. She noticed the effect and twirled on her toes to repeat it. She checked to see if I was watching, and smiled. "I know something you don't know."

I started to walk away.

She said, "Friends of Greta Stenholm tend to get dead."

I stopped. "What?"

Pavich laughed, swung the straw basket around, and skipped back to her car. She made a big deal of backing out, smirking the whole time.

I leaned against the bars and watched her drive off.

Jesus, I thought. I'd found the body thirty-six hours ago, and I was already way out of my depth.

CHAPTER
SEVEN

Father was bombed. My sister had mashed herself into the corner of the booth and was picking at a piece of cheesecake.

The Pacific Dining Car was an old-fashioned steak house on the edge of downtown. It catered to business and City Hall people, and the movie stars who still ate meat. My father's Dining Car routine never varied. He always sat in the darkest room. He always sat on the same side of the same booth, so he could see into the bar and catch the game on TV. He always ate a shrimp cocktail, a T-bone, and onion rings; and when he paid the check, he always told the waiter he'd rolled a drunk for his credit card.

They both spotted me as I came in. Father said, "Well, if it isn't my long-lost daughter, by god! Hello, stranger!"

I shook his hand and slid in next to Sis. She said under her breath, "You came—I can't believe it."

I said, "Howdy, pardner. Texas still hot to secede?"

Father said, "It sure the hell is. You still writing for that commie rag?"

"'You have nothing to lose but your chains.'"

Father laughed and I took a good look at him. He'd aged since I'd seen him last. He was going red in the face, and running to fat on his scotch and fried-everything diet. More and more he looked like what he was: an old-style Texas oilman.

Father signaled the waiter. "Name your poison, child."

I said, "Just a Perrier. I've eaten."

Father rolled his eyes and pointed to his half-empty scotch. "Put this up on its feet, Diego, and bring two *Perriers* for the girls here."

The waiter took Father's glass away. I was bored already; I wanted to be somewhere else, thinking about other things.

I'd stopped by the paper on my way to the restaurant. Mark was in and I asked him to help check the computer archive for murders in Greta Stenholm's circle. I searched Vivian's filing cabinet for more Lockwood background. But everything she had, I already had. I raided Barry's office and struck out: the guest list for the party was nowhere.

Sis nudged me under the table and pointed at my bruised cheek.

I dipped my head in Father's direction, then shook it. That meant he wasn't responsible. Sis glanced at him and blinked three times. That meant he was so loaded that we could talk in code all we liked. I nodded and ate a strawberry off her plate.

My sister looked bad.

I watched her pick at her cheesecake. She hadn't looked happy or well for a long time. Two years to be exact.

Two years ago she tried to commit suicide. It was the second time she had tried. The first time was right after our mother's inquest. We were both flipped out; I quit college and wanted to leave the country, and Sis took a bottle of sleeping pills. When she recovered I asked her to come to Europe with me. She wouldn't because she thought Father shouldn't be left alone. So she'd lived with him for the next ten years — until she'd tried to kill herself again. I had flown to Texas, sprung her from the hospital, and brought her back to L.A. by force.

She and I used to resemble each other. We were both blue-eyed and built small, and we had curly brown hair that we didn't like to comb. My jaw was stronger than hers, which always made her the "pretty" sister. I could only be "attractive" because, as our mother had liked to say, there were too many opinions on my face.

We didn't look like each other anymore. Sis was sober, but boozing and depression had ravaged her. She was sallow, limp, and too skinny, and her spine had settled into a permanent curve. She looked older than me, not younger, and so sad.

I hated to see her like this, but I was also tired of worrying. I'd done what I could to help; after that, I figured it was up to her. She was an adult—her happiness was her responsibility. But she wasn't getting better and it had put a strain on our relationship.

The drinks came. Father lit a cigarette and took a swallow of scotch. He said, "Sara Lucille, tell your sister what we were discussing."

Sis sighed. "Daddy wants us to move back to Fort Worth."

"It is a mystery why daughters of mine would live in this armpit. *Hollywood*, for Christ's sake. It's nothing but Hebrews and homosexuals—"

I stuck my fingers in my ears; Sis copied me. It was one of our oldest gags. Father shook his head. "I have raised two bleeding hearts, to my undying chagrin."

I dropped my hands and changed the subject. "Sis says you're here about gas leases."

"I'm scouting properties for an old boy in Houston."

Sis piped up. "Better California than Alaska."

Father guzzled more scotch and launched into a rant about the state of the oil business. He had been on the skids ever since the domestic oil industry went bust. He refused to work for the big companies, so he'd wildcatted dry wells and flopped a string of get-rich-quick schemes. Natural gas was his latest inspiration. I didn't know how bad business was until I went to pay for Sis's rehab. I found out that he'd been looting our trust fund for seed money. I called him on it, and Father's response was that *rob* and *loot* were strong words: he preferred *borrowed*. Sis and I used to joke about being minor-league heiresses, but there was nothing to inherit now. Our money was gone.

Father took a swipe at environmentalists and stood up without a pause. He leaned against the booth for balance.

The waiter saw Father stand up and came over with the check. Father signed the credit card slip and left a gargantuan tip. He said, "I count on seeing you next Wednesday, Elizabeth Ann."

I said, "Have you heard from our lawyer?"

Sis looked at me and frowned. Father said, "I had the authority to borrow from you girls."

"You know you didn't. You forged those releases."

"Oh, horseshit, Ann!"

He turned away too fast and had to grab the booth again. He steadied himself, focused his eyes, and walked out of the room using the booths as his plumb line.

Sis was still frowning at me. I said, "I called a lawyer. I knew you wouldn't go for it, so I didn't tell you."

"I won't sue him, Annie."

"I'm not talking about a lawsuit, I'm talking about a crime. DA, grand jury, prison—groovy stuff like that."

"I'll never—"

"Don't get upset, it's probably a waste of time. What's this about next Wednesday?"

Sis sighed. "He wants to take us out to the San Andreas Fault, you know, one of his famous geological expeditions. He leaves next Friday."

"That's easy—I'm not going and neither are you." I looked at my watch and slid out of the booth. "I've got things to do."

"You have to drive me home first."

"Where's your car?"

"I sold it."

I leaned against the booth. "Sold it? Jesus—why?"

"I needed the money."

"Why didn't you tell me?"

Sis reached up and rubbed my arm. "They cut back my hours at the bookstore, and I've just started with a new therapist, but she's expensive and my insurance only covers partial psychiatric, and I..."

She hung her head.

I said, "How much do you need?"

Sis kept her head down. "Five hundred. They're going to cut off my phone, and I don't have the rent for next month."

Christ, *five hundred*. Something in me snapped. I'd bailed her out for two years and suddenly I wanted to slap her.

"Sis—"

"Please don't call me that. I'm not a baby anymore."

"Then why don't you get a real job? Why don't you get on with your life instead of trying a new shrink every other minute? You're paralyzed by too much therapy."

Sis got her know-it-all look. "*Any* therapy is too much therapy, according to you."

"Don't we have the same past, and don't I earn a living? Don't *I* function in the world?"

"You function because you don't think about it. You use movies as a substitute for your emotional life."

I'd heard that one before. The room was empty, but I lowered my voice. "Hell, yes, I think about it. I think I've got better things to do than wallow in a goddamn psychological swamp with you!"

Sis mumbled, "Go screw yourself."

I lost it completely. *"Am I supposed to be like you? Am I supposed to get some intermittent, sorry-ass job so I can go to group therapy five times a day? So I can consult seventeen zillion 'health professionals'? Why don't I just quit my job? Why don't I sit around at the beach trading horror stories about asshole fathers? Then who'd pay for all the shit that's supposedly curing you?!"*

Sis tried to take my hand; there were tears in her eyes. I jerked my hand away, opened my wallet, counted out six bills, and dropped them on the table. Six hundred dollars from the Greta Stenholm research fund.

I said, "Rent—and a taxi home."

Sis wiped her eyes. "I love you, Annie."

I shook my head. I said, "Sorry, not tonight," and walked out of the restaurant.

I DROVE INTO Hollywood and parked in front of the Chinese Theater. I came here to calm down. To calm down and get a fix on Greta Stenholm. This was her old neighborhood.

The scene at the Dining Car had upset me. Even on a good day nothing made me madder than Big Bill Whitehead. I shouldn't have taken it out on my sister, but she could be so *helpless* sometimes.

Tilting the seat back, I watched people go into the late show.

I felt exhausted and overwhelmed. There was too much to absorb and too much to do. A lot to be afraid of, too: I hadn't forgotten about that.

I shut my eyes and tried to empty my mind. I wanted to concentrate on Greta Stenholm.

My mind wouldn't empty. I heard my sister say, "I love you," and flashed on our arguments about family feeling. I tried to picture Stenholm, and pictured my mother instead. She was the only dead body I'd ever seen before.

I'd never discussed her death with anyone except Sis and the cops at the time. People knew she was dead, that was all. I'd been matter-of-fact with Lockwood because nothing else was called for. But I hadn't felt matter-of-fact. I didn't want to dredge up that story. I didn't want to remember what I thought when I saw my mother dying.

I'd been home on vacation and heard the argument from another part of the house. The gun went off just as I ran into the kitchen. The explosion shattered glass, and I got caught by a spray of blood. Sis was screaming; Father let her go and watched Mother collapse. She'd blown a big hole in the side of her face. Blood gushed everywhere. I could see the frayed stump of her tongue and bone fragments piercing her cheek and eye. Her chest was still moving, and she made a horrible whistling noise as she tried to breathe. I tasted her blood in my mouth, saw the red blood on my clothes, and my first thought was: This is the most painful moment of my life — *and I can't feel any pain.*

It was almost as bad as the shooting.

I'd waited years before I told my sister about it. She'd had all kinds of therapy by then and she wasn't surprised. She said that the experience was common and encouraged me to talk about my childhood. I had tried, but I didn't remember much. I remembered getting punched and ducking flying objects. I remembered being thrown across rooms and down flights of stairs. I remembered blacking out, temporarily deaf from a smack to the ear. I remembered getting locked outside during a Canadian winter when it was sixty below with the windchill.

My sister said that memory loss was normal in cases like ours. But my memory loss wasn't total. I remembered the atmosphere of my childhood distinctly. And I remembered the emotions I grew up on. I remembered the constant fear. I remembered the desire to understand and escape; I remembered the contempt. The only emotion I ever felt for Father was contempt. And I felt contempt for my mother because she stayed with him and didn't fight back.

Sis never fought back either. She took more of Father's crap than I did because she was a passive target. But when she got sober, she made it her life's work to forgive him—and to make me forgive him, too.

Sis's favorite movie was *The Prince of Tides*. She watched it twice a year as a ritual. A line from the voice-over had become her mantra: "In families, there are no crimes beyond forgiveness." That made me furious. In the first place, some crimes were unforgivable. In the second place, forgiveness wasn't the issue. It wasn't my job to find a way to forgive Father: it was his job to act right. My sister believed that her forgiveness would change him. So far it hadn't—and I knew it wasn't going to. Sis and I argued about it, but the arguments always ended the same way. Sis said that we had to love our parents. I said that I loved the movies.

That's why she decided that movies were a substitute for my emotional life. I'd tried to explain what movies meant to me; Sis chose to simplify.

A tour bus pulled in at the curb ahead. I checked the time. It was late but the buses kept coming. I watched tourists fan out through the forecourt and thought just how complicated the explanation was.

When I left for college I swore I'd never look back. And I didn't, until Mother shot herself. Then I knew that college wasn't far enough, not even the States were far enough. I had to get clean away. If I didn't cut myself off, the family would catch me and crush me and I'd become a casualty like my sister.

I'd dropped out of school and taken off for London. I had my life savings, some people's names, and no plan: I just wanted to get lost. I partied all the time. I smoked dope day and night, and slept with every guy who appealed to me. Months went by in a haze, and one morning I woke up in West Berlin. I didn't remember how I got there—and didn't care. Sometimes I slept with someone because I had no place to stay. In Berlin one of those guys hit me. Nobody'd hit me since Father and I went ape. I grabbed an ashtray and beat him unconscious. I jumped on a train after, and wound up in Paris with my last fifty bucks and the name of a friend of a friend who was studying film.

The friend of a friend lived above a revival house near the Sorbonne. The revival house was running a retrospective of Michelangelo Antonioni films. While I waited for her to come home, I'd gone to see *The Passenger*.

I felt my forehead get hot. Even now, the memory of what happened in *The Passenger* brought on a sweat.

It was the first show of the day and I was alone in the theater. I'd never seen an Antonioni movie, so I didn't know what to expect. I was hungover; I was fried from sitting all night in the train; I was having paranoid fantasies where the Germans charged me with murder. Strung out and unprepared, I stared at the screen and couldn't understand what was happening. I couldn't understand how I couldn't understand. I moved closer to the front—and still couldn't understand. Half an hour in; I freaked. I burst out screaming. The projectionist ran into the theater to see what the matter was. I babbled about the movie. He said it wasn't me; he'd shown *The Passenger* for a week and didn't understand a thing. He said his favorite Italian director made *Meet Me in St. Louis*. When I didn't get the joke, he offered to stop the film and buy me a brandy next door.

I sent the projectionist away and stayed where I was. I forced myself to watch to the end. By the end I still didn't get it—but I was calm. I knew that *The Passenger* was a test. I knew that my whole crazy year in Europe had been a test. I'd fought the family and I'd fought fear. I'd burned out a lot of ugly, useless shit, and I was ready to start again.

After the film I went back to the booth and seduced the projectionist. He was a sweet guy who couldn't believe his luck. He told me what he liked about Vincente Minnelli and disliked about Michelangelo Antonioni, and let me watch *Mystery of Oberwald* for free.

I moved in with the film student, the friend of a friend. I gave up booze and dope, and never missed them. I met more film students and became part of a gang that lived for movies. Father cut off my allowance when I left the country so I was forced to find work. My only options without a permit were cash jobs like housecleaning or English conversation with widows and lechers. The jobs paid nothing; I was broke a lot and didn't always eat. Some friends started a culture 'zine, and I became their critic. That led to freelance subtitling, then to subtitles full-time. I'd learned French in Canada — I never thought it would pay the bills some day.

When I wasn't working for money, I was working for free: I wanted to see if I had any filmmaking talent. I worked as a production assistant. I wrote student shorts, cowrote some longer scripts, and directed a two-minute comedy sketch. I even joined a women's cooperative before I realized I wasn't made for collaboration. What I really loved was reviewing. I loved the solitary dark, and I loved being alone to think and write. I discovered that writing channeled my violence. I thought I'd left that stuff behind, but I saw the world in violent terms and it showed in my reviews. An editor once said that I wrote like every sentence was my last. I had laughed. Any sentence could be your last, I'd told him. But I didn't say that my mother died like that.

I'd discovered something else: my ability to love another person had been screwed at the root.

I had a passion for men. I'd sleep with someone just to touch his hair or hear a funny story about Jean-Luc Godard. Sometimes it was ninety minutes in the back row of a theater, sometimes a month of nothing but bed. I'd also had serious relationships. The breakup of the last, and most serious, ended my seven years in France. He was a director I met after raving about his films in print. Things went fine until he mentioned marriage and children. Our final fight was over the word *love*. He said that I'd never told him I loved him. He was right. I could say it about movies or books, but I couldn't say it to a man I really adored.

The breakup was hard but I didn't regret it for long. My sister said that our mother soured me on a conventional woman's fate. That was partly true. Another part of me was just numb; when people talked about *Love* love, I knew I'd never felt it. But I felt plenty of strong feelings. And a life full of men and movies was the only life I wanted.

I looked up at the facade of the Chinese.

L.A. had been a shock at first. I'd gone from a *Cahiers du cinéma* crowd who talked like Abel Gance and Sergei Eisenstein were still alive, to the Hollywood of "event" pictures and corporate marketing tie-ins.

Movies were a lot of things for me. Window on the world, fortress over the void, magic carpet, aphrodisiac, microscope, telescope, and sometimes an antidote for the pain. But they weren't an excuse to ignore my past. They weren't a substitute for emotion.

Damn Father for coming to L.A. *Damn* him and Sis for reminding me about the past.

But they hadn't started it. Lockwood had, when he made an issue out of the Colt.

Jesus—

I just remembered—

Lockwood hadn't returned my call. I'd gone all day without telling him about the ambush at Greta Stenholm's apartment.

I checked my watch: 12:30 A.M.

I got out Lockwood's card, picked up the car phone, dialed the police station, and left another message at the desk. This time I said it was urgent.

CHAPTER
EIGHT

I woke up thinking about Isabelle Pavich and her taunt: "Friends of Greta Stenholm tend to get dead."

It was now Thursday morning. Greta Stenholm was murdered Tuesday and I had a major urge to shake some answers out of Pavich. I spent an hour on the computer, searching the *Times* archives for murders. After an hour of frustration I decided to call Pavich. Then I changed my mind. I had USC names of my own, and Pavich gave me the creeps. I'd exhaust every possibility before I made a deal with her.

Vivian left a message while I was at the Chinese. The LAPD had no record of a break-in at 7095 Hawthorn; and she'd try to get more background on Lockwood, but she wasn't optimistic. I left a return message. I told her about the Lockwood-watcher journalists, and the information trade I wouldn't agree to. Maybe *she* could get something out of them, I said.

I checked my face in the mirror. My cheek was better; it felt more stiff than painful now. I popped four aspirin, dosed the bruises with arnica cream, and had toast and coffee. The dead-friends remark nagged at me. The burglary nagged at me. Why would Stenholm not report it? There were only two reasons I could think of. Either nothing happened, or something happened that she didn't want to tell the police.

I packed up my notes, raided the attic for more money, and

headed out. First stop was the bank, to change the hundreds into smaller bills. Next stop was the gun store.

Gun Galaxy backed onto a liquor store just east of Beverly Hills. The owner was a mild-spoken black man who hated whites and made his money arming them. I always bought my shells from him — although he disapproved of the Colt as old-fashioned and unwieldy.

He was unlocking his doors as I pulled into the parking lot. He greeted me with his usual pitch for a Lady Smith & Wesson. I laughed and laid out my problem: the cops had seized my gun and I needed immediate, concealable protection. He didn't ask questions; he just listed everything he had in stock, legal and illegal. It was a substantial list.

I bought a can of Mace, brass knuckles, a sap, and a pair of handcuffs. I might have bought a Lady Smith & Wesson if it hadn't been for the fifteen-day wait and the fact that I couldn't manage an automatic without practice. As it was, I walked out of the store with a miniarsenal. It made me feel nervous but safer.

The ambush the other night had been educational. I learned that my reflexes were rusty; I'd gotten out of the habit of self-defense. And being jumped by a stranger was different from being jumped by someone you knew. When the little goon grabbed me, I seized up: that had never happened before. I'd have to prepare myself to fight back, like I'd done with Father all those years.

Neil John Phillips, Stenholm's writing partner, was next on the agenda. He lived in the Fairfax District not far from the gun store. I drove over there.

Phillips's block was lined with old Spanish duplexes. I knew that he'd filed for bankruptcy, but these places ran three grand a month at least. I parked in front of his address. It was a ground-floor apartment on the corner. An engraved business card was taped to the mail slot: NEIL JOHN PHILLIPS — WRITER OF SCREEN PLAYS.

I banged the lion-head knocker and waited. Nobody answered. I circled around to the back door and knocked again. The screen was latched from the inside. I stood on the steps and tried to see in the kitchen window. The louvers were frosted glass and shut tight.

The backyard was all pavement and a row of garages. They were marked with the duplex numbers. I walked over, lifted Phillips's door, and got hit with a blast of hot air.

The garage was crammed with cardboard boxes. It was so full there almost wasn't room for a car. But there was no car. I went to the nearest stack and opened the flaps on the top box. It held hundreds of brittle yellowing memos, stamped with the Metro-Goldwyn-Mayer logo. I picked one up and the edges crumbled in my hand.

The memo was dated June 6, 1944, and was sent by Louis B. Mayer to a Mrs. Chadwick. It began "Re: Miss Garland's weight" and continued with detailed dietary instructions. The studio was putting Judy Garland on a stringent no-fat regime, and prescribing more amphetamines. I tried to think how old Garland would have been in 1944. Twenty?

I dug through the rest of the memos. Lots of them mentioned famous stars and seemed too valuable to be sitting in someone's garage; they were crumbling to dust. I caught references to Miss Crawford's freckles, Miss Garbo's large feet, and Mr. Gable's chronic infidelity. Louis Mayer had sent some; heads of production units and departments had sent others. There were even a couple signed by Irving Thalberg, MGM's legendary head of production.

I circled the garage looking into the most accessible boxes. All I found was old MGM paper—routine bureaucratic stuff of no interest.

One box contained a dozen bound scripts. The first few were authored by a B. N. Hecht. They were new scripts, not collector's items, and it took me a minute to figure them out. I realized that "B. N. Hecht" must be a pseudonym for Neil John Phillips. The blackballed Phillips must have borrowed a name from MGM's classic years: Ben Hecht was one of Hollywood's great screenwriters.

I found a copy of *The Last Real Man*. That was the script that had caused the controversy and ended Phillips's career. I opened the cover to take a look. A large piece of paper fell out from between the pages. I caught the piece of paper and unfolded it.

It was a pencil sketch of some kind of floor plan. The structure had long approaches from three directions, a central courtyard, and rooms labeled EDITING, and PROJECTION. There was a kitchen, a commissary, several offices, and a long hallway lined with bedroom suites. It was a weird hybrid, a cross between an open-air house, it seemed like, and a rudimentary movie studio. But there was nothing to identify the sketch—no address or name. I flipped the drawing over: the back of the paper was blank. I couldn't tell if the building existed, or if it was a film geek's vision of nirvana.

I heard footsteps on the pavement and looked up. A guy loomed in the garage opening. Before I could react, he snatched the script and the floor plan out of my hands, and backed away glaring. It all happened very fast.

I dusted myself off and stepped out of the garage. He slammed the door down and kicked it shut. I could see the guy better in the sunlight. He wore chinos, moccasins, and a polo shirt. His mouse-brown hair was thinning and receding, and he had a weak, spoiled face.

I said, "You're Neil John Phillips."

The guy pulled out an expensive miniature cell phone. "No, I live next door. You're trespassing. Give me one reason why I shouldn't call the fucking cops."

"My name's Ann Whitehead and I work—"

"OoOOoooo, the *movie critic*. I *know* who *you* work for."

What a prick, but I stayed cool. "Do you know where Phillips is?"

The guy nodded his head. I waited for more, and finally said, "Where is he?"

"Out of town."

"Where out of town? How can I reach him?"

"You can't."

"Why not?"

"Because he's writing—he goes underground when he writes."

I stuck out my hand, palm up. "Can I borrow your telephone?"

"What for?"

"To call the cops. Phillips's ex-writing partner was murdered, and you can't dick the cops around."

I took a step toward him. He said, "Desert Hot Springs."

"Where in Desert Hot Springs?"

"I don't know."

I faked a grab for his phone; he jerked his arm back. "I don't! Neil checks in every couple of days!"

I got out a pen and a business card and wrote my home number on the front. "Have him call me next time he checks in. Tell him it's urgent."

He took the card without reading it or looking at me. I shrugged and walked away. As I walked up the drive, I looked around. He was folding the floor-plan sketch and putting it back between the pages of the script.

I SAT IN my car on Phillips's street and made a load of phone calls.

I started with Edward Abadi—the agent of both Stenholm and Phillips. I called Creative Artists. The receptionist at CAA said that Abadi no longer worked there. I asked every way I could think of, but she wouldn't tell me when, why, or where he'd gone.

I called Abadi's Malibu number. A machine picked up, and a woman's voice said, "I'm not here right now. If you want to speak to Arnold Tolback, he's moved to the Chateau Marmont."

Arnold Tolback?

I hung up and rechecked Abadi's number off my notes. I *had* dialed it correctly. I called Information; there were no Edward Abadis listed in the L.A. area. I tried the other big talent agencies. ICM, William Morris—no go. I tried UTA—no go. I tried the Marmont on a slim hope. Arnold Tolback was not in his room, the restaurant, the lobby, or out at the pool.

That was very strange. Hollywood agents were the most locatable people in the world. You might not be able to talk to them, but you could always find them.

I gave Edward Abadi a rest and tried Stenholm's two USC classmates. Hamilton Ashburn Jr. wasn't home, but Penny Proft agreed to see me "toot sweet." She knew Stenholm was dead because the morning *Times* had published a second squib with the victim's name. She gave me the address, and I drove over to talk to her.

Proft lived in a pint-sized bungalow in the crowded flatlands adjoining the Beverly Center. A stout woman answered the front door. She was talking into a cordless telephone and held up one finger to say, almost done. I followed her into the living room and took a seat.

"...A *breast cancer* movie for *cable*? No frickin' *way!*..."

She had a brutal New York accent and wore baggy warm-ups. With her round face and round body, she looked like a comic career-woman troll.

"Uh-huh...yeah, yeah, uh-huh...Okay, if you can get my price, I'll do it....Yeah, thanks for nothing, you hump."

She mashed down the aerial and looked at me. "I never dreamed I'd get a breast cancer movie and meet our notorious bad girl all in one day. You were way right about *Moulin Rouge* and *Shrek*, Ann, but so not right about *Bridget Jones's Diary*. *Bridget Jones* was a howl, and Colin Firth, pass me a spoon, I'd eat him with fudge sauce any day. I've heard he's straight, tell me it's true. Luckily, you've never reviewed a movie of mine, but that's only because I've never had a script produced—a minor technicality."

What could I do? I laughed.

"Holy Mother of God, it laughs! The gals down at the Guild will never believe this." Proft threw herself on the couch and tucked the phone into her pants.

I said, "Let's talk about Greta Stenholm."

"I warn you, I never liked that woman. It doesn't surprise me one bit she got whacked. Cherchay le homme, is what I say."

She pronounced *homme* like "homey" and kept going. "Don't tell me, you're looking for the killer and a Pulitzer Prize, right? Or maybe you want her life story for a movie. It's been done before, but the world loves a dead blond—"

I cut in. "Do you mind if I say something?"

Proft made the zipper sign across her lips. "Be my guest, chiquita. I'm just tickled you're here."

"You went to SC with Stenholm."

"For three unforgettable years. The women loathed her and the guys groveled at her feet while she acted like Little Miss I-Live-For-My-Art all the time. I heard she was frigid."

"Were she and Neil Phillips a couple?"

"That dweeb? Euuuh, no way." She pretended to brush an insect off her leg. "The only person Neil wants to nuzzle is Irving Thalberg."

I flashed on the memos in his garage, and the lion-head knocker. "I understand he's a fan of the old MGM."

"A *fan*? He's positively *cracked* about it. They were a pair, those two, with their pet obsessions. He was going to be the greatest screenwriter who ever lived. She was going to direct wide-screen adventure movies. What a yutz—you can count on no hands the number of women who've directed adventure in the entire history of the studios."

I said, "Better to stick to breast cancer and other female complaints?"

Proft laughed. "Hey, I'm not here to change Hollywood. I just want my slice of the pie."

I said, "What happened after Stenholm graduated? She and Phillips sold one screenplay, and then she dropped out of sight."

"Hah! That's the best part! Miss I-Live-For-My-Art was headed straight for the top. I heard she fucked everybody and their spotted dog—"

"She was frigid *and* promiscuous?"

Proft shrugged. "I'm just telling you what I heard. And the great part is, she never got anywhere. She slept her way to the bottom!"

I smiled. "What happened exactly?"

"Do I care? I never saw her after SC, thank the Lord. I could speculate, though."

I said, "So speculate."

"Only an actress gets anywhere by being a slut. Women writers have to pick their affairs. The best bet is to hitch your wagon to a director, or producer, or another writer—male, of course. That's when women really go places around here. Greta and Neil broke up after school, and lone females scare the doo-doo out of movie executives."

Proft paused. "I hate to sound sympathetic, but you also have to think that Grets was too beautiful. A town like this and a shikse like that? The guys don't want her to direct their precious movies, no sirree. They want her to suck their cocks and show her bosom to the camera."

"I think she became a feminist, too."

Proft whistled through her teeth. "That's the Kiss o' Death right there. You have to be super-ultra-hyper-careful how you're a feminist in Hollywood. If I know our Greta, she'd spout off about it."

I was digging Proft's candor. Industry women almost never talked about sexism to the press; I knew because I'd tried to get them to. "So Stenholm was ambitious and talented, but not very realistic?"

"Exactemente — no concept of what she was up against. 'Oh I go to be Steven Spielberg, tralalalala.'"

I said, "Do you know who she slept with?"

Proft shook her head. "I can't remember any names offhand. It's just gossip I heard over the years — you know, in one-car-out-my-mouth kind of thing."

"But you said, 'Cherchez l'homme.'"

"Well, there's a story about her and her agent that made the rounds last year."

"Edward Abadi?"

"That's him. He was a CAA comer and West Bank wet dream, if you get my ethnic drift. It appears Mr. Ted was slipping Greta the schnitzel behind his fiancée's back — his fiancée being Hannah Silverman, Oscar-winning art director and world-class witch. And I heard recently that Greta was playing bury the brisket with Hank's *new* boyfriend, I forget his name, some producer. The name ends in ack — Prozac, halfback, something-ack."

I took a guess. "Arnold Tolback?"

"Voilà! Tolback."

"What happened to the affair with Abadi?"

Proft hooted. "You are *really* out of the loop, babycakes." She flattened her nose to one side and made a gun with the other hand.

"Bang! Bang! I heard Greta fucked him not two hours before it happened, in the house he shared with gnarly Ms. Silverman. Edward is sleeping the big sleep, Ann—somebody shot him."

I CALLED MARK when I got back to the car. He'd been trying to reach me for hours. He'd heard about the murder and had looked up the original news item. It was dated July 13, 2000, and he read it directly off his computer screen:

"'The Los Angeles County Sheriff's Department confirmed today that Edward Abadi, thirty-five, a movie agent, was found dead at his Malibu Beach home late last night. The cause of death has not been released. Sheriff's detectives are investigating.'"

That was it, apart from two short obituaries in the trade papers. Mark had phoned around for more information. Abadi was a Lebanese American from Encino who'd started as a gofer at CAA and rocketed to junior agent. Smart and ruthless—that was the book on Abadi. Conflicting rumors had him dying of a congenital heart defect, and a gunshot to the head. CAA wouldn't discuss him or the circumstances of his death. He had merely "left the organization."

I asked if the murder rumor was ever confirmed in print. Mark said no, it never was. He also said he couldn't do any more work for me—Barry's orders. He'd gone in to ask about the guest list and Barry got pissed. Barry claimed there wasn't any written list and pressured Mark to tell him what we knew. Mark appeased him with a few scraps, but he was finished as my researcher. I was supposed to call Barry ASAP. He told Mark to remind me that *Lockwood was due Tuesday.*

Mark hung up and I sat in the car thinking.

Why had Abadi's death barely made the papers? One: it was a congenital heart defect. Two: it was murder. Either Abadi's family or CAA put a lid on publicity, or the killing went unsolved. There were a lot of murders in L.A. The dailies only wrote up the crime, the arrest, and the conviction—unless it involved a celebrity or some baroque circumstance. If there was nothing else in the archives, it probably meant they'd never made an arrest.

I started the car and headed out for Malibu. I used one hand to drive and dialed my phone with the other.

I punched in the Palm Springs area code and sweet-talked an operator with hints about multiple murder and police bungling. I got her to give me the names of every hotel and motel in Desert Hot Springs. There were a ton—it was a resort town. The drive took an hour, and I scribbled names and numbers the whole time. I *had* to talk to Neil John Phillips.

Finding Edward Abadi's address was no problem. His former house sat on the beach, on a side road just off the coast highway. I parked opposite the house and ran across the street.

The house was protected by a stockade fence. There was a door, a mail slot, and an illuminated bell set in the fence. I leaned on the bell and waited. I leaned on it again: nobody. I jumped in the air, but I wasn't tall enough to see over. I debated, checked around for neighbors, and thought, Fuck it.

Backing up, I ran at the fence, jumped, grabbed the top, and pulled myself up. I swung my legs over and dropped down to the patio.

The house sat north-south, perpendicular to the beach. It was a weather-worn, shingled job perched on pylons sunk in the sand. I reached into the mailbox and pulled out bills and liberal junk mail for Hannah Silverman and Arnold Tolback. I put the mail back, checked the garage, and found a shiny black Humvee. I wrote the license number on my hand.

I knocked at the front door. Nobody answered. I tried the knob; the door was locked. I pressed my face against a window. I could see straight through the house—the whole back wall was glass. I held very still. There was no sound or movement inside.

A sloping stone path led to the beach. I followed it out to the sand. A sundeck jutted off the back of the house, high over my head. I stood behind a pylon and checked both directions. There were people way down on the public beach; nobody close.

I took the wooden stairs up to the deck. The main floor had

sliding glass doors; one was unlocked. She must be home, I thought. I slid the door open and called Hannah Silverman's name. No one answered. I waited, listened, looked both ways again, and slipped inside. I stood there a second to slow my breathing down. I was feeling some nerves.

The rooms were big and flowed together to show off the ocean view. The furnishings were designed and coordinated down to the last lamp shade. I found the one bedroom by process of elimination. It was a pigsty. There was an open Vuitton suitcase on the bed, and women's clothes thrown everywhere, like someone had been packing in a fit. I checked a few labels: pricey stuff.

An office adjoined the bedroom, and it was a pigsty, too. Drawers stood open; the desk was covered with messy junk. On the floor I found a half dozen framed photographs. The glass had been smashed to slivers.

The pictures showed the same loving couple posed in trendy locales. I recognized Bali and the waterfront at Cannes. The woman was too thin, and she had a snotty way of standing with her chin in the air. Hannah Silverman. Her companion was shorter, younger, and clearly having a better time. He looked like a fraternity boy; she looked like a prime neurotic.

I glanced around and saw bare nails sticking out of the walls. Only one photograph was still hanging and intact. Hannah Silverman stood beside an exotically handsome, Arab-type man in what looked like a hotel ballroom. They both wore business suits and she held a folder that said SUNDANCE FILM FESTIVAL. There was a marquise diamond on the third finger of her left hand.

The fraternity boy had to be Arnold Tolback. The Arab-type man had to be Edward Abadi. Like Tolback, Abadi looked ten years younger than Silverman. He held a cell phone and stared past her as if he'd spotted his next deal coming through the lobby. I studied the picture up close. Abadi and Stenholm would have made a spectacular pair.

A second room led off the office. I walked in and found a combination gym and sex playpen.

Twin stair-step machines faced a ceiling-high entertainment

center. The center featured a massive TV set, a smaller set, a DVD player, a VCR, a tuner, a six-CD player, and a pair of speakers taller than me. Bookcases lined another wall. They held videos, DVDs, CDs, magazines, free weights, mats, towels, yoga props, Evian vaporizers . . . and bondage paraphernalia.

There were whips and leather masks, collars, leashes, and padded handcuffs—all looking brand-new and sitting in plain sight. Mirrors covered one entire wall. A video camera stood on a tripod in one corner. A big hook was screwed into the ceiling, with chains dangling off. The effect was so corny and antiseptic that I had to laugh.

An unlabeled tape was sticking out of the VCR. I pushed it in and turned on the small TV.

An image jumped onto the screen. I caught a vignette in progress.

The scene was set in a brick cellar. A small window was inset high in the back wall, and a harsh light glared down from the ceiling. A ratty curtain partly hid an iron cot. A fake-platinum blond was parading around in Gestapo drag. She pointed a toy pistol at a naked young guy who was kneeling by the cot. He wrapped his arms around her ankles and pressed his face into her leather boots. Tears streamed down his cheeks.

I hit the volume.

He was sobbing, "Oh, please, spare my life! I'll do anything you want, only spare my life!"

The she-wolf leered at him. He crawled up her jodhpur leg and revealed a hardening penis. He stroked it to a full erection.

The she-wolf slapped him. She said, "It iss zo zmall," in a silly accent. "It muss be ffery larch to mekk pleashure to Helga."

The guy sobbed and stroked his dick. It was plenty large in my opinion, but Helga had different standards. She snarled and pressed her pistol into his neck.

I burst out laughing.

A voice shot from the front of the house. "Is that you, Arnie, you faithless son of a bitch?!"

Hannah Silverman.

I recognized her from the answering machine. The front door slammed; keys jingled. She yelled, "I turned you in to the cops yesterday! Ask me if that felt good!"

I lunged for the sliding door, ran out to the deck, and took the stairs two at a time. I hit the sand hard and tripped forward on my face.

The voice came closer. *"Arnie, you bastard!"*

I rolled under the deck out of sight. Jumping up, I raced for the path, up to the street, and threw myself over the front fence. I landed off balance and almost fell into traffic.

I looked over my shoulder. Hannah Silverman was nowhere. I dodged across the road and ducked behind my car. I was panting. I peeked around the bumper.

The front gate opened and Silverman stuck her head out. The look on her face was hilarious: a snarl worthy of Helga.

I said, "Dilettante perverts," and laughed again.

SILVERMAN TOOK off while I was hiding behind my car. I tailed her along the coast road and lost her at a light. I wandered around Malibu, saw no black Humvees, gave up, and drove back into Hollywood.

I parked in an alley by Greta Stenholm's and walked to the Chinese Theater. Hollywood Boulevard was the usual zoo—a cleaned-up zoo since the big rehab and new subway. The tourists were out in force like always, but the street freaks had been displaced by hip and happening locals.

I'd shelved Neil John Phillips and Arnold Tolback for the moment.

I'd called hotels in Desert Hot Springs on my way in from Malibu. I didn't find Phillips. I'd also dropped by the Chateau Marmont: Tolback wasn't around. But I did a lot of interviews at the Marmont and knew the desk staff there. The guy on duty said that Tolback checked in the week before. I made a note of the date: August 23. I promised him twenty bucks if he'd call me the minute Tolback showed up. He said he'd rather have a tape of my interview with Clive Owen. I said fine.

Hannah Silverman was not shelved. I didn't know which movie she won the Oscar for; I didn't remember ever hearing her name. A world-class witch, Penny Proft had said — with a thing for younger men and corny discipline games. And the third party in two love triangles, if Proft's gossip was reliable. Stenholm had slept with Edward Abadi *and* Arnold Tolback. That was more than coincidence; it looked deliberate. But why would Stenholm want to mess with Silverman?

Lockwood knew why.

I'd called from Malibu and caught him at the station. He didn't like it that I knew about Edward Abadi. He confirmed that Abadi had been shot, but wouldn't expand or explain. I asked him straight out: why would Greta Stenholm want to mess with Hannah Silverman? Lockwood said he'd meet me at my place later, named a time, and hung up. He hadn't gotten my messages and didn't give me a chance to mention them.

I walked into the forecourt of the Chinese, glad I hadn't agreed to his one-way "cooperation" deal. I would have known exactly nothing right now.

The forecourt was jammed with people. They were pouring out the theater exits, lined up behind velvet ropes, and taking pictures of the footprints in cement.

I stopped to remind myself why I'd come.

Last Friday, four days before she died, Greta Stenholm spent a chunk of time seeing movies on the Boulevard.

I was filling in the blank week in her calendar. On Thursday she went to the library and read about herself in the *Hollywood Reporter*. She saw movies all day Friday and vandalized candy machines on Saturday.

The question was: Why would Stenholm come *here*? Maybe she still lived in the area; the movies she saw, except the documentary at the Cinematheque, were playing citywide.

Was it another way to celebrate the sale of her script? Was she saying good-bye to five years of failure? Was it an act of triumph and revenge, like defacing the *Reporter* piece? Or was she a fan of movie history like her ex-partner Phillips? The El Capitan was a landmark. The Cinematheque was in the Egyptian Theater. The Egyptian was Sid Grauman's first theme palace in Hollywood, the Chinese was his second, and both theaters had been restored to their kitschy '20s splendor.

I didn't know the history of the Vine, but she went to see a Steven Spielberg double feature there.

Where did she get the cash to buy tickets? She was bouncing checks and stealing from candy machines, and she died broke. Did she spend her last dime on *movies*?

I walked up to the main doors of the Chinese, flagged down an usher, and asked him to get the manager. The kid ducked into the lobby and came back with a frazzled-looking man. I showed him my press card. I said I was doing a piece on Hollywood hopefuls and trying to locate Greta Stenholm. He didn't register the name, so I showed him the *Reporter* photograph.

He smiled when he saw it. She was a regular at their discount matinees, he said. "A lovely young lady, crazy for movies and very bright." The day shift loved her and wished her luck with the new screenplay. He hadn't seen her last Friday, but he knew one of her haunts: a pizza place across from the Egyptian.

I walked east and found the pizza place. It was a biker hangout with brown Naugahyde booths, but it was clean and it smelled good. I showed my Stenholm picture to the guy at the counter. He identified her right off. He knew her first name and said she was a longtime customer.

According to him she'd talked about nothing but her script for the past month. She'd also looked more and more ragged because the studio negotiation was driving her nuts. She'd made calls from the pay phone, and gotten calls back—from her agent, she'd said. And she'd eaten there every day for the past two weeks. The counterman admitted he was feeding her for free. He couldn't let her starve, he said, when her script was going for hundreds of thousands of dollars. He saw her last on Monday, the night of Barry's party. She'd made a few calls, eaten a calzone, and gone to a movie down the street.

I ran back to my car and drove down to the Vine Theater.

There was no place to park, so I left the car in a loading zone. I by-passed the box office and asked an usher to get her boss for me. The usher wanted to know why; she was busy. I told her my "Hollywood hopefuls" story and showed her the picture of Stenholm.

The usher turned to a shaggy surfer boy who was working the concession stand. He wore a beaded choker with his uniform. She called, "Yo, Harrison! She's got your *girlfriend* here!"

The usher giggled at the look on the surfer kid's face. He left his popcorn popper and came over.

He said, "Hi, can I help you?" His face was tight. I steered him away from the giggly usher.

I said, "It's about Greta Stenholm."

His face changed. He whispered, "But I talked to the cops yesterday. Is this going to start again?"

"Is what going to start again?"

He shook his head and clamped his lips together. I showed him my press card. "I'm not the police."

The kid just shook his head. I said, "She saw a movie here last Monday and I know for a fact she was broke."

The kid sagged against the wall. "Oh, man. I'm going to get fired this time—I'm going to get fired."

I pulled a twenty out of my pocket and put it in his hand. "Tell me everything, from the beginning."

He passed the bill right back to me. "I don't want money."

"Then I'll have a few words with your boss."

He said, "No!" and moved to block my way.

"Then talk. *What* is starting again?"

The kid hesitated. "A dude...like...got iced last year."

"Her film agent?"

The kid nodded.

"And?"

"And, like, she was here when the deal went down."

"Here at the Vine?"

"Uh-huh, watching movies. She used to come every week, sometimes more than once. Sometimes she'd be low on cash or whatever, and I let her in for free."

I saw what he was getting at. "You let her in free that night, so she had no proof she'd been here, no ticket stubs."

The kid nodded. "But Greta covered for me down the line. She told the cops she lost her stubs, and anyway, two of us saw her that night—me and this other girl."

"Did the cops suspect her of the killing?"

The kid rolled his eyes. "Oh man, like, for *real*. They wouldn't leave us *alone*. They kept coming back until the other girl quit because she couldn't take it anymore."

I said, "Now Greta's dead and the cops are back again."

The kid smiled for a second. He was missing teeth. "But not the same ones. These dudes are, like, cool. I told them about the ticket stubs and they believed me, and they won't narc me to my boss."

I described Lockwood and his partner. The kid nodded. "That's them."

"Did they know that Greta had been here Monday night?"

"Nuh-uh—not until I told them." He looked over at the concession stand. The line was getting long and there was only one other kid to handle it.

I poked his arm. "Greta was here last Friday for two shows. Were you working that night? How did she act?"

"She was, like, strange, man. She asked if she could sleep in the ladies' lounge."

"Why?"

He shrugged. "She couldn't go home maybe."

"Do you know where she was living?"

The kid shook his head.

"Did you let her sleep in the lounge?"

"Nuh-uh—I'd get in trouble."

I said, "Do you know where she *did* sleep that night?"

He shook his head and pointed at the lines. "I can't talk anymore. I have to go."

"One more question. What happened Monday night?"

"Monday I let her watch *A.I.* for free."

"Didn't she see it on Friday?"

"Uh-huh, but she did stuff like that, like, see the same movie over and over. But she left in the middle of the show to meet somebody about a movie she wrote."

"What time was that?"

He shrugged. "Nine-thirty?"

"Was she going to meet her agent?"

The kid shrugged. "That's all I know. She said she was seeing somebody about *GBDB*."

"G-B-D-B?"

He shrugged again. "Whatever—I guess it's the name of her movie. Now, like, I *really* have to go. And don't talk to my boss, okay?"

He ran back to the popcorn machine. I pulled out my pen and wrote "GBDB—???" on the palm of my hand.

As things got more complex, I got more excited.

A film-school star reviving her dead career. A beautiful blond, flat broke and scrounging free meals and movies. Two murders, a burglary, a blackmail scheme—and a six-figure film script that told the truth about the condition of women.

My Hollywood story.

One article wasn't going to be enough. Greta Stenholm would need a series, and I already had the title. I was going to call it "A Bright Young Woman."

Everything was dark when I got home. I'd left in such a rush that morning, I forgot to turn on the floodlights around the mansion. I always left lights on if I was going to be late. The place could be eerie at night.

I pulled down the drive and parked by the garage in back. Checking my watch, I decided to leave the driveway gates open. I was exactly on time. Lockwood was due any minute.

I walked around the pool, trying to pick out my door key by feel. My head was down and I was squinting at my key ring as I walked up to the pool house. There were bushes beside the front porch. I heard leaves rustle. I looked over; it was too dark to see. On instinct I ducked and threw up one arm.

Branches snapped. A figure crashed out of the bushes. I yelled and faked to the left. He fell past me, waving an object in the air. A heavy iron bar grazed my shoulder.

I dodged sideways and tried to run. He grabbed my bag and jerked me back. I twisted away from him. He swung the iron bar; I caught a glancing blow. It stung. I twisted and ducked and dug for my sap. Swinging wild, he hit me on the wrist. I screamed and dropped my bag. The guy stumbled backward with it. I took off running. The guy came after me. I heard his breath as he closed in.

I could have outrun him. But it was dark, and I was frantic, and I ran straight into the swimming pool. My feet hit air and I smacked the water face first.

The guy jumped in on top of me. Something rammed my head. I saw starbursts and almost blacked out. We both went under. The guy grabbed my neck and started to strangle me.

I tried to scream. I opened my mouth and sucked in water. I thrashed and kicked and clawed for the surface. The hands squeezed tighter.

I banged my head on something hard. It was the cement lip around the pool. I flailed and kicked, trying to throw the guy off me. I couldn't *breathe*.

Suddenly my neck was free. Water sucked and churned—squishy footsteps raced across the lawn. I grabbed the edge of the pool and held on, choking, spitting water, and gasping for air.

Someone touched me.

I screamed and struck out blind. Two hands latched on to my wrists. I tried to kick away from the edge. The hands grabbed me and pulled me over the side. I was yelling. I fought; I twisted my body and squirmed backward. Then I heard a familiar voice:

"It's me! I've got you! *Stop!*"

I went limp on the cement. Lockwood rolled me over, put his thumbs along my spine and pushed. My stomach heaved. I rolled onto my side and threw up pool water. The chlorine stung my mouth.

Lockwood jumped up and took off across the lawn. I lay there panting for breath. He ran to the back wall, grabbed some ivy, hauled himself to the top, and jumped down into the vacant lot behind.

I lay there a few minutes, then made myself sit up. I was soaking wet and shaking hard. I was dizzy. My lungs ached, my neck ached, my nose and throat burned. I tried to pull a clump of hair out of my mouth. My right fingers were numb, and my right wrist wouldn't bend.

I rested a few more minutes, then made myself stand. My head started to spin and I almost fell down again. I caught myself on a chaise lounge, gave it another minute, and walked to the pool house very slowly.

I found my bag in the bushes where the guy had dropped it. I bent slowly and picked it up. I had to keep my head level or else I'd fall. Reaching into the front room, I hit the wall switch. The ceiling light went on.

I stared at the chaos.

All the furniture had been shoved out of place. The daybed was torn apart—mattress, pillows, blankets, everywhere. The rugs were wadded up. Drawers and cupboards were open, the bookshelves had been emptied. My things were flung all over the floor.

I crawled up on my writing table and tried the slats of the attic fan. The guy hadn't searched there. I got the envelope of money, climbed down, and set it on the table. I waded into the bathroom to get my flashlight. The bathroom had been trashed, too.

I walked out to the back wall, careful not to move fast. I tucked the flashlight in my jeans and climbed slowly to the top. The vacant lot was dark. I shined the light down along the outer wall.

There was a crack of dry branches. I lifted the flashlight. Lockwood was coming through the vacant lot, straightening his necktie. He saw me and pointed off to my right.

I swung the light around and saw a ladder propped against the outer wall. That was how the guy got in.

I said, "Look." I aimed the light low on the ladder.

Lockwood stooped to examine the ground. The dirt was too packed and dry to show footprints. I leaned down closer. The light beam started to sway back and forth. Lockwood glanced up. I dropped the flashlight and grabbed some ivy to steady myself. My ears were ringing.

I slowly lowered myself to the ground. Lockwood climbed over the wall and jumped down beside me. I was just standing there, holding my head, fighting the dizzy sensation. I felt sick, I was so dizzy. Lockwood put his arm around me. I wrapped both arms around him and pressed my face into his jacket. I almost wanted to cry.

Lockwood started to walk me toward the pool house. He said, "We better get you to the hospital."

I made a no noise. Lockwood said, "You can't stay here. I can put you in a hotel, or give you around-the-clock guards. Which would you prefer?"

We walked up onto the porch. He stopped when he saw the mess inside. I spotted a long object on the cement. I let go of him, bent down carefully, and picked it up. It was a carpenter's pry bar. I wasn't worried about fingerprints because the guy had worn gloves. I'd felt the material around my throat.

I tapped the pry bar on the door, just a light tap. It made a dent in the wood. The guy would have crushed my skull if he'd had better aim. *Crush my skull*, I thought—and laughed out loud. It sent pain through my whole body. I stopped laughing, grabbed the door for support, and gritted my teeth.

I gave the pry bar to Lockwood. He tested the heft of it. I told him about the attack, the sequence of events as I remembered them. I had to stop every so often to gather my strength. While I was talking, he walked into the pool house and looked around. He stuck his head in the kitchen and the bathroom. Three times he turned to stare at me. I finally said, "Is something wrong?"

He nodded. "I don't understand you."

"What do you mean?"

"I've never seen a witness act the way you did the other day. You made jokes at our first interview." He held up the pry bar. "Then someone tries to kill you and you laugh."

I smiled. "People say I only get emotional about movies. Maybe I don't feel the gravity of the situation."

Lockwood did not smile. "No, I think you don't feel fear."

I stuck my hands out. They were shaking so badly, he could see it from across the room. I said, "I need to dry off."

I went into the bathroom and shut the door. I stripped naked in front of the mirror. There were red marks in a band around my neck. They'd turn into bruises soon. My right shoulder had a welt where the pry bar grazed it; my right wrist was numb and already swollen. I dosed myself with more aspirin and arnica, and took two drugstore sedatives to calm down. For the first time in years I wanted a drink.

I threw on dry clothes and opened the door. Lockwood had found the Burger King file in the mess. He'd put the mattress back on the bed and sat there, flipping pages. He held Vivian's note in one hand and seemed to be engrossed.

I didn't have the energy to clean up just yet. Aftershock was setting in; my legs were rubbery and I felt hot and weird. I sat down in a chair and watched Lockwood read Vivian's note. He reread it a couple of times. I thought he'd react to the gossip about his Mexico trip and love life, but his expression didn't change.

I said, "I'd like to do a piece on you."

Lockwood shook his head.

"Why not? You could tell your side—"

Lockwood closed the file and pointed to the mess. "We have more important things to discuss. I've spoken to your family."

I almost laughed. "You can't still think I'm involved in the murder, not when Stenholm *and* her agent are dead."

"I hear that you've brought a legal action against your father."

"Not yet I haven't. He stole some money from my sister and me, and I'm seeing if there's a criminal case."

"Your father says that you hate him. You've accused him of murdering your mother, and you've assaulted and threatened to kill him on several occasions. Now you're trying to put him in jail, he says."

I tracked the logic. "And Father happened to be in L.A. during the time frame of Greta Stenholm's murder."

Lockwood nodded. "Your sister believes he's capable of murder."

"That's because she doesn't understand him. How much did she tell you about the family?"

"We had quite a long talk."

"Then you know that my father's a coward. He might dream of killing me—just like I've dreamed of killing him—but he prefers a helpless target. He wouldn't fly out here to kill me in cold blood. Moreover, he'd never do it with a knife. Moreover, the guy who jumped me tonight was smaller and younger."

Lockwood frowned. "Do you have any proof that the individual tonight was Miss Stenholm's murderer?"

I just looked at him. "Isn't it obvious?"

"Nothing's obvious." Lockwood set the Burger King file down and leaned forward. "Here are my four best explanations for what just happened."

He counted off on his fingers. "One, your accomplice in Miss Stenholm's murder wants to eliminate you—"

"That's preposter—"

Lockwood talked over the objection. "Two, the killer *was* after you, and he came back to finish the job. Three, something was left at the crime scene, and a witness, an accomplice or the killer himself, came back to get it. Four, sometime between Tuesday evening and now, you did something or saw somebody who *is* the killer, or who alerted the killer to your connection to this case. You've learned something that our guy considers dangerous to himself."

Lockwood got out his pen and notebook, and opened the notebook on his knee. "What have you done since I saw you last?"

I gave him a rundown of the relevant items: Stenholm's old apartment to the popcorn kid at the Vine Theater, omitting only my stop by the gun store. I didn't apologize and Lockwood didn't interrupt. He got names, numbers, times, places—all the minutiae that he thrived on. At the end, I pointed to the envelope on my desk.

Lockwood pulled out latex gloves and got up to examine it. He counted the separate bundles, then all the bills in one bundle. I saw him say, "Eighteen thousand," under his breath.

He peeled off his gloves. "This incident at the Hawthorn apartment happened two nights ago. Why didn't you call us?"

"I did. I left messages at the station."

He frowned, jotted in his notebook, ripped out the page, and handed it to me. There were two cell-phone numbers: his, and his partner Smith's. He said, "Next time call us directly. I don't want to not get a message again."

I stuck the paper in my jeans. "Anyway, the timing proves that the blackmail and the murder aren't related. It makes no sense to deliver the money after you've killed her. And the guy didn't even know what Greta Stenholm looked like."

"Regardless of timing, blackmail constitutes a possible motive." Lockwood rubbed his eyes. He looked tired, and disgusted with me.

"This is why I asked you not to interfere. Bad guys screw up— their actions aren't always logical. The date to deliver the money was probably set prior to her murder, with no further communication between the extortion victim and the third party delivering the payment. Remember, Miss Stenholm's name wasn't published until today. If the victim decided to have her killed, he isn't going to confess it by canceling the delivery before her death was common knowledge."

I thought that over—and dismissed it. "But the murder wasn't planned. The killer used my kitchen knife and left the blackmail pictures behind."

"So that the murder would appear unplanned, perhaps, and the pictures would appear unrelated."

I lay my head back on the chair; talking made me feel faint. Lockwood said, "Where's the rest of the money?"

My voice came out faint. "What do you mean 'the rest'?"

"Eighteen thousand is an odd number. Where's the rest?"

"There is no 'rest.' Maybe—"

Lockwood held up his hand. "Miss Whitehead, do you know the difference between right and wrong?"

I flushed and didn't answer him. Lockwood said, "My guess is that you kept part of the money and hid it in the same place you hid the xeroxed copies of Miss Stenholm's personal papers."

He nudged a pillow with his foot. "Do you think that money's still here?"

I did not look up at the attic fan, or at my bag. "It's still here— and I know it's wrong to keep it. How do *you* justify keeping my Colt?"

"I justify it by long experience. I justify it by a sense I have of you."

"A sense of me?"

He nodded. "I believe that you would use a gun if circumstances required it. I intend to prevent that if I can."

I DIDN'T HAVE to ask; Lockwood volunteered the bare facts of Edward Abadi's murder.

He had died between 9 P.M. and midnight on July 12, 2000, at the beach house where he lived with his fiancée, Hannah Silverman. Silverman came home the next morning and found his body on the living room couch. His appointment book was still open on his lap. He'd been shot once in the right temple with his own gun. There were no signs of forced entry and nothing was stolen.

The Sheriff's detectives ruled out suicide. The powder burns, the angle of the entry wound, and the gun's final resting place all indicated murder. Abadi was shot by a person who stood a short distance away and slightly behind him. The signs also said an intimate setup: Abadi and the killer had probably known each other.

The Sheriff's thought that Greta Stenholm or Hannah Silverman did it. They thought jealousy was the motive. But no physical evidence linked them to the killing, and both women had alibis that were never broken down. Silverman spent the night at her father's house; Stenholm was watching movies at the Vine Theater.

The women accused each other of the crime. Silverman said Stenholm did it—because Abadi had ended their affair and dumped her as a client. Stenholm said Silverman did it—because Abadi had broken off their engagement.

The case was still unsolved.

The telephone rang and interrupted him. I let the machine pick it up. After the beep, came:

"Ann, it's Nicholas at Marmont reception. Mr. Tolback just—"

I quick grabbed the phone. "Nicholas, I'm here." Lockwood leaned over and tilted the receiver so he could listen in.

"Mr. Tolback just went up to his room."

I checked the clock; it was almost 11 P.M. "Was he alone?"

"Yes."

"What kind of car does he drive?"

"It's a Porsche, new it looks like, black."

Lockwood spoke into the mouthpiece. "This is Detective Lockwood, Los Angeles Police Department."

The line went quiet. Lockwood said, "Did Mr. Tolback say he was in for the evening?"

"... Yes, he did."

"Thank you for your trouble, Nicholas. Good night."

Lockwood took the receiver and hung it up. "I want you to promise that you won't bother Hannah Silverman or Arnold Tolback."

I looked at my hand. I'd written "GBDB" and Silverman's license number on it: the ink had washed off.

Lockwood said, "Promise."

I smiled. "Shouldn't I steer clear of my father, too?"

"Promise me."

"I'll promise, if it's renegotiable and you'll answer some questions."

Lockwood rubbed his eyes.

I said, "Why didn't the Sheriff's believe the kid at the Vine Theater?"

"No comment."

"Did they fumble it? Were they too attached to the idea that one of the girlfriends did it?"

"No comment. They're excellent detectives in general."

"Are there other people besides Hannah Silverman who cross over from the Abadi killing to Stenholm?"

Lockwood said, "Yes—but I won't discuss names at this point."

"Silverman looks good, doesn't she, with Stenholm out stealing her boyfriends and only a father for an alibi?"

Lockwood said, "No comment."

I said, "Stenholm came to Barry's party to meet someone about GBDB. Do you know the name of her new agent?"

Lockwood shook his head.

"There might be a copy of the script in the trunk of her car."

Lockwood shook his head. "There were scripts there, yes, but no GBDB."

"It would also be on computer disk."

Lockwood shook his head.

"Did you get any fingerprints from the back office?"

"Partials for Miss Stenholm and rubber glove marks that we assume were you. A range of latents we can't identify."

"What do you know about the burglary at her apartment last winter?"

Lockwood shook his head. "We weren't called in. Nobody knows what was taken, if anything." He scribbled a note, tore the page out of his notebook, and passed it to me. He'd written, "Parker Center/RHD/3rd fl." and a phone number.

"I want you there at 9 A.M. to talk to our composite artist. We need a picture of the man who gave you the money."

I said, "Where was she living? She got thrown out of her apartment two months ago, and she tried to sleep in the ladies' lounge at the Vine Friday night."

"We believe she was living in her car."

I was silent. Jesus.

"Our people rousted her in Griffith Park last Sunday for sleeping in her car. She told the officers she didn't want to leave it unattended because it had been broken into in Hollywood the previous Friday and suitcases and other personal items were stolen. Traffic Division confirms the story in part. She was issued two tickets for meter violations on Ivar Avenue Friday night."

I said, "And Ivar is right by the Vine. So her apartment broken into, her car broken into..."

It explained the dented trunk lock and smashed passenger window. It explained the dirty fingernails and body odor. She might have come out to the pool house just for a bath.

Lockwood took the envelope by one edge, put his notebook away, and stood up. His slacks and sport coat still had damp spots from me. He said, "What have you decided?"

"I'm not going to the hospital."

"Regarding protection, I meant. A hotel or a guard?"

"The mansion has an alarm. I'll be fine in there."

He shook his head. "I'd prefer—"

"Really, I'm fine."

He decided not to argue. "Then I'll send someone for the ladder, and I'm going to get a car to watch the front."

I put out my hand to him and said, "Thanks for saving my life." Lockwood touched it briefly. "I'll see you tomorrow morning."

He stepped over a wadded rug and walked out, shutting the inside door behind him. I stared at the door and felt myself blush. That was embarrassing; I'd made the gesture and he hadn't returned it. He hadn't even looked me in the eye.

I heard his car pull out of the drive and got up to close the gates. On my way back I hit all the floodlights, including the pool and the flower beds. Nobody was going to catch me in the dark again.

I felt wasted, but I was too wound up to sleep. I studied the mess in the front room. Nothing was torn or broken that I could see. The guy was looking for a specific thing, I bet—this wasn't just terror tactics or helter-skelter. It would take hours to clean. If Lockwood weren't such a *cop*, I would have asked him to stay and help: I would've liked some company right about now. Company, and a nice stiff drink. But there was no alcohol in either house.

I locked the screen, bolted the inside door, and shut all the windows.

Bending down, I picked a cushion up off the floor. There was a dirty shoe print on the fabric.

Lockwood had offered four explanations for the attack tonight. I liked the fourth one best. Sometime in the past two days, I'd learned something that was dangerous to Greta Stenholm's killer.

And now he wanted me.

CHAPTER
TEN

FIFTEEN YEARS ago Creative Artists was at the top of the Hollywood pile. Mike Ovitz and his partners had combined Asian martial philosophy with the totalitarian packaging of Lew Wasserman and come up with a talent agency more powerful than any studio. Ovitz had since left CAA—for browner pastures, some said—and CAA wasn't the omnipotence it used to be. But it was still considered the best-run agency with the strongest roster of talent. And it was still located in the monument that Ovitz had built to his success: the specially commissioned I. M. Pei building in the commercial district of Beverly Hills.

I was reviewing recent history as I walked into CAA's lobby the next day.

Greta Stenholm and Neil John Phillips graduated from film school in 1996. Being recruited by Creative Artists, getting a comer like Edward Abadi for an agent: Stenholm and Phillips would've been very hot with the Industry.

I took off my sunglasses and looked around. I'd never been in here before, although I'd heard plenty about it. The lobby was high, simple, and light—Eastern minimalism translated into expensive spatial art. I thought of Mark, who liked to rag Ovitz's pretensions. He said that Mike Ovitz worshipped Art everywhere except in movies.

The light was too much for my headache. I put my sunglasses back on and walked over to reception.

The woman there looked up. I told her I didn't have an appointment, I just wanted some information. She checked out my bruises and slipped her fingers under the rim of her desk. A security guard appeared from behind a pillar. He wore an Italian suit and looked like a karate instructor.

I turned right around and walked out of the building. The bum's rush didn't surprise me. A place like that was as protected as a studio lot; I'd only hoped to get the receptionist to talk.

The guard followed me outside and asked where I'd parked. I asked him if he'd known, or had heard of, a junior agent named Edward Abadi. Did he know who'd taken Abadi's clients after his death? The guard put an arm out to direct me away from the building. I shrugged and walked back to my car. The guard followed three feet behind.

He waited to make sure I actually left. I pulled out, circled the block, and turned onto Wilshire. A banged-up Trans Am pulled up level in the lane beside me. The fenders were primer gray, which caught my attention. I looked at the driver.

It was the goon from Greta Stenholm's apartment building. He was wearing the same Hawaiian shirt—purple palm trees on an orange background.

He saw me see him. He took one hand off the wheel and rubbed his thumb and forefinger together. He mouthed, "MY M-O-N-E-Y." I read his lips from ten feet away.

I punched the gas and shot through a yellow light. The goon got caught at the red. Traffic on Wilshire was heavy; it jammed me up on the next block, and I crawled along in first gear. Not stopping to think, I grabbed the car phone and dialed Parker Center.

A man answered on the first ring. "Robbery-Homicide."

"Is Detective Lockwood there? Tell him it's Ann Whitehead."

The man put me on hold. Lockwood picked up within seconds. "You were supposed to be here at nine."

I cradled the phone on my shoulder; I'd remembered too late why I didn't want to talk to him. "The blackmail guy is following me! You said someone would watch the house!"

"He must have picked you up on Los Feliz."

"He's driving a rusted-out Trans Am with primer fenders."

I checked my rearview mirror. The light had turned green, but the Trans Am was hemmed in by Mercedes sedans.

Lockwood said, "Have you got his license number?"

"Not yet."

"What's your exact location?"

I looked for a street sign. "I'm going east on Wilshire, between Beverly Drive and Cañon."

"I won't ask what you're doing so far from downtown. Stay on Wilshire past San Vicente—as soon as you're in City territory, I'll have our guys pull him over."

I checked my mirror again. *"Damn!"*

The Trans Am had turned down a side street. I dropped the phone and cranked a hard right. It was all residential south of Wilshire. I hauled down a parallel street, ran the stop sign at the end of the block, and made another right. The Trans Am was bombing at me head-on.

I slammed on my brakes. He slammed on his brakes. Our cars screeched to a stop five yards apart. We stared at each other, motionless, right in the middle of the street.

He made a fist and pretended to punch me. Then he let off his brake and started to roll forward.

I hit the gas, swerved around him, and did a big U-turn in the intersection. I memorized his rear license plate. He threw the Trans Am into reverse and tried to ram me. I swung the wheel right, took off, and ran a four-way stop going fast. I was lucky: no cars, no pedestrians. The Trans Am was half a block behind.

I spotted my chance up ahead.

A delivery truck was parked on the street; it was blocking the entrance to an alley. I hit the brakes, bumped over the curb, and squeezed between a light pole and a fence corner. I bombed down the alley and checked my mirrors.

The Trans Am was too wide to follow me. The guy tried anyway. I saw his fender smash as it caught the pole. The Trans Am stopped dead, wedged between the pole and the fence.

I slowed down and watched the guy jump out of his car. He yelled, "*Cunt!*" and started to come after me on foot.

I gunned my engine and hung a left at the end of the alley. I zigzagged back to Wilshire, checking my mirrors all the time. The Trans Am did not reappear. I pulled into the curb to catch my breath. I was feeling dizzy.

I wiped the sweat off my palms, picked up the car phone, and called Vivian's mobile number. I caught her running around at city hall. I asked her to tap her cop sources again, this time for information on the Trans Am. I gave her the license number. She pumped me for whys and whos. I told her I'd get back to her and hung up.

The phone rang immediately. I knew it had to be Lockwood, and I was sorry I'd called him. I'd only done it on reflex.

When I couldn't sleep last night, I decided that he'd behaved like a jerk. I understood that he was pissed. He hadn't received my messages; I'd lifted a few thousand out of the blackmail money. But he could have shown a little sympathy about a guy with a pry bar trying to kill me. I didn't need to be babied, but he could've managed something warmer than "I'll get you a hotel room." That's why I hadn't gone to Parker Center to meet the composite artist. Lockwood ignored it when I'd tried to thank him. And he'd left me alone after the attack as if I weren't worth worrying about. He was a jerk.

I switched the phone off in midring.

I CUT THROUGH Beverly Hills to Progressive Properties and Artists on Robertson. Their office was an old-fashioned brick cottage with flower boxes and white shutters. It was two doors up from The Ivy, an Industry watering hole.

The lobby was cozy and wood paneled, there were no security guards, and the receptionist was smiling.

I walked over to her desk. I said, "I'd like to speak to Mr. Ziskind about a woman named Greta Stenholm. I don't have an appointment."

She registered Stenholm's name: a little blink gave her away. She pressed a button on her telephone and lifted the receiver.

Cupping her hand around the mouthpiece, she whispered, "There's someone here about—"

Her voice dropped lower.

A door opened across from reception and a guy stuck his head out. It was Jack Nevenson. He was the Yale tie I'd offended at Barry's party by wondering if smart people made good art. Nevenson recognized me and was equally unthrilled. I pointed to his office. He stood aside and motioned me in.

The office was windowless and paneled in wood. Nevenson shut the door and sat down behind his desk. He didn't ask me to sit. I stayed standing and tried to catch his eye, but he kept his head turned. He looked irritated and/or scared—and/or like he was waiting for help to arrive.

Help arrived almost instantly. A connecting door opened and a chubby middle-aged man in stocking feet walked in. He was carrying an open script and a pair of reading glasses.

Nevenson said, "Len." Ziskind stopped and looked at me. He said, "What's the problem, Jack?"

I cleared my throat. "Mr. Ziskind, my name is Ann Whitehead. I work for the *Millennium* and I'm researching a piece on Greta Stenholm."

Ziskind was smoother than his employee. He pulled up a chair for me and sat down on the edge of Nevenson's desk. He smiled. "You've been very unkind to some of my clients in print."

I said, "Only when they deserve it, I'm sure."

Ziskind smiled and twirled his glasses. "What is it you wanted to know?"

"I'd like to see a copy of *GBDB*."

Nevenson did a huge double take. Ziskind shot him a look, and Nevenson took a sudden interest in his penholder.

I said, "You're agenting the sale of her screenplay, aren't you?"

Ziskind smiled. "There's been some kind of misunderstanding. The police seem to think that Greta and I had a personal relationship."

"According to her calendar, you saw her three times since the first of the year."

"Yes, we supposedly had lunch on January eighth and April twenty-first, and dinner on July tenth." Ziskind shook his head. "On January eighth I was in Aspen with my family. On April twenty-first I worked through lunch, and on July tenth I ate at Mr. Chow with two producers. All of this can be checked."

I shook my head. "But you worked at CAA. You must have known her agent, Edward Abadi, who was murdered last year. Greta must have gotten a new agent at that point—you, for instance. Then she followed you to PPA."

Nevenson gripped the arms of his chair. "It's not *true*."

Ziskind smiled. "Please, Jack, she's just fishing, and I'm sure if we ask her nicely, this will be off the record. I'm asking you nicely, Ann."

I nodded. I didn't want to, but I had to.

Ziskind said, "Jack, run to my office and get the letter from Greta's file."

Nevenson trotted out and Ziskind laid on the smooth talk. "What you don't realize is that Greta was no longer Teddy's client at the time of his murder. Her career was in the toilet by then, and the agency had fired her. She only came to us this past May when she read about my new agency in the trades. As I understand it, she'd had no representation since Teddy died."

Nevenson came back. He handed Ziskind a sheet of paper, which Ziskind handed to me.

It was dated May 25, 2001, and it went:

"Dear Mr. Ziskind: You left Creative Artists in order to make a different kind of Hollywood movie. The unexpected success of *Crouching Tiger, Hidden Dragon* and *Charlie's Angels* should tell you that there is a large untapped audience for women's adventure films. I don't mean more family-in-jeopardy films or quasi-B chick flicks. I mean films in the tradition of *Thelma & Louise*—ambitious adventure stories with A-list artists and an implicit political message. Hollywood has let in black and Latin men to speak to a constituency, and their movies have made money. Why not let a woman tell exciting stories about the condition of women?

"I'm writing a script called *GB Dreams Big* that would be ideal for PPA. It's based on the true story of a young woman murdered in L.A. in 1944 and her best friend's search for the killer."

The plot synopsis ended there. Stenholm gave her academic stats but no film credits, and reminded Ziskind that she'd been with CAA for three years. Her signature was forceful and stylized.

I reread the letter and handed it back to Ziskind. He said, "We set up a meeting. I remembered her very well from CAA. She was a beautiful girl, and showed a great deal of promise at one time."

I said, "What happened at the meeting?"

"She pitched her story, which we liked, minus the preaching."

"Who is 'GB'?"

Ziskind smiled. "I don't recall at this point. Jack?"

Nevenson shook his head. Ziskind said, "We didn't sign her, but I told her to bring in the finished script and we'd discuss it."

Nevenson couldn't contain himself. "And she never came back! I saw her at Barry Melling's party, but she acted like she'd never met me!"

Ziskind smiled. "What Jack says is true. We didn't see her again, and we are not her agents."

I shook my head. "But she went to Barry's party to talk to someone about her script."

Nevenson glanced at Ziskind, and Ziskind gave him a "Go" nod. Nevenson said, "Scott Dolgin."

I said, "Scott Dolgin?"

Ziskind nodded. I said, "It can't be Scott Dolgin. Her script was going to a studio for six figures—the sale was almost final."

Nevenson frowned at Ziskind. Ziskind tapped his reading glasses on his front teeth.

I said, "What is it?"

Nevenson said, "Should I, Len?"

Ziskind nodded.

Nevenson said, "At the party, Scott told me he was developing several projects with Greta. I assumed that the story she'd pitched us was included. Then Scott called the agency two days ago, looking for her script about the murdered girl. He seemed to think that Len was representing it."

Ziskind stood up and put his glasses on. He smiled. "That's all the time we can spare, Ann. To summarize—PPA has no connection with Greta Stenholm, none whatsoever, and this conversation never happened. If I see anything about it in that ass-wipe paper of yours, I'll turn you upside down and screw you seven ways from Sunday."

I PULLED IN at a minimall to buy a quart of grapefruit juice and a bottle of extrastrength aspirin.

Standing outside, I washed down six pills and drank half the juice. I laughed because I was a wreck. My cheek still hurt from three nights ago, my head ached from last night, and I'd wrenched my wrist again during the car chase. None of it was terminal. But it made me want to lie in bed, not drive around town getting dumped on by movie-biz cruds.

I leaned against the car and started making calls.

Barry had said that Scott Dolgin didn't know Greta Stenholm. But Dolgin did know her, and Barry damn well knew it. Him and his Hollywood ambitions: "She was murdered at *my* party—it's an embarrassment for everyone involved." No wonder he'd fought me on the Stenholm piece.

I called In-Casa Productions. A machine answered and I left a message. I called Information for Dolgin's home number; he wasn't listed, of course. I called the newspaper and tried to worm the number out of Barry's assistant. She wouldn't give it to me. She told me to hold the line: Barry was anxious to talk. I said I'd call back and hung up.

I dialed Vivian's mobile number. She had the information I wanted on the Trans Am.

The owner's name was Dale Wendell Denney. He was forty-six years old and lived on Earle Avenue in Rosemead. His criminal record went back decades. He had six drunk driving convictions, a statutory rape arrest, a burglary arrest, and an assault-and-battery arrest. He also had two convictions for assault with a deadly weapon:

he'd pistol-whipped a bookie at Santa Anita, and knifed a guy in a bar brawl in Duarte. He'd done county time on both charges.

A scum for all seasons, Vivian called him. He used to repossess cars for a living. Now he hired out as cut-rate movieland muscle. He played bodyguard and alleged "fixer" for Hollywood people who couldn't afford bigger names like Gavin de Becker or Anthony Pellicano for their security needs.

I wrote it all down, put off Vivian's questions, and hung up. An LAPD black-and-white cruised by on Beverly Boulevard. The passenger cop stared at me, but I didn't think anything of it. I shut my eyes and pressed the juice bottle against my forehead. The cold glass felt good. I stood there enjoying the sensation.

Someone said, "Ann Whitehead?"

I opened my eyes. The patrol car had turned into the minimall parking lot. The passenger cop was standing right in front of me. His car was blocking my car, and his partner was talking into a two-way radio.

The cop said, "Give me your telephone, please."

I gave him the telephone. He set it on the hood of my car.

"Turn around, place both hands on the vehicle, and spread your legs."

I did like he asked. He frisked me up and down, then took my arms, bent them behind my back, and handcuffed my wrists.

It hurt. I tried to readjust the handcuffs, but he gripped my arm and marched me to the black-and-white. He opened the back door and I tipped myself onto the seat. The driver cop climbed out of the front to guard me.

I watched the passenger cop walk back to my car. Reaching through the window, he picked up my bag and proceeded to search it. He found the sap, the Mace, the handcuffs, the brass knuckles, and laid them in a row on the hood. He opened my wallet and found the wad of fifties and twenties I had there. He lined up the wallet on the hood.

A beige sedan swerved into the parking lot and skidded to a stop. Lockwood jumped out with the engine running and walked up to the black-and-white. His face was set hard.

"Uncuff her, Officer."

I levered myself out of the backseat. The driver cop reached around and freed my hands. Lockwood pointed at my car and almost pushed me toward it. The passenger cop moved out of our way.

Lockwood grabbed my arm and dragged me in close. He was angry—and the emotion showed for once. He said, *"Why can't you do what I say?"*

He shook me. I struggled, trying to pull away. *"Don't touch me like this! I hate it!"*

Immediately he let go and stepped back. I leaned against my car, feeling woozy. Lockwood told the other cops to take off. The black-and-white pulled out of the parking lot and booted it down Beverly.

I shut my eyes and willed the wooziness to pass. I heard paper rustle and opened them again. Lockwood had searched my bag and found the xeroxes and crime-scene notes. His expression was back to normal.

He said, "I'll leave these. I assume you have more copies."

He dropped the papers on my front seat. He examined the row of weapons, opened my wallet, pulled out the wad of money, and counted the bills. All that was done with theatrical slowness. Looking at me, he put the money in the pocket of his sport coat. He was daring me to argue.

I didn't intend to argue: he'd run me down and nailed me again.

He said, "What happened after we were cut off this morning?"

I pulled out my notes on Dale Denney and passed them over. I said, "He's a Hollywood bottom-feeder with a criminal record that includes burglary and knifing."

Lockwood gave the notes back without reading them. I said, "You mean you already identified the guy."

Lockwood nodded.

"How? From my description?"

Lockwood shook his head.

"Were there fingerprints on the money envelope?"

Lockwood shook his head again.

"Does that mean no, or that you're not going to tell me?"

Lockwood said, "Yes."

I looked at him. Was he actually being funny? Somehow I got the wild idea that he was.

CHAPTER
ELEVEN

W<small>E LEFT</small> my car at the minimall and drove out to Northeast Station in Lockwood's. I didn't know what he wanted because I hadn't asked and he hadn't said.

I sat staring out of the window. What *was* the matter with me, in fact? I felt all edgy and emotional. Why *couldn't* I do what Lockwood said to do? I knew he knew better than I did how to catch a killer. I hated to think I was so prejudiced against cops that I couldn't admit their expertise. If that was it, I was a bigot, and just as wrong as the cops I called bigots.

Something else hit me.

It wasn't only politics with Lockwood. I thought back to the day we met. It hit me that since the first day, I'd wanted to resist him. I'd wanted to smart-mouth him, to puncture his official reserve and make him *see* me —

Oh Jesus, no . . .

I groaned and bent forward, hiding my head between my knees. My face had flushed painfully hot.

Lockwood said, "Are you all right?"

I nodded but didn't lift my head.

That was the answer. That was why I acted so volatile around him. I would've realized sooner, except he was a cop. How awful — how truly mortifying. A cop — Jesus. A *cop.*

I covered my head and burst out laughing.

Lockwood did not comment. I sat hunched over covering my head until I heard the car engine stop and him say, "We're here."

The police station was a cut-stone bunker in a tough section of Glassell Park. Lockwood walked me inside and found his tubby partner Detective Smith. I asked for a drink of water. Lockwood brought a mugful, and left me on a hall bench while they made notes for a telephonic search warrant. I watched them through a glass partition, trying to read their lips. I didn't succeed. But I took it that a regular search warrant wouldn't happen fast enough, and that they didn't want me to hear the extent of their case.

A couple of times I laughed out loud.

Lockwood came and got me after an hour. A judge had granted the warrant, he said, and they were headed to Dale Denney's. I asked if he was stranding me there without a car. He said that I would go with them. He wasn't letting me out of his sight until further notice.

Whatever the reason, I was happy to go.

Rosemead was four suburbs east of downtown. It looked hot and nasty from the freeway, like the towns on either side of it. Smith used his cell phone to call the Temple City Sheriff's for jurisdictional clearance. They gave him a green light and even offered to help; the local cops knew Dale Denney and hated him.

Denney lived in a scuzzy apartment building that stood between a topless bar and a check-cashing place.

Smith circled the block looking for the Trans Am, then parked in an alley behind the building. Lockwood grabbed a set of lock picks and told me to stay close. We took an outside stairwell to the second floor. There was nobody around. The second floor had an open walkway like a motel; Denney's apartment faced the topless bar. Lockwood and Smith unbuttoned their jackets and kept one hand near their guns. They approached apartment number eight quietly. I stuck close behind them and realized I was nervous.

They took up positions flanking the door. Lockwood knocked. We waited. He knocked again: nothing stirred in Denney's place. I tried to look through a window. The glass was filthy and the curtains were drawn tight.

Lockwood examined the doorknob. Even I could tell it was shoddy hardware. He jammed two picks into the hole and jimmied the lock with no trouble. Smith pulled me into the apartment after him. Lockwood shut the door and locked it again. Smith told me to stand by the window and keep track of activity outside.

I cracked the curtain. Lockwood turned on a light and dropped a copy of the search warrant in a chair.

I glanced around the living room. It was a lowlife's place. It reeked of Denney's cologne. The walls were stained with tobacco smoke; all the upholstery was synthetic plaid. Gun and skin magazines were piled on the coffee table, and a crappy pair of loafers sat on the floor underneath it.

Smith walked into the bedroom. He came back holding a framed picture. It was a glossy eight-by-ten head shot of a fake-platinum blond. A gushy dedication was scrawled at the bottom: "To Dale, my biggest fan! XXXXXOOOOO Shelly!"

Smith showed it to Lockwood, then to me. I recognized the blond right away. She was the actress who played Helga. Helga, the Gestapo size-queen in the video at Hannah Silverman's house.

I said so to Smith and Lockwood. Lockwood frowned, but Smith laughed, clicked his heels, and mimicked a *"Sieg Heil"* salute. Lockwood had obviously filled him in.

Still frowning, Lockwood pulled up a chair. Smith propped "Shelly" against the magazines and sat down on the coffee table. They started to debate their next move — right in front of me. I couldn't believe it. I asked if I should leave but Lockwood shook his head. They needed me to watch for Denney.

The problem was they couldn't take the photograph. My break-in at Hannah Silverman's wasn't lawful; any seizure they based on an illegal search would be thrown out in court. There was no way around it.

They'd talked to Silverman two days ago, I learned. She had an alibi for the night of Stenholm's murder. It was the same alibi she'd had for Edward Abadi's murder: she spent the night with her father. She still accused Stenholm of killing Abadi. Her big theory now was that Arnold Tolback murdered Stenholm. A lover's quarrel, Silverman told the cops.

But Lockwood had talked to Tolback at the Chateau Marmont last night. Tolback could prove his whereabouts during the time of the murder. He also denied Silverman's claim that he was having sex with Greta Stenholm. He denied it categorically, and Lockwood couldn't budge him.

I spoke up.

Tolback moved out of Silverman's house just five days before Stenholm died. There had to be a connection. I'd heard Silverman call him a faithless son of a bitch. And according to Penny Proft's gossip, Tolback and Stenholm were sleeping together. Either Tolback was lying or Silverman was imagining things.

I'd asked Lockwood once before: why would Greta Stenholm want to mess with Hannah Silverman? I'd since learned the answer. Because she thought that Silverman murdered Edward Abadi. Reason enough to seduce Arnold Tolback, I argued.

Lockwood nodded his head. He said the point was logical but not necessarily reflective of actual events. They had yet to discover evidence of a Tolback-Stenholm affair. Smith said they were still looking.

I shut my mouth and they went back to the Dale Denney problem.

It'd be premature to brace Hannah Silverman about Denney; they agreed on that. But he was a link to Greta Stenholm and the blackmail, and he had a history of violent crime: they needed to find him *now*. They thought he was probably hiding out, and they'd have to start "doorknocking" his known associates. *Doorknock* was a police verb, I guessed. They said that doorknocking Denney's KAs would take time and manpower.

I listened to their talk while I watched the walkway outside. Listening to them, a crazy plan popped into my head. It was not only crazy, it was dangerous. But it seemed like an effective shortcut to

Dale Denney. I thought it over, weighing the pros against the cons. The pros won. At a break in conversation I spoke up again and offered myself as bait.

Lockwood and Smith just looked at me. I explained what I had in mind.

Dale Denney was a desperate man. Whoever hired him for the blackmail drop wanted their money back. His reputation, maybe even his life, hinged on getting it back. He'd followed me from home that morning, and he'd stake me out again, maybe as early as tonight. He'd come after me for sure—if it seemed safe.

Here was the deal, I said. I'd go home to the pool house. I'd leave the driveway gates open, my car out, the yard lights off. Unmarked surveillance cars could cover the street. Lockwood could come through the vacant lot and climb the back wall; we'd time it to arrive at the pool house together. Lockwood could hide in the kitchen, or somewhere, while I puttered around the front room. I'd open the doors and windows and light all the lights. I'd be a superbly vulnerable target.

Lockwood and Smith didn't even think it over: they vetoed the plan flat. Lockwood cited my injuries from last night and asked if I wanted to risk another attempt on my life. I said I didn't see the risk if he was right there. They remained adamant, so I tried a bluff. I said I would do it with or without their help. I didn't give a damn who I flushed out. I was tired of being jumped, chased, punched, and almost drowned. And I had nonlethal weapons to defend myself.

Lockwood shook his head N-O—emphatic. Smith gave me a patronizing smile, like I was some plucky young chick, too cute for brains.

I reminded them that the doorknock approach took time and manpower. I reminded them—

They ignored me, stood up together, and went to search the rest of the apartment.

I could hear them talking. They found garish clothes and more skin magazines in the bedroom; condoms and drugstore cologne in the medicine cabinet; eight cans of malt liquor and a carton of cigarettes in the fridge. They didn't find an address book, or any letters or bills. There was nothing to tie Denney to anyone or anyone to Denney—except the picture of "Shelly."

I argued for my plan on the ride downtown. It was a one-sided argument: neither Lockwood or Smith would discuss it. They filed the results of their search at the county courthouse, drove me to the minimall, and dropped me at my car.

I climbed out of the backseat. I was thinking that my bluff had been called and I was on my own. Screw them, was my next thought; I'd prove I had the chops to trap Dale Denney myself.

I started to slam the door. Lockwood looked at his watch and said, "Meet me by your back wall at nine o'clock."

LOCKWOOD APPEARED at 9:00 P.M. sharp. I'd stopped to eat, swung by the office to check in, and was only a few minutes ahead of him. I heard a low whistle from behind the wall. I whistled back, and he came up and over. The hanging ivy made too good a ladder—I'd have to get it trimmed. Or sprinkle broken glass along the top of the wall.

I waved. Lockwood crossed the lawn to meet me, looking around the whole time. It was dark; but he scanned side to side as if he had the yard gridded in his head. He spent longest on the trees and bushes. The shadows there were the darkest.

He said low, "We checked Denney's prints against the latents in the pool house and the back office. No match."

"I didn't think there would be." I pointed to the street. "What about extra help?"

"I have three unmarked units in the area—yours, plus two more. Nobody's seen Denney's car. You still want to do this?"

He reached for my hand and held it a second. His hand was warm; mine was clammy. He said, "You're sure?"

I started to walk away. He took my arm and walked along with me. I was waiting for final comments or instructions, but he didn't say a word.

I went into the pool house first. He let go of me and headed for the bathroom. He had his bearings, I noticed; he didn't trip over anything in the dark. I heard the bathroom louver squeak. He'd set up to watch the front drive.

I dumped my bag, turned on all the lights, started coffee, and played my messages.

Sis had called to ask if she and Father could come by. She also wanted to talk about her interview with Lockwood; she wanted to know how I'd gotten involved in a murder case. I pressed fast-forward before she finished. Barry called four consecutive times, demanding to know where the *fuck* I was and what the *fuck* I was doing. He was in a twist. He'd never nagged me about a piece before.

Barry's messages were the last. The reporters had given up, for one day at least. There was no return call from Scott Dolgin, and no calls from Isabelle Pavich. I was surprised by that. I thought for sure I'd hear from her by now; she'd struck me as the pest type.

I poured some coffee and took a few sips. It wasn't what I wanted; I wanted to lie down. I kicked off my shoes and stretched out on the daybed. The minute I was horizontal, a dizzy spell hit. I was getting used to the spells—I'd felt dizzy off and on since last night. After it passed, I wedged the can of Mace under my leg and took deep breaths to relax. A night breeze blew in the screen door. I stared out into the dark. My eyelids got heavy and my mind began to drift....

A noise—

My eyes jerked open.

The noise came from the driveway side of the pool house. Something had brushed against the bushes.

I checked the clock: 10:05. I wrapped my fingers around the Mace.

A dark shape on the porch. *The stink of cologne.*

Dale Denney was suddenly at the screen. He yanked it open and lunged for me.

I had no time to think. I pulled up my knees and kicked out. I hit him in the chest and knocked him back. Lockwood came running from the bathroom. Denney smashed into him. They tipped over a chair and crashed to the floor.

I jumped off the daybed, grabbed my sap, and started swinging. I couldn't get a clear shot at Denney. He was tangled in with Lockwood.

They rolled and thrashed and banged the furniture. Lockwood was tall and fit, but Denney was one compact muscle. My bookcase pitched over. A lamp smashed against the wall. The shade exploded; glass flew. Lockwood ducked it, raised up, and kicked Denney in the groin. It was a vicious kick. Denney screeched and bent double. Lockwood knee-dropped him in the back. Denney hit the floor, spitting blood.

Lockwood grabbed Denney's fingers and bent them backward. He said, "Don't move or I'll break them." He was breathing hard.

Denney coughed blood and lay still. Lockwood kept him pinned, trying to catch his breath. Blood oozed from cuts on his face and neck. Suddenly I felt sick. I weaved and sat down on the daybed. The room was tilting out of focus.

Denney said, "She stole my money."

Lockwood bent his fingers back. Denney squirmed. Lockwood leaned into his kidneys. Denney arched and lay still again.

Lockwood pulled out his badge. He hung it in front of Denney's face. Denney whispered, "*Cunt.*"

I'd had it with that. I leaped up and swung the sap at him. My ears started to ring. I missed Denney, lost my balance, dropped the sap, and reached for Lockwood. He put an arm out to catch me.

Denney saw his chance and shook loose. He staggered to his feet, snatched a chair, and swung it at Lockwood. A leg caught Lockwood in the head. He sprawled into me and knocked us both to the floor. Denney kicked Lockwood in the ribs and took off running.

The last thing I heard was "*Cunt!*"

CHAPTER
TWELVE

THE DOCTOR at Hollywood Presbyterian said that I had a mild concussion and bruised bones in my right wrist. He prescribed Percodan, plus a day in the hospital for observation.

It ended up being longer than one day. I'd never taken prescription painkillers before and I dug the warm, woolly high; but I was so exhausted from nerves and everything else that it wiped me out completely. I could hardly think straight by Saturday night, much less get up and go home. To tell the truth, I was also happy to sleep somewhere safe for two nights.

Lockwood came by three separate times to check on me. He hadn't been hurt in the fight with Denney. I heard this from a nurse; I was asleep and missed him all three times. The last time, he left a note on my bed stand. It said that Denney had escaped. The unmarked units picked him up outside my place, then lost him on the downtown freeways. They'd found the Trans Am later, abandoned in South Pasadena, and were now checking stolen-car reports. Denney's apartment was under surveillance, and they were trying to locate his known associates. Rest, Lockwood wrote — rest and feel better. He'd had an officer drive my car to the hospital; I'd find the keys at the nurse's station.

By Sunday morning I was better and ready to be gone. The weekend was half over and I had a lot to do. I had to shelve Greta Stenholm and start serious work on the Lockwood piece. If I didn't

get my research done that day, I'd never make Barry's Tuesday deadline. And so far I had nothing publishable on him — not a thing.

I drove home and found a pair of men installed in the mansion.
They said that Lockwood had copied my keys and put the two of
them there. They were anonymous-looking cops from Metro Squad
whose job was to watch for bad guys and protect me. On Lockwood's instructions, they'd moved my stuff out of the pool house
into the bedroom I used as caretaker. I found everything I needed
upstairs: my computer, my books, my clothes. My writing desk and
reading chair were arranged like I liked them. They'd put my soap
and towels in the adjoining bathroom. They'd even brought up the
telephone, fax, and coffeemaker, and plugged them in.

I couldn't resent Lockwood's interference.

While I was tripping on the Percodan, I'd had a few revelations. One: I'd been nuts to use myself as bait for Dale Denney.
Smith and Lockwood were right to try and stop me. It was a dumb,
reckless idea, and I was lucky that Lockwood and I weren't seriously injured. If Denney'd had a knife or a gun, anything might
have happened.

Two: I was afraid.

I was physically sore from all the attacks and I didn't look forward to more pain, or worse pain. But my fear wasn't just physical.
I was afraid because I didn't know what the hell was going on.

Greta Stenholm wasn't murdered by her blackmail victim.
Lockwood's attempt to justify that theory was flimsy and convoluted. Hannah Silverman hadn't murdered her either. Silverman
might have murdered Edward Abadi out of jealousy — that remained to be proved. And she might have murdered Stenholm, in
theory, for the same reason. But I wasn't jumped at the pool house
by Hannah Silverman. I'd seen her pictures and I'd seen her live;
even in the dark, I could tell the difference between a tall, stringy,
middle-aged woman and an average-sized man. The man might
have been hired by Silverman. That was always a possibility, since
the pool house attack happened the same night I searched her
beach house. She could have seen me or my license plate and

hired a killer. But the killer was not Dale Denney; Denney's cologne was too unmistakable.

Or there might be a third motive. Not blackmail or romantic revenge—a third reason for Stenholm's death that I had no hint of. And I couldn't defend myself from something I had no hint of. Someone was going to try to kill me again—and I didn't know what or who to look out for.

But I wouldn't let the fear paralyze me; I refused to let it. And Lockwood's Metro Squad guys were a comfort. They'd set up watching posts at both ends of the second floor. One watched the front yard and street, the other watched the back. My room was in the middle, between them, but the house was so big that we couldn't see or hear each other. Anyway, they weren't there to confine me or keep tabs on my movements. They'd said so when I asked.

I showered off the hospital smell, changed into fresh clothes, and went straight to work. I must have needed the rest. I felt stronger and clearer than I'd felt since Denney punched me in the face.

Vivian was still asleep when I called. She answered on a groggy, "What is it?"

I said, "I need a strategy for Lockwood."

Vivian's voice got louder. "I'm not helping you, sister, until you tell me your news. I'm tired of being pumped for information with no quid pro quo."

I could trust her with confidential stuff, so I told her my news, every last bit except the part about my crush on him. For once in our five-year friendship, Vivian was speechless. I used the silence to talk. "Did you get anything out of those reporters—"

Vivian blurted, "*Shit!*"

"—who wouldn't—"

"No, I mean really, *shit*, Ann. Maybe you shouldn't—"

I stopped her because I knew what she was about to say. "Would you give it up if you were me?"

There was another silence. I heard domestic noises in the background; it sounded like Vivian was out of bed, making coffee.

She came back on the line, wide-awake. "You have to talk to a cop-groupie named Karen. I met her at the Ray Perez trial — she's older and sort of a groupie doyenne."

"What about those reporters who wouldn't talk to me?"

"They wouldn't talk to me either. They wanted information and I wouldn't play."

"Then I thought I'd try Parker Center and the police academy—"

"Ann, it's *Sunday*, and besides, random polling is the most frustrating and time-consuming way to do research. Talk to Karen. She's Lockwood's oversexed admirer I wrote you about — the one who provided the 'divine but unfuckable' quote. Those groupies know things, and Doug Lockwood is their idol."

I DIDN'T TAKE Vivian's advice right away. I should have, but I didn't believe her and didn't have enough reporting experience to know better.

I drove to Parker Center, then to the police academy in Elysian Park. There weren't a lot of people around and the people who were around wouldn't talk to me.

At Parker Center they wouldn't let me up to Robbery-Homicide. Anyway, I was told, the offices were closed. I spoke to a secretary in Personnel who was catching up on work; she was polite but not helpful. In the parking lot I tried some patrol cops. They were willing to flirt but not to talk about Lockwood.

At the police academy, I found some guys practicing at the outdoor pistol range. I never made it to my first question. The name of my newspaper alone got me three deadpan stares, a shrug, and a rude suggestion.

Like Vivian said, it was frustrating and time-consuming. I wasted the morning and part of the afternoon, and finally called Karen-the-groupie. She lived in Reseda, way out in the Valley. Her roommate said that Karen wasn't home; she was at a bar in Elysian Park called The Short Stop. The roommate started to tell me the cross street. I said thanks, I knew it.

The Short Stop was only a few blocks down Sunset from the police academy. The pink sign said COCKTAILS, and the exterior was boarded-up white. I walked in and let my eyes adjust to the lighting. It was almost empty on a Sunday afternoon, and the guys at the bar were definitely not cops. They looked more like neobeatniks, readers of the *Millennium*. I checked the booths for someone with very long hair. That's how Karen's roommate had described her.

There were three women giggling in the booth nearest the door. All three wore navy blue LAPD windbreakers, tight jeans, and dress shoes with heels. One was noticeably older and had long, streaky blond hair. Peroxide had turned it the texture of straw.

I walked over to the booth and said, "Karen?"

They stopped giggling and looked at me. I got the female once-over, then Karen looked at her two colleagues. They were glossy little Latinas wearing press-on nails and gold bracelets. Barely out of their teens, I guessed. A telepathic message passed among the three: I didn't meet any of their standards for beauty or fashion, therefore I was no threat. They burst out giggling again.

The older woman said, "I'm Karen. Who are you?"

She was a track-worn thirty, with a breathy, fakey voice. I told her who I was and how I'd gotten her name. I said, "I'd like to talk to you about Douglas Lockwood."

That brought on a big giggle fit. The Latinas nudged each other and Karen flipped her hair over her shoulder. She said, "Doug Lockwood is one of our *favorite* subjects, isn't he, ladies?"

The Latinas giggled and nodded. I sat down in the booth and pulled the tape recorder out of my bag.

"I'd like to know what you know about his career."

I set the tape recorder on the table. Karen wrapped her hand over the microphone. She said, "You know what we don't understand about you women in the media?"

I said, "'We' being who?"

She pointed to the Latinas. "'We' being friends of law enforcement—'we' being the wives and girlfriends of police officers."

I checked for a wedding ring on her finger. She saw what I was doing, and giggled. "Not at the moment—I just divorced my second one."

For sleeping with groupies? I wondered, but didn't ask. I said, "What is it you don't get about us women in the media?"

"I'll show you, watch."

She pinched the skin on her neck and down her arm. She squeezed her own thigh, then she took one of the Latinas' hands and held it.

She said, "See this? See this?"

I didn't see, and my expression told her so.

She dropped the Latina's hand. "Bodies, get it? Everyone has a body, and you women act like cops don't have bodies because you don't like them. But law enforcement isn't just a political issue or something to criticize on television, it's men's live bodies standing between us and harm, and we love those bodies and worry about them being killed, and you women in the media act like they don't mean anything."

She looked to the little Latinas for backup; they both nodded. To me, she said, "Do you think Doug Lockwood is a handsome guy?"

"I'd rather talk about his police—"

"Come on, woman. Is Doug a hunk or what?"

"I don't—"

Karen rolled her eyes. "Jeepers, see what I mean?"

She reached into her windbreaker and pulled a newspaper article out of the pocket. Unfolding it carefully, she laid it on the table in front of me. The two Latinas slid around the booth and crowded Karen for a look. The four of us looked at it together.

It was a full-color *Times* photograph that hadn't made it into Barry's Burger King file.

The caption read, "Hero of siege receives medical attention after ordeal." Lockwood was lying on his back in a patch of grass. His eyes were closed, and his face was so pale he looked unconscious. The paramedics had removed his jacket and shirt, and stretched his left arm over his head. The gunshot wound ran horizontal under one nipple: a long, thin gash that spilled blood across his stomach. One paramedic knelt on the grass beside Lockwood. He was staunching the flow of blood with gauze.

Karen took her fingertip and traced the outline of Lockwood's torso. His body was lean and mature. She caressed the newsprint with the kind of feeling, I assumed, that she wanted to spend on him. The Latinas followed the path of her finger and looked ready to swoon.

Karen's tracing stopped at Lockwood's waist. Blood from the wound had soaked his belt and the top half of his jeans. She stroked his waist with a dreamy finger. Her voice was dreamy:

"Everyone eats at Burger King. Any of us might have been there that day, and it was only by luck that we weren't. But if you had been, or I had been"—she nodded at the two Latinas—"or Vicenta or Rosa had been, he would have stopped that bullet to save our lives. He put his own body between us and a crazy with a gun. Doug is bleeding for *us*."

The Latinas chimed in, "For *us*."

IT TOOK awhile, but Karen finally gave me the information I wanted.

She'd waited a long time to lay her cops-bleed-for-us speech on one of us women from the media. Once she'd made her point, and I didn't argue, she was willing to talk about other things besides Lockwood's looks.

But she wouldn't let me tape or take notes. She didn't trust me, and she was afraid of being misquoted. I said she could talk anonymously; she wouldn't relent. I explained how proof works in journalism, that her testimony alone wouldn't be enough to base a piece on, and I'd use other people for corroboration. I didn't think she understood, but she refused anyway: no tape recorder, no notes. So I bought a pitcher of margaritas for the table, and she talked for two hours. Two solid hours—I was amazed by what she knew. She knew so much that I started feeling sorry for Lockwood, who, in Karen's own words, was a "very private man."

Afterward, I raced home and jammed it all into the computer. I started with the chronology of his police career. I couldn't remember all the jargon she'd used, the P1s and P2s, but I did the best I could.

1976 — joined LAPD.

1977–1982 — worked patrol out of Central and Wilshire Divisions; also loaned to Detectives during that time (loan to Detectives at this stage the sign of a talented officer).

Early–mid '80s — earned law degree from Southwestern U. going to night classes — passed CA bar.

1983–1984 — eighteen-month tour in Wilshire Vice.

1984–1986 — on loan to Wilshire Detectives.

1987 — promoted to detective. Assigned to Hollywood Division. Moved around the various desks (Burglary, Vice, Auto Theft) but mostly worked the "big" desks, Robbery and Homicide.

1995 — became D3, the highest grade of detective. Assigned to Major Crimes Unit at Robbery-Homicide downtown (RHD). Working as lead detective.

1996 — twenty years on Department.

2000 (Dec.) — Burger King siege.

2001 (May, June, July) — leave in Mexico.

2001 (August) — assigned to Homicide desk at Northeast Division. Given duties of a Detective 2 (D2). Demotion perceived as politically motivated, and temporary.

I typed on.

Karen had seen the contents of Lockwood's personnel file; she wouldn't tell me how. His record was spotless. The file was full of letters of commendation and A-1 rating reports. He'd never been accused of excessive force or had any contact with Internal Affairs. Until he shot Juan Pablo Marquez, he'd never even fired a gun in the line of duty.

Karen didn't know why Lockwood hadn't pursued the law. She had two theories about it: police work was more exciting, and Lockwood was a natural-born detective. According to her he had an 82 percent solve rate, which was exceptional. He'd cracked the Turner-Matusek case; he'd cracked the Bronson Caves murder. He'd worked LAPD strands of the *Cotton Club* case, and the Night Stalker killings, and a lot of the city's toughest homicides of the past ten years. One case *had* taken him into Rampart territory, but he was *not* involved in the mess there. He'd been scheduled to take the lieutenant's exam in late 2000. Then the Burger King siege happened. Before that, there was no telling how far he'd rise in the Department; but Burger King had postponed or derailed his advancement.

Which was totally not fair, Karen had said. Not fair, not fair.

An Officer-Involved-Shooting team investigated the siege. The shooting team submitted their report to a review board. The board cleared Lockwood of any wrongdoing in the death of Marquez. But the Department was afraid to release the findings. They were afraid of the media and public opinion. They thought they'd be accused, yet again, of protecting their own. They didn't want that while Rampart was still open.

I'd asked what Lockwood did right at the siege. I remembered the answer, and the way Karen gushed police language. I tried to capture it verbatim:

"There are rules in police work, you know, there's a Department manual, and training bulletins, shooting policies, *rules.* Under what conditions is an officer justified in the use of deadly force? That's the question you have to ask with Burger King, but none of you media people asked it. When danger is imminent is one condition, and defense of self and others is one. In extreme cases, an officer isn't required to identify himself or warn anybody that he's going to shoot. That whole time Doug was inside with the hostages, he was weighing the different variables of his chances of taking the guy alive, but the guy was psycho, and Doug had to take him down. That hostage lied who said Doug shot the guy when he was surrendering, and the media just listened to him because they hate cops. The review board heard all the evidence, and even commended Doug for resolving the situation with so little loss of life. If SWAT had gone in, a whole lot of people might have died, a *whole* lot."

She'd finished on an escalating note:

"Doug's the *very best police officer there is,* and his life is *ruined,* and the Department won't *help!* They're just *covering their butts because of Rampart!*"

I had used Lockwood's ruined life to turn the conversation. I said that I'd heard he came back from Mexico a changed man. Did he talk to Karen about it?

The three women had burst out giggling. When Karen could control herself, she said she'd never talked to Lockwood personally. He wasn't your standard cop. He didn't hang around The Short Stop drinking, or date the girls who did. His thing was brainy lawyers; brainy lawyers were what turned him on.

I'd mentioned his wife, the senior deputy DA for Orange County. Karen said she was the latest in a short line of legal women. They'd only been married five years, and it was his first. He waited so late to marry because he'd had a long affair with a federal judge, starting when he was a rookie detective. Karen wouldn't name the judge, but she was older and went back to her estranged husband in the end. There'd also been two other affairs that Karen knew of—with a famous crusading attorney, and a prosecutor in the DA's office downtown.

Lockwood was no "horn dog": Karen had wanted to make that clear. He wasn't like a lot of cops; he didn't sleep with witnesses or bereaved relatives, and he didn't participate in the orgiastic local courts scene. Those three affairs were serious, monogamous deals. Again, Karen wouldn't name any names. As if I'd call up Lockwood's ex-lovers for a quote.

I would, however, try the current wife. But Karen confirmed Vivian's gossip: the current wife was history. The Burger King scandal wrecked the marriage. Lockwood had moved back from Orange County and now lived in bachelor digs in Hollywood. If Lockwood was innocent, I'd asked, why was his marriage wrecked? Karen didn't know and couldn't guess. But she was happy to blame the media for it.

I'd pressed again on the subject of Lockwood's post-Mexico change.

Karen told me to put myself in his position. Publicly labeled racist and killer; a fine career in limbo, maybe destroyed for good; a marriage on the rocks. Wouldn't that change somebody?

I'd agreed that it could. She'd launched into the details of his latest case: a woman murdered in a Los Feliz mansion. She must have talked to someone who saw the crime scene — all her information came from the day I'd found Greta. I played dumb and asked a few questions, but she hadn't known anything I didn't.

I stopped typing. My head and wrist were aching. I'd switched from Percodan to aspirin to keep my mind sharp. I was determined not to switch back.

I scrolled to the top of the file and reread my notes.

Was Karen reliable? How could I verify what she'd said? If the journalists wouldn't talk, where could I find someone who was critical of Lockwood *and* knew the insider police facts? Ranking cops had come out against Perez, and other Rampart figures. But the LAPD hierarchy had never condemned Lockwood that way.

I thought about phoning Hollywood Station. Lockwood had spent a lot of years there; maybe I could rustle up a former colleague or ex-partner. Then I remembered my treatment today and decided, Forget it. No cop was going to talk to me; it would just be more wasted time. Unless Lockwood had enemies — and how was I going to locate an enemy?

Another problem:

I felt confused.

Barry didn't want just a profile of Lockwood — he wanted a hatchet job. But so far I didn't have the material for a hatchet job. And my feelings were starting to get in the way. Jesus, that picture of him in the *Times*, half-naked and covered with his own blood. I shouldn't satirize the groupies' swoon; that picture had gone through me like electricity. I was a big girl, though, and I could resist raw sexual attraction when I had to. It was only a fever and it would break. In the meantime I worried that it was skewing my judgment. Even without Karen's information, Lockwood didn't seem like a dirty cop to me.

I'd seen for myself that he was smart and good at his work — I'd seen it, and paid for it. I hadn't witnessed any thuggery or racism; I hadn't heard any lunatic notions about law and order. All our fights had been fair fights: when I pushed him, he pushed back.

And when he was a jerk, he'd always made up for it. He left me alone after I got jumped at the pool house, but he baby-sat me the entire next day just because Dale Denney tailed me to Beverly Hills. He wouldn't return the Colt, but he let me keep the sap, brass knuckles, handcuffs, and Mace. One minute he wouldn't say how they identified Denney. Next minute I watched them search Denney's apartment.

As a journalist I'd seen no evidence that Lockwood was the cocksucker Barry wanted him to be. At the same time, as a journalist, I had to admit that Lockwood wasn't the type of subject I was used to.

I'd only done profiles of movie people, and I knew the shallow requirements of the genre. You spent a few hours with your subject in a hotel room or production office. If it was for the cover, you might get two sessions and a treat: artist at home, artist on the set. A few hours was enough time to get a feel for the personality you were dealing with. Correction: to get a feel for as much of the personality as anyone sensible would expose to strangers. It helped that the artist *wanted* you to get a feel. It helped that press attention sold movie tickets.

I counted the number of hours I'd spent with Lockwood since Tuesday. Seven plus three plus eight: eighteen altogether. We'd spent eighteen hours in different settings under intense circumstances. I'd even seen him lose it once, when he grabbed me and shook me: "*Why can't you do what I say?*" The Burger King file provided facts; Karen had maybe provided facts. Despite all that, I couldn't begin to say who Lockwood was. He'd shown me nothing of himself. Nothing that would make his story more than a description of the official man. Nothing to give me an emotional entrée, however shallow, to the piece.

It was a variation on the movie-star problem. Movie stars were an elaborate facade; Lockwood was a wall. My job was to go over, under, or through that wall. But *how?*

I sat at the computer thinking.

I could try to provoke a personal moment with him. I'd done that before in interviews. If I thought I was boring, or getting someone's predigested spiel, I'd try to jolt us both. I'd exert my non-journalist self to see what it would spark in the other person's nonpublic self. I'd used all sorts of strategies to do it—a joke or silly remark, a leap off the topic to current events or jungle animals. Sometimes it worked and sometimes it didn't. Some interviews were just doomed to formula.

I had a flash: I'd already tried for a personal moment with Lockwood. When I offered myself as bait to Dale Denney, I was reaching for something extreme to thaw Lockwood's ice.

But the strategy hadn't worked. It only put me in the hospital.

Lockwood was a bigger challenge than a jet-lagged movie director. He was a controversial figure. He had no incentive to talk to me, and there was more at stake in murder—

Right then, I knew what I should do.

I jumped off my chair and ran down the hall. The guy watching the backyard was camped in a corner bedroom. I knocked and found him on the floor doing leg lifts. I asked if he'd escort me to the pool house. He said sure, a change of scenery would be nice. I hurried him outside and waited on the porch while he went in, turned on lights, and checked around. Then he motioned me to come in.

The front room was empty except for the rug and the daybed. And the kitchen stool. My kitchen stool was standing in the middle of the room, directly underneath the attic fan.

The Metro guy posted himself in the doorway. I climbed on the stool and examined the slats. There was a trick to the attic fan, which was why I'd picked it as a hiding place. Most attic fans were electric; the interior vent opened automatically when you turned on the fan. But this fan dated from the '20s and the vent was manual. At some point someone had broken the lever that opened the vent. To open it now, you had to hit the fourth slat at one end. Only one end of one slat would do it; otherwise the slats seemed to be stuck shut.

I hit the fourth slat. The vent opened. I reached up and felt around for the money.

It was gone.

No, it wasn't. It was there: someone had moved it.

I pulled out the money and wiped the dust off. There was only a part of one bundle left—six hundred dollars out of Greta Stenholm's twenty-thousand-dollar blackmail payoff. Lockwood had the rest. All except the nine hundred dollars I spent on my sister's rent and the weapons from Gun Galaxy.

The Metro guy was watching me. I asked him who'd been up there, and got the answer I expected: Detective Lockwood. Lockwood had supervised the moving of my furniture, noticed the attic fan at last—

And left the money there to test me.

I jumped off the stool and dragged the Metro guy back to the main house. I asked if he knew where Lockwood was. As it happened, he did. Lockwood had called in thirty minutes ago for a progress report, he was at the station.

I gathered up my things and drove out to Glassell Park in a rush. But I just missed Lockwood. Detective Smith said he'd gone home for a few hours of sleep. Smith looked like he needed sleep himself. He had black circles under his eyes, and his shirt was stained with chicken grease. An empty take-out box sat on his desk among the paperwork and files.

I told him I wanted to leave something for Lockwood. He asked if it involved new information in the Abadi or Stenholm cases. I said it didn't, and could I borrow a manila envelope? He shrugged and passed me an envelope.

I would've loved to know how their end was going, but I knew it was useless to ask. I stuck the money inside the envelope. I added my crime-scene notes, and the xeroxes of Greta Stenholm's address book and Filofax. Then I sat down at Lockwood's desk and wrote an apology. I tore up a couple of starts. I remembered what happened when I thanked him for saving my life; he didn't like effusion. And he had no belief in my sincerity. I'd screwed that when I screwed with his crime scene.

In the end I kept it plain. I didn't list everything I was sorry for, I just said I was sorry. I said I owed him nine hundred dollars, which he'd get back in installments. And I told him what I wanted to do next: pursue Scott Dolgin about Greta Stenholm's screenplay *GB Dreams Big*. Did he object? If he did, he should call me before 8 A.M. tomorrow.

I folded the note and clipped it to the envelope. It was funny, I thought. I took the Lockwood assignment to prove I could do it, and to get the story I really wanted: Greta Stenholm. But things were different now. Now I had to know. I had to know who Lockwood was, and how he'd changed, and whether his life was ruined. I could feel his drama—and it was just as exciting as Greta Stenholm's rise and fall on the fringes of Hollywood. If I had to give on Greta to get his story, I was ready to give on Greta.

The money in the attic was a good sign. Lockwood could have impounded it but he didn't. He left it, and the stool, for me to find. It was his version of a personal moment. He'd ignored his official duty to make a personal gesture from him to me. He'd asked explicitly once before: did I know right from wrong? With the money he asked the same question another way.

I had to show him that he could trust me. He'd never talk to me unless he trusted me first.

CHAPTER
THIRTEEN

I RECEIVED LOCKWOOD'S answer early Monday morning. He sent it via the new surveillance team to pass on when I woke up. Just be careful, the message said. That was all. No acknowledgment of the package, or anything I said in my note: be careful.

What a sphinx the guy was. But he hadn't discouraged my Scott Dolgin plan or warned me off other lines of action. So I decided to look on the bright side.

I cleaned up, popped some aspirin, and headed out for Culver City. I bought a coffee and muffin en route, and checked my mirrors constantly to make sure I wasn't followed.

Culver City was a middle-class dump on the south end of West L.A. What it lacked in aesthetics, I'd always thought, it made up for in movie history. The movies built Culver City. Hal Roach, Thomas Ince, and D. W. Griffith settled there in the teens. Sam Goldwyn followed, then the newly merged Metro-Goldwyn-Mayer moved into Goldwyn's facility in 1924. By the '30s MGM was It: Culver City's largest industry and the biggest, most "Hollywood" studio. When MGM declined in the '60s, so did Culver City. It wasn't a ghost town now; it was still crowded and commercial, and they'd done a lot of cosmetic updates. But the place felt worn-out to me — like it had shot its civic wad once and for all.

In-Casa Productions had a five-digit Washington Boulevard address. I assumed it would be on the old MGM lot, which Sony

Pictures had bought ten years ago. I figured Scott Dolgin had a deal at Sony or one of its subcompanies, Columbia or TriStar.

I was wrong. I found 10203 Washington on the block across from Sony. I parked out front and remembered seeing this place a thousand times. It faced the east end of the studio lot, opposite the Thalberg Building where I often went for press screenings. I'd logged it as another movie-inspired architectural folly—the kind L.A. was full of.

It was a Spanish-style courtyard apartment painted champagne color and trimmed in red. You entered the court under a stucco arch inscribed CASA DE AMOR. Eight matching bungalows, four to a side, faced each other across a central walkway. The walkway was lined with every shade of red rose. There were red roses everywhere—in pots, on bushes, on climbing vines. The back wall of the court was a solid trellis of roses.

I stopped inside the arch and laughed out loud. The whole thing was too wild.

The motif of the courtyard was Love. A pair of interlocked hearts, molded in stucco, hung over the front windows. Wrought-iron railings featured wrought-iron hearts; hearts were painted on the porch tiles. All the front doors had heart-shaped knockers, and all the windows had heart-red awnings. Halfway down the walk, a stone Cupid dribbled water into a heart-shaped fountain.

The bungalows weren't numbered or lettered, and there was no one around to ask. I checked for a tenant directory but saw something better. The first bungalow to my left had a shingle on the porch rail. The shingle said IN-CASA PRODUCTIONS.

I started up the stairs right as the screen door of the bungalow opened. I fixed my face to greet Scott Dolgin and—

Lockwood stepped onto the porch. He was wearing latex gloves, and he looked fresh and rested.

I was only surprised for a second. I started to say, "Where's your car?" A slight sign from him, a slight shake of the head, shut me up. I waited for my next cue.

He said, "Can I help you with something?"

I got the immediate drift. I said, "My name's Ann Whitehead. I'm here to see Scott Dolgin."

"For what reason?"

I improvised. "I was supposed to see him this morning about an interview—I'm a journalist."

"If you would come with me, please, Miss Whitehead." Lockwood held the screen open and followed me inside.

Dolgin's living room was crammed with men in latex gloves. Detective Smith had the search warrant in his hand and stood reading a list into the telephone. One guy packed plastic bags into a cardboard box; another guy closed up a fingerprint kit. There were traces of fingerprint powder on every flat surface. A lab man was down on his knees examining the coffee table. A photographer stood over him with a camera ready.

Lockwood took my arm and pointed out the picture window. The venetian blinds were down but open. I sited along his finger at the bungalow across the way. A woman was standing on the porch. I hadn't noticed her before because of the climbing roses. She was a well-preserved older woman dressed in dirty gardening clothes. Her eyes were riveted on Dolgin's place. She didn't blink or move.

Lockwood said low, "That is Mrs. Florence May. She's owns these apartments. I didn't want her to know that we knew each other."

"Why not?"

He said, "Come and look."

Lockwood walked me back to the bedroom. I checked the place out. The interior wasn't absurd like the exterior; it was museum-grade '30s Moderne. The furniture was chrome, velvet, and leather, and the colors matched in pale greens and creams. The floor plan was typical for a courtyard bungalow. Living room and dining room in front, kitchen and bedroom in back, and a bathroom squeezed into the hall.

Two suitcases lay open on Dolgin's bed. The clothes inside belonged to a woman. Lockwood flipped through the clothing to show me. T-shirts and jeans, underwear and sweaters—nothing fancy. And nothing to identify an owner, except the tags on the suitcase handles. Greta Stenholm.

Lockwood held the tags for me to see. I said, "This means—"

He cut in. "Have you heard of someone named Isabelle Pavich?"

"Jesus, Isabelle Pavich!"

"I thought you might help." Lockwood took me back to the dining room. He steered me along ahead of him; he was walking fast.

Dolgin's dining room doubled as his business office. There had obviously been a fight there. The table was shoved off-center; two chairs were knocked over. A curtain had been ripped off the rod. Dried, rust-colored stains trailed across the carpet onto the floor in the kitchen.

I stopped to stare at the stains. Lockwood caught me staring and pressed my arm. He wanted me to look at an object on the table. It was a straw basket. I stood still. It was—it had to be—Isabelle Pavich's purse. She was carrying it the day she came to see me. The purse was splattered with the same rust-colored stains.

Lockwood got out his notebook and pen, and I told him what I knew. How I'd seen Pavich at Barry's party. How Pavich had been tugging at Dolgin's sleeve. How she'd come to the pool house two days later. How she'd angled for movie material and information about the murder. How she'd put me onto Edward Abadi with "Friends of Greta Stenholm tend to get dead." How I hadn't seen or heard from her since. How I hadn't told him about her visit because I thought she wasn't relevant.

Lockwood didn't look up from writing. "She stated to you that she met Mr. Dolgin at the party."

"But she acted odd about it."

"In what way, 'odd'?"

"When she rang at the back gate, I couldn't place her. Then I remembered the party, and her trying to get Dolgin's attention, so I said, 'Did you ever talk to Dolgin?' I thought it was innocuous, but Pavich dodged the question. She said, 'What? We haven't . . . No, what do you mean? I never met him before the party.' I hadn't asked her when she met him. Ergo, odd."

Lockwood wrote fast, flipped back a page, and made another note. He said, "Someone searched Mr. Dolgin's filing cabinet. I need you to go through the contents and tell me what you see."

The filing cabinet stood by the door to the kitchen. A big old photograph hung beside it; it was a tinted enlargement of the Thalberg Building under construction. Lockwood went to talk to Smith. I opened the top drawer of the cabinet.

The drawer was full of financial records. I skimmed through the bank statements first.

Dolgin appeared to be personally solvent. He had fifteen grand in his checking and savings accounts. But In-Casa Productions seemed to be broke.

I looked for bank letters, articles of incorporation, deal memos—any paperwork to prove that In-Casa was a viable entity. All I found was a letter of agreement between Scott Dolgin and Barry Melling dated March 2001. Barry agreed to advance Dolgin ten thousand dollars to get In-Casa started. He also agreed to additional funding for a six-month period, to be repaid as Dolgin made his deals.

I found In-Casa's bankbook. It showed no record of a ten-thousand-dollar deposit last March. Only small additions were noted over the six-month period—five hundred to nine hundred dollars, tops.

I went through the middle drawer. I found back issues of *Variety* and *Hollywood Reporter,* and a voucher book filled with coupons. Dolgin was paying off a 2000 Range Rover; he was into his fifth month.

The bottom drawer contained chewed-up screenplays. There were two by Penny Proft, three by Hamilton Ashburn Jr. And two by "B. N. Hecht"—also known as Neil John Phillips. They were duplicates of scripts I'd found in his garage. I looked twice, but there was nothing by Greta Stenholm.

I stood up and brushed the fingerprint powder off my hands. Lockwood came back with his notebook open.

I said, "She thought In-Casa was a farce, and it looks like she might've been right. It looks like Dolgin spent Barry's seed money on a swanky truck. It also looks like Dolgin was working with some SC people, including Greta's old writing partner, Phillips. But there's no evidence of any producing deals, or anything that proves Dolgin was working with Greta. I didn't expect to find *GB Dreams Big*, because Dolgin called PPA looking for it. But he told Jack Nevenson at the party that he was developing several projects with her."

Lockwood was writing. "How do you know that?"

I told him about my talk with Len Ziskind and Jack Nevenson last Friday morning. Dale Denney had pushed it right out of my head.

I said, "Do you believe Ziskind? Why would Greta's calendar say she had meals with him if she didn't?"

Lockwood shut his notebook. "We're going to the residence of Miss Pavich right now. I want you to meet us there."

He gave me Pavich's address and hustled me out of the bungalow. As I drove off, I checked the side street by the Casa de Amor. There were the cop cars, and Pavich's little roadster.

I WAITED FOR Lockwood on the sidewalk in front of Pavich's building. She lived in West Hollywood, a block off the Boys' Town strip. The street was quiet, and her building was bland and new. The front gate was set in a tall security fence with surveillance cameras mounted on top.

The police arrived in three separate cars—Lockwood and Smith together, and another crew of technicians. Lockwood had Pavich's straw purse with him. He rang her buzzer a couple of times, then used her keys to open the security gate. Her apartment was on the fifth floor. Lockwood knocked at the door and called Pavich's name. When nobody answered, he started trying keys in the dead bolt.

One key finally did it. The door opened, and the group of us walked into a narrow foyer. Smith called Pavich's name again. Lockwood hung back to give me a pair of latex gloves. I put them on. He told me to stick by him and not to disturb anything.

We fanned out through the apartment. The tameness of the place surprised me, given Pavich's personal style. Nothing was cute and the furniture was ordinary outlet-store stuff. D-girl for a small production company couldn't pay much. She probably spent her money on rent and making the scene.

Lockwood pointed to the tables at either end of the couch. They were covered with framed photographs of Scott Dolgin. Some were candid, some posed, some taken in crowds, some just Dolgin alone. Lockwood picked up one of the pictures. It was labeled and dated on the back. I checked a couple more: all of them were labeled and dated. The dates ran back to '95, and the pictures commemorated movie premieres, parties, and holidays.

Lockwood leaned forward to examine faces. I studied the faces over his shoulder. Pavich only appeared in some of the photographs. When she did, she was always clinging to Dolgin and he was always looking bored.

A glass étagère stood by the doors to the balcony. There were more Dolgin photographs there. On the middle shelf, in the place of honor, sat an engraved announcement. It was the invitation to Barry's party for In-Casa Productions. I touched Lockwood's arm and pointed. He lifted the card off its easel, read it, and turned it over. The reverse side was covered with handwriting:

Isabelle Dolgin. Isabelle Pavich Dolgin.
Isabelle P. Dolgin. I. P. Dolgin.
ISABELLE PAVICH-DOLGIN.

Pavich had drawn star bursts and comet trails around the names. Underneath she'd printed: HEAD OF DEVELOPMENT — IN-CASA PRODUCTIONS.

Lockwood tapped the card and set it back on the easel.

The kitchen was divided from the living room by a waist-high wall. Detective Smith had been searching the kitchen; I'd heard the cupboards and drawers open and shut. The noise stopped and Smith called out. Lockwood went to see what he'd found.

He'd found several things.

There was a doodle pad sitting next to the telephone. Pavich had practiced the possibilities of her married name there, too:

Isabelle Pavich-Dolgin. Isabelle P. Dolgin.
I. P. Dolgin.

And she'd created various designs for the initials "IPD." Lockwood riffled through the pad. There were other IPD logos on other pages.

An answering machine sat next to the telephone. The red light was flashing and Lockwood hit PLAY.

Pavich's boss had called twice — once on Saturday and once that morning. He wanted to know why she hadn't come to the office. His second message sounded anxious: "Isabelle, you *never* miss work. Where *are* you?"

Lockwood and Smith exchanged a look. Smith indicated one last item.

It was a movie-themed 2001 calendar, open and flat on the kitchen counter. Lockwood flipped back to January. Scott Dolgin's name appeared everywhere — but August was the real jackpot.

On Friday, August 24, Pavich had scribbled: "Fight!!!" On Monday, August 27, she wrote: "8 P.M. Barry/Scott party."

The next day — the day after the party — Tuesday, August 28, Pavich drew a big round happy face.

She'd spent some time on the drawing. The face was a perfect circle, and the smiley mouth was a perfect half circle. She'd even colored the face with a fluorescent yellow marker.

Smith looked at Lockwood, put his finger on the happy face, and kept it there.

LOCKWOOD DIDN'T let me hang around for the Pavich discussion. I'd told him what I knew; there was nothing in her apartment he couldn't interpret himself. He also had a job for me:

Scott Dolgin was gone.

If they had a theory about Dolgin's nonpresence, Lockwood wasn't sharing it. But that's why he'd played that charade at the Casa de Amor. The landlady claimed that Dolgin had taken a short trip. He needed a rest, she said, from the police and the trauma of Greta Stenholm's death. She refused to say where Dolgin was, and she couldn't be moved.

Lockwood wanted me to break Mrs. May down. He asked me to go back to the Casa de Amor and see what I could get out of her. I should pretend to be pro-Dolgin, Lockwood said. He thought she might talk to a sympathetic woman.

So I left them in West Hollywood and drove back to Culver City as fast as I could.

I found Mrs. May sitting in a wicker chair on Scott Dolgin's porch. The police had left, and she recognized me as I came through the archway. I didn't have to invent a pretext to stop. She patted the chair beside her and said, "Your name is Ann—come and sit. You may call me Flo."

She smiled. I saw from the steps how youthful she was. She had white hair and a dancer's body, and she could have been anywhere from fifty to seventy. She looked like she'd made skin preservation her raison d'etre; skin preservation, and roses. Her gardening clothes had rips all over them.

She said, "I just spoke to Scottie on the telephone. He apologizes for missing your appointment, but he said he'll be home tomorrow. He'd like to reschedule if he might."

I sat down, set my bag down, and smiled back at her. What an actress; she had a trained voice and impeccable delivery. I hoped I could keep up with her.

I said, "And screw the cops, right?"

Mrs. May blushed. "Your *language*, dear."

"But you did tell Scott they were here today."

She nodded, patting my knee. "Of course I did—he's aware of it. For whom do you write, my dear?"

"The *L.A. Millennium*. You might know Barry Melling—he's a friend of Scott's."

"Friend and mentor—he's been very helpful to Scottie's career. If you don't mind my saying, you're awfully darling for a reporter."

I smiled. "Where was Scott when he called? We could reschedule right now."

She went vague suddenly. She said, "Where was he?"

"I mean, where can I reach him?" I pulled out my pen to write down a phone number.

She smiled and patted my pen hand. "Oh, no, no—not *now*, dear. Call him tomorrow. He said you should ask me about the Casa. It's an important inspiration for him."

I knew that Lockwood would want me to humor her, to see where it led. I leaned down and pulled out my notebook. "Scott must have named his company after the Casa de Amor."

Her smile got beatific. "The Casa de Amor is my whole life." She lingered over the *l*s in "whole" and "life." Wholllle llllife.

I said, "I've always been curious about this place. I'm over at the Thalberg a lot."

"We're going to be declared a historic landmark."

"Really? What's historic about it?"

She smiled. "The Casa is a Temple of Love."

Too wild, I thought. I wrote down "TEMPLE OF LOVE." Mrs. May liked that; she waited until I finished to go on.

"It was built in thirty-seven by people from Metro—as a lark, I think, because it is a bit much, honestly, all the hearts and whatnot. Even I'll admit that."

"Nineteen thirty-seven. So it's the same age as the Thalberg Building."

She nodded. "Metro owned this land and the bungalows were built as a trysting spot for studio executives. They kept their lady friends here, or rendezvoused in the units that were empty. It was a wonderful, magical retreat from the world."

Or a cross between a casting couch and an extramarital romper room. I said, "How did the men get here without being seen?"

"...How?...Oh, yes, how? Well...in those days, you're right, there was no wall and you could see the Thalberg plainly from here. The men drove, yes...and they parked behind....We had open carports in back that led to the courtyard. They were closed years ago, when we closed off the rear for security reasons."

I was watching Mrs. May; something was bothering her. As she answered my question, she looked away and lost focus. I said, "What's the matter?"

"No, no, nothing, dear." She looked back, smiling. "One's memory goes at my age. Heavens, I'd forgotten all about those old carports."

I said, "How did you come to be here?"

"I? Do you mean the Casa, or Hollywood?"

"Both."

"Oh, you've heard my little story many times. Little ballerina from the sticks wins a beauty contest and goes to Hollywood with big dreams. I was lucky, though. I met a producer, an adorable but very married man, rest his soul. He found me a place at the Casa."

"And now you own it."

"I do, dear. Harry passed away and left me comfortably off, and I bought the Casa in '69 when it was put up for sale. It's sad, don't you feel, that the greatest studio of all has come to the worst end? Metro hardly makes pictures anymore. When you think of their glory days, it's very sad."

She looked to me for agreement so I nodded. Since the late 1960s MGM had been raided and sacked, mismanaged and chopped into pieces. Kirk Kerkorian sold the back lot to developers, auctioned the movable property, and co-opted the lion logo for hotels and airlines. United Artists was added, subtracted, and added again. Ted Turner took the film library. MGM the company moved, and rented out the lot. The last renter, Lorimar Telepictures, bought the lot, then sold it to Sony. A shifty Italian moneyman owned MGM for awhile in the early '90s. He was foreclosed by his French bank, who sold the company to I forgot who, and now Kerkorian owned it again. MGM hadn't shown a profit in thirty years.

Mrs. May said, "I've tried to keep the Casa just as it always was, and I only rent to fallen women with pasts as spotted as mine." She smiled.

"Scott Dolgin isn't a fallen woman."

She stopped smiling and her eyes misted. "I think of Scott as the son Harry and I could never have. Scottie's my special boy."

She folded her hands and stared into space. I didn't think she was acting: Dolgin *was* her special boy.

I said, "Are you sure I can't call Scott now? I really have to nail down an interview."

She wasn't listening. I said, "Mrs. May, can't I call—?"

"Flo, dear."

"Flo, can't I—?"

She turned to me. "What did the police say about Scottie this morning?"

"They wanted to know if I knew where he was."

"You were with them a long time."

I shrugged. "Scott's a friend, and I think their suspicions are stupid. Just because he was working with Greta Stenholm."

Mrs. May patted my knee. "That's what I think, too."

She reached for her bucket of garden tools and stood up. I said, "Did Scott go alone?"

She patted me again. "It was nice to meet you, dear. Don't worry, everything's fine."

She walked across to her bungalow and went inside. I waited a minute to see if she'd come back.

When I decided it was safe, I got up, walked down the path, and started ringing doorbells. I rang and waited, moved on to the next bungalow, rang, and waited. I'd been sent there to debunk the landlady's story, and I was determined to do it. Some other tenant might have seen Scott Dolgin, or Isabelle Pavich, or the two of them together.

I worked my way around the courtyard and rang all the bells. Not one single person opened up.

I stood beside the fountain, scanning front doors. There were people inside the bungalows; there had to be. The signs came slowly. Venetian blinds separated, and old women peered out. I walked up to the nearest window. The blinds snapped shut, but I caught a glimpse of glassy eyes and a gray Medusa head. I crossed to another window. Another glimpse: sloppy dye job and flowered housecoat. I took off running. I ran up to the end of the courtyard and ran back. Blinds snapped shut as fast as I could arrive.

But I'd seen enough.

Mrs. May only rented to women with pasts? This looked like the harem of the living dead.

I'D LEFT my car in front of the Casa de Amor. I walked out to use the car phone, and glanced across the street toward the Sony lot. I tried to picture the view before Sony put up the high wall and even higher trees. The Thalberg Building was invisible from the bungalows.

I followed the line of the wall. There were two men standing together on the far corner of Washington. I stared: *I knew them.* One was Jack Nevenson. The other was Neil John Phillips's neighbor—the obnoxious guy who caught me in Phillips's garage and wouldn't tell me where Phillips was.

Nevenson and the neighbor turned down Madison and headed for the lot entrance. Without thinking, I started across Washington. Brakes squealed and people leaned on their horns. I jumped back on the curb, took a look at traffic, and ran up to the corner. I punched and punched the crosswalk button, but the light was long. When it finally changed, I sprinted across the intersection, ran down Madison, and stopped at the lot entrance. I craned for a look inside.

I couldn't see them.

The street entrance was guarded by a kiosk and a gate. Access was easier for pedestrians. A car pulled up and distracted the guard. I slipped behind the kiosk, ducked into the trees, and ran to the front of the Thalberg. Nevenson and the neighbor weren't around. I kept running, past buildings with false fronts and up the road between the soundstages. I checked the side alleys off the road. They were nowhere—*damn.*

I ran back and tried the gift store. I tried the commissary across from it. The café and restaurant were empty after lunch hour. I searched both rooms, and even tried the emergency doors. They weren't there either.

I ran back to the Thalberg. It said COLUMBIA PICTURES over the entrance, and the lobby was lined with Oscars won by Columbia movies. I walked up to the reception desk and asked the guard if two guys had just come in. The guard shook his head.

The lot covered thirty acres—I could run all day for nothing. But I didn't want to give up so soon. I walked outside, picked a bench, and sat down in the shade. From there I could watch the street entrance and the Thalberg at the same time. I tried to be inconspicuous; I'd get kicked out without a pass.

I sat watching people go by. A studio lot was a busy place, but I got bored real fast. After a while my eyes moved automatically and I let my mind wander.

I started thinking about the Thalberg, looming up in front of me. The Irving G. Thalberg Memorial Building.

It was a massive, bright white Moderne building, with streamline and WPA influences thrown in. I'd never been a starry-eyed lover of classic Hollywood, not like some movie fanatics. But when I went to my first Thalberg press screening, even *I* had felt the glamor and the weight of movie history—

Two men walked up the ramp from the Thalberg basement. It wasn't my guys. It was two Japanese men with attachés stamped SONY PICTURES ENTERTAINMENT.

Irving Thalberg...

Metro-Goldwyn-Mayer's first head of production. The studio system's first boy wonder. The Academy had named an Oscar after him, and posterity elevated him to a god. I'd even heard a local historian argue that Irving Thalberg invented Hollywood as we knew it.

I didn't think I'd go that far. But if the film industry was founded on the conflict between Art and Commerce, then Thalberg was the first producer with enough power, taste, and profits to take the fight to its highest level. He was the creative force behind MGM for eight years; his philosophy and methods established the new studio and an Industry standard. He oversaw hundreds of the types of film that Hollywood still considered its best achievement. He took the big-budget star-studded studio movie as far as it would ever go. He also showed what Hollywood could never do because of the constraints of business, and the business mentality.

When he died in 1936 he was only thirty-seven. Louis Mayer had hated Thalberg by the end. He hated the Thalberg legend; he hated the Industry perception that Thalberg, not Mayer, had made MGM. At the funeral Mayer supposedly said, "Isn't God good to me?" But they named the new administration building after Thalberg...

...and set the Art-Commerce battle in stone.

I reached for my notebook. Against all predictions, and despite some rough years, Sony had not tanked in the motion-picture business. There was a "Ghost of Irving Thalberg" piece in there somewhere.

I started making notes.

The building stood by itself, outside the original studio walls, on the eastern tip of the lot. The architecture was not imaginative. It looked more like a post office or a bank than the center of red-hot artistic activity. But that was the point. Art happened inside the studio walls, on the soundstages and back lot west of the building. The Thalberg was administration, the Thalberg was Commerce. It guarded the studio gates and anchored the rest of the lot—a counterweight to ephemera, a reminder of what Art cost. If you want to send a message, the Thalberg Building said, you buy your stamps here.

I stopped writing and smiled. I'd had a cynical thought. Commerce had triumphed over Art in corporate Hollywood. The battle now was Commerce versus Commerce: conflicting ideas about how to get the most return on the studio's investment. There was a Thalberg quote I read once—I didn't recall it exactly. Someone brought him an oddball idea and Thalberg said something like, "Sounds interesting, let's do it. The studio made enough money this year." It was a different planet.

I looked up.

Irving Thalberg had been bugging me ever since Neil John Phillips's garage. I remembered Penny Proft's remark: the only person Phillips would nuzzle was Irving Thalberg.

He was a strange hero for a guy like Phillips. Nobody cared who Irving Thalberg was anymore except film cognos and Industry fossils. Besides which, Phillips aimed to be the greatest screenwriter who ever lived. But he had to know that MGM was a producer's studio. Thalberg's treatment of writers was famously bad, although he worshiped literary talent and routinely overpaid for it.

I watched two men walk out the main doors of the Thalberg. They weren't who I was looking for.

That coincidence was strange, too. What was Jack Nevenson doing with Neil John Phillips's neighbor on Phillips's sacred MGM turf?

I shut my notebook and jumped up. Jesus, I was dumb. *How could I be so dumb?*

The neighbor guy *was* Neil John Phillips.

CHAPTER
FOURTEEN

I SAID, "WHAT does Neil John Phillips look like?"

Hamilton Ashburn rubbed his nose. I'd tracked him down across town at Raleigh Studios. He was directing a movie; that's why he hadn't returned my phone call last week. He'd made it clear that he was *extremely* busy, and could only talk between camera setups.

The soundstage was freezing. Ashburn had on a big parka and woolen mitts. I suggested going someplace warm — outside in the sun, or under the lights of the set. But Ashburn wouldn't leave the stage, and he didn't want me to see what he was filming. So we stood in a dark, cold corner. I turned up my collar and held it closed around my throat.

He said, "Neil is medium. He's medium-sized, and his hair's medium brown. He's hard to describe — there's nothing to distinguish him physically."

Ashburn was pretty medium himself. There was nothing to distinguish him from a jillion other young directors. He wore the usual accessories — baseball cap and wire-rim glasses — and had a typical beard. He also disliked Phillips: that much was obvious from his tepid testimonial.

He spoke into his walkie-talkie. "Lisa, bring my binder."

An assistant rushed up, gave Ashburn a binder, and rushed off again. Ashburn opened the binder and showed me a group photograph he kept inside the front cover. It was the USC Film Class of 1996.

I spotted Penny Proft and Greta Stenholm. Ashburn pointed to a face in the second row. He said, "Neil."

It was him: the obnoxious neighbor. He had the same spoiled expression, but a lot more hair.

Ashburn closed the binder and checked his watch for time. "Why do you care if Greta was murdered? What is she to you?"

"She wrote a screenplay that she said tells the truth about the condition of women."

Ashburn nodded. "*GB Dreams Big*."

"What do you know about it?"

"I know that Neil cowrote the script."

I shook my head. "Penny Proft said their partnership broke up years ago."

"But Neil couldn't get work after *The Last Real Man*, and Greta needed structural advice. Neil told me he did a complete rewrite but left his name off the final version. Greta agreed to split the fee and share credit once the script sold."

"Do you know who's agenting the script, or who bought it?"

Ashburn rubbed his nose. "Neil was letting Greta handle that part. I haven't read anything in the trades."

"Do you know if Scott Dolgin was involved at any point? I heard you were doing work for In-Casa Productions."

Ashburn curled his lip. He didn't like Dolgin either. "*Charity* work. All you need to start a production company is a telephone and some friends, and Scott has no friends. He scraped up backing somehow and came to the SC crowd for material. We unloaded all the stuff our agents couldn't sell. Only Neil was writing original work on spec."

I said, "Why'd Dolgin come to the SC crowd in particular?"

"Because he knew us. He was in the producing program until they asked him to leave."

That connection clicked into place. I knew Dolgin had been thrown out of film school; I should have put it together sooner.

Something else clicked. I said, "Do you know Isabelle Pavich?"

"Who?"

I described her. Ashburn listened, and shrugged. "I'd forgotten the name. She's Scott's girlfriend—works some nothing development job."

"Did she go to USC?"

"Not with us." He checked his watch again.

"Greta thought In-Casa was a farce but Dolgin told people he had projects going with her."

"If he did, it's because Greta had no choice. She hated Scott. He's been in love with her since school, but she hated him."

Ashburn's assistant appeared, holding up five fingers. Ashburn checked his watch and waved her away.

I had to hear it again. I said, "Scott Dolgin was *in love* with Greta Stenholm?"

"And Greta was in love with Ted Abadi. You know what happened to Ted?"

I nodded.

"I still wonder about his death. The police suspected Greta, which is insane. She was devastated by the murder, as Neil was—as we all were. It was a tough break for Neil. He never got another agent, and nobody thinks his career will recover."

"Greta never got another agent either."

"But CAA had already let her go. It was her own fault—she made herself unmarketable with her ball-busting ideas. That's why Neil broke up with her in the first place."

I said, "He agreed to rework *CB Dreams Big*."

"Neil would do anything to get his career back. He saw the commercial potential of the script and wanted to attach himself to it."

I shivered and rubbed my hands. "If Phillips is so career minded, why did he sabotage himself over *The Last Real Man*? Why's he so nutty for the old MGM? What does that get him when Hollywood's frame of reference is hit movies from the past two years?"

The walkie-talkie crackled: "Ham, we're ready."

Ashburn switched it off. "Neil's always had one problem—he

cares too much about movies. Hollywood isn't about movies, it's about relationships. Neil was golden after he sold *The Last Real Man*. It didn't matter if the star trashed it, or it flopped domestically and the critics blamed the script—Neil was in bed with the right people. You've heard the old saying, 'The deal is the sex, the movie is just the cigarette.' Neil cares too much about the cigarette."

I STOOD OUTSIDE the soundstage and jumped around to get warm. When my hands thawed, I grabbed the car phone and paged Lockwood.

I waited for him to call back. It occurred to me they might still be at Pavich's. I dialed Information to get her number, and tried the apartment. A machine answered. I pretended to leave a message for Pavich, hoping Lockwood might hear and take the call. Nobody picked up.

I started the car and headed over to Neil John Phillips's place. It wasn't far from Raleigh, and he'd had enough time to get home from Culver City.

Ashburn said that Phillips owned a black three-series BMW. I checked the street for it as I drove up to the duplex. I parked blocking the drive in case Phillips tried to dodge me again. I knocked on his door. I peeked through the mail slot and over the hedge in front of his front window. No one. I walked around back to check his garage.

I lifted the door . . .

All the boxes were gone. The scripts and the old MGM paperwork: gone. The garage had been cleaned out.

I just stood there staring. There were footsteps behind me. I thought it was a replay of the other day, and turned around. But it wasn't Phillips. A woman stood on the second-floor landing above me: Phillips's upstairs neighbor. She asked what I wanted. I told her who I was looking for. She said that Phillips had done a flit— skipped out on his lease and disappeared. I mentioned that there was furniture in his living room; she said his place rented furnished. I asked if she had any clue where he might be. She shook her head. She knew he had an office in West L.A., but she didn't know where.

I stared into the empty garage and felt myself shiver. It was not from the cold.

DIRECTORY ASSISTANCE didn't have a Neil John Phillips in West L.A. The Writers Guild didn't give out information about its members. PPA blew me off: Jack Nevenson was in a meeting, and the receptionist wouldn't put me through to Len Ziskind. Hamilton Ashburn wasn't taking calls. I tried a long shot—Penny Proft.

She answered with a vampy "Hellooooo?"

I said, "It's Ann Whitehead. How are you?"

"High hard ones are scarce, I'm sorry to report. And yourself?"

"I'm looking for Neil John Phillips."

"Try Hollywood Cemetery—they buried his career there."

"Seriously, do you know how to reach him?"

"Seriously, get a shovel and dig. He dead, dat boy."

"Do you know anyone who knows how to reach him?"

"I'm getting buphes from you today, Ann."

"*Do you know anyone who knows how to reach him?*"

Proft stopped the jokey voices. "I've heard he still hangs with Scott Dolgin and Ham Ashburn. They're a couple of pukes from SC."

I said, "I just spoke to Ashburn."

"The Hamster must be thrilled—he's the last man standing."

"What do you mean?"

"I mean, color him green. He was en-vee-us of Neil and Greta at SC. They were the wunderkids, Ham was the drudge, and he's the last one left."

I said, "If Scott Dolgin is such a puke, why'd you donate two scripts to In-Casa Productions?"

Proft whistled. "You get around, hermana."

"Why did you?"

"I was just covering my bases. Today's puke could be tomorrow's studio boss."

I didn't buy it; I had started to mistrust her humor. I was debating how to break her down when Proft said out of the blue, "Guess who I saw two Saturdays ago at Farmer's Market?"

"Who?"

"I'll give you a hint—she's dead."

"What's your point?"

Proft put on a broad stage whisper. "My point is, *La Stenholm* was not alone."

I said, "Quit it. Stop fucking around."

"Okay, okay, sheesh! Greta was friends with a professor, a real tombstone in Culture Studies named C. Margaret Kerr."

"Jesus, not her."

Catherine Kerr was a condescending, contentious, pain-in-the-ass film expert. I'd tangled with her on panels, and dreaded her letters to the editor. All the critics dreaded them.

"Aha, you obviously know C. Margaret. Well, I spied C. Margaret and C. Greta eating pancakes together. They were having a, shall we say, difference of opinion, and C. Greta stomped out in a huff."

"You said you hadn't seen Greta since school. Why didn't you tell me this before?"

"Let's see, why *didn't* I tell you before? Could it be that I forgot? Or could it be that Ms. Kerr, who I've spoken to maybe twice in my life, called me after the tragedy? Could it be that she *begged* me not to say anything about The Fight At Farmer's Market, which she claimed was just a teeny-weeny contretemps that wouldn't interest the El Lay PD? Now that my conscience is clear, I'll let you draw your own conclusions. Have a gas—ciao."

Proft hung up. I made a couple of quick calls, to Information, then to Kerr at home. I caught her coming in from classes. She was hard work, even just to arrange an interview. I did learn that she hadn't seen Neil John Phillips in years. But I couldn't follow the directions for getting to her place. To curtail the conversation, I said I'd find it myself.

Kerr lived in a pain-in-the-ass part of town, of course. I sat in the car outside Phillips's place and studied the map. Mount Washington was over the freeways from Los Feliz; it was a long trip by surface streets. I took off headed north, and cut over to Western. I was on Western, almost at Los Feliz, when the phone rang.

I picked it up, thinking it must be Lockwood. But an unfamiliar voice said, "Miss Whitehead?"

"Yes?"

"This is Officer Garcia speaking, up at the house. There is a dispute in progress here. We believe it involves members of your family—"

"I'm coming, thanks."

I dropped the phone and stepped on the gas. I was only two minutes away. Traffic wasn't bad, and I pushed it past fifty, screeching the left turn onto my street.

A red car was sitting in the drive. I could see it from down the block—a red Ford economy car. When Father was flush, he rented monster Lincolns. The puny set of wheels showed that he'd hit a record low.

I got closer. The driver's-side door was standing wide open. Father had his back to me, bent over. He was straining with something. He was pulling a heavy object out of the front seat.

My sister.

I slammed on the brakes and jumped out of the car. Father was roaring. His face was purple and he had a glazed look I knew from experience: his liquid-lunch look.

Sis was hugging the steering wheel with both arms. Father leaned back on his heels and yanked hard. His Stetson flew off. Sis gave in; she let go of the wheel and fell out of the seat.

I sprinted up the driveway, shouting. Sis spread-eagled facedown on the pavement. Father had her wrists and was dragging her away from the car. The cement scraped her bare skin bloody.

I took a leap and plowed straight into Father. His knees buckled. I smashed him on the back with my fists. He staggered sideways and let Sis go.

He roared my name, swung around, and looped a punch at me. I ducked and shoved him into the car. He thudded off the driver's side and fell on his hands and knees.

I stooped to help Sis up. She was sobbing; her whole body heaved and shook. I was shaking, too. I helped her through the driveway gate and slammed it behind us. Blood was dripping off her.

She leaned against me, wiping her eyes and catching her breath. She tried to say something, tried again, and couldn't manage. I knew what she wanted. She wanted me to go with them—put Father to bed and talk this out.

Father yelled, *"I'm leaving now!"*

We watched him crawl into the front seat and start the car. He floored the gas, revved the engine, and honked the horn simultaneously. Sis turned toward the gate.

I grabbed her: "Don't go!"

She pulled away with more strength than she used against Father. She wouldn't look at me.

Father blasted the horn again. Sis unlatched the gate and ran. Father's Stetson had rolled into a flower bed. She picked it up, ran around the car, and climbed in the passenger seat.

Father jammed the car into reverse and shot out of the driveway. I ran out the gate waving my arms, but Sis refused to look up. She was brushing the dirt off Father's hat.

THE TRIP over to Catherine Kerr's gave me time to calm down.

Whitehead cardinal rule: no matter how blitzed Father was, he always drove. Sis and I used to joke about the family's designated driver, and arranged cars so that we never relied on him at night. But this was afternoon, and I'd only seen him that drunk this early in the weeks after our mother died. He might be drinking like that now, I didn't know. But Sis got stuck riding with him and probably got scared; which was why she'd tried to break the cardinal rule.

After that scene maybe she'd listen to me.

I called her machine from the car phone. I reviewed our mutual past and reminded her that predinner drinking was a bad sign with Father. I said he was out of control. She had to stay away from him—and she absolutely had to cancel the San Andreas trip, if it was still happening. I made every argument I could think of until her machine switched off. I called back and went over the same territory again. Every time the machine beeped off, I called back. I filled ten minutes of tape, hoping that it would do some good. Sis had gotten used to life with no violence; she'd told me so herself. I hoped today had been a lesson to her. Father was never going to change.

Mount Washington was a hilly old neighborhood east of Los Feliz. The roads were overgrown and badly marked but I found Kerr's address with only one wrong turn. It was a shingled Crafts-man house tucked up under the eucalyptus trees.

I parked the car and climbed a rickety set of stairs to the ve-randa. The wooden railing creaked. A voice called, "It's open!"

I walked into the living room. Catherine Kerr was spread out on a couch, reading a book. She said, "Is that blood on your shirt?"

I looked down. Sis had left a red smear on me. I said, "I must have cut myself thinking."

Kerr went, "Ha-ha."

She was somewhere around fifty, and absolutely humorless. Ethnic dresses and folk jewelry were her trademark. She also chain-smoked cigarillos; she had one going now.

She pointed me to a chair. I sat down and glanced around. Her place looked like I'd expected: books, books, books, videos, papers, more books. Books were stacked in piles on the floor, and she had two computers set up on a long table.

I said, "What were you and Greta Stenholm fighting about at Farmer's Market two weekends ago?"

Kerr's hand froze by her mouth. "Penny Proft, that cow. Has she told the police?"

"I don't know. But I will, if you don't tell me what the fight was about."

Kerr sucked on her cigarillo and shrugged at me. "It was noth-ing. I would have come forward, but I didn't want to get embroiled with the police for no productive reason."

Her tone was way too casual. I shook my head. "Try again."

Kerr sighed. "All right, Greta called me that morning. She wanted to get together, so I proposed breakfast."

"How often did you see her?"

"That was the first time in months. We'd been in regular contact since SC but had fallen out of touch because she was working on a new screenplay."

I said, "*GB Dreams Big*. What do you know about it?"

Kerr stubbed out her cigarillo; she never finished one before she started the next. "It was a period drama, set in wartime Los Angeles. That's all Greta would say except that she wanted it to be a wide-screen adventure story told from a feminist perspective. When I saw her that morning, she said she'd sold it for a lot of money."

"To who? Was it Universal, Paramount, or Columbia?" I named the three studios run by women.

Kerr shook her head and fished around for another cigarillo. "Greta wouldn't say until the deal closed. She didn't want to jinx it."

I said, "So what about the fight?"

Kerr took an age, putting the cigarillo in her mouth, striking the match, lighting the cigarillo, tossing the match into the ashtray, setting the matchbook down. I'd never seen her stall a conversation before.

She exhaled smoke and watched it float away. Finally she said, "It was a Saturday morning that Greta called. We met at Farmer's Market and she told me that someone had broken into her car the night before."

"Did she know who did it?"

Kerr shook her head. "She said she didn't, but I had the distinct impression she suspected someone. She didn't report the incident to the police even though her clothes were taken and they ransacked the glove compartment. I found that peculiar."

"But you have no idea who she suspected, or why, or what they were looking for?"

"None."

"Did Greta tell you that someone broke into her apartment last winter?"

Kerr shook her head. There was a pause. I waited. Kerr acted like she had nothing to add.

I said one more time, "And the fight?"

"Oh, all right, damn it. Greta had no clothes, no money, and no place to live. I wanted her to move in with me, but she refused. She wouldn't accept a loan or even come here to clean up."

"And you fought why? Because she refused your help? Did she have other offers?"

Kerr turned to gaze out the front window. I said, "*Why* wouldn't Greta stay with you?"

She ignored the question.

I stood up and blocked the window. "*Why* wouldn't Greta — ?"

Kerr burst out: "Because she wasn't being reasonable! She was jittery and distracted, she could barely sustain a conversation! It was because of her studio deal! The lawyers were finalizing details, and the process was driving her crazy!"

I sat back down. Kerr ground out her cigarillo and showed me the book on her lap. It was the first volume of English director Michael Powell's autobiography, *A Life in Movies*.

She opened it. "Listen to what Powell says."

"'I am speaking in 1986 about talkies that I was directing in 1931. Fifty-five years a long time in movies? Perhaps. But it is certainly a long time in art. The Impressionist movement, the Pre-Raphaelite movement, the Romantic movement, came and went in less than fifty years. But in the movies, nothing has changed. People go into films in this day and age to make money. And so long as money is the only yardstick, there will be no advance in any art. There will only be the surge of the wave on the pebbles on the shore, which sounds very impressive, until you realize the tide is going out.'"

Kerr stopped reading and shut the book. "Has it occurred to you that you don't have a future?"

I laughed. "You're changing the — "

"You can laugh, but look at reality. The era of serious film criticism for a general readership is dead. It was a historical phenomenon of short duration, linked to the rise and fall of a thriving counterculture and the cinema that came out of it. Nobody cares about the meaning of movies anymore. Nobody wants reasoned negativity. Thumbs up/thumbs down — that's film criticism now.

Industry buzz, per-screen gross, celebrity profiles—that's how movies are discussed today. Review space shrinks while the Tom Hanks story runs ten thousand words and business experts analyze the demographics of the summer blockbuster audience. Critics are losing their jobs as media chains consolidate, and soon the only people left will be cheerleaders and junketeers."

I said, "You forgot quote whores."

"That's how low your profession has sunk. Studios send a choice of quotes to an unaffiliated critic, and ask them to sign their name to one for the ad campaign. The studios like corrupt critics—they'll manufacture one if they have to. And the independents are almost as bad. You're supposed to applaud them just for being independent, which means what anymore? Chiefly, it means nonstudio financed, not ideologically or artistically different from mainstream values. The movies don't want you and they don't need you. So where do you go from here?"

I would not be sidetracked. I said in an extremely slow voice, "Why-did-Greta-Stenholm-refuse-your-help?"

Kerr slapped the Michael Powell book. "Greta wanted to take *you* to Hollywood!"

I said, "What?"

"She sold *GB Dreams Big,* and it convinced her that Hollywood was ready for what she had to say!"

"What's that got to do with me?"

"Greta was going to ask you to quit the *Millennium* and sign on with *GB Dreams Big*. She wanted to storm Hollywood, and she wanted *you* to come with her!"

CHAPTER
FIFTEEN

I COULD NOT make Kerr connect the dots. Greta refused Kerr's help because she wanted to take *me* to Hollywood? It didn't make sense; a logical step was missing. But Kerr wouldn't explain it. I finally called her a liar, and she kicked me out of the house.

I knew Kerr was lying. If Greta wanted to take me to Hollywood, why didn't she mention it at Barry's party? I remembered our conversation word for word. Greta didn't say a thing about teaming up. She wanted me to review her movie when it got made. And she definitely said, "I will beat the System." Not "*We* will beat the System," "*I* will beat the System."

After Kerr, I dropped by Los Feliz to change shirts and check the answering machine. I still hadn't heard from Lockwood, but I didn't have voice mail on my car phone and thought he might've tried me at home. He hadn't. There was an old message from Sis. She asked if she and Father could drop by after lunch, and asked again why Lockwood had interviewed them. And there were six new messages from Barry. Each one was nastier and more profane than the last. "Where are you?" turned into *"Where are you?! What the fuck are you doing?!"* The final message was a threat: *"Call me, or else I'll pull your assignments and put you back on reviews."*

I didn't bother paging Lockwood again; I phoned him at the station. He wasn't in and neither was Smith. I got passed around until I found a detective who agreed to take a long message. Lockwood would know what was happening, at least.

I gave him a rundown of the day. I started at Mrs. May, ended at Catherine Kerr, and reviewed all the speculation in between. I hadn't located *GB Dreams Big* but I'd begun to think that everyone was lying—a little or a lot. I told Lockwood so. I told him that my next stop was Barry Melling, and after Barry, the Casa de Amor.

I thanked the detective for taking the message. He laughed, said, "Everyone's lying," and hung up.

Okay, I was stupid. It hadn't occurred to me to doubt every person I talked to. Now I knew.

I phoned the *Millennium* to see if Barry was still there. It was 8 P.M.; the night watchman said that Barry had gone home.

He lived in the hills above the Sunset Strip, in a funky chalet stuck out over a canyon. I thought about him the whole way over. He had lied to me, too. He was Scott Dolgin's mentor. He'd lent Dolgin seed money and thrown a party for In-Casa Productions. How could he not know about Dolgin and Greta? He probably knew Greta herself. That's why he tried to stop me from writing the piece. That's why the nasty messages demanding updates—and the threats.

His street was one lane of steep hairpin turns. A wide truck was parked in front of his house. It had two tires in the ivy and still blocked half the road. As I squeezed by, I checked it out. A shiny black Humvee.

Hannah Silverman's Humvee.

I parked on the dirt shoulder and walked back down. Keeping low, I leaned against the Humvee to look in the driver's window. An antitheft device beeped; I ducked and jumped back. I held my breath, waiting for someone to come out. A minute passed, but no one did.

I snuck through the ivy and looked into Barry's kitchen. Barry was standing at the counter in a kimono. His chest and feet were bare, and he was pouring wine as he talked to Hannah Silverman. They were too absorbed to hear an electronic beep outside.

Silverman wore one of Barry's kimonos and nothing else. She towered over him like she towered over Arnold Tolback in pictures—but Barry was closer to her age. And just like the pictures, she held her chin at a snotty angle. Penny Proft had called her a world-class witch. From this distance she looked it.

Barry went on talking. I stood up as much as I dared and pressed my ear to the window. I could only catch a few words. I heard "father." I heard "midwifing the sale." I heard "asking price" and "other projects together." Silverman's voice was more shrill, but I watched her lips and couldn't make out her answer. They were discussing business, that's all I could tell.

Barry corked the bottle and they took their wine into another part of the house. I walked over, rang the front doorbell, and waited.

Barry came to the door. He cracked it to see who it was; his expression changed instantly. *"Where have you been?! I've been calling for days!"*

I said, "Let me in and I'll tell you."

"I'm entertaining."

I pointed at the Humvee. "The Joint Chiefs of Staff?"

Barry stepped outside and shut the door behind him. He wrapped his kimono tighter. He said, "I want Lockwood by tomorrow noon."

"I need another week."

"No!"

"Listen, the piece isn't time linked, and I'm getting the most amazing stuff on him."

Barry lit up.

"It's stuff that's never been printed. I've found a new source on his police record and sexual past, and I've got access to the LAPD's findings on the siege."

Barry clenched his fist. "We're going to nail that cocksucker!"

"But I need more time for verification, and I need your help. Some of the reporters won't talk to me because I won't talk about the murder. I need you to twist arms."

Barry reached for the doorknob. "Call me tomorrow about the reporters. I'm giving you one more week."

He opened the door. I said, "Do you know where Scott Dolgin is?"

"Why?"

"Well..." I faked hesitation.

Barry shut the door again. "What is it?"

"I..."

"What?"

"It isn't good..."

"*What* isn't good?"

"...Dolgin lied to you."

Barry tensed. "He did not. What about?"

I said, "It turns out that he knew the dead woman. They were actually working together, and I think he knows where I can find a script of hers. That's why I'm looking for him—the script."

Barry relaxed. "Oh, that. Yes, Scott told me."

"About the script?"

Barry shook his head. "After you and I spoke, Scott told me he knew her. He lied because he was worried about fallout. He doesn't want to hurt In-Casa."

"Where can I find him?"

"Forget Scott—Doug Lockwood's your job."

Barry opened the door and stepped inside. Silverman yelled, *"Hey! I'm waiting here!"*

Barry slammed the door and I heard him throw the dead bolt. I counted backward on my fingers. Arnold Tolback checked into the Marmont on the twenty-third of August. It was eleven days by my calculation: Hannah Silverman broke up with Arnold Tolback eleven days ago. But she'd known Barry longer than that. They didn't look like brand-new lovers to me.

AT NIGHT the Casa de Amor was pink. The porch lights were pink globes, the roses were lit with pink baby-spots, and CASA DE AMOR was lit with pink floods on the archway. The bungalows stood out very pink in the darkness. Traffic on Washington slowed down to stare at them.

I found the side street west of the Casa empty. Pavich's roadster was gone, and there were no cop cars. I parked, walked around to Mrs. May's, and knocked at the door. Her front blinds were open. I leaned over the porch rail and looked in. None of her lights were

on, but the TV set was; it was playing the Home and Garden channel. The courtyard was completely quiet.

I knocked again and listened: nobody was coming. I opened
the screen. An LAPD card had been wedged under the brass
knocker. It was Lockwood's. I knocked on the inside door, then
tried the knob. The knob turned, the door was unlocked. I pushed
it open and called Mrs. May's name.

Calling my name, I walked into the bungalow. Mrs. May's
front room looked exactly like Dolgin's except the greens and
creams were reversed. The sound was down on the TV. A rose cat-
alog lay open on the dining table. Beside it was an empty teacup
and a plate of sandwich crusts.

I walked into the kitchen, calling Mrs. May's name. I felt
around for a light switch and hit the light.

I stopped dead.

Sitting on Mrs. May's kitchen counter: khaki pants, and a pair
of white sneakers. The pants had a rust-colored patch on the right
leg. The sneakers were spotted that same rust color, and there was
dried mud on the treads. I got up close to look. I could smell
chlorine.

My first thought was: *Don't touch anything*. My second thought
was: *Protect the evidence*.

I ran to the kitchen door. Grabbing a dish towel, I covered my
hand and slid the chain into the slot. Nobody would come in the
back way.

I ran through the rest of the bungalow. Mrs. May's purse was
sitting on a shelf in the bathroom. It had her money and car keys
in it. I checked there and everywhere else for door keys—a landlady would have a lot of door keys. There was a Cupid hook stuck
in the wall by the front door. It looked like it might be a key-ring
holder; but the key ring wasn't there.

My heart was pounding. *The murder pants. The murder shoes*. I
wiped the sweat off my hands and told myself to think. What
should I do next?

I ran out to the porch, closed the inside door, and made sure it
locked behind me. I wanted to call Lockwood, but I didn't want to

leave the bungalow unguarded. I realized I should have used Mrs. May's telephone. I twisted the knob and pushed — too late. *Damn.*

Where was she? She couldn't be far. Door open, television on, purse there: she'd only stepped out for a minute.

I looked across the walkway. Scott Dolgin's bungalow was dark. I ran over and tried the door. It was locked.

I ran up the walk to Mrs. May's neighbor. The neighbor's front door was open. Through the screen, I saw a fat woman wedged into one of the Casa's velvet chairs. She wore a turquoise muumuu and fluffy slippers, and had a candy bar in one hand and a bottle of bourbon in the other. It was small-batch bourbon — the most expensive stuff you could buy. Her eyes were closed; she was engrossed in chewing.

I rapped on the screen door. The woman opened her eyes and screeched, "Go *away!*"

I cracked the screen. "Do you know where I can find Mrs. May?"

The woman sloshed her bottle at me. "Looking for Flo, looking for Scott, looking for Ben. Is everybody lost?" She bit off a mouthful of candy bar.

I said, "Who's Ben?"

She screeched, "*Ben!*" spewing chocolate. She pointed toward the back of the courtyard. "Last on the right!"

Ben? The Ben of Ben Hecht? The Ben of "B. N. Hecht" — the pseudonym Neil Phillips was using on his scripts?

I ran up to "Ben's" bungalow. The porch light was on but the place was dark. Lockwood had stuck another business card under the knocker. The blank side faced up. Lockwood had written: "Mr. Phillips, please contact us at your earliest convenience." So Lockwood knew; and Mrs. May lied about Scott Dolgin being her only male tenant —

I heard a noise inside Phillips's bungalow. It sounded like footsteps. I listened hard. It *was* footsteps.

I knocked on the door. The noise stopped. I knocked again, called Phillips's name, and tried looking in his front windows. The venetian blinds were shut.

A stucco wall closed off the rear of the courtyard. It ran flush up to the bungalow, and it was thick with roses. I couldn't get to Phillips's back door from that end.

I tiptoed off the porch and broke into a run. I ran under the arch, turned left, and looked for a back way into the bungalows.

Behind Mrs. May's I found a wooden gate and a cement path. The path led past back doors, garbage cans, and a line of cat-food bowls. I ran down the path on my toes. At Phillips's place, I crouched below the kitchen sill. The louvers and door were shut. I jiggled and pried, but it was no use. I got right up to the window and listened. I couldn't hear footsteps or anything else.

I ran back to the gate, slammed it shut, twirled, and ran smack into a man. The man grabbed me. I yanked away and tried to punch him. The man ducked and caught my fist. In the light from the rose beds, I saw that it was Lockwood. I grabbed his jacket and pulled him close. My heart was pounding.

"*Neil Phillips is home! I heard him but he won't answer the door!*"

Lockwood held on to me. He whispered, "Take it easy. Phillips can't be home—I have Culver City watching the apartments, and they haven't seen him tonight."

"*Are you sure?*"

Lockwood pointed to a car parked on the opposite side of Washington. I made out two silhouettes in the front seat.

I lowered my voice. "*Scott Dolgin's the killer. I was inside Mrs. May's. There's a pair of pants and a pair of sneakers in her kitchen. They're covered with dry blood—and the sneakers smell like a swimming pool.*"

I started pulling Lockwood toward the archway. He let himself be pulled. I said, "*He was in love with Greta. He sent Pavich to my place to see what the police knew. He broke into Greta's car and stole her suitcases. He's Mrs. May's 'special boy,' and she's protecting him. He's disappeared and no one's tried to kill me since.*"

Lockwood stopped me at Mrs. May's porch. "Calm down, please."

"*I am calm! Did you get the message I left at the station?*"

Detective Smith appeared from the back of the courtyard. Lockwood raised his eyebrows at him, but Smith shook his head.

Lockwood walked me onto the porch and made me sit in a wicker chair. I jumped up. *"We should check the garages!"*

Lockwood pressed me back into the chair. "You calm down first."

I looked at him, and then at Smith. I could tell that they both thought I was hysterical. I shut my eyes and took some slow breaths in and out. I felt Lockwood's hand cover mine. I breathed in and out. When I opened my eyes, he and Smith were still looking concerned. I smiled at them. I wanted to make a joke but nothing came to me.

Lockwood let go of my hand. "Now, tell us what you saw."

I told them what I'd found in Mrs. May's bungalow. Smith wrote the notes; Lockwood just listened. Neither of them seemed jazzed.

I said, "What's the matter?"

Lockwood looked at Smith. "I don't believe it, do you?"

Smith shook his head. Lockwood said, "Let's assume that Mrs. May removed these items from Dolgin's residence because she suspected, or knew, that they incriminated him. That doesn't explain the existence of the items. A murderer will generally dispose of bloodstained garments as soon as possible after the crime."

Smith nodded. I said, "You think they're a plant?"

"It could be."

"By who?"

Lockwood and Smith played that poker-faced. I said, "Let's kick down Mrs. May's door and get the stains tested."

I started to stand up, but Lockwood held me back. "We can't go in there. We don't have a warrant."

"You didn't have a warrant for Isabelle Pavich's."

"That's what is called 'exigent circumstances.' We believed Miss Pavich was the victim of an assault and kidnapping."

"Is it her blood on Dolgin's carpet?"

Smith said, "We don't know yet."

I said, "*But something's happened to Mrs. May.*"

Lockwood almost nodded. "Mrs. May called this afternoon to say she had information for us. We thought it might be because she'd talked to you and changed her mind. She'd overheard an argument a few days before Miss Stenholm was murdered—"

I jumped on that. "The notation in Pavich's calendar— 'Fight!!!' And Greta's car was vandalized the very same night!"

Lockwood tapped Smith's notebook. "Friday the twenty-fourth. Write it down, would you, partner?"

I said, "What else did Mrs. May tell you?"

"She said, quote, 'They found it,' but wouldn't explain further. When we arrived for our appointment she wasn't home, and the neighbors weren't able to help us."

I stood up. "No wonder, with one foot in the grave and both hands around a bottle. Can't we check the garages?"

Lockwood didn't argue that time. He stood up with me. Smith said, "I'll stay here," and took Lockwood's chair.

Lockwood and I crossed the lawn and walked down the side street. I was walking faster than him. The garages backed onto the rear of the Casa de Amor, perpendicular to the bungalows. There were eight garages—four on each side of an old strip of asphalt. All eight garage doors were padlocked.

Lockwood pointed to Dolgin's garage. He said, "His vehicle isn't there. We've put a want out on it."

I said, "Which one is Mrs. May's?"

Lockwood pointed to the garage opposite Dolgin's. He said, "We've put a want out on her vehicle, too. Unfortunately, surveillance wasn't in place when she called us. She had time to leave before they came on."

I said, "I found a set of car keys in her purse. Did I mention that?"

Lockwood nodded. I walked up the right-hand row and found a gap between the second and third garages. The gap was a covered walkway that led to the back wall of the courtyard. Lockwood switched on a flashlight and followed me into it. The wall had a wooden gate, and the gate had a working lock. I tried the handle. The gate was locked. Roses hid the door on the courtyard side, I guessed.

Lockwood touched me and pointed his flashlight at the ground. There was a rectangular wooden board embedded in the asphalt. It was flush with the surface and the size of an ordinary door. I stepped on the board, then jumped with both feet. I shrugged at Lockwood. He frowned at the board and stepped on it himself. His weight didn't make any difference: the board was anchored solid.

We toured the rest of the garage area. There wasn't much to it, but I registered something I hadn't before. The Casa de Amor's closest neighbor was a school. The playground had a chain-link fence that surrounded the Casa on two sides, and the fence was fifteen feet high. With a car watching on Washington, there was no way to get in or out of the courtyard without being seen. The foot sounds inside Phillips's bungalow must have been something else — stray noise or the girl ghoul next door.

Lockwood walked me back up the side street. I said, "Barry Melling's sleeping with Hannah Silverman. I saw them together tonight."

If that surprised Lockwood, he didn't show it. I said, "Do you have any idea what's going on?"

He stopped beside my car, and I could tell he didn't intend to answer the question. I pointed across Washington. "Let's look around the Sony lot."

Lockwood shook his head. "I want you to go home and go to bed. When you're overstrained, you don't think clearly and you —"

I finished his sentence. " — flip out and imagine all sorts of crazy stuff?"

"Nerves will always catch up with you. You might not feel them for days, and then the accumulation will hit."

I said, "I'll go straight home after Sony, I promise." I shook his arm. "I *promise*."

Lockwood checked his watch. He looked dubious. But after a pause, he nodded.

We walked back to Mrs. May's and he told Smith the plan.

Smith was staying put. Someone had to watch the bungalow: until they had grounds for a search warrant, they were making sure the pants and sneakers weren't removed. My testimony wasn't enough for the warrant. I was all over this case, Lockwood said; any judge would suspect collusion between me and the cops. And if the judge didn't, the defense attorneys would.

Lockwood and I jaywalked across Washington and followed the Sony wall around the corner. He loosened his necktie while I ran down what I knew about Neil John Phillips and Jack Nevenson. Lockwood had heard it before—I was just hoping to find out what he knew. But he didn't comment, he listened.

It was late and there was nobody around. We walked up to the kiosk at the entrance to the lot. Lockwood badged the security guard there. The guy yawned, put down his sports section, and came out to talk to us.

Lockwood had some photographs with him. They were enlarged DMV shots of Greta Stenholm, Scott Dolgin, Neil John Phillips, Isabelle Pavich, and Mrs. May.

Lockwood said, "Do you recognize any of these people?"

The guard went through the pictures and pointed to Phillips. "That's Ben."

Lockwood said, "Ben who?"

The guard yawned and leaned against the kiosk. "Don't know his last name—used to work in the Columbia mail room back six, eight years ago. Quit that job to write movies I heard, but still hangs around the lot. Eats in the cafeteria quite a bit—I see him when I'm on days. Kind of a mascot, a fixture, you might say."

Lockwood took back his photos. "Is Ben friends with anyone in particular, do you know?"

"Weeell, I'd say Dick, one of the projectionists. Old guy, older than me, union man, been around donkey's years. Told me Ben's always wanting to talk about old movies."

It was 11:25 by my watch. I said, "Were there any screenings tonight?"

The guard nodded, then shook his head. "Locked up the theaters half an hour ago."

Lockwood said, "Can you tell me how to reach the projectionist?"

The guard leaned into his kiosk and checked a clipboard. Lockwood whispered in my ear, "Don't talk unless I say so."

"Sorry."

The guard read off the projectionist's name and home phone number. Lockwood wrote it down. Another security guard rolled up in a golf cart, a young guy. Lockwood identified himself. The guy snapped to, leaping out of his cart and standing at attention. He looked like an ex-soldier or ex-cop. Lockwood showed him the photographs. He picked "Ben" out of the pack right off.

Lockwood said, "What can you tell me about Ben?"

The guard pointed to Scott Dolgin's picture. "He's buddies with this guy, sir. I see them together."

Lockwood said, "Doing what?"

The guard shook his head. "I don't know, sir—walking, talking."

"In any particular location?"

"No sir, not in particular. I've seen them all over the lot."

Lockwood said, "Can you recall anything else?"

The guard screwed up his forehead; he really wanted to help. Lockwood said, "At some point, Ben removed a large number of boxes from the property. Do you know anything about that?"

The guard said, "I recall the boxes, sir. That was years ago, after the Sony outfit bought the lot."

Lockwood said, "And?"

"And they were throwing out old papers that Ben wanted. I thought he was nuts—it was just paper—but I helped him haul the boxes away and stash them. Then he brought his car and took the boxes home in dribs and drabs. It took weeks—I really thought he was nuts, sir."

Lockwood stuck the DMV photos in his pocket. "Would you show me where Ben hid the boxes?"

"Yes, sir!"

The guard jumped into the golf cart. Lockwood took the passenger seat and motioned me in behind him.

We rolled across the parking lot. Lockwood looked around and

I thought about Phillips. A true MGM fan *would* be nuts with COLUMBIA PICTURES on the Thalberg Building, and a bronze bas-relief of Harry Cohn on the building next door. Cohn's small, cheesy Columbia would've been beneath the great MGM's contempt.

The guard rolled onto the sidewalk and turned right, down the first road parallel to the old studio wall. Sony had kept the MGM building names; we passed the Kelly and the Poitier; but particle-board fronts transformed them into police precincts and clothing stores. The guard kept going until we hit the famous colonnade gate that faced Washington — the original studio gate from the '20s. This part of the lot hadn't been renovated. The original guard kiosk was used for bicycle storage, and the two-story buildings were cramped and decayed.

The guard rolled to a stop beside the old kiosk. He said, "This is called Cutter's Row, sir. Ben told me it's the most historic part of the lot."

Lockwood nodded and climbed out of the cart. The guard jumped out; I followed him. He started down a narrow alley be-tween the buildings. It was a dump back there; junk sat every-where. The guard pointed behind a wall that concealed large gas mains. He said, "Ben put boxes here, sir, until it rained."

Lockwood and I looked behind the wall. The guard kept walk-ing to a utility shed in an alley beside the Hepburn Building. The guard got out his keys and unlocked the shed. Lockwood stuck his head inside.

He said, "Did Ben have the key to this?"

The guard nodded.

"How did he get it?"

The guard shook his head.

"Does he still have it?"

"I don't know, sir. I believe he has a number of keys, but we don't mind. He treats the old studio like a church."

Lockwood nodded and walked back to the golf cart. The guard hurried to lead the way. We climbed into the cart and the guard hung a U-turn, stepped on the gas, and drove us back to the parking lot.

Lockwood said, "Where are the theaters?"

The guard jogged right and stopped. He pointed to the ramp at the near end of the Thalberg Building. Lockwood got out of the cart. The guard fumbled at his belt and handed a key ring to Lockwood.

"The keys are marked, sir. There's four you want—one for the theaters, one for the projection booths, one for the washrooms, and one for the emergency exits. Keep them as long as you need to, please. It's...it's..."

He said in a rush, "It'sanhonortomeetyousir." He whipped another U-turn and took off before Lockwood could react.

I pulled Lockwood's sleeve. "Walk this way."

I led him down the curving ramp into the Thalberg basement. I knew all the screening rooms on all the studio lots: this was home to me.

A very long hallway led to the screening rooms. The office doors were closed and the lights were low for the night.

I turned down a short hall into the upper lobby of the theaters. The decor was a contemporary version of the Casa de Amor's Moderne: muted colors and stylized simple furniture. Posters from forgotten Columbia movies lined the walls. The lights in the lobby were on half power, too.

I pointed out the washrooms to the left, the coatroom to the right, and, down some stairs, the screening rooms off the lower lobby. Lockwood went to check the washrooms. I headed for the theaters. The doors were locked, like the guard said, and I waited for Lockwood to come with the keys. He unlocked and searched the rooms in sequence. There were six theaters, A through F, and six projection booths. The theaters were identical except for decor: deep, cozy, high-ceilinged rooms, with rows of comfortable chairs.

I followed Lockwood into each theater, around, and out. I turned lights on and off when he asked. He never talked otherwise; I'd noticed that he liked his searches quiet. We didn't find anything of interest except the personal quirks of the projectionists. One was a neatnik. Another was a Myrna Loy fan: the corkboard walls of one booth were covered with her picture. She was an arcane taste and I wondered if that was Neil Phillips's projectionist friend.

We circled back to theater D. Lockwood unlocked the door again and walked down the aisle to the curtained area below the screen. Looping back the curtain, he unlocked the emergency door and stepped into the passage behind. He signaled me to follow him.

The passage was low and lit by red bulbs in scallop-shell sconces. Half the bulbs were burned out, and Lockwood had to turn on his flashlight. He shined it around the walls and across the ceiling and floor. The passage wasn't just bare cement. The floors were bare, but the walls had been finished, and the old paint and plaster were in good shape. Nothing had cracked or leaked, so the passage didn't have the damp dirt smell of underground places. There were also exhaust vents; Lockwood reached up to inspect a grate. That's why the air wasn't stale.

Lockwood stopped and listened. I held still and listened with him. The passage was silent. I couldn't hear any building noises, no furnaces or water in pipes. Lockwood stepped on a chunk of loose cement. The sound didn't echo. I imagined a million tons of earth and stone all around us; I imagined the old-fashioned workmanship that went into the Thalberg. Maybe the emergency exits were soundproofed like the theaters. We weren't that far underground, but the silence was absolute.

Lockwood whispered, "Stay close."

I stuck behind him as he followed the passage behind theaters E and F, to a dead end. The passage there branched off right and left. I pointed to the right and whispered, "That's the way out. We had a fire alarm once — it comes out at the back of the building."

Lockwood nodded and made the left. His flashlight caught a painted arrow on the wall. The arrow said EMERGENCY ACCESS — THEATERS A, B, C.

We kept going along the passage, and hit another dead end. The only choice was left. We made the left and found ourselves behind theater C. The passage continued straight and dead-ended behind theater A. There was nowhere to go from there. We turned around. Lockwood swung his flashlight side to side as we walked back.

He stopped and pointed. There was an old maroon door across the passage from theater C. The paint had faded, and peeled in parts, but we could still read the PRIVATE, in Deco lettering. The knob had a brass plate and an old-style keyhole lock. Lockwood checked the key ring. He saw that none of the keys would fit and kneeled down to examine the keyhole. He put his eye right against it, then pulled back and twisted the knob. The door didn't budge. He pulled harder and couldn't move it. He ran his light around the frame, looking for obstacles. The door was sealed tight.

I bent down to look at the floor. Lockwood saw what I was doing and aimed the flashlight for me. I found patches of green fuzz. It was heavy and stiff like carpet fiber, except none of the theater carpets were green. Cigarette butts and cigar stubs were scattered everywhere; they were flattened by age and the shoes that had crushed them. I picked up one of the butts. It was nonfilter and had faint lipstick stains around the tip. The old paper crumbled and spilled dry tobacco.

Lockwood picked up some green fuzz. I leaned closer to him. "How much do you know about MGM?"

Lockwood shook his head.

"In its heyday it was run like a fascist state. It had its own police force and internal spies. They bugged employee offices and monitored left-wing political activity—they even kept track of the actresses' periods. Louis Mayer had a private elevator that he used to keep his meetings and movements secret. The elevator ran from his office on the top floor to these screening rooms. This was probably an entrance."

I tapped the maroon door. Lockwood sat back on his heels and studied it. He ran the flashlight beam back and forth over the whole surface. I watched him get to the bottom sill, stop, and frown at the door.

A voice reached us, muffled by walls. "Detective! Detective, sir!"

Lockwood stood up, and we took a shortcut through theater C to the lower lobby. The security guard from before was looking for us. He seemed flustered. He was with an old guy wearing a tool belt.

The guard explained that he'd gone to disarm the emergency system so that Lockwood and I could move freely. He discovered that someone had tampered with the alarm fuses. Someone had also tampered with the emergency door leading outside from the passages. Lockwood asked the guard to show us. He and the maintenance guy led us back through theater C and along the passage to the outside exit. There was a steel door at the bottom of a long flight of cement stairs. The catch on the door had been jammed so the door could be opened from the exterior.

The four of us walked up the staircase into the night air. It was more parking lot back there, a high wall and Culver Boulevard. Lockwood asked the two men about Louis Mayer's private elevator. The maintenance guy, a veteran, said that they'd discovered the elevator shaft in the late '60s when a wall in theater C started to leak. The elevator had been taken out and the shaft sealed. Its approximate location was the ladies' restroom next to theater C.

Lockwood thanked the men and asked how soon the alarm system would be fixed. They said a couple of hours, and took off.

Lockwood backed up to survey the rear of the building, then sat down on the top step of the emergency stairs. I sat down beside him. He shined his flashlight down the staircase.

I said, "Someone is using the basement to hide."

Lockwood put his finger to his lips. I lowered my voice. "Should I not talk?"

"Please, talk—but try a different subject. I need to think about this."

It was a perfect opening. I gathered my nerve and said, "I wish you'd let me write your story. You really should defend yourself. From what I've heard, you did the right thing at the siege."

Lockwood was silent. I said, "If it's because you don't trust me—I'll have the rest of the blackmail money in two months maximum."

He said, "It's not that."

No, I actually knew it wasn't that. The signs that he trusted me, at least some, had been there since morning.

I said, "All right, I'm the enemy and you hate me. But I can still write a great piece."

Lockwood squeezed my wrist and didn't answer. The light was too dark to see his face clearly, but he looked like he was smiling.

I said, "I can be objective—"

Lockwood moved the flashlight; he *was* smiling. I said, "Is something funny?"

He shook his head. "It isn't about trust or liking. Other journalists have offered to write my side of events."

"Really?"

"I have a few supporters in the media, believe it or not."

"So why didn't they?"

"Because I wouldn't let them."

"Why not?"

Lockwood's smile went away, and he paused. He said, "People who commit crimes lie. I'm used to lying—I'm not only used to it, I expect it."

I said, "Unlike gullible me."

Lockwood squeezed my wrist again. "You're a bad liar, baby, that's why good liars fool you."

I flashed back to the scene with Barry tonight. I could do a certain kind of lying when I had to. I'd left Barry with several wrong impressions.

Lockwood was talking. "In my experience, it's a rare criminal who isn't aware of his own lies. You see the pathological cases, sure, the guys who've lost touch with reality. But people usually know they're lying when they lie to me. They know what the truth is, they're just choosing to hide it. But they can be trapped with evidence. That's why we have courts and trials—to present evidence to neutral arbitration and prosecute the guilty."

I said, "That's the theory."

"I agree—that's the theory." Lockwood played with the flashlight beam.

"But the media is a different breed of liar. Criminals have

fallen from truth, whereas the media doesn't seem to give a damn about it. The truth has no power with them unless other considerations make the truth convenient to tell. They run with the herd and call it 'reporting the facts'—even when the herd changes its mind the next day.

"I'm accused of many things by the people I arrest, but I don't dignify them with an answer. If I did, it would give them credibility they don't have. The media would love for me to defend myself because it would give them credibility. It would mean I acknowledged their charges as something that should be dealt with. But I don't acknowledge it. People who know the facts know I did what was possible in the circumstances."

I said, "Some say you did better than that."

Lockwood shook his head. "If nobody had died, that would have been better."

He realized he was just playing with the flashlight, and switched it off. He didn't talk for a minute; but he wasn't done.

"The media hates me now, and I couldn't change their minds if I wanted to. I think they hate me in part because they've painted me as evil and they know I'm not. It also goes beyond me—this is also about LAPD in general, and Rampart. I've been advised to ask forgiveness publicly, even if I'm not sincere. But then the dishonesty would come full circle. I'm not looking for forgiveness or vindication—I didn't do anything wrong. I want no part of notoriety I didn't ask for, or an image that the media fabricated in bad faith."

I said, "But if you don't defend yourself, they win."

"They win either way, is what I'm saying. If I play, I lose. My words on a page have the same weight as their words on a page. The game is rigged and can't be redeemed. I won't waste my time with it."

I sat looking at him. There was no self-pity in his face. He wasn't angry or bitter: he'd said all that in his normal way. And I understood exactly what he was talking about.

I grabbed the railing and pulled myself up. Lockwood said, "Where are you going?"

"Home to bed—I'm overstrained."

He stood up and stopped me. "What's the matter?"

I blurted, "Did the siege scandal change you?"

I felt the abruptness of the question, but Lockwood didn't hesitate. He said, "Yes, it changed me."

"How has it changed you? What were you before? Did it wreck your career and ruin your life?"

Lockwood glanced down the emergency staircase. "Let's solve these murders first."

"If I help, will you talk to me?"

He said, "You've already helped."

"So will you talk to me?"

Lockwood nodded.

I started to clap my hands. Lockwood reached out and held them closed. He said, "I'll talk to *you*. Not to your newspaper—you."

CHAPTER
SIXTEEN

The Los Angeles District Attorney's office today confirmed rumors of a secret grand-jury probe into the ongoing Rampart corruption scandal. The announcement came after weeks of speculation. Sources close to the probe say that Douglas Lockwood, the LAPD detective involved in the controversial 'Burger King Siege' of last December, has been called to testify about his Rampart links."

Jesus, I thought. *Shut up!*

I covered my ears to stop the sound of the anchorman's voice. The TV boomed through the student union and added to the racket of kids between classes.

I shifted around, trying to get more comfortable. All the couches were taken and I was napping in an armchair. But the chair was lumpy, the fabric made my skin itch, and I was surrounded by eating, drinking, yakking kids. I opened my eyes to check the time. It was only ten-thirty. I was so tired and over-amped that I wanted to scream.

I'd slept a total of forty-five minutes all night. Lockwood had been right about how nerves accumulate. After I got home from Sony, I just bounced around the mansion—I didn't even feel like lying down. I'd talked to the surveillance guys a bit; mostly I stared out of windows and replayed the end of the evening.

I was convinced that someone was using the Thalberg basement to hide. Lockwood had disagreed. Someone was using it to pass through, he said, but there was no practical place to *hide*—not in the screening rooms, or the upper floors. I'd said there was plenty of access between the theaters and the floors above it: three elevators and two staircases connected them. He'd said the lobby was guarded and the fire escapes were grilled and locked; the only way in and out of the building without trouble was the basement. I wasn't convinced. Why use the basement at all, then? Come in by the west ramp, leave by the south emergency stairs, or vice versa: what did it get you? A tricky escape hatch, Lockwood said.

But people had disappeared, I argued—where did he think they were? The more time wore on, the more dire things looked. And why, I had asked, did he care about Neil John Phillips and his boxes of old MGM memos?

I knew I'd made progress with Lockwood. He'd agreed to talk to me: that was an important concession. But it didn't mean he was going to answer all my questions.

He wouldn't comment on Phillips's boxes. He refused to say who or what he suspected; he wouldn't agree that the SC crowd was key to Greta Stenholm's death. He'd only discuss concrete measures. They were fixing the Thalberg's alarm system. He'd issued a broadcast listing Isabelle Pavich as a possible kidnap victim. He'd attended roll calls at Culver City PD to get their help locating Mrs. May, Scott Dolgin, and Neil Phillips. Mrs. May was a priority. He wanted to search her bungalow and bag the bloody clothes.

He'd left it between us like this: if anything crucial happened, he'd call me or I'd call him. Otherwise I should be careful and we'd talk when we talked. *Be careful*, I'd thought for the billionth time. Careful of what? Of who?

By dawn I had worn myself out on hypotheticals. I decided to take a swim. I swam until I couldn't lift my arms, then collapsed on the bed and slept for a whole forty-five minutes.

I was back on the road at 7 A.M.

Catherine Kerr had slammed her door on me. Hamilton Ashburn was in transit between his house and the set, and his cell phone didn't answer. Penny Proft made a couple of lame jokes and invited me to breakfast. The receptionist at PPA said that Len Ziskind and Jack Nevenson weren't in yet. I'd dodged past her to check their offices; she started dialing the cops. I left the building voluntarily and drove up to the Writers Guild on Sunset. The Guild registered written material to protect it from plagiarism. I claimed to be Greta Stenholm's sister and tried to finagle a copy of *GB Dreams Big.* The desk person just laughed at me.

From there I'd swung down to the Casa de Amor and talked to the surveillance guys sitting across Washington. They hadn't seen anybody we wanted.

At that point I was totally out of ideas. Then I'd remembered a name Mark gave me way back at the start: an Academy librarian, film teacher, and screenwriter named Steve Lampley. Lampley knew Greta from Kansas.

I'd found Lampley's phone number and called him at home. He was giving a lecture at a college in Malibu. Could he meet me out there beforehand? Unlike everyone else that morning, Lampley had seemed anxious to talk.

I sighed. The nap just wasn't happening.

I sat up, stuck out my legs, stretched, and checked around. I saw an older guy walk into the student union and stand looking for someone. On the phone Lampley told me "black suit and salt-and-pepper ponytail." This guy had both. I waved an arm. He spotted me and headed over.

He was small and fortyish, with a grievance on his face. I could even guess what the grievance was. He didn't want to be lecturing at Podunk colleges; he wanted to be earning seven figures per screenplay.

I pointed to an alcove away from the TV set. He nodded and we went and sat down on a couch.

Lampley said, "I just realized I might have killed Greta."

I'd barely gotten settled. I dropped my bag and just stared at him. He said, "You were one of her best friends so I'll tell you first."

I tried not to gape. First Catherine Kerr and her news: Greta wanted to take *me* to Hollywood. And now *I* was one of Greta's best friends? I'd play it as close to the truth as I could.

I said, "Greta and I weren't *friend* friends. I mean—"

Lampley cut in. "No one was really friends with Greta—you don't need to explain. We both know she only had one idea in her head and nothing else mattered, certainly not friendship. But she talked about you more than anyone else before she...toward the end."

He had a hard time with "end." It was the only sign of whatever emotion he felt. He was a tight, controlled guy.

He said, "But you can't put this in your article. It makes Greta look bad."

"What if I don't agree with you?"

"Wait until you hear—you'll agree."

I shrugged and Lampley cleared his throat. "You know her fiancé was murdered a year ago and the murder hasn't been solved."

I corrected him without thinking. "You mean Hannah Silverman's fiancé."

Lampley shook his head. I thought I'd blown my best-friend status, but he just said, "It's incredible the things Greta didn't tell people. When I first met her, you know, she was a sweet, straight-ahead Midwesterner. She never lied and she trusted everybody."

I glossed over my gaff. "I've also heard two different stories. Greta said that Abadi broke off his engagement with Silverman, but Silverman says that Abadi dumped Greta—"

Lampley cut in. "Hannah's a liar. The fact is, the same day Ted was killed he had dumped Hannah and asked Greta to marry him."

"I never heard the marriage part."

"It's true, but the engagement was going to be secret until Greta revived her career. See, when the agency dropped Greta, Ted dropped her, too—that's when he started dating Hannah. He was nothing if not ambitious, Ted was."

I couldn't peg Lampley's tone. It felt like he wanted to sneer at Abadi—then it hit me why. Mark had said that Lampley followed Greta from Kansas. Maybe he'd torched for her all these years. Maybe they'd had an affair—although if I knew Greta, I doubted it. Lampley was the loser, Abadi was the winner. Abadi had looks and killer drive, and a primo foothold in the movie business.

I said, "How long were Abadi and Greta together initially?"

"Three years, ever since he signed her at film school."

"And how soon did they hook up again after Abadi started seeing Silverman?"

At that, Lampley did sneer. "Ted never *broke off* with Greta at all. See, that's the thing—he couldn't let her go. Hannah was the *official* girlfriend, because she was a better career move. But even Ted couldn't stomach her, or her demented father-daughter act."

I said, "Who's Hannah Silverman's father?"

Lampley paused. "You're kidding."

"I'm not kidding. Who's her father?"

"Jules Silverman. Her father is Jules Silverman."

Yow, *Jules Silverman*. My mind started to race.

Silverman was a very gray Hollywood eminence; only Lew Wasserman was grayer. He'd made a fortune as a producer in the '50s and '60s. Then American movies got too gritty and he retired to philanthropy and liberal causes. He was now past eighty and a semirecluse; he never left his Malibu estate. But he still had clout. The studios still listened to him, and he played a major role in local politics. Barry knew him. I'd heard Barry call him "Julie" not long ago.

I said, "What's the 'father-daughter act'?"

Lampley shook his head. "I can't give you details. I only know the two of them are unnaturally close."

Maybe I was tired, but I didn't see where this was going. I said, "So Hannah and Jules are unnaturally close. And so?"

Lampley said, "And so it looked like the police weren't going to solve Ted's murder, and so Greta decided to solve it herself."

"How?"

He said, "See, Jules was Hannah's alibi for the night of the murder. I should have guessed that Greta might try to pressure him—I could kick myself for not guessing. But Ted was such a worthless asshole, and I just couldn't believe she'd do something illegal—"

I got it. I saw Greta's whole plan in a flash. I saw the spanking picture, and I saw the old guy in it. The old guy was Jules Silverman.

I said, "She was going to break down Hannah's alibi by going after her father. Is that it? Greta thought that Jules was covering up for her."

Lampley nodded. "And I gave Greta information that she could have used to blackmail Jules. See, I don't have absolute proof that she tried to extort him, but I do know that she asked your boss, Barry Melling, to publish the information in the *Millennium*, and Melling wouldn't do it."

The word *information* threw me. Was a dirty picture "information"? I said, "Greta never told me she knew Barry."

"They met through a mutual friend, Scott Dolgin. Dolgin introduced them, and Melling wouldn't leave Greta alone after that. He said he'd print her information, but only if she slept with him. Fortunately, Greta wasn't stupid."

I shook my head. Dolgin and Greta; now Barry and Greta. I'd been lied to yet again.

"What exactly is this information?"

Lampley said, "You know I work at the Academy Library part-time."

I nodded.

"I was put in charge of cataloging old material that had never been organized. In the process, I came across transcripts from an abandoned book project, an oral history of the blacklist at MGM. The subject interests me, so I read the transcripts. Over and over, ex-employees identified Jules Silverman as a HUAC stool pigeon. It was widely known at the time, apparently, but never discussed. And because of Silverman's public profile, some of the people still wouldn't confirm the story for print."

It *wasn't* the spanking picture. Still: fifty-year-old blacklist revelations? It didn't strike me as a viable wedge.

Lampley said, "You see what something like that would do to Jules Silverman's reputation."

I shook my head. "The blacklist is ancient history. People don't care about it anymore."

"You're wrong—Silverman has enemies who would care. The evidence is all there, and contradicts Silverman's own story of how he opposed the blacklist covertly by employing the unemploy-ables. See, according to this, Silverman got his break at MGM by squealing on his competition, most of whom were liberal or left-leaning Jews. People don't realize how anti-Semitic HUAC was, underneath the anticommunist rhetoric. And Silverman handed the committee a lot of Jews."

I said, "Barry would never print that. Not even if there were five Gretas and they all slept with him simultaneously."

Lampley didn't smile. He said, "It gets worse. According to the transcripts, Silverman was a major suspect in an unsolved murder from 1944. The victim was a USO hostess named Georgette Bauerdorf, who was killed in West Hollywood."

The initials hit me full-on. *GB. Georgette Bauerdorf. Georgette Bauerdorf Dreams Big.*

I didn't jump up and dance around. I sat very still and said, "Where are those transcripts? I'd like to read them."

Lampley made a tight face. "They're gone."

"What do you mean 'gone'?"

"It's my fault—I told Greta about them and I shouldn't have."

"When was this?"

"Late February, around the time Tolback fired her."

I said, "Arnold Tolback?"

Lampley looked at me. "She took that job to get close to Hannah's new boyfriend, but Hannah found out and made Tolback fire her. Did Greta ever tell you *anything*?"

I shrugged. "We never talked about our personal lives. We talked about movies."

Lampley nodded like, Of course. He knew about the One Idea in Greta's head.

He said, "Greta told me she wanted the transcripts to show to Neil Phillips. You know Neil?"

I nodded. "And his MGM jones."

Lampley nodded. "I was an idiot to believe her. I lent her the transcripts and said I needed them back right away. But she kept them for weeks, Neil says he never saw them, and then they were stolen from her apartment—"

Lampley suddenly couldn't go on. He leaned forward and put his head in his hands. He said, *"Oh, god."*

I said, "And you think she was murdered for the transcripts. You think Jules Silverman stole them, and killed her because she knew what they contained."

Lampley didn't look up. "He's too old. I think someone did it for him."

"But you don't have proof."

Lampley didn't answer.

I sat and studied his bald spot. Until yesterday I would've bought the act whole: repressed guy under emotional strain hides eyes as he confesses guilt. "Oh, god" was a nice touch. But now I didn't believe him. Some, most, or all of what he said could be false. There was no way to check if the transcripts even existed. So the question became: why was Lampley telling me this? If I believed him, what did it accomplish?

I glanced over at the TV set. The anchorman said, "And those are the top news stories for Tuesday, September 4, 2001."

It was Tuesday already. Greta had been dead for a week.

HANNAH SILVERMAN lived across the coast highway a half mile south of the college. Lockwood had warned me not to bother her or Arnold Tolback. But Lockwood wasn't reachable and Silverman was close: I decided things had changed enough that I could take the risk. Leaving Lampley to his lecture, I drove down to Silverman's house, parked, and rang the fence bell.

Nobody came. I went to the car, dialed Silverman's number from the car phone, and got her machine. I thought about hopping the fence one more time. But a neighbor was washing his car, and I had to think again. I looked around and saw some letters sticking out of Silverman's mail slot. I checked a return address: it was outgoing mail.

I turned my back to the neighbor and quickly flipped through the letters. One to TreePeople, one to a plastic surgeon in Beverly Hills. One to Mr. J. Silverman, Ramirez Canyon, Malibu.

Two miles away.

I slipped the envelope out, opened it, and skimmed the card. Hannah had written: "Daddy, you're always in my thoughts. Love, love, love, forever and ever and ever."

Not hard to memorize. I stuck the card and envelope back, got in the car, and made a U-turn onto the coast highway going west. At Ramirez Canyon I made a right into the hills.

The road climbed and climbed, and changed from asphalt to gravel. Way up the gravel, I found the entrance to Silverman's estate. Two huge granite pillars flanked a huge wrought-iron gate. A wrought-iron fence fronted the property for hundreds of yards. You couldn't see the house: it was hidden by a forest of imported trees.

I drove past the entrance, turned around, and parked on the side of the road. I set the emergency brake and settled down to watch the gate.

That got old real fast. It also made me sleepy.

I shook myself awake and picked up the car phone. I called Information, then the Producers Guild. They gave me the name and address of Arnold Tolback's company—AT Productions in Burbank.

I dialed the AT Productions number. The woman who answered said that Mr. Tolback wasn't in. I kept her talking and led around to the subject of Greta Stenholm. She said that Greta worked at ATP for four months as assistant to one of Tolback's assistants. She said that Greta was very competent; it was a surprise when Tolback fired her. I asked where Tolback might be found and the woman said, "Try the Chateau Marmont."

Jules Silverman's gate wasn't moving. I started the car, put it in neutral, and rolled down to the coast highway. At the highway I stepped on the gas. I turned on Sunset and took it all the way into West Hollywood.

There was a black Porsche parked in the Marmont's breezeway. I pulled around in front of it. A valet was holding the driver's door and a guy was just getting in. It was the guy from the smashed pictures in Hannah Silverman's office. The fraternity boy—shorter, younger, and having a better time than her.

I jumped out of my car and ran to the Porsche. Tolback was fooling with his shoulder harness. He heard me coming and looked up.

I said, "I want to ask you some questions about Greta Stenholm."

He said, "And you are?"

"Ann Whitehead. I work for—"

He laughed. "Yeah, I know you. You're that loudmouth critic everybody hates."

I said, "Why'd you fire Greta last February?"

Tolback was wearing a blue blazer; he got a pen out of the breast pocket. "Give me something to write on." He snapped his fingers.

I dug into my jeans and found a gasoline receipt. Tolback grabbed it from me, wrote on it, and passed it back.

"Go to that address after eight-thirty tonight. Tell Lynnda I invited you, and tell her I said they can all kiss my ass. Say it exactly like this, loudmouth—'Arnie says, *Kiss my pimple-free kosher ass!*'"

Tolback laughed and peeled out of the breezeway. The engine noise rattled my teeth. I read what he'd written: "Lynnda-Ellen, 3617 Whitley Terrace, Whitley Heights."

I stuck the receipt in my pocket. Just what we need, I thought: another new name.

I WALKED INTO the lobby of the newspaper. Mark and Vivian were standing by the switchboard, huddled together. I walked up behind them and said, "Hey."

Vivian turned. "There you are! We wondered if something had happened." She squinted at me. "You don't look so hot."

I said, "Eating and sleeping might help."

Mark patted my arm. "Welcome to real journalism. Have you solved the murders yet?"

I gave him a sarcastic smile. Vivian said, "Did you find my groupie at least?"

"I did, thanks, at The Short Stop with two teenage groupettes."

"What'd she tell you?"

"You were right—those girls know things. Can you guys spare any cash?"

Vivian shook her head, but Mark reached for his wallet. Vivian said, "You'll tell me later about the groupie."

I nodded as Mark handed me thirty bucks. He said, "When are you coming back to the section?"

"Thanks." I stuck the money in my jeans. "I don't know—tomorrow, next month, I don't know."

I turned to leave. Vivian held on to me, lowered her voice, and pointed. "Speaking of finances, get a load of that."

She was pointing across the lobby to the accounting office. Three strange men were inside; they had briefcases open and calculators out. The *Millennium*'s head accountant hovered over them, and the desks were stacked with files.

I said, "Is that why you guys are huddled up here?"

Mark whispered, "There's a rumor going around that the paper's for sale."

I said, "That rumor's been going around since the Hollywood gang recruited Barry for—"

I stopped because I'd remembered something. I'd remembered the fragments of conversation I overheard between Barry and Hannah Silverman: father, asking price, midwifing the sale.

I said, "Who does Jules Silverman know who would want to buy the paper?"

Vivian said, "Jules Silverman?" Mark raised his eyebrows and started humming the theme to *The Godfather*.

Vivian nodded. "Jules Silverman knows everyone in the country with that kind of dough."

Mark stopped humming. "If the rumor is true, it explains why Barry wants to mainstream the film section. He's trying to make the paper more attractive to buyers."

Vivian said, "Why do you think Silverman's involved?"

A banging noise interrupted us; it came from the far side of the lobby. We turned to look, and Barry came rushing down the stairs from his office.

Vivian whispered, "Doug Lockwood was just here with another detective—they just left."

Barry had his car keys in his teeth and he was zipping his coat.
I stuck my hand out to grab him. I said, "Wait—you wanted the
names of those reporters—"

Barry brushed past us. "Not now, Ann!"

He ran across the lobby and out the front door. I waved at Mark
and Vivian and ran after him.

I saw him pull out of the parking lot and bomb by, going south.
He didn't see me. I raced to my car, jumped in, gunned it, and followed him.

He rolled through the stop sign at Franklin and turned left,
then right on Vermont. I turned left, then right, and stayed in the
curb lane three car-lengths back. He was driving crazy. He zigzagged through traffic, changing lanes, not signaling, cutting
people off. I was forced to do the same. People honked their horns
and yelled at both of us.

He was still driving like that as we hit the Hollywood Freeway.
He turned left at the entrance, southbound, and accelerated down
the ramp. I hit the ramp two cars behind him. I had broken a sweat.

He hopped lanes all the way into downtown. It wasn't easy for
me to keep up. Traffic was heavy, and Barry had a new Lexus. He
could punch it through openings where I couldn't.

The freeway split up at the downtown interchange. I stayed in
the middle lane, since I didn't know where we were going. At the
last minute Barry swooped into the right lane. I floored the gas, cut
over, and kept him in sight. We curved south and hit the Santa
Monica Freeway going west. Barry stepped on it, started to change
lanes, and almost sideswiped another car. They honked and
swerved apart. Barry slowed way down. I watched him wait, then
ease into the fast lane when it was clear. He sped up to seventy and
held it there.

I stayed behind him two lanes over. I didn't need to be that
careful—Barry wasn't paying attention. Once he hit cruising speed
he picked up his car phone and started to talk. He talked and

drove, talked and drove: it went on for miles. And it wasn't just one call. He must have redialed eight or ten times.

We kept going west. We passed exit after exit. By La Cienega I was sure where we were headed.

Barry shot off the freeway at the Robertson exit. I was prepared for it and dropped back to follow him. A red light stopped us at the bottom of the ramp. The light took awhile to change. I'd learned something about car chases. They weren't fun or exciting: they made you sweaty, and sick to your stomach.

The light turned green and Barry turned south on Robertson. He'd calmed down and was driving the speed limit. I still kept two cars between us. He turned onto Washington Boulevard going west. We were in Culver City now. Barry's state only showed at intersections. He ran two yellow lights, which forced me to run the reds. I almost hit a motorcycle at one of them.

Barry pulled up in front of the Casa de Amor. He jumped out of the car, left his door open, and ran under the arch. I pulled over and stopped at the end of the block. There was a new surveillance team parked across the street. Their heads turned to watch Barry.

He reappeared inside a minute. He jumped back in his car and took off down Washington. I pulled out behind him.

This time he sailed right through a red. I got there late and had to slam on my brakes: the cross traffic was too heavy.

I sat and watched Barry's taillights shrink. But Washington Boulevard was flat and straight, and I could see a good distance. He turned north at Overland.

My light turned green. I floored it up to Overland and made the right. Barry had pulled into the Starbucks on the corner. He left his car in a loading zone and went inside. I parked behind a pole and watched him through the plate glass. He checked every table and counter seat, and came out alone. He stood in the lot and clawed his hair. He scanned the parked cars and the passing traffic.

I ducked down and peeked over the dash.

He got in his car and took Overland north again. There was construction on both shoulders. The street narrowed down to one lane, and Barry was boxed into a line of cars doing twenty-five. I slowed down to twenty-five myself. He worked his way up to Isabelle Pavich's place in West Hollywood. It took us half an hour on surface streets and I kept thinking I'd lose him, but I never did. It was safe to follow him close; he was absorbed by the road in front of him. I watched him get out and buzz at Pavich's security gate. He was not let in.

From Pavich's he drove to Neil John Phillips's duplex. He knocked at Phillips's front door, then walked around to the back. He wasn't gone very long—two minutes tops. I couldn't see what he did, but I figured he hit the logical points: kitchen door, garage, maybe upstairs neighbor.

After two minutes he walked around front and climbed into his car. I saw him start dialing his car phone again. I hoped it would be another marathon. I picked up my phone to call Lockwood; he should know what his visit did to Barry. But Barry pulled out before I finished Lockwood's number.

I dropped my phone and followed him.

We took surface streets out to Burbank. Barry skirted the Warner lot and parked at a building across from the studio entrance. I recognized the address. I rolled past slowly and watched Barry walk inside. I gave him time to get upstairs, parked around the corner, ran into the building, and checked the directory to make sure. Yes, suite 219: Arnold Tolback and AT Productions.

I ran back and hid at the corner. Barry came out of the building five minutes later. He was not happy. He kicked his car, got into it, and squealed off.

I ran to my car and followed him.

He was driving fast again. I sped up and tried to keep two cars between us, but sometimes it was four or five. He got on the Ventura Freeway going west. Traffic was bad, like normal, and it was easy to keep him in view. I wanted this to end, but I couldn't give up now. I stopped thinking, I stopped worrying, I just drove.

Barry got off at a canyon exit and took back roads through the hills to Malibu. I checked my gas gauge. We were covering a lot of territory.

Barry turned right at the coast highway, and right again at Jules Silverman's street. I made both rights and pulled over to the side of the road. There was no traffic on Ramirez Canyon—no cars to hide behind.

I counted a minute on my watch, then floored it. Silverman's gates were just closing by the time I arrived. I saw Barry's taillights swing around a bend and disappear.

This time I was going in.

I parked and ran to the fence. I checked the pillars for surveillance cameras: none. I picked up a rock and rubbed the iron to see if it sparked. It didn't. I hoped that meant it wasn't electric.

I braced myself and grabbed two bars, but didn't get zapped. Sticking one foot through, I squeezed between the bars. I dropped to a crouch and listened for alarms or dogs. All I heard was the ocean breeze.

I started to run. The trees were great cover.

Silverman's property was immense. The drive switched back and forth as it climbed the hillside. The hill was too steep to cut straight up. I slowed down and jogged parallel to the drive for half a mile. Finally I saw a clearing. I ducked and crept up to the edge of the tree line. I was breathing hard.

The drive leveled out into an immense paved forecourt. A huge stone fountain stood in the middle; it was carved with dolphins and nymphs. A monster house sat on the far side of the fountain. It was all glass and granite and looked like a first-class chain hotel. The view was unbelievable—south to Catalina, west to the horizon. We were way high in the air.

Barry was talking to two people on the terrace of the house. I couldn't hear what they said because the fountain was too loud. But I could see them perfectly.

One: Hannah Silverman. Wearing a terry-cloth robe and thongs, holding a glass of carrot juice. Her hair was tied back with a sweat sock. She stamped her foot while Barry talked.

Two: an old man. Thin and tall; tanned to a crisp; one arm linked through Hannah's. Wearing a terry-cloth robe and thongs, holding a glass of carrot juice.

I'd never seen Jules Silverman in person. He never appeared in public anymore, and the press always ran archive shots of him as a younger man.

Silverman turned his head my way.

He looked different with clothes on, and he wasn't wearing the dark wig or sunglasses. But he *was* the guy in Greta's picture—the old guy getting spanked in the dinosaur bedroom.

CHAPTER
SEVENTEEN

SHERIFF'S HOMICIDE was in a retail park in the City of Commerce east of downtown. It had taken me two tries to locate it.

When the Silvermans invited Barry inside, I decided not to hang around. I'd driven to the Malibu Sheriff's substation to find the detectives who handled Edward Abadi's murder. There were no detectives there. A deputy informed me that the Sheriff's wasn't the LAPD; it had one central homicide bureau instead of homicide teams at every station. He'd given me directions to City of Commerce and told me that parking was easy.

Maybe parking was easy, but the drive from the ocean was hellish. I walked into the lobby in a bad mood. The offices had generic white walls and industrial floor covering. A plainclothes cop at the front desk asked if he could help. I peeked into a big room behind him. It had long rows of desks buried under paper and computer terminals. Circulars, charts, and chalkboards covered the walls. The room was pretty empty; six or so detectives sat around talking into telephones. The quiet surprised me.

The desk cop had a pizza box beside him. I could smell the hot pizza and it made me hungry.

I said, "I'm interested in two unsolved murders. One's from 1944 and—"

"Sheriff's case?"

"I think so. It happened in West Hollywood."

The guy pointed through a doorway to the right of the desk. "Through there. You can't miss it."

I thanked him and followed his directions. "It" turned out to be a separate room with UNSOLVED stenciled on the door.

I knocked and walked in. The room was tiny; three desks took up all the space. The nameplates on the desks read SGT. McMANUS, DEP. GADTKE, SGT. SCARBORO.

None of them were in.

I stood looking around. There was a corkboard on the wall, covered with tacked memoranda. Among them was a color enlargement of *my* DMV photo. Below it was Edward Abadi's name, date of death, and Sheriff's case number. Below that was Lockwood's name and telephone numbers.

I looked closer and burst out laughing. Some joker had defaced the display. He'd printed, "ACHTUNG!" at the top of the page. He'd given me pointy ears and vampire fangs, and written, "She Walks By Night!" above my head. Over my shoulder was a coffin with the lid open. The lid said, "Bloodsucking Liberal Media!" Next to Lockwood's name, the comedian wrote, "LAPD Sucks Donkey Dick!" Below it was a cartoon of a donkey with an obscene erection dragging the ground. A photo of Bernard Parks was pasted under the donkey's belly. Parks had his mouth open, as if to swallow the donkey's appendage.

I couldn't resist. I got out my pen and drew a thought balloon by the donkey. Inside it I wrote, "I hope he's better than Sheriff Baca!" I drew a frown on the donkey, too. The donkey should be worried.

I walked back to the front desk and told the cop there was nobody in Unsolved. He checked his watch. "Then they've left for the day. Give me your name and number and they'll call you tomorrow."

I said, "It's more urgent than that. Can you page them?"

A second deputy heard me; he'd come for a slice of pizza. He said, "Stevens Steak House."

I said, "Where is that?"

He gave me the address; it was close by. "McManus and Gadtke will be there."

"What do they look like?"

"You'll know Gadtke. He puts plastic vomit on the floor by his bar stool."

I said, "Jesus." Both cops smiled and nodded.

I walked out, checked the directions on my map, and drove to the restaurant. It sat on a frontage road off Atlantic Avenue. I parked in back and used the rear entrance like other people were doing. Inside it was dark: dark red and dark wood paneling. I stood in a large room filled with booths, and a bar along the wall to my left. Male and female cops jammed the place. Everybody looked like a cop, except the women who looked like secretaries just off work. It was a big swinging scene.

I laughed to myself. Before Greta, I had no idea that the law enforcement community was so profligate; journalists had nothing on them. I cruised the bar area, looking down for plastic vomit. The bar was crowded and the light was bad . . .

I stepped right in it.

A florid man had been watching in the mirror. He swiveled his stool around and grinned at me. I picked up the vomit and tossed it on the bar. The man elbowed the guy next to him. That guy had sad eyes, a lot less flesh, and the walrus mustache you saw on a lot of cops. Both men were somewhere in their fifties.

I made fangs with my two index fingers. "I valk by night."

The florid man laughed out loud; it blew the smell of liquor in my face. The sad-eyed man said, "We can't let you look at the Abadi file."

I said, "Orders from Detective Lockwood."

They both nodded. The florid one had to be Gadtke. The other one had to be McManus. I sized him up as straight man and conscience of the pair: he was drinking ginger ale.

I said, "You've reopened the case, haven't you?"

McManus nodded. Gadtke slurped his whiskey and leaned into me. I was pinned between them.

Gadtke said, "The Abadi file is not for little newspaper girls. It's for big policemen like us."

I squeezed away from him. McManus leaned forward and freed me. I said, "There was a second unsolved murder. The victim was named Georgette Bauerdorf and she died in 1944."

The two cops looked at each other. McManus shook his head. "She knows about Bauerdorf."

He reached into his suit coat and pulled out a cell phone. I tried to back away, but Gadtke stuck out his arm and stopped me. He said, "The Los Angeles Police Department sucks donkey dick."

I said, "And the donkeys don't dig it." Gadtke was delighted. He laughed and lowered his arm.

McManus was saying, ". . . we have your reporter here, Doug. She's asked about Georgette Bauerdorf. What do you want us to do?"

McManus listened, nodded, and handed me the cell phone. I got on. "I leave a million pages and he reaches you just like that."

Lockwood said, "Sergeant McManus caught me at my desk. Do you think you could say hello?"

I stuck my finger in my other ear to block out noise. "Has anyone shown up at the Casa de Amor? Hello."

Lockwood might have chuckled. "Not yet. Tell me how you heard about Bauerdorf."

I ran down the productive part of my day, from Steve Lampley to the epic tail job on Barry Melling. I was getting better at verbatim recap—he said, I said, he did this, I did that. McManus shook his head like he couldn't believe it. At the end I brought up my promise to lay off Hannah Silverman and Arnold Tolback. I explained why I'd broken it, and waited for Lockwood's reprimand. I deserved a reprimand: what was I going to say to Silverman if I'd found her at home? I hadn't thought it through at all.

But Lockwood digested everything without comment.

I said, "How long have you known about Georgette Bauerdorf?"

He was on a different track. "You're saying 'transcripts,' as opposed to the memos you found in Mr. Phillips's garage."

"Transcripts of interviews about the blacklist at MGM. So transcripts *and* memos—both related to the old MGM, and possibly containing the same information about Jules Silverman. If the transcripts exist, that is, and Lampley isn't just making it up for some reason. Does Barry have an alibi for the night of Greta's death? Does Scott Dolgin?"

I slipped those questions in, not really hoping. But Lockwood said, "I wondered when you'd get to that. Yes, they do."

"Which are?"

"After the party they took separate cars to Melling's and discussed business until late. Mr. Dolgin had too much to drink and stayed overnight instead of driving home."

I went, "Woooo."

Lockwood said, "Our thought exactly. Now, while you were tailing Melling, did he stop at the Sony studio lot?"

"No. I would have said so."

"Did he visit Progressive Properties and Artists?"

"No. I told you everything."

There was silence at Lockwood's end of the line. McManus sipped his ginger ale and watched me.

Lockwood said, "Go ahead, sorry. I needed to think."

I switched phone ears, and plugged the other one. "You already knew it was Jules Silverman in that spanking picture, didn't you? How long have you known?"

"Since last week."

"How did you find out?"

"I won't discuss that at this point. I want you to read the Bauerdorf file—I think you'll find it interesting."

"How did *you* find out about her?"

"Miss Stenholm went to Sheriff's Unsolved to ask about the murder. I found out from the detectives who worked the Abadi case. They were keeping tabs on her."

"Is there any chance I could see the Abadi file?"

"That's not my department. But if you want something out of Sergeant McManus and Deputy Gadtke, I suggest you soften them up—offer to buy them a nice meal. Put Sergeant McManus back on, if you would."

I handed the phone to McManus. He said, "Yes, Doug . . . No, there's no problem. . . . No, we didn't refile the material. . . . I'll warn them. . . . Fine, yes, you're welcome. . . . I'll tell her."

McManus hit a button and folded up his cell phone. "Detective Lockwood says he'll see you later."

"Did he say where?"

McManus just put the cell phone away. I didn't push. I said, "Are you and Deputy Gadtke free for dinner?"

Gadtke smiled and sat forward. McManus looked at me. I said, "You pick the restaurant and the newspaper buys."

McManus smiled. "How about the Pacific Dining Car?"

I'D TRIED very hard to talk them out of the Dining Car. I suggested a dozen other places, including Stevens—but the detectives ate at Stevens all the time. I wouldn't agree to the Dining Car until I'd called to make sure Father wasn't there and wasn't expected. The maitre d' told me that he and Sis had been in for lunch. So much for my advice to stay away from him, I thought. My sister was hopeless.

I arrived at the restaurant ahead of the detectives. They'd gone back to their office for the Bauerdorf file. I'd asked if they would bring the Abadi file, too. They said no, categorically. They said they'd never show an active case file to a journalist.

While I waited for them, I ordered mineral water and worried about time. Arnold Tolback had said to go to Whitley Heights after 8:30 P.M. I didn't know how much later than 8:30 I could be.

I heard Gadtke's laugh before I saw him. He appeared at the table and pointed his finger:

"You wrote that on my burro, didn't you? 'I hope he's better than Sheriff Baca!'"

I shook my head. Gadtke winked and flopped down across from me. McManus took the seat beside him. Gadtke laid his plastic vomit on the tablecloth, snagged the wine list, buttonholed a waiter, and ordered a double whiskey and a two-hundred-dollar bottle of red wine. I winced, even though it would go on expenses.

McManus was embarrassed by his partner; he looked it as he handed me the Bauerdorf file. The folder was tan and scuffed up, and the contents were an inch thick. I moved my silverware to clear space for it.

I said, "If the LAPD sucks donkey dick, why are you cooperating with Lockwood?"

Gadtke flagged another waiter. "Food first."

He ordered two shrimp cocktails, the porterhouse-and-lobster combination, and a chocolate sundae for dessert. He wanted chocolate soufflé but had to settle for ice cream. McManus ordered filet mignon and rice. I ordered a salad. The waiter was brilliant about the vomit: he ignored it.

The whiskey and wine arrived together. Gadtke shooed the wine steward off before he could serve a taste. Smacking his lips, Gadtke made a grab for the bottle. McManus beat him to it and held the bottle out to me. I put my hand over my glass. He shrugged, poured himself half a glass, then poured for Gadtke.

Gadtke tipped the bottle to make sure he got filled to the top. He wrapped one hand around the wineglass and drank his whiskey with the other. He smacked his lips again. He said, "We're cooperating with *Detective* Lockwood because he's a righteous white man. LAPD are shitheads and gloryhounds—"

McManus set the wine down. "Let's just say they don't like to share information or credit. Whereas Detective Lockwood is an excellent investigator who'd rather catch bad guys than promote himself."

Gadtke said, "And he was jobbed on that siege."

I said, "What do you know about the siege?"

Gadtke waved his whiskey. "What *don't* we know—we had it in umpteen training bulletins. We know all about sight lines, ingress and egress, disposition of counters and booths. Who was where, when, for how long."

I said, "I'd like to see those bulletins."

McManus said, "Why?"

Gadtke laughed. "Yeah, why? So you can job him some more? Your newspaper would never defend a cop."

He slurped his drink for punctuation. I looked at McManus. His face told me that he thought the same.

I opened the Bauerdorf folder. McManus said, "Start at the end. The paperwork is entered chronologically."

I flipped to the bottom of the file. It smelled like mildew and six decades of hand soap. It contained official correspondence, interview transcripts, mug shots, teletypes, and detective reports on yellow, pink, and blue paper. There were fingerprint cards, stray notes, anonymous letters scrawled by obvious psychos, and a letter signed by J. Edgar Hoover.

I started reading. The paperwork was chronological but the facts were all over the place. As I strung them together, I thought of Greta and her script. The file was packed with character and drama.

Georgette Bauerdorf was born in New York and spent her early years in a Long Island convent. Her father was an oilman and Wall Street figure named George Bauerdorf; she had a stepmother and a widowed sister named Connie. When or why the family moved to L.A. wasn't said, but Georgette graduated from Bel Air's ritzy Westlake School for Girls in 1942. Except for a housekeeper and a chauffeur, she'd lived alone for most of her senior year. Her school friends thought Georgette was lonely and unhappy—a "poor little rich girl" who lacked parental guidance and a proper home life. But she wasn't wild or boy crazy; she was quiet and hard to know. She also smoked too much and bit her nails.

In October 1944 Georgette was twenty and living by herself in the family's apartment at Fountain and La Cienega. Her father, stepmother, and sister had gone east on business in August; they were staying at a hotel in New York City. Georgette was driving her sister's '36 Oldsmobile and devoting her time to war work. She was a registered member of the Hollywood Canteen, the Volunteer Army Canteen Service of Beverly Hills, and other soldiers' aid societies. She also corresponded with twenty-four servicemen on ac-

tive duty. Her only other interest was flying. She took expensive flying lessons in the desert outside L.A.

Wednesday, October 11:

Georgette had lunch with her father's secretary. After lunch
she got a scalp treatment and a manicure. At 2 P.M. she went to a
tea party at Pickfair — Mary Pickford's home in Beverly Hills. She
left the party at 5 P.M. with a female friend and two Marine pri-
vates. The Marines were up from San Diego to work as movie
extras at Twentieth Century Fox. Georgette dropped them off
somewhere east of Beverly Hills.

6:30 P.M.:

Georgette met her friend Nance Carter at the Hollywood
Canteen. They talked in Georgette's car while Georgette knitted.
Georgette wanted Nance to read some letters from Private Joseph
Allen — a soldier stationed in El Paso, Texas. Georgette was going
to fly to El Paso on Friday. She was engaged to marry Private Allen,
but she didn't want her family and other friends to know. Georgette seemed tense and asked Nance to spend the night at her
apartment. Nance declined: she didn't understand what Georgette
could be nervous about.

Georgette and Nance spent the evening together at the Canteen. At one point an unidentified soldier danced a jitterbug with
Georgette. He was about twenty-nine, five eight, 175 pounds, with
a scar on his left ear. He had black hair combed straight back, dark
eyes, and an olive complexion. Nance got the impression that
Georgette didn't want to dance with him.

11:20 P.M.:

Georgette leaves the Canteen. Eight other hostesses check out
at the same time. Georgette picks up a hitchhiker on her way
home. He's an Army sergeant on fifteen-day furlough. She tells
him she's hurrying home to wait for a phone call from Texas. She
picks the sergeant up at Sunset and Vine, and drops him a block
east of Laurel Canyon.

Midnight:

The caretaker couple in Georgette's building hear someone
walking around Georgette's kitchen. They recognize the sound of

Georgette's slippers. They hear water in the sink and Georgette drop a tray—

I looked up from reading. The main course had arrived; the waiter was handing out plates.

Gadtke dived into his lobster without waiting for McManus or me. He'd already demolished his shrimp cocktails and most of the wine.

I said, "There aren't any pictures of her."

Gadtke said, "Sickos get into the files. They like famous cases with dead women, especially the mangled ones."

McManus pulled a paper out of his pocket. "We copied this off microfilm for you."

I took the paper. It was a professional head shot of Georgette Bauerdorf. She looked like a polite young lady. She might have been intelligent or not, pretty or not: her face was still unformed. She had dark hair arranged in the shoulder-length '40s style. Barrettes held the hair in place.

Gadtke said, "A Black Dahlia with class." He dribbled lobster meat.

I said, "How much more is there on microfilm? The paperwork stops in early '45."

McManus nudged the folder with his fork. "We only showed Miss Stenholm what you have here."

I ignored my dinner and went back to reading.

Her body was found on the morning of October 12. The caretaker saw that Georgette's front door was open and walked in to clean. She went up to the second-floor bathroom and found Georgette dead. Sheriff's deputies arrived and radioed in an apparent suicide. The detectives arrived at 11:30 A.M. They saw Georgette's body resting facedown in the bathtub—

I shut my eyes a second. A *bathtub*. Jesus—

The tub was empty because the caretaker drained it before the cops came. Georgette's head was resting at the spigot end. Her left foot was resting on the ledge at the opposite end; her right leg was resting on her left. There was a small amount of blood on the bottom of the tub under Georgette's face. The lower part of her buttocks were bloodstained, and she had bruises on her: she'd fought for her life. She was wearing a pink pajama top and nothing else.

A coroner's man removed the body from the tub. He found a piece of cloth sticking out of her mouth. Her teeth were clamped around it. The cloth had thin red borders; it appeared to be torn or cut from a towel end. Deputies searched the apartment but couldn't find a matching towel or fragments of one.

Georgette's bedroom adjoined the bath. Her pink pajama pants were laying on the floor, ripped. The cops found a blood spot on the carpet near the bathroom door. The carpet around it was wet; someone had tried to remove the spot. There was no blood on the bathroom floor or the bed, and no signs of any struggle in the bedroom. They found Georgette's diary and address book. Her jewelry box hadn't been touched, but three items were missing from her purse: an amethyst ring, seventy-five dollars in cash, and her car keys. The Oldsmobile was gone from the basement garage.

How they knew about the ring and the cash, the file didn't say.

Detectives questioned Georgette's neighbors. Some had heard a scream; some hadn't. Someone heard, "Stop, you're killing me!" at 2:30 A.M., thought it was a marital spat, and went back to sleep. The detectives read Georgette's diary and address book, and talked to her girlfriends. They talked to all the hostesses who worked at the Hollywood Canteen on October 11; there were 120 of them, although no movie stars were named. They called in the U.S. Provost Marshall, and Naval and Army Intelligence, and tried to locate every serviceman who knew or corresponded with Georgette. There were dozens and dozens—but her closest friends were fliers.

They talked to the three servicemen she gave rides to on October 11. They checked out every hospital, canteen, and recreation center where she volunteered. They chased a Navy cook who was barred from the Hollywood Canteen for "abnormal sexual tendencies" and "heckling."

The coroner's report came in. Georgette died between one and two in the morning. Cause of death: strangulation. The piece of cloth had been pushed down her esophagus until she choked. She'd also been raped.

The Oldsmobile turned up in a black neighborhood ten miles east of the crime scene. The keys were in the ignition, the tank was empty, the rear license plate had been removed. The cops modified their operating theory. They had wanted a white serviceman. Now they were looking at black men, too.

They canvassed the black neighborhood and came up with zero. They broadened the investigation. They checked out burglars, rapists, dishonorably discharged soldiers, sex offenders, and general black arrestees. They wrote to the FBI; the FBI ran cross-checks on the latent prints found in Georgette's apartment. They got fingerprint cards, mug shots, and rap sheets from police departments all over the country. Deserters, drifters, and car thieves were grilled and eliminated. They checked out two female bathtub deaths in New Orleans and New York. A man in San Francisco confessed to the killing. They took a train up there to find out he didn't do it. He'd blown his inheritance money in Reno and just wanted the gas chamber.

Every man in Sheriff's Homicide worked the case. They checked out all the silly tips; everyone knew someone who hadn't come home the night of October 11. Women squealed on their ex-husbands out of spite. One letter accused a Beverly Hills gardener because "he had big hands and liked to look at white girls."

They found the soldier who made Georgette dance a jitterbug—and eliminated him. But they never identified one guy, a wounded soldier who claimed to be in love with Georgette. Georgette had told her friends that she was afraid of him. She'd called him psychopathic.

They finally identified the cloth that asphyxiated her. It was a Tetra Brand elastic bandage, ten inches wide, European made, and obsolete. A Chicago company imported the bandage. They'd only sold five ten-inch rolls in '42 and '43—but they were still used in foreign hospitals. Maybe a soldier had brought it home: the possibilities were too numerous to follow up.

Georgette's father, stepmother, and sister came back to L.A. after Christmas. Detectives walked them through the apartment and fingerprinted them for elimination purposes.

Private Joseph Allen wrote to the cops in February 1945. His letter was the last item in the file. He said he was Georgette's former fiancé and wanted to know what progress they had made on her case. He'd misspelled Bauerdorf.

I closed the folder and squared it with the edge of the table-cloth. Gadtke had pushed back from the table; he looked flushed and sweaty. McManus was finishing a piece of pie.

I tapped the file. "Where's Jules Silverman?"

Gadtke giggled. I said, "I heard Silverman was a major suspect, but his name's not in here."

McManus put his fork down and looked away from me.

I said, "Lockwood."

Gadtke swirled the ice in his whiskey. I said, "Lockwood had you pull the part about Silverman. You discussed it on the telephone."

McManus looked at Gadtke. Gadtke shrugged: "Your call, partner."

McManus cleared his throat. "This has to be off the record."

I said, "Forever?"

McManus reached for the file. "Or until Detective Lockwood says otherwise."

I nodded.

McManus flipped pages. He found a summary report dated November 1, 1944, and pointed to a paragraph at the end.

I'd skimmed right over it. It said that the unit had one major suspect but the information pertaining to him was highly confidential and couldn't be disclosed at that time. The report was written exclusively for the eyes of Sheriff Eugene Biscailuz.

I said, "Is that Silverman? They talked to so many people — there's a million names mentioned."

Gadtke nodded his head. "Needle in a haystack. Your worst fucking nightmare."

McManus said, "Jules Silverman was a pilot for the Navy and frequented the Hollywood Canteen during a leave in October of '44. Several hostesses placed him there on the night of the eleventh. He was also seen in the parking lot after 11:20 P.M., talking to the victim. The chief hostess had to caution him and Miss Bauerdorf because the girls weren't allowed to make dates with servicemen or see them off-premises."

I said, "A deranged sexual atmosphere."

McManus nodded. Gadtke giggled and nodded; he was pretty plastered. I said, "What's confidential about a nobody Navy pilot?"

Gadtke kicked his seat further back. "Silverman had powerful friends even then."

McManus said, "That's our assumption. When Miss Stenholm came around asking about the case, we reviewed the file. We were familiar with the Abadi case, and when we read that a Jules Silverman—"

Gadtke said, "Shitbird."

McManus said, "—was a major suspect on Bauerdorf, we paid special attention. We guessed that Miss Stenholm had learned of Silverman's involvement from some other source. We almost let her see the Silverman material, to see if she'd shake the Abadi tree for us, but we decided it was too risky. From what you told Detective Lockwood, she went after Silverman anyway."

I said, "Maybe."

Gadtke said, "He shipped out of Long Beach on a Navy transport at six in the morning on the twelfth. Our guys had a hell of a time tracking him down in the middle of the Pacific. The first time he was interviewed, he couldn't account for his whereabouts between midnight and four the night of the murder. Then the file hems and haws, and there's that shit about confidentiality."

McManus said, "At the third interview, Silverman suddenly produced an alibi. He claimed he attended an orgy in Culver City with executives from the movie studio Metro-Goldwyn-Mayer. He worked there before the war—and *orgy* was his word, not ours."

I had a premonition. "Where in Culver City was the orgy?"

McManus said, "You know the place yourself, the Casa de Amor. Back then it was a high-rent private whorehouse."

I whispered, "Wow."

Gadtke said, "Something went down. The studio put the screws on—Biscailuz handled Silverman through unofficial channels, told the Homicide guys to lay off, something."

I said, "It could be Silverman was covering for some married men, not that his alibi was phony."

McManus nodded. "That was our first thought."

Gadtke smiled. "But remember the loose lightbulb?"

I remembered. The night after the murder, the caretaker noticed that Georgette's porch light was off. He tested it, saw the bulb was loose, and told the detectives. They'd assumed that Georgette opened her door voluntarily, since there were no signs of forced entry. Now they knew: the killer probably jumped out of the dark and surprised her.

I said, "The bulb went in for fingerprinting, but I didn't see the results."

McManus said, "The lab identified one latent. It matched Jules Silverman's left thumb."

I whistled. "How did Silverman explain it?"

Gadtke banged the table; an empty glass tipped over. "He didn't explain it! Or if he did, nobody filed a report of his explanation, and the investigating officers are dead!"

McManus said, "Silverman claimed he'd never been to Miss Bauerdorf's residence. But Nance Carter said he showed up twice in early October and Miss Bauerdorf had trouble keeping him out."

Gadtke leaned toward me. "You know the motto of Sheriff's Homicide?"

I said, "'It isn't as hard as it looks'?"

Gadtke guffawed. McManus said, "'Our day begins when yours ends.'"

Gadtke banged the table again. "Fucking right! And the day has just begun for Mr. Jules Silverman!"

I put my head down on the Bauerdorf file. She was mine now, too.

CHAPTER
EIGHTEEN

THE NEIGHBORHOOD of Whitley Heights sat back in the hills west of Los Feliz. Like Los Feliz, it was a former movie-star enclave intact from the silent era. Whitley Terrace was a dark street that stopped and started, turned corners, stopped and started again. I found 3617 after a long trip to the wrong end. I expected the house to be a fake Italian villa, the kind that made the neighborhood famous. It wasn't. It was a big, straggling ranch stuck on a hillside planted with cactus instead of ivy or grass.

Luxury sedans lined the street below it. I parked in a red zone and rechecked the name on Arnold Tolback's note. "Lynnda-Ellen." I remembered his message to her: You can all kiss my ass.

I stuck the note back in my pocket. I was still buzzing from Georgette Bauerdorf. I would've been happy to punt this errand, stay at the restaurant, and go through the file again. But McManus decided that his partner was drunk enough. He'd packed Gadtke out after coffee and taken the file with him.

That didn't stop me from thinking about it.

The bathtub.

Georgette died in one; Greta died in one. Edward Abadi didn't, but his killer tried to disguise the murder as suicide, and Greta's killer tried the same thing. The methods might not connect Bauerdorf to Abadi to Stenholm. But one name did: Jules Silverman.

Days ago I'd wondered about a third possible motive for Greta's death. Blackmail seemed iffy; romantic revenge looked better but not ironclad. What if the real motive was Georgette Bauerdorf? What if Georgette was the reason *behind* the reason?

What if the Sheriff's never got near the motive in Abadi's death. What if the Abadi motive and the Stenholm motive were the same. What if Edward Abadi stumbled onto Jules Silverman's old secret. What if Hannah Silverman shot her fiancé to protect her father. What if Jules Silverman shot him — with jilted Hannah standing by to deflect suspicion. What if, one year later, Jules arranged Greta's death to protect his secret again.

I bounced *what if*s around while I watched Lynnda-Ellen's house.

A party was in progress. The front drapes were open and I had an excellent view. The living room was full of guys standing around in pairs and groups. They wore dark suits with dark shirts and I put the average age at thirty-five. Adding that to the luxury sedans, I figured it had to be an Industry crowd.

The stink of cologne.

It blew in the car window. I turned my head: Hawaiian shirt. Purple palm trees on an orange cotton —

The car door flew open. Dale Denney grabbed my collar and jerked hard.

I reacted fast. I braced my feet and hooked one arm through the steering wheel. Denney started to drag me out. I grabbed my bag; I found the brass knuckles. I slid my right hand into them and round-housed a shot. It caught Denney low. He wheezed and doubled over.

He dragged me with him. I thrashed and swung wild. I caught his nose flush. It split the tip in two.

Denney screamed. Blood sprayed out on the doorsill and asphalt. Denney let go and clutched his nose. Blood foamed over his hands down his face.

I grabbed the handcuffs, grabbed Denney's wrist, and clicked a cuff on. I yanked him forward by the cuff. He fell on his knees. I locked the other cuff to the steering wheel.

I grabbed my sap, slid out the passenger side, ran around the car, and tried to push him inside. He whipped around to slug me. He saw he was cuffed and let out a yell:

"*You cunt!*"

I went nuts with the sap. I sapped his neck, I sapped his shoulders. He dipped and dodged, throwing elbows, twisting around on his knees. I aimed for his nose. He protected it and crawled backward onto the front seat. I slammed the door on his legs—once, twice, three times. He howled and pulled his legs inside.

I slammed the door shut. Denney kicked his foot out the window. It missed me. He kicked the door, coughed up blood, and said that word again.

I couldn't do anything about it. My knees gave way suddenly; I sat down in the street. I was shaking and panting. I was dripping with sweat. I dropped the sap and slumped against the car.

It took me a good long while to recover. The shaking slowed down and stopped, and I got my breath back. I checked around to see if anybody had heard us: the street was dead quiet. Reaching for the door handle, I hauled myself up. I looked in the driver's window. Denney was lying on his side, cupping his nose in his free hand. His eyes were closed and he was breathing through his mouth. Blood bubbled from his nostrils.

I circled the car and opened the passenger door. Denney didn't move. I didn't trust that—I kept my eyes on him. I got a rag and a water bottle off the backseat, and wiped my arms and face. I dumped my jacket; it was ripped and spattered with blood. My jeans and shirt were bloody, too. Wetting the rag, I rubbed at the stains. They came out—but I soaked my clothes to do it.

The car phone was sitting beside Denney's head. I reached in, grabbed it quick, and pulled the cord as long as it would go. Denney still didn't move. I'd dialed Lockwood's pager before I realized it wasn't practical: I didn't want to wait there for a return call. So I canceled the page and left an urgent message at the station. I told Lockwood where Denney could be found. I also told him to bring the paramedics.

I unplugged the phone, grabbed my bag, and threw everything

in the trunk. I realized that I felt happy. That's all I could think: I
was *happy*. Nobody called me a cunt and *nobody* laid violent
hands on me. Dale Denney and I were even now.

I crossed the street and walked up Lynnda-Ellen's driveway.
There had to be a back way into her house. I couldn't waltz into a
party looking the way I looked.

A side porch was locked. But the side yard led to the backyard,
which had a door leading to the garage. Inside the garage another
door led to a utility room.

I tiptoed across the utility room and cracked a second door. I
was looking down a long carpeted hallway with more doors. I listened for party noise; I couldn't hear any. If I had my bearings
right, the living room was at the other end of the house. This end
was silent.

I walked down the hall, opening and closing doors as I went. It
was funny — I didn't feel a bit nervous about trespassing. My adren-
aline must have been all used up.

Behind one door I found a room crammed with costumes and
props. Painted scenery flats were stacked upright against the walls.

I found a large room filled with tables and mirrors. It looked
like a backstage dressing area. A sign beside the light switch said,
"You have <u>15 mins.</u> between shows. Be quiet. Be quick. Be neat.
NO SMOKING." Makeup and accessories cluttered the tabletops;
the mirrors were bordered by spherical bulbs. A portable shower
stood in one corner, with a curtained changing room attached.
Street clothes hung from the hooks that lined one wall.

I began to suspect that Lynnda-Ellen was a special kind of
hostess.

The next door had a plaque reading MAXIMUS IN LOVE. I stuck
my head into the room. It was dark. I slid inside, shut the door, and
waited for my vision to adjust.

The air was warm and close; I was standing in a tight space.
The wall facing me had a sort of glass porthole at eye level. I
stepped up to the porthole and looked through.

I almost whistled.

It was a stage set — a facsimile of the field tents in *Gladiator*.

Silk draperies hung on the walls; animal skins covered the floor and divan. Classical busts and candelabra stood around on pedestals. A couple in Roman costume lay on the divan. She was made up to look like the emperor's sister; he was beefy and tan like Russell Crowe. They were feeding each other grapes from a gold plate.

Someone sneezed. The sound came from my right.

The floor was inlaid with track lights. I followed them around a corner into a second room. I was walking soft. My eyes had adjusted and I could tell that someone had divided up a bedroom to create this arrangement.

In the second room I found a row of individual viewing booths. A wall separated the booths from the stage; tufted screens divided the booths from each other. The booths were backless, so I could see into them. Each booth contained an upholstered chair and each chair contained a spectator. The spectators were all men. They were watching the *Gladiator* scene through individual glass portholes. They wore miniheadsets to hear the dialogue.

I didn't know what to think. The whole deal looked like pornography, but it didn't *feel* like pornography. There wasn't that atmosphere I associated with triple-X theaters or the back of porn stores. The management did not provide towels; the floor had nice carpet. And the men sat with their legs crossed and their hands folded—like they were viewing dailies, not getting their rocks off.

I tiptoed out of "Maximus in Love." The plaque across the hall read AG'S PLAY ROOM. I could hear the party now.

I opened the door to "AG's Play Room." The setup was the same: a glass porthole in the wall in front of me. I looked through the porthole. I looked . . . then I stared.

Hannah Silverman's video down to the last corny detail. The brick cellar. The window in the back wall. The iron cot and ratty curtain.

The fake-platinum blond was wearing her Gestapo uniform and waving her prop pistol. The young guy was sobbing and hugging her leather boots. I didn't need headphones to hear the dialogue. I knew it already and I could read her lips: "It muss be ffery larch to mekk pleashure to Helga."

This time I didn't laugh about dilettante perverts. I was too busy putting things together.

I ran out to the hall. The party had gotten louder—I heard voices and saw a slice of living room through an archway. I didn't care if somebody saw me. There was one last door, and that door nailed it. The plaque read SPIELBERG PRESENTS. I got so excited I almost forgot to be quiet.

I ran in and pressed my face to the porthole.

A kid's dinosaur bedroom. Spielberg movie posters covering the walls. Toys all over the floor; a toy battle pitting miniature soldiers against towering toy dinosaurs. A brunet in a nightgown spanking an actor in dinosaur pajamas. It was the *same* brunet as Greta's picture. The actor lay across her lap in the *same* Jules Silverman position. The brunet's mouth was moving. She repeated something over and over as she spanked her colleague. I figured out what it was. She was saying, "Bad boy! Bad boy!"

I tore myself away and tiptoed around to the viewing booths. There were only five, and I didn't recognize any of the spectators. I tiptoed out to the hall and checked my watch. Almost 10 P.M.

I ran back to the dressing room. It was still empty. I ran across and squeezed into the space between the portable shower and the wall. From there I could see the door and most of the room.

This was it, I thought. This was how Lockwood identified Dale Denney. Lockwood once worked Vice in Hollywood. He would have drawn a straight line between Greta's photograph, Lynnda-Ellen's parties, and Dale Denney. Denney *had* to be a Lynnda-Ellen associate. I knew he was—not just from the glossy portrait of Shelly/Helga in his apartment. "To Dale, my biggest fan! XXXXXOOOOO Shelly!" I knew it because he couldn't have tailed me all day and night. He found me at Lynnda-Ellen's because he was already *at* Lynnda-Ellen's.

And Dale Denney had a record of burglary and knifing.

And Jules Silverman was a Lynnda-Ellen client. Arnold Tolback would have told the cops that—if the cops weren't already familiar with Lynnda-Ellen's client list.

And Jules Silverman had a secret.

Two secrets, if you counted the spanking gig. But that was minor compared to Georgette—

The door of the dressing room opened. I squeezed back and watched the actors pile in. They were all in their early twenties and had the look of recent MFA grads: buff and earnest.

They grabbed their clothes and headed for the sink or the makeup tables. They seemed too tired, or too embarrassed, to talk. The "Maximus in Love" guy recombed his centurion do. The other people stripped off their costumes, threw on their street clothes, and left with their makeup still on.

Shelly came in and collapsed on a chair. The spanking brunet walked in last. She looked mad. She sat down beside Shelly, pulled her nightgown over her head, and chucked it across the room. Her hair was done up in a maternal bun. She started jerking the pins and ribbons out.

Her hair fell to her shoulders and I got a jolt. With her hair down, the brunet looked like Georgette Bauerdorf.

Something hit me:

The brunet wasn't wearing a frumpy nightgown in Greta's Jules Silverman picture. She was wearing pink satin pajamas.

Shelly got up and shut the hall door. She whispered to the brunet, "I don't understand why she fired you, Debbie. Everyone loves your work."

Debbie shrugged and spread cold cream on her face. Shelly took off her Gestapo tunic and cold-creamed herself in the mirror. She said, "Lynnda's been acting strangely since Greta died, have you noticed?"

Debbie shrugged again. Shelly whispered, "Dale says she knows something about Greta's death."

Debbie wiped her face with a Kleenex. Shelly reached into the shower and turned on the hot water full blast. It sprayed over the top and scalded me. I jerked sideways; the shower stall went *thunk*.

Shelly stuck her head around the corner of the stall. When she saw me, she made a squeak noise. I shushed her. I said, "Shut off the water—I want to talk to you."

Shelly just stood there blank. Debbie turned, saw me, and stared. They looked like a couple of airheads.

I squeezed out of my hiding place and shut off the water myself. I said, "Does Lynnda ever come back here?"

Debbie blinked. "Are you after Lynnda?"

I nodded.

Debbie said, "Good." She turned back to the mirror, smiling. Shelly saw the smile and said, "Don't, Deb. You better not get involved."

Debbie tossed her Kleenex and picked up an eyeliner. She said, "Lynnda won't come — she's busy with the customers."

"Debbie!"

Shelly ran and cracked the hall door, checked outside, then shut the door and locked it. She leaned against it for insurance.

I sat down in Shelly's chair. Debbie was lining her eyes. I watched her in the mirror, and said, "I think you were fired because you did your 'Bad boy!' routine with an old man, and Greta Stenholm took pictures."

Shelly whispered, "Don't talk to her, Deb, *please*." She checked the clock on the wall.

I said, "How did Greta and Lynnda get along?"

Debbie said, "None of us like Lynnda, but Greta especially didn't like her. She turned Lynnda's shows into a joke on purpose. One of the new shows is 'AG's Play Room.'"

I said, "I saw it."

Debbie threw down the eyeliner. "AG stands for Amon Goeth, the Nazi sadist in *Schindler's List*."

I covered my mouth; it was breathtakingly sassy.

Debbie said, "Lynnda doesn't know, neither do the customers."

Shelly whispered, "Ralph Fiennes played the role. It was his breakthrough part."

Debbie said, "Greta turned 'Mother's Little Man' into 'Spielberg Presents.' Lynnda wouldn't let her call it 'Saving Private Ryan from the Dinosaurs.' The actors thought the new script was sick, but Lynnda loved the changes."

Another connection clicked. The two trips to see *Jurassic Park III* at the Vine. She was probably researching another level of satire.

Shelly whispered, "It's the most popular show now."

Debbie had worn her own clothes under the nightgown. She rolled down her pants. Shelly realized she still wore her jodhpurs and boots; she ran to the hooks and grabbed her clothes.

Debbie started tossing makeup into a bag. She said, "Mommy comes in and catches little Steven playing movie director when he's supposed to be in bed asleep. I don't know why people don't see it's a joke."

I said, "And a comment on Lynnda's clientele?"

Debbie nodded. "Greta was out there. There was something strange about her."

She stood up, packed and ready to go. Shelly was arranging her Gestapo costume on a hanger. Debbie said to me, "Lynnda wants the artists out in fifteen."

I said, "What do you care what Lynnda wants?"

Shelly looked around and didn't whisper. "*I* care."

Debbie said, "Lynnda tells everyone we're being seen by important people, we'll get acting jobs out of this, but it never happens."

Shelly whispered, "That you *know* of, Debbie. And it's less work than nonunion theater, and Lynnda pays better." Shelly headed for the hall door with her coat.

I checked the clock. "Two more minutes. When did Greta start work here?"

Shelly stopped. "Oh, Debbie, that's enough!"

Debbie dropped her bag and sat back down. She said, "She started in March, but she didn't live here until a couple of months ago. We could never figure that out. Lynnda's a bitch."

Greta had lived *here*. She must have moved in after she lost her apartment. I said, "What exactly did Greta do? She changed the shows and what else?"

Debbie said, "The shows were always changing. Greta rehearsed the actors, and rewrote dialogue all the time. She always wanted to make the shows better. She should have been a director. We've worked with a lot worse, and we thought she was good."

I said, "What about the old man?"

Debbie shrugged. "He's just some old guy who came for private sessions. I never knew who he was because of this disguise he wore. If Greta took pictures, I didn't know. I don't know how she found out about him because Lynnda made me promise not to tell."

"Did he ask for you because of your looks?"

"I didn't want to do it. I've played the mommy since Greta rewrote the part, but Lynnda forced me. I wore a different costume and left my hair down. I was supposed to put these in."

She dug through the junk on her table and found two old-fashioned rhinestone barrettes. She used them to clip her hair behind her ears.

"I curled my ends under like this." She showed me.

I said, "So, a 1940s hairstyle."

She shrugged, "I guess."

Shelly whispered, "Come *on*, Debbie. Let's go."

Debbie said, "There's a rumor that Lynnda knows more about Greta's death than she says."

Shelly slapped her leg. "I told you that in confidence!"

I said, "Lynnda and Dale Denney. What's the story there?"

Debbie said, "Dale works her parties. He parks cars and checks invitations—"

She stopped. The sound of pounding feet came down the hall-way. The dressing-room door shook on its hinges. A man yelled, *"This is the back way!"* It sounded like a stampede.

Debbie jumped up. *"The cops!"*

Shelly unlocked the door and peeked out. Debbie lunged for the knob and threw the door wide. A stream of men raced past us; they were headed for the utility room. Debbie grabbed Shelly and pushed her into the hall. They ran.

I plunged in behind them. Nobody gave us a second look. I fol-lowed the crowd up the hall, through the garage, around and out to the front. Doors banged; everybody was breathing hard. Men slipped, tripped, and flew down the driveway. They fanned out for cars parked on both sides of the street. I slowed down. I saw Shelly and Debbie make it to an old Toyota and take off. A few guys came barreling out the front door. They leaped down the stairs and raced for their cars. They disappeared around corners and down side streets.

I looked around for what caused the panic: it *was* the cops. Lockwood's car was parked on my bumper. Dale Denney was sitting up. He held his bloody nose with one hand and watched the commotion.

I cut across the cactus beds to Lynnda-Ellen's front door. Detective Smith stood in the vestibule. He was showing three customers the way out. They jostled past him and ran for the stairs.

Smith laughed at them, then saw me. He said, "You're a menace to public order. The keys to the cuffs, please."

I pointed at my car. "They're in the trunk."

Smith noticed my hand as I pointed. It was swelling and scraped raw where the brass knuckles fit. I flexed my fingers to keep them loose.

Smith said, "Where'd you learn your technique?"

I said, "He tried to pull me out of my car." I started into the house; Smith barred the door and shook his head.

I said, "But I have things to tell him."

Smith said, "Then don't leave."

He closed the door on me. I jumped off the porch to look in the living-room window. Smith crossed the dining room and walked into the kitchen. I ran around the near end of the house, climbed a fence, and heard voices. Ducking, I snuck up to an open window. I peeked over the sill.

A stacked scrawny woman was leaning against the kitchen counter. She wore a tight black dress and her bleached hair was spun up into cotton candy. Cheap, but shrewd-looking: Lynnda-Ellen. Lockwood stood and faced her. Smith had posted himself by the exit to the dining room.

Lynnda-Ellen said, "It's a private party, Doug—you can't just come in like this."

Lockwood passed her a photograph. "We aren't here about your 'party.'"

She squinted at the picture, holding it close, then at arm's length. She gave it back to Lockwood. "I don't have my reading glasses, sorry."

There was a clatter in the dining room and Hannah Silverman burst into the kitchen. She shouted, *"Don't talk to them, Lynnda! Don't say one fucking syllable!"*

Lockwood deadpanned her. He said, "Detective Smith, would you show Miss Silverman to her vehicle?"

Smith reached for Silverman. Silverman glared. "Don't you dare touch me! I'll sue! Lynnda, don't tell them anything!"

Lynnda opened her mouth. Lockwood shot her a look that shut her up. Silverman tried to stare Lockwood down. She was no match for him: Lockwood just looked at her. She stamped her foot, stuck her princess chin in the air, and stormed out of the kitchen.

She yelled, *"I'm calling my lawyer!"* The front door slammed.

Smith shrugged. "Must have been in the ladies' room."

Lockwood refocused on Lynnda-Ellen. He held up the photograph. I could see what it was now. It was a blowup of Greta's blackmail picture. A little blurry at that magnification — but the important elements were clear.

Lockwood said, "Arnold Tolback introduced you to Greta Stenholm this past March. Business was falling off and Mr. Tolback said Miss Stenholm could help. He had one condition — you weren't allowed to tell Hannah or Jules Silverman that Miss Stenholm was working for you."

Lynnda made her face a blank. She refused to look at the photograph.

Lockwood said, "The Silvermans are two of your best customers. Miss Silverman attends your weekly 'parties,' but Mr. Silverman comes for private appointments because he doesn't appear in public. You wondered why Mr. Tolback would want to keep Miss Stenholm's presence a secret. You asked around and learned the gist of Miss Stenholm's history with the Silvermans — or maybe you asked Miss Stenholm herself."

Lynnda switched from blank to bored. Her expression said, Ho hum, this has nothing to do with me.

Lockwood said, "Miss Stenholm revamped your acts and business picked up. She became a valuable employee and you couldn't afford to tell the Silvermans who was responsible. When she was evicted from her apartment in June, you invited her to move in with you."

Lynnda examined her fake fingernails; they were scarlet with sparkly silver designs. She picked on one to chew.

Lockwood said, "Mr. Tolback informed Miss Stenholm of Mr. Silverman's sexual tastes. He had his own bone to pick with the Silvermans—something you realized too late. Miss Stenholm discovered the exact time of Mr. Silverman's private appointments. Maybe the actress involved told her, maybe she saw Mr. Silverman arrive or leave—or maybe you told her, since she was so close to your business. Whichever the case, she discovered the secret and took photographs covertly of Mr. Silverman."

Lockwood jiggled the picture. Lynnda said, "Will you be done soon?"

Lockwood said, "Miss Stenholm sent Mr. Silverman the photographs and moved out of your house on the day he received them. That would have been Thursday, August twenty-third—twelve days ago. She asked for twenty thousand dollars."

August 23: the day Hannah gave Tolback the boot and he checked into the Marmont. Tolback must have spilled all the beans. Lockwood's information was *detailed*.

Lockwood said, "The Silvermans blamed you for the extortion. To appease them you did two things. You recommended Dale Denney to deliver the blackmail payment, and you promised to throw a scare into Miss Stenholm. Denney was too much of a clown for the scare job, so you deputized a second man to hunt her down. He braced her at a party, but he went too far and killed her. Maybe the guy took a powder, and you read about Miss Stenholm's death in the papers. Maybe the guy came to you with the story, but you couldn't tell the Silvermans, so Denney delivered the money to the wrong woman on the night following the murder. You'd tried to keep Miss Stenholm a secret, and Denney didn't know what she looked like."

Lynnda started on a fresh fingernail. It was ennui, not nerves.

Lockwood said, "The woman who received the payment reported her encounter with Denney to us, and exposed the blackmail angle. Now the Silvermans want their money back, and you are all concealing knowledge of a felony. You may be concealing the murderer."

His pitch was measured and impressively succinct. But I didn't know how much of it was factual. The second-man theory was news. Did Tolback tell Lockwood that Scott Dolgin was the "second man"?

Lynnda said, "Are you finished?"

Lockwood handed her a business card. "You have twelve hours to tell me everything you know, or I'll shut your ass down permanently."

Lynnda yawned. "You've tried it before."

Lockwood said, "We have Dale Denney in custody. I think he'll be willing to cooperate."

That worked; that got to her. Lockwood and Smith walked out of the kitchen. She waited until they'd gone, then kicked a cupboard and swore.

I ran around to the front and met Lockwood and Smith walking down the stairs. Smith said, "There she is."

Lockwood saw me and shook his head. "You could have killed him."

"Would you have cared?"

He shook his head, deadpan. "We'd clear it as self-defense."

Smith nodded. "Piece of cake."

"*Cunt!*"

Dale Denney jerked at his handcuffs. His face and arms, neck and shirt, were covered with blood.

I made a fist and started for him. Lockwood held me back. He said, "We have to get him cleaned up. Meet us at the station in an hour."

———

"CARJACKING?!"

Dale Denney thrashed in his chair. The chair was bolted to the floor; he was cuffed to one arm. His eyes were black and blue, his nose was a mass of stitches, and there was a wad of cotton up one nostril. The hospital had given him a clean shirt from their Lost and Found.

Smith hovered over him; Lockwood sat on a table. I sat in the next room, watching through a two-way mirror. A wall speaker supplied the sound. I nursed my right hand with an ice pack.

"I never carjacked nobody! That's a crock of shit!"

Smith coughed in his face. "We had a carjacking-homicide downtown, and you match the description of the suspect."

Lockwood shuffled papers. "He's a six-foot-six African American weighing approximately three hundred forty pounds."

Smith said, "They call him 'Slim.'"

Lockwood said, "His hairline is similar to yours. As you probably know, hairlines are critical in these kinds of identification."

Denney jerked his cuff chain. "Fuck that hairline shit! That's a crock!"

Lockwood said, "You tried to pull a woman out of her car tonight, so we're holding you on probable cause."

"That cunt!"

Lockwood said, "Watch your mouth."

Smith said, "Be nice, Dale."

Lockwood told me their strategy beforehand. If I filed an assault charge, Denney would bail out in no time. But they could hold a homicide suspect for forty-eight hours without a formal arrest or the possibility of bail. And the LAPD really did have an unsolved carjacking-homicide where the suspect matched Denney's general description. I laughed when I heard how general; the guy was a dark-haired male Caucasian.

There was also the pool house. Once Denney had seen Lockwood's badge, he was supposed to surrender. He hadn't, and for that they intended to screw with him. I'd reminded them about the lesson of Rodney King, and Lockwood asked if I had a video camera with me. For the longest time, I hadn't recognized his humor for what it was; I was getting used to his deadpan style. Or maybe it was just cop humor, because Smith was good at it, too.

Smith said, "Lynnda's cutting you loose, Dale. You're a liability now."

"That's a lie! I delivered the money, that's all—the *money!*"

Smith said, "What money would that be, Dale?"

Denney slumped. "Ask the cunt."

Smith said, "Be nice, Dale."

Lockwood said, "Watch your mouth."

Smith said, "Lynnda shared a theory with us, and we think it's a good one."

Lockwood said, "Lynnda sent you out to deliver a package and lean on Miss Stenholm a little. You leaned too hard, killed her, then tried to cover it up. You delivered the package the following night and pretended not to know what Miss Stenholm looked like. You were betting that between the money and the assault, the story would get back to us."

Denney shook his head and banged his fists on the chair arms.

Lockwood said, "You told Lynnda that Miss Stenholm got her money. Then the papers ran the news of Miss Stenholm's death. You played dumb to Lynnda. You told her what 'really' happened—that you never located Miss Stenholm, and you mistook one woman for another when you delivered the money. Lynnda didn't believe you. She figured you killed Greta Stenholm and stole the twenty grand."

Denney shook his head and rattled his handcuffs.

Smith said, "*We've* got the money, Dale. But we didn't tell Lynnda that."

Denney said, "I *didn't* kill her."

Lockwood said, "You're a knife man from way back. You've got the ADW on your rap sheet."

"*I didn't kill her. I delivered the money and a message.* I didn't count the money, and I don't know what the message meant."

Smith said, "How did you fuck up so badly, Dale?"

Lockwood said, "You had it in for Miss Stenholm. You hate smart women—they make you feel like the dipshit you are."

"I hate cunts, is what I hate! I'm not through with that one neither!"

Smith said, "Women should be seen and not heard, right, Dale?"

Lockwood said, "You broke into Miss Stenholm's apartment nine months ago. What did you steal?"

"I didn't steal *nothing. I didn't do it.*"

Smith said, "Come on, Dale—no panties to sniff in your lonely moments? No Russian novels to improve your mind?"

Lockwood said, "On Friday night, August twenty-fourth, you broke into Miss Stenholm's car while it was parked in Hollywood. What did you steal?"

"Fuck you guys! Ask me where I was the night of the carjacking!"

Lockwood said, "You followed Miss Stenholm to a party on Monday night, August twenty-seventh. She got smart on you, and you killed her."

"*I didn't kill her. I didn't steal nothing. I didn't do NOTHING!*"

Smith said, "Lynnda wants the money back. She's called all the people you work for and told them what a fuckup you are."

Denney thrashed in his chair. "That cunt—it's her fault!"

Lockwood said, "Watch your mouth."

Smith said, "Watch it."

Denney said, "*She's a—!*"

He didn't finish. I saw Lockwood stiffen. I saw him exchange looks with Smith; I saw Smith give him permission and move aside. It only took a split second, then Lockwood stood up, stepped forward, and slapped Denney across the mouth. It was a nasty backhand swipe. Denney grunted—his head whipped sideways and fell on his chest.

I leaped up, holding my breath. Lockwood stepped back and stared straight at me through the two-way mirror.

CHAPTER
NINETEEN

I BLEW OUT of the station without saying good-bye. A mile down the road, I pulled in at the curb and parked. The streets were deserted.

I wished I had something to put between me and the damp seat. I'd washed off Denney's blood with car rags and bottled water. I was lucky he'd lain down; most of the mess was on the passenger side and the floor mats. I should've grabbed a towel to sit on when I stopped for clothes after Lynnda's.

I draped my arms around the steering wheel and stared out the windshield. I couldn't get the image of Lockwood and Denney out of my head.

I wanted to treat the thing like a political lesson. I'd never in my life considered the cops' side of the story. Police brutality was police brutality: the cops were always wrong. But here was a case where Denney purposely provoked them—and *I* had beaten him much worse. Knowing the contents of Lockwood's personnel file, I knew he didn't hit suspects as a matter of routine—

I whacked the dashboard.

I was lying to myself and I knew it. Political lesson, my ass. The honest fact was: Lockwood hit Dale Denney *for me.*

I leaned my forehead on the steering wheel. We'd gotten beyond political differences, the detective and I.

I started to blush. I wanted to laugh it off—and realized I couldn't. I didn't know what I felt.

THE DASHBOARD clock said past midnight, but I had no desire to sleep.

I got my notebook and the car phone, and dialed Steve Lampley's number. He was awake and sounding upset. I asked him one question. Did Greta have proof that Jules Silverman killed Georgette Bauerdorf? Not old rumors or hearsay testimony from abandoned book projects—proof.

I didn't get an answer, I got a half-sobbed monologue. The controlled guy I'd seen that morning let it all hang out.

I had no compassion, he said. I didn't respect his suffering and pain. He'd taught Greta at Kansas, he was her oldest friend in L.A, he hadn't slept or eaten since he heard she was murdered. He'd worried and debated and finally called the cops, he felt so guilty, so guilty—what if the transcripts had killed her? I didn't care about Greta, I just wanted fuel for my career. He'd tried to organize a memorial service for her, but only Catherine Kerr would come, everyone else was covering their butt, no one wanted to associate with failure. Two people in all of L.A. cared that Greta was dead, then I call in the middle of the night with intrusive questions. He bet I wouldn't attend a service for her, nobody'd loved her like he did, I was a lousy friend, insensitive, shallow, opportunistic...

He finally ran out of steam. I asked my intrusive question again. Did Greta have proof that Jules Silverman killed Georgette Bauerdorf? Lampley said he didn't know and to leave him alone—and hung up.

I started the car and headed for Mount Washington. Catherine Kerr was expert at not answering questions, too. I hoped that a guilty conscience had kept her awake late.

The neighborhood was dark, but Kerr's front windows were lit up. A black BMW coupe was parked in her driveway: Neil John Phillips drove a black three-series BMW. I pulled in behind it and parked. I climbed Kerr's steps as quietly as I could, careful not to touch the railing that creaked. I heard a voice from inside:

"You're crazy, babycakes—it ain't worth it."

Penny Proft.

I peeked through the screen door. Catherine Kerr and Penny Proft were sitting at one end of the computer table. Their end was a postmeal mess: coffee cups, cake plates, and, for Kerr, overflowing ashtrays. Proft had changed her baggy warm-ups for baggy overalls. The air was thick with tobacco smoke.

Proft smacked her forehead. "Dumb-kopf—you have tenure! Why give that up on a crapshoot?"

I opened the screen and walked in. Proft looked up. She said, "Uh-oh, Jill Webb! Hide the murder weapon!"

I pointed at Kerr. "'A real tombstone in Culture Studies'—who you've talked to 'maybe twice' in your life?"

Proft smiled and shrugged. Kerr puffed on a cigarillo. She said, "Get out of my house."

Proft said, "Now C. Margaret, don't sulk. What gives with the hand, Annsky?"

I flexed my fingers. The ice had kept the swelling down, but the blues and greens were starting to show. I might have broken a bone this time.

Kerr said, "She hurt herself thinking."

Proft's eyes widened. "Did you just make a joke, C. Marg?"

Kerr wasn't her usual self; she didn't look like she wanted to beat the world in an argument. She puffed on her cigarillo and fiddled with a coffee cup.

Proft said, "She's the Halley's Comet of comedians. Every eight decades she makes a joke."

Kerr didn't react. Proft said, "C. Margaret is sulking at you, C. Ann, because—"

Kerr said, "Don't."

"—because C. Greta chose you—"

"Don't!"

"—for her Hollywood running mate, and C. Margaret wanted the nomination." Proft framed a movie screen with her hands. "It's an epic saga of two women against an unjust system! Never in motion picture history has the tragic plight of—"

Kerr cut in. "You little cow."

Proft grinned: she seriously disliked Kerr. I said, "Does that have anything to do with the fight at Farmer's Market?"

Kerr mashed out her cigarillo and lit another one. Proft said, "It has *everything* to do with it. Grets had signed a deal to direct her own script. C. Marg wanted Grets to take her along, Grets wanted you. They saw me eating, I swear, a strict low-calorie breakfast, and called me over to referee the bout. I hadn't said word one to either of them since SC."

I sat down across from Proft. I said, "Go on."

Proft shrugged. "I didn't pick sides — I thought they were both mental. Greta had this idea that the moviegoing public was ready for . . . How did she put it?"

I said, "The truth about the condition of women?"

Proft cupped one hand Italian-style. "Ecco — la condizione delle donne. And C. Marg wants on the Hollywood hayride. Gretissima was her ticket in."

I looked at Kerr. "What happened to Michael Powell and the twilight of cinema? I thought the tide was going out."

Kerr wouldn't look at me; she exhaled a cloud of smoke. Proft flapped it away with her napkin and pretended to cough.

She said, "I told the girls that if I had to do it over, I'd pick another line of work. I wish they'd warned us at film school. It takes a certain kind of woman to suck poison dick every hour of every day and still want to succeed in the business that makes her swallow."

She caught the self-pity in the last sentence, and laughed. "Boohoohoo, poor Penny. Overpaid and underlaid."

I said, "Did Greta mention Jules Silverman that morning?"

Kerr sat forward. "Greta knew *Jules Silverman?*"

Proft mimicked, "'Greta knew *Jules Silverman?*'"

Kerr frowned. Proft pointed a fork at her. "She wants to ditch academics for the movie biz, so she calls me over for an intimate din-din, then snores through my poils of wisdom until she hears the magic name of Silverman."

I said, "Did his name come up or not?"

Proft went to a stage whisper. "*Greta mentioned Big Jules while*

C. Margaret was powdering her nose. Greta knew C. Marg would do a somersault up Julie's derriere if she had half a chance. Talk about a ticket in—"

Kerr said, "Get out, both of you!"

She grabbed two ashtrays and shoved them at us. They tipped off the table into our laps. I jumped up to brush the butts away; Proft just sat there laughing. Kerr stumped down the hall and we heard a door slam.

Proft reached for one of Kerr's computer keyboards. Standing up, she dumped cigarillo butts all over it. She shook the keyboard so that the tobacco flakes settled between the keys.

I said, "What did Greta say about Jules Silverman?"

Proft put the keyboard back and dusted herself off. "A lot of wacky shit, man, no kidding—that sister was fugued. Scott 'The Puke' Dolgin, In-Casa Productions, the Casa de Amor, some mishigas about the Casa de A and making Silverman pay. World War Two was in the ratatouille, but then World War Two is everywhere since Sir Steven reshot D-Day to rave reviews. Rat-tat-tat, 'Argh, ya got me, ya stinkin' Kraut bastids!'"

Proft clutched her stomach, faking a beachhead death. "Grets wasn't talking jobs, though, or Oscar-winning movies. I don't think she'd ever met Jules the Large."

Kerr yelled, *"Get out of my house!"* It was muffled by a door.

I said, "Is there a romantic angle I should know about? Did Kerr have a thing for Greta?"

Proft hooted. She grabbed a pen and paper from Kerr's workstation. I said, "What are you doing?"

"It's a note to C. Margaret. I'm suggesting lesbianism as a career move—Industry dykes are powerful like you would *not* believe."

Proft laughed to herself as she wrote. "I heard Hannah Silverman goes for girrrlz. C. Marg could deploy some strategic poontang and meet C. Jules that way."

I said, "Greta slept with everyone and no one, Hannah Silverman is straight and gay. You think your rumors are reliable?"

Proft shrugged and kept writing. A door opened down the hall. I didn't wait around; I ran.

EVERYBODY WAS in bed at the Casa de Amor. The pink outside lights were on, Mrs. May's TV set was still on, but the rest of the bungalows were dark and quiet.

It was 2:20 A.M.

I'd talked to the surveillance guys across Washington. They were more conspicuous without traffic going by. They'd said there'd been no sight of Scott Dolgin, Neil Phillips, or Mrs. May. They'd said Mrs. May's bungalow hadn't been searched. And they were sick of the smell of roses.

I walked up the central path and sat down on the edge of the fountain. I looked around the courtyard. The harem of the living dead. But I'd only seen two of the female tenants up close: Mrs. May, and Mrs. May's muumuu neighbor who loved candy bars and small-batch bourbon. Either of them could be old enough for my purposes. The woman, or women, I needed would have been at least eighteen years old in 1944. Eighteen, I *hoped*. They'd be seventy-six, minimum, today.

I got up and walked to the nearest bungalow. I rang the doorbell; I leaned on it hard and long. I went around the courtyard, ringing bells where I knew someone was home. I leaned on the bells hard and long. I wanted the harem wide awake and glued to their front windows.

Nothing moved, so I did a second circuit of the courtyard. I gave every doorbell ten seconds. I walked up and down until there were signs of stirring. I didn't expect them to open their doors for me. But lights went on, and venetian blinds spread apart. I saw the pale blob of unrouged faces and the glow of cigarettes.

I climbed up on the fountain and raised my voice:

"There was a wild sex party at the Casa de Amor on October 11, 1944. I know that's almost sixty years ago, but I also know one or more of you were there. I want the details. I want to know which of you was there, who the guests were, and what happened at the party."

The door to my right opened. The muumuu neighbor screeched, "Leave us alone!" and slammed the door with force. There was a feeble "Go away, go away" and knuckles rapped on glass.

I made a megaphone with my hands. "I am *not* going away! *Someone here* was at that party! *Someone here* told Greta Stenholm about it! *Someone here* knows why the party's important!"

The muumuu neighbor banged her front window. "Go *away!*"

"*I'm not leaving until—!*"

I stopped because I heard footsteps on the path. A uniformed cop appeared in the archway; he was Culver City PD.

He crooked his finger at me. I jumped down off the fountain. He took my arm and escorted me out to a patrol car.

CHAPTER
TWENTY

IT WAS TURNING into the longest day of my life.

I lay in the holding cell and counted how many consecutive hours I'd been awake. From 7:30 A.M. Monday to 3:15 A.M. Wednesday: almost forty-four hours in a row, minus the nap Tuesday morning after I swam. The nap probably broke the streak. But it was still a lot of hours with nothing like real rest.

I'd had drug-assisted marathons before. I remembered plenty of times when I'd staggered around Paris, fried from having sex all night instead of sleeping. But I'd never stayed up this long with no help from chemicals or men. I'd never stayed up this long *doing things*. I'd been running flat out since Monday.

I sat up, took off my jacket, folded it for a pillow, and lay back down. I was alone on the women's side of the jail. The place was ugly and overlit. My bunk was a steel slab bolted to a wall; the walls and bars were glazed an institutional green; the cell stunk of old vomit. I could hear snoring sounds from the men's side. Two different guys were snoring.

I'd asked the Culver City cop who squealed on me. He said it wasn't the old women, it was the surveillance guys. I'd started to complain at him. He told me to relax, no one was pressing charges. They'd notified Lockwood where I was. He was coming to spring me — but it might be awhile before he could get there.

My eyes wanted to close. I knew if I let them, I'd sleep for a week. I rolled off the bunk and started to pace the cell. I was pacing when Lockwood arrived. The booking officer unlocked the cell door and Lockwood walked in.

He put out his hand and said, "Come on. I'm taking you home."

"I THINK GRETA found independent corroboration of Silverman's guilt. Before that, she was going on the MGM-blacklist transcripts and the partial Sheriff's file. The transcripts are just hearsay, and she didn't know about the orgy alibi, or Silverman's thumbprint on the lightbulb. I think she stumbled into something at the Casa de Amor. I think one of the tenants gave her something that implicated Silverman unequivocally—i.e., that he definitely did *not* attend the orgy that night. I think she went to Silverman with the evidence, *after* she'd sent the spanking picture. I think she tried to use it to pry something big out of him—like the Abadi killer or a confession on Georgette Bauerdorf. That was the second part that wasn't doable, and that's what got her killed."

I waited for Lockwood's reaction. He was in the bathroom. I was on the couch, looking at the view; I had a bowl of ice cubes for my hand.

When he'd said he was taking me home, he hadn't meant my place, he'd meant his. He lived in an old clapboard cottage on a cul-de-sac near the Hollywood Bowl. The cottage had been updated. It was two good-sized rooms and a wall of windows facing west. He'd hung a collection of crime photographs—gangsters dead and alive. But the furniture looked like leftovers from a lady DA with taste: cushy chair, antique end table, and the leather couch I was sitting on. It was sparse but comfortable.

I said, "Did you hear me? What do you think?"

The bathroom door cracked. Lockwood said, "Help yourself to coffee."

I got up and walked into the kitchen. The kitchen had a view, too. I poured coffee and stood at the sink sipping it. I wondered if I'd get to bed before dawn. Lockwood joined me after a few minutes. He'd showered, shaved, and changed into fresh clothes. Since I'd known him he'd worn nothing but starched white shirts, and dark jackets and slacks.

He dropped his jacket on a chair and poured himself coffee. He said, "I'd like you to call in for your messages."

He brought the telephone over and set it on the table. I sat down with my coffee, he sat down with his. But I didn't reach for the phone.

Lockwood looked at me. "Why did you run out on us? You're not upset about Denney."

I shook my head. Lockwood said, "My partner thinks you turned squeamish, being a liberal journalist and all. He's expecting a lynch mob from the ACLU."

I felt myself start to blush. To hide it, I grabbed the telephone and punched in my number. The machine picked up; I hit my remote-access code.

Lockwood said, "Put it on the speaker, if you would."

I pushed the speaker button. The computer voice said, "You have six new messages." I punched in the play code. Lockwood stirred his coffee.

"Monday, 6:30 P.M. 'He's out of control because of *you*, Annie, because of the lawyer–trust fund thing. Today was *your* fault. He *never* drinks like that before dinner.'"

I said, "My sister." Lockwood nodded.

"Monday, 6:33 P.M. 'You *have* to come with us on Wednesday. He's here for ten days, and you can't just see him once.'"

Sis again. I made a face: my warnings had done exactly no good.

"Monday, 6:35 P.M. 'I forgot—you still haven't answered my question. Why did Douglas Lockwood interview Dad and me? How are you involved in a murder? You can't be—you'd tell us. Call.'"

"Tuesday, 4:01 P.M. 'Where *are* you? Dad and I are making plans for the San Andreas trip. *Call me.*'"

"Tuesday, 7:49 P.M. 'Annie...Annie...he's...*You have to come tomorrow.* We're meeting early....He's been...He's...'"

The machine cut her off; it only allowed so much silence. I checked my watch to see when I could call her. She sounded badly upset. I had to try and talk her out of that trip.

"Tuesday, 10:18 P.M. 'Ann, Barry. I need those reporters' names you were supposed to leave with me. I want to cover every angle on that pigfuck Lockwood—'"

Before he could finish, I hit the disconnect button and cradled the receiver. Lockwood's face had gone chill; the official mask was back on. I leaned toward him to explain. "I'm not—"

Lockwood held up his hand.

I said, "But I—"

Lockwood shook his head. "We have business to discuss."

I gave up and sat back. "Business with my answering machine?"

"I wanted to see who was keeping tabs on you, or if you had any odd hang-ups. I also wanted to see, frankly, if you were running any schemes without my knowledge."

"Barry doesn't know—"

Lockwood stopped me again. "Did you learn anything useful at Lynnda's tonight?"

I sighed. "Nothing you didn't hear from Arnold Tolback except that Lynnda fired the actress in the spanking picture. Which proves she knows about the blackmail—if Hannah Silverman crashing around giving orders didn't prove it already."

Lockwood sipped his coffee, thinking. I said, "I'm right."

"About what?"

I sat forward. "Look, every time you try to link the murder to the blackmail, your reasoning gets absurd. I heard you with Lynnda-Ellen. Do you really think she hired a second guy to scare Greta? Do you really think Denney murdered her by accident, then pretended with me the night after? I know you're just rehearsing possibilities, but they're all convoluted and preposterous when you start with blackmail as the motive."

Lockwood sipped his coffee.

"But if you start with Georgette Bauerdorf as the motive, everything gets simple. Bathtubs, murder disguised as suicide, Jules Silverman, Edward Abadi, Greta, Mrs. May, the Casa de Amor, all the people who've disappeared—everything ties together. Have you identified the blood in Scott Dolgin's dining room?"

Lockwood nodded. "O-negative. Miss Pavich's type."

"See! And when you get a warrant for Mrs. May's you'll find those khakis and tennis shoes aren't a plant. I'm sure it's Scott Dolgin's clothes and Greta's blood, and everything ties back to Georgette Bauerdorf! It could be that Mrs. May told Greta about the orgy in 1944. That's why she's disappeared!"

Lockwood was thinking. I sat back, light-headed. I was too tired for much effort.

Lockwood said, "What makes you think Miss Stenholm found corroboration on Silverman at the Casa de Amor?"

I repeated my talk with Catherine Kerr and Penny Proft. I used both hands to show how Kerr shoved ashtrays at us. Lockwood frowned at my right hand and said, "You need ice."

He got up, poured out the melted ice, went to the fridge, and broke more ice into the bowl. He came back with the bowl and a dish towel. He dried my hand and examined the swelling.

"Bend your fingers."

I bent them as far as they'd go. I felt a sharp pain in two knuckles. Lockwood saw me flinch. He said, "You're going to need X rays. Do you want more aspirin?"

I shook my head. He tossed the dish towel, refilled our coffee cups, and sat back down. He looked me straight in the face; he was studying me.

I said, "What?"

He said, "From the first you've acted like a lightning rod. It was you who exposed the blackmail for us. Where would we be if you hadn't ignored me that first night and gone to Miss Stenholm's apartment?"

I pointed at my hand in ice. "*I'd* be in better shape."

Lockwood didn't smile. He wasn't in great shape either. Fatigue showed in his face and around his eyes. He'd been cut wrestling Dale Denney, but the cuts were healing.

"You're also a capable burglar." Lockwood ticked off a list. "Mr. Phillips's garage, Miss Silverman's premises, Mrs. May's premises, Mr. Silverman's property."

I said, "I try not to do anything halfway."

"I believe it. You dived into the Bauerdorf case with your usual abandon."

"Do you like my theory?"

"If it's true, you shouldn't be broadcasting it at the Casa de Amor. And true or not, you have no proof."

I repeated again what Penny Proft had said.

Lockwood sipped his coffee. "That's interesting, but Miss Proft was wise to mistrust Miss Stenholm's mental state at the time. If we theorize Miss Bauerdorf as the motive in our two crimes, we have the problem of establishing that Edward Abadi knew of the Bauerdorf murder, knew for a fact that Jules Silverman was guilty, and threatened to use it against Mr. Silverman for a reason yet to be determined."

Lockwood held up two fingers. "Second, who pulled the trigger on Abadi? There's no evidence it was Silverman, but it's more likely that he'd use a gun at his age than that he'd drive from Malibu to Los Feliz, hope he found Miss Stenholm alone, knock her out with a heavy object, and slit her wrists."

I said, "Scott Dolgin did it for him."

"Why would Dolgin do that?"

I shrugged. "For a reason yet to be determined? Maybe he did it for his movie career. Silverman's a sure ticket into the business, to quote Penny Proft."

Lockwood stared at his coffee cup; he was taking that idea seriously. I nudged his leg. "You know things about Dolgin and Silverman that I don't."

Lockwood held up two fingers again. "We have two sets of phone records — Dolgin's residence, and your main house from the night of Melling's party. Dolgin called Silverman's unlisted number at least once a day for the past month, and someone called Silverman several times from the party."

Barry: it had to be. He was back and forth to the telephone all night. Lockwood said, "Our guess was Melling, based on your account of the proceedings."

"And Barry knows that Greta knew about Jules and Georgette — for whatever that's worth."

Lockwood nodded. "I'm not saying you're wrong about Silverman, it's just that we have no proof. And there are other factors you aren't aware of. You haven't read the Abadi file, for example."

"Not for lack of trying."

"Your next plan was to go to the original investigating officers, correct?"

"It hadn't crossed my mind."

"I'll save you the trouble. Sergeant McManus and Deputy Gadtke are handling the case now, and most of our players were questioned for Abadi. Not just the major people — Dolgin, Miss Stenholm, and the Silvermans — but others such as Leonard Ziskind, Jack Nevenson, Neil Phillips, and Steven Lampley."

"Penny Proft or Catherine Kerr?"

Lockwood shook his head.

"In the month before he died, Mr. Abadi had appointments with Dolgin, Melling, and Lampley. All of them were looking for work in films. But try this for size — Scott Dolgin murdered both Abadi and Stenholm out of sexual jealousy. It's the simplest solution. If Dolgin's our guy, the disappearances at the Casa de Amor make sense logically and logistically. Neil Phillips was Dolgin's alibi for the night of the Abadi murder. Only Phillips's testimony stands between Dolgin and serious police scrutiny. Dolgin might have coerced that alibi — "

I broke in. "Maybe in exchange for career help. I told you how Phillips was blackballed."

"Possibly. At the moment it's moot, since we can't locate Phillips."

I said, "I thought you had more on Scott Dolgin. How'd you get a search warrant for his place?"

Lockwood frowned. "It was an anonymous tip through RHD. An unidentified caller said we'd find Miss Stenholm's belongings and the murder clothes at Dolgin's place. I hope it doesn't bite us in the ass in court."

"Why would it?"

"Anonymous tips are shaky. How does the court know we didn't engineer it ourselves just for a look around Dolgin's?"

"But a judge signs the warrant."

"Search warrants can be challenged in court. They can be thrown out."

I flashed back to the groupie, Karen. She'd told me about the downtown courts scene and how everybody slept with everybody. She'd told me about "friendly" judges who'd sign borderline warrants because they were doing a detective involved. She'd also told me something I forgot to write down. Lockwood avoided that kind of collusion; he liked to win too much. He'd almost never had a warrant overturned at trial.

I changed direction. "What about what Mrs. May said about a fight and 'They found it'? 'It' could be proof of Silverman's guilt."

Lockwood shook his head. "'It' could be anything—the fight could be anything. If Dolgin's our guy, he's running scared, and so are the people around him. Maybe Phillips was threatening to go to the police, or maybe Miss Stenholm was. Maybe she found proof that Dolgin snuffed Abadi, or Miss Pavich did, or—"

He rubbed his temples. "There are too many suspects and too many motives. At least your father's alibi checked—that took your family out of the equation."

I said, "They shouldn't have been there to begin with. Did the Sheriff's look into Silverman's orgy story in 1944?"

Lockwood nodded.

"So the file must list witnesses from the Casa de Amor."

He nodded.

"Who were they? Is it Mrs. May? At least one of them lives there now."

"McManus and Gadtke are on it."

"Greta—"

Lockwood leaned across the table. He said, "I noticed you started calling her 'Greta.' You're wasting your sentiment. Miss Stenholm was not only a blackmailer, she was a liar."

He covered my hand. "You should know that her address and appointment books are more or less complete fabrications."

I HAD WALKED out of the kitchen and gone to stand at the picture window. It was still night. I could see the skyscrapers of Westwood and Century City, and the lighted flatlands in between. I pressed my forehead against the glass. I almost didn't need his evidence. The minute he'd said it, I knew absolutely it was true.

Lockwood came and stood beside me. "At the party you noticed Miss Stenholm going through the office Rolodex. It's common to steal the private numbers and addresses of famous film people—there's a black market in that kind of information."

Who's Who of Hollywood 2001: the sheer quantity of big names should have tipped me off.

Lockwood said, "We spoke to the film people she allegedly saw in the weeks preceding her death. All of them have denied knowing her except Mr. Ziskind. He admits to knowing her but denies having seen her on the three occasions mentioned in her book. His story checked out."

I closed my eyes and filled in the blank days in Greta's calendar.

Thursday, August 23. She leaves Lynnda-Ellen's house. Jules Silverman receives two-part extortion demand. She moves into her car and visits the Academy Library to relive her student success.

Friday, August 24. An argument at the Casa de Amor. She sees five movies on Hollywood Boulevard. Her car is vandalized, her suitcases are stolen.

Saturday, August 25. She eats breakfast with Catherine Kerr and Penny Proft. They fight over me, and Kerr's ambitions. She steals change out of the candy machines in her old apartment building.

Sunday, August 26. The cops roust her in Griffith Park for sleeping in her car.

Monday, August 27. She eats a free dinner at the pizza place. She sees *Jurassic Park III* for free at the Vine Theater. She goes to Barry Melling's party.

More squalor than stellar. No wonder the last week of her calendar was blank: fantasy and reality had split too far apart.

Lockwood put his hand on my arm. I opened my eyes. "I'm fine—I believe you."

He said, "You understand she was mentally unstable in the latter months of her life."

"I talked to her. I understand."

"And you know her film script doesn't exist."

That hit me in the stomach.

"You *do* know it."

I couldn't think—I just stood staring. I must have looked funny, because Lockwood took my arm and led me over to the couch. He sat down and made me sit next to him.

He said quietly, "Don't be upset."

I laid my head back. I had no idea I'd attached such importance to GB *Dreams Big*.

Lockwood said, still quiet, "Add up the facts. We can't locate a copy of this supposed script. Nobody seems to have seen it, and the Hollywood trade papers never reported a sale. The people at Progressive Properties and Artists thought Scott Dolgin had it, while Dolgin thought PPA had it. Her book mentions meetings at studios, but never which studio or with what individuals. She claimed to various people that you two were best friends, and she wanted to take you to Hollywood. And yet when you met at Melling's party, she didn't mention anything of that nature."

I lay there, feeling like a jerk. He didn't want to upset me even though he thought I'd sold him out to Barry behind his back.

Lockwood pressed my arm. "Are you listening?"

I rolled my head sideways and looked at him. He said, "I'm sorry."

I said, "I haven't told Barry I'm not doing the piece on you. I haven't told him about our conversation at the Thalberg the other night. I'm in some trouble at the paper and I can't piss him off right now, so I'm letting it slide until the deadline."

Lockwood said, "What kind of trouble?"

I said, "The script exists."

Lockwood reached for my hand. "What kind of trouble?"

I held on to his hand and shifted around to face him. I had to make him see what I saw.

"Everything else might be a lie, but she wrote that script. I *know* she did. You forget that Neil Phillips worked on it—he told Hamilton Ashburn so."

Lockwood looked skeptical.

"Phillips stinks, I know." I counted off five fingers. "He lied to me about who he was, he skipped out on his Fairfax place with those boxes, he's talking to Jack Nevenson on the Sony lot, he lives at the Casa de Amor under a fake name—and where the hell *is* he? But why would he lie to Ashburn about *GB Dreams Big*? I can't think of a reason, can you?"

Lockwood thought about that. "If he wanted to juke his career, it's the last lie he'd tell. If the script didn't exist, then Miss Stenholm's Hollywood hopes wouldn't exist, which means she couldn't help Phillips. You might be right."

I got excited.

"She wrote it because she *had* to write it, and I know why. I understand what Greta wanted—I know who she *was*. Look, we were born on the very same day two years apart. We were both raised on a prairie. We both craved movies and the big, wide world—we both fell out with our fathers, partly because of that. I started at the *Millennium* the same year she graduated from film school. We *did* go to Hollywood together, only I didn't know it."

Lockwood was looking out the picture window. He said, "You aren't the same type. I think she was cold, and more mercenary than you'd like."

"Maybe. Was Edward Abadi a real emotion or part of her career plan? I don't know."

Lockwood shrugged.

"Penny Proft calls her 'Little Miss I-Live-For-My-Art.' Steve Lampley said she only had one idea in her head. Making movies—that's all she wanted, that's all she cared about. But she wasn't realistic about how to get it. I haven't done the research yet, so I don't know details. But I think she thought she could succeed on her own terms, the way talented men can. I think her looks hurt her. Five years after film school she's a wreck, living in her car, delusional, a blackmailer, and a liar, raging about the condition of women."

Lockwood said, "She couldn't write a film script in that state."

I shook my head. "She wrote it before she was too far gone. She started months ago when she read about Georgette Bauerdorf. I think Georgette focused Greta's whole life. She could avenge Georgette and Edward Abadi, write a woman's adventure story, and salvage her career all at once. I think that script will tell us what Greta Stenholm thought and felt. I think it will tell us about her five years in Hollywood. I also think it's a message to me. In the script, Georgette's best friend finds the killer. In real life, Greta cast *me* as her best friend. It's my job to help find the killer, hers and Georgette's."

Lockwood said, "If Jules Silverman is so powerful, how would it help her career to expose him?"

"The script exists, Detective. I will bet you the nine hundred dollars I owe the blackmail fund that *GB Dreams Big* exists."

Lockwood smiled at me. "I'll take that bet. If you win, I'll replace the nine hundred dollars myself." He checked his watch.

I dropped his hand and stood up. "Don't tell me the time—I don't want to know."

Lockwood pulled me back down beside him. He loosened his tie and unbuttoned the top button of his shirt.

I didn't understand what he was doing. I said, "Aren't you going to work?"

Lockwood leaned forward and kissed me.

I couldn't believe it; I leaped up off the couch. Lockwood tried to hold on to me, but I was headed for the door.

He jumped up and followed me across the room.

I broke into a run. I opened the front door, stopped dead, did a complete turn, shut the door, and stood facing it like a fool.

Lockwood walked up behind me, but didn't touch me. He said, "What's wrong?"

Like a dope, I said the first thing that came to me. "I thought you went for lawyers."

I hid my face against the door. Lockwood pulled me around and kissed me again. He kissed me until I gave in and kissed him back.

BUT I JUST couldn't do it.

I had wanted him for the longest time—it was a relief to finally let my feelings go. The real experience of his mouth and his hands was a strange and intense pleasure—more intense than anything I could've imagined, if I'd allowed myself to imagine. But I found I couldn't respond with everything I had. My mind wouldn't give in. It was running wild with counterthoughts, and disbelief. Was this *me*, making love to *Douglas Lockwood*? Between my desire for him and my resistance against him, I felt like I was going to implode.

He started walking us toward the bedroom. He was taking off his tie. Suddenly I couldn't stand it anymore. I pulled free of him and backed away. He tossed his tie on the chair. If I'd thought he was handsome before, it was nothing like he looked with his mouth wet and his hair mussed up.

I said, "Could we talk?"

It sounded so lame; I knew I was destroying the mood. He nudged me toward the bedroom.

I said, "I can't!"

He saw that I was serious, and his face changed. I took hold of his sleeve and led him to the couch. He was willing to be led, but he wouldn't sit. He lay down on his back, put out his arm, and made me lie down next to him. I lay down on my side. There was just room for both of us. The whole front of my body pressed into his left side, but I was stiff from tension. He took my arm and draped it across him. Reaching up, he switched off the lamp.

He said, "It's because I'm a cop."

I said, "Until tonight I didn't think you'd noticed me."

Lockwood laughed; it was quiet. I had never seen him laugh before. He said, "Your Colt first caught my attention." He paused. "No, I believe it goes back further than that."

And so he told me the story of the Burger King siege.

His account was more detailed than what I'd read, but the gist was the same. Juan Pablo Marquez had terrorized a restaurant full of people for two hours, until he lost it and fired into the kitchen where his former girlfriend worked. The customers panicked and Lockwood couldn't get off the shots he wanted. He was sorry for Marquez's death but it didn't trouble his conscience. Marquez played by the rules of crime and punishment, and Lockwood might have died himself.

It wasn't the shooting and killing that changed his life: it was the controversy that followed. Not because of his treatment in the media, although that had made his professional life more difficult. A grand jury was after him even though he'd only passed through Rampart Division on a case. Trash like Dale Denney lipped him off, something that didn't happen before the publicity. The controversy hadn't derailed his career, however — I'd been misinformed about that. He could have taken the lieutenant's exam years ago; he just didn't want to be a lieutenant. He didn't want to push paper or run a division: he wanted to solve murders.

What the controversy changed was his attitude toward his work. It had started him thinking about the larger context of law enforcement. He'd spent three months in Mexico, thinking and reading. He decided that L.A. had become impossible to police, and that LAPD wasn't the cause, or the solution. The Department had serious problems — problems of philosophy and practice, problems of leadership and budget. But what could they do about economic and social factors that produced poverty and a permanent criminal underclass? Or do about a widespread disaffection with authority, which extended to police officers themselves? Or do about the cynicism of lawyers who played on race prejudice to free a guilty client? Or do about a Juan Pablo Marquez who took strangers hostage because his love life went bad?

The police were swamped by problems that weren't police matters. He'd always known it, like most cops did — but he'd never had time to reflect on the bigger picture. And his reflections had changed him. He'd always been such a strict law-and-order guy; he'd always felt so responsible. Now he'd begun to see how much couldn't be solved by the criminal justice system. Now he didn't know how he felt about police work in general. Catching killers was essential, but he didn't believe in the job like he used to. He had lost his faith.

He stopped talking and stared at the ceiling. I didn't ask if that's what ended his marriage; I didn't want to bring up other women. I said, "But how did that lead to here?"

He tightened his hold on me. I put my head on his shoulder — it was more comfortable. His shirt smelled of aftershave and laundry starch. I had stopped feeling tense.

He said, "When we met at the crime scene, I didn't automatically think 'liberal pain-in-the-ass.' It's surprising how fast your ideas can change, once the process is under way."

He'd liked my looks, he said. He'd liked my bare feet and bed hair. He even didn't mind the lies; he was too busy trying to figure out my game. But the Colt had clinched it: the Colt upset all his preconceptions about journalists. It made him want to know more. He'd fixed it so I never dealt with his partner, only him. He'd talked to my family right off, when there were a hundred party guests to interview. He'd let me keep the sap and everything; he'd left the money in the attic. After the guy tried to kill me, he'd waited down the street to see if I'd call him back and admit I was afraid. And he'd gone along with my plan to trap Dale Denney to see if I'd really do it. He'd done all that to test me. He wanted to see who I was and what I'd do next; he'd taken chances with his case to find out. His only worry was that he repelled me because he was a cop.

I lay pressed against him and listened. I should have been astonished: he liked me from the first, and I didn't have the slightest clue. But only part of me was listening now. The other part was feeling his physical nearness.

I shifted my leg and felt myself flush up hot. He was still talking; he was saying how frightened he'd been those two nights at the pool house. It barely registered. I reached one hand and slowly unbuttoned the rest of his buttons. He broke off talking but made no effort to stop me. I sat up, pulled his shirt out of his slacks, and pushed it open. I put my hands on his chest and just looked at him.

He was looking at me.

I bent over and kissed the scar under his nipple. It was a long, thin ridge that showed pink against his faded Mexico tan. I kissed the ridge of flesh from end to end, then kissed the skin around it. I closed my eyes and licked along the scar. His breathing speeded up. He ran his fingers in my hair to press my mouth closer. He laid his head back, and I heard him say my name.

CHAPTER
TWENTY-ONE

WE NEVER made it off the couch. He was a wonderful lover, laughing and passionate, and once we got started again, it was way too urgent to think about moving to the bedroom.

We'd almost just fallen asleep when the telephone rang.

I would have ignored it, but I felt Doug stir. I cracked an eyelid. Sun was pouring in the windows; the room was filled with light. Doug reached for the phone on the end table. I buried my face in his neck.

"Lockwood speaking . . . Yes, partner . . . What time is it now? . . . I know her. I'll go while you do that. . . . Good idea, good."

He hung up the phone. He said softly, "Ann."

I tightened my arms around him and said, "*Sleep.*" He kissed my ear. "I know, baby, but Lynnda called the station. She's ready to talk."

I let go of him. He kissed me again and rolled off the couch. I watched him walk into the bathroom. I said, "I'm coming with you."

He turned. "To Lynnda's or to shower?"

I sat up, rubbing my eyes. "Don't tempt me. I'll fix coffee and shower second."

He shut the bathroom door. I heard water splash and braced myself to stand up. I couldn't manage it.

Our clothes were thrown all over the floor. I picked up my

shirt. I couldn't find the energy to put it on—I just sat there stupe-
fied. I tilted sideways and lay back down . . .

The sound of laughter woke me up. Doug was standing beside
the couch. He leaned over and shook me. He said, "Hurry."

I didn't move. "I'm hurrying."

He laughed again and walked into the kitchen. I dragged myself to the shower. I blasted the cold water, got dressed, dragged to
the kitchen, and guzzled a cup of coffee that Doug had made
strong. The coffee didn't make a dent at all. My head wouldn't
clear—I felt bleary and sluggish.

I also had problems working my right hand. Doug doctored it
for me. He applied pain cream and wrapped an Ace bandage over
top. I thought he might discuss Lynnda-Ellen while he was working; unlike me, he was awake and lucid. He brought up my trouble
at the paper instead. I said that his powers of recuperation were
sickening, but he wouldn't let me duck the question. So I told him
I was temporarily tired of movies—how I'd refused assignments
and missed deadlines, and how my reviews had gotten spiteful. I
told him it wouldn't be serious except that Barry was blanding out
the film section to prepare for a possible sale, with Jules Silverman
as the possible broker.

Doug frowned at the new connection. I told him I wasn't worried: Barry was just going through a phase. He'd forgotten why he
started the *Millennium* but he was bound to remember sometime.

As if Doug cared whether the paper ran pro-studio fluff, or
blew up in a big mushroom cloud.

I said so and he smiled.

We took separate cars to breakfast and to Whitley Heights.
When I was alone, I was overwhelmed by a sense of unreality. I
tried to absorb the change in our relationship. It was hard. It was
hard to adjust to the other Lockwood—the real live man under the
official exterior. It was especially hard since I felt so tired and I still
wanted him. I didn't feel like the night had ended, and here it was
morning and we were up and dressed and back to business.

Doug stood waiting for me at the bottom of Lynnda-Ellen's
stairs.

Detective Smith couldn't make it; he'd had to organize a lineup to maintain the fiction that Dale Denney was a carjacking suspect. We climbed the stairs and Doug rang the doorbell. He squeezed my arm without turning his head.

Lynnda answered the door in full makeup and a lacy lounging ensemble. The top was open and her breasts were very evident. They were too perfect and taut; she'd had them enhanced by surgical means. She took one look at Doug and lost her simpery smile.

"Oh, it's you."

He said, "Yes, so you can put those away."

Her mouth turned down. Closing her top, she tightened the belt and jerked her thumb at me. "Who's this?"

Doug said, "Miss Whitehead is a witness. I thought her presence would be useful."

Lynnda stepped aside to let us in. Her living room was like her — a bunch of money spent on gaudy effect. It had a wet bar and a grand piano, and we sat down on pom-pommed, faux leopard-skin chairs.

Lynnda had a lace hankie; she started dabbing her eyes with it. The backup act, I guessed: from sex to light tragedy. Doug got out his notebook and pen. I forced myself to pay attention.

She said, "It's all been such a terrible shock. I thought I knew Greta but I've discovered things about her that have surprised and saddened me."

She hadn't talked like that yesterday night. Her delivery was stilted and the formal phrases sounded phony.

Lynnda balled her hankie. "Arnie Tolback only told you part of the story. You said yourself that he has a bone to pick with the Silvermans — that's why he only told you part. He didn't say that Greta and him conspired to embarrass the Silvermans and extort money from them."

Doug started writing. Lynnda said, "Arnie *did* bring Greta to me in secret. She did help with the shows, and I did ask her to come live here. But Arnie didn't tell you that him and Greta planned the blackmail together. Arnie told her about Mr. Silverman's visits, because he had an interest in embarrassing the Silvermans."

Doug didn't look up. "What was Mr. Tolback's interest?"

"Arnie's a user. He used Hannah to get Mr. Silverman's help in the movie industry. But Mr. Silverman's a smart man—he always knows when he's being used and he wouldn't help Arnie. So Arnie conspired with Greta to embarrass the Silvermans and extort money from them."

She was recycling her pat phrases. Doug said, "What was Miss Stenholm's interest in the scheme?"

"Greta was broke—"

Doug cut in. "You still pay your people shit, Lynn?"

Lynnda had her hankie and wasn't going to be baited. She sniffed. "Greta and my's arrangement was she worked in exchange for rent. Looking back in retrospect, maybe it wasn't quite fair."

Doug said, "So she needed money. Why would she want to embarrass the Silvermans?"

"She hated the Silvermans—Hannah worst. Hannah stole her boyfriend and has a good position in the Industry. Greta was a nothing going nowhere."

Doug said, "You deny any knowledge of her murder."

Lynnda dabbed her eyes. Her hankie was dotted with mascara, not moisture.

"I admit that Dale delivered the money for the Silvermans—people of their level don't dirty their hands with details. But I didn't send a second man to threaten Greta. She'd taken off, I didn't know where. Naturally I did what I could to repair the damage. I fired the actress who appeared in the pictures, and I provided Dale to deliver the money. Dale screwed—pardon me, mishandled—the delivery, but he's assured me he will rectify that situation. If you want my opinion, Arnie did her. I think they had a fight and he did her."

Doug reviewed his notes. "Let me get this straight. It is your belief that Mr. Tolback and Miss Stenholm conspired to . . ."

He let the sentence dangle. I saw the trap; Lynnda didn't. She finished the sentence. ". . . to embarrass the Silvermans and extort money from them."

I burst out, "Who wrote your lines?"

Lynnda ignored me and looked at Doug. Doug said, "Answer the question."

Lynnda twisted her hankie. "I'm sure I don't know what she means."

I said, "'Surprised and saddened'? 'Dirty their hands with details'? 'Rectify the situation'? Did Hannah write that stuff or did her lawyer?"

Doug stood up and walked to the telephone. Lynnda lost her fake-o dignity. She jumped up, shrill.

"Arnie did her! He whacked her! She was a greedy bitch! They were screwing! They planned it together and the deal went bad!"

Doug punched a number. Lynnda said, "*What are you doing?*"

Doug spoke into the telephone. "Partner, it's me. Let's try tax evasion—call your contact at the IRS. Denney says there's maybe four hundred grand a year in unreported income— "

Lynnda shouted, "*No!*"

Doug said, "Hold on a minute," and covered the mouthpiece. Lynnda was white. She said, "I need to make a call."

She rushed out of the living room. Doug uncovered the mouthpiece. "It worked. I'll call you back... Yeah, they're magic."

He put the phone down. I said, "What's magic?"

"The letters *IRS*. This might take awhile—you should go look for your film script."

I stood up and headed for the door. I suddenly remembered my sister and that damned San Andreas trip. I stopped, frowned, and checked my watch. They'd probably left hours ago. Father liked to get an early start.

Doug read my mind. He said, "You missed your family."

I lowered my voice. "Making love with you."

He kept his face deadpan. "First things first, Miss Whitehead."

I said, "Detective—first things *always* first."

I TURNED OFF Robertson and swung down the alley behind Progressive Properties and Artists. I'd been tossed out last time I came by; I wasn't going to attempt the front entrance.

I had gotten a second wind. I'd heard about herbal speed from the hippie who wrote the *Millennium* health column. Vivian had tried it for fun and told me it worked. So I'd stopped at a health food store and bought a bottle of pep pills. I also bought arnica for my hand, and washed everything down with organic espresso. By the time I hit Beverly Hills I felt awake and lucid as hell.

I called my sister at home on the off chance she didn't go. There was no answer; and there was no answer at Father's hotel.

PPA's parking lot was just a tight place between dumpsters. The parking slots were labeled by name: Leonard Ziskind and Jack Nevenson were in. They both drove BMW sedans. A BMW ragtop stood in the visitor's space. There was no other parking, so I left my car on the hash marks reserved for garbage trucks.

The alley door was locked; it had a buzzer and an intercom. The window beside the door was cracked an inch. I checked around for people, removed the screen, pushed up the sash, and climbed inside. Breaking and entering had become routine.

I paused on the carpet to orient myself. PPA was a small operation—a few offices off a main hall. I saw the front reception area, and the receptionist with her back to me. I heard voices closer by. They came from the office adjoining Jack Nevenson's.

I tiptoed down the hall toward the voices. When I got close enough to hear distinct words, I ducked into a paneled niche. The receptionist couldn't see me there if she turned around.

I peeked in the office door. Len Ziskind sat behind his desk; he was tapping his teeth with his glasses. Jack Nevenson and Hamilton Ashburn Jr. sat facing him. Ashburn was dressed for the set, except for parka and mitts.

Ashburn was talking.

"Neil is no friend of mine, Len, not after that stunt he pulled in the trades. But he asked me to relay the message, so I'm doing it. He wants credit on the script and half the money."

Ziskind spread his hands. "We didn't agent the sale. We never saw a finished screenplay."

Ashburn turned red and looked at Nevenson. Nevenson nodded. "I've told Neil we thought Scott Dolgin had the property and was developing it himself."

Ashburn said, "Not Scott—Greta and Neil hated him."

Ziskind said, "Hate him? Why?"

Nevenson cleared his throat. "Len's considering Scott for a client."

Ashburn said, "A client? I don't think you want him as a client."

Ziskind tapped his teeth. "Why not?"

"Scott turns people off, and if he had any talent, he'd be somewhere by now. You don't want PPA associated with Neil or Greta either. Everyone says that Greta peaked at film school, and Neil blew it with *The Last Real Man*. He showed me his rewrite on *GB Dreams Big*, and I think he's lost it."

Nevenson read a dismiss signal from Ziskind. Nevenson stood up. "Thanks for coming, Ham."

Ashburn took the hint; he stood up and shook hands with Ziskind. He said, "You know my agent, Joel Rothman. Joel heard you're packaging features for cable, and we'd love to talk to you about it. I'm currently directing my third HBO movie."

Ziskind was cool. "Have Joel call me."

I ran down the hall, squeezed through the window, put the screen back, and waited for Ashburn in the alley. The ragtop had to be his. I thought of Penny Proft on the subject of Ashburn, Greta's death, and Phillips's aborted career: "The Hamster must be thrilled—he's the last man standing."

The back door opened and Ashburn walked out. His mouth was clamped shut. He saw me and kept walking.

I followed him. I said, "Neil sure sent the right guy to plead his case."

"He's lucky I came at all with his reputation."

"He's lucky you wanted to meet Len Ziskind."

Ashburn unlocked his car; he wasn't curious in the least. I said, "I have to talk to Phillips. You know where he is."

"I'm going to meet him right now."

"I want to come."

Ashburn got in his car. "You go, then. *You* tell Neil they never saw his script, and tell him no more errands. I was humiliated in there."

"Where is he?"

"8493 Fountain Avenue, corner of La Cienega. *Move.*"

I moved. Ashburn backed out and drove off up the alley. I watched him, recovering from the jolt. 8493 Fountain was Georgette Bauerdorf's old address in West Hollywood.

I PAGED DOUG from the car and prayed he was close to a telephone. He was; he hadn't finished with Lynnda-Ellen. I told him I was on my way to meet Neil John Phillips and told him the address. He recognized it with no help. He said to keep Phillips talking and he'd come as soon as he could. He said play the journalist, pretend you only know one-tenth of what you do. And please, he said, don't scare Phillips or try to muscle him. I hung up the phone laughing.

I pulled into a space in front of 8493. They were called the El Palacio Apartments. The building was two stories and wrapped around three sides of a wide lawn. It was vintage Spanish, preserved in its original condition down to the last molding and tile. It would have been swank in 1944; it was still swank in 2001.

I didn't see Neil Phillips as I walked up the stairs from the street. I also didn't see any apartment numbers and wanted to find Georgette's number six. I started with the near wing. The apartments were built in pairs with a shared ground-floor vestibule. I found number five and number six inside the third vestibule. The vestibules were stucco, and this one had a mural of the Spanish countryside. I looked up at the ceiling. The light fixture hung from a chain. I stood on my toes to try and reach it. My fingertips fell about eighteen inches short of the bulb. Anyone less than six feet tall would need a ladder to unscrew it. Jules Silverman was six one or two—

A whisper: "What are *you* doing here?"

Neil John Phillips's voice.

I jumped and turned. It had come from the shadows at the back of the vestibule. I squinted to see. There was an alcove under the staircase that led to the second floor.

I walked back to the voice. The alcove had a velour bench and Phillips was sitting on it. He whispered, "*What are you doing here?*"

I said, "'OoOOoooo, the *movie critic.*'"

It just popped out. We'd been chasing the guy for a week, but I couldn't help myself. He'd been so obnoxious the other time. Phillips didn't react badly, though. He smiled and spoke in his normal voice.

"I apologize for that, Ann—I wasn't thinking straight. You cats at the *Millennium* were the only ones who ever defended me, I should have been more grateful. I always meant to give Mark a call."

He pointed at the bench for me to sit down. I stayed standing and looked him over. He wore jeans and a baseball cap, and relaxed against the wall like we were old friends. This wasn't the Neil John Phillips I'd built up in my mind. I'd built up the image of someone spoiled and arrogant; an embryonic filmland monster— obnoxious in success and obnoxious in failure.

I said, "Hamilton Ashburn sent me."

Phillips jerked forward to look outside. I said, "No, I ran into him at PPA. He told me to tell you that Len Ziskind never saw *GB Dreams Big.*"

Phillips frowned. "Fuck."

He leaned back and pulled his legs and feet into the shadow. He wasn't obvious about it, but he was clearly hiding.

I said, "What happened to *GB Dreams Big*? I thought PPA handled the sale."

Phillips shook his head, but not at me. He said, "Terrible title, too clunky. I couldn't convince Greta to change it."

I checked outside. The vestibule didn't have a door; it had an open arch that faced across the lawn toward Fountain. I expected Doug any minute.

Phillips said, "Do you want to help me?"

I looked at him. "I was hoping *you* could help *me*. I want to read *GB Dreams Big.*"

Phillips shushed me and pointed to the bench again. I sat

down at an angle so I could watch out. I lowered my voice. "What's going on?"

Phillips hunched my direction. "How close are the cops to catching Greta's killer?"

He might've seen me around the Casa, but I decided to pretend all the way. I shrugged. "I don't even know who they suspect. What did the cops tell you?"

"I haven't talked to them and don't intend to."

I played shocked. "But you and Greta were—!"

Phillips shook his head. "Why do you think I didn't identify myself that day at my place?"

"You were pissed that I searched your garage."

Phillips shook his head. "I can't afford another scandal, Ann, I cannot. First there's *The Last Real Man*. Then Ted is murdered— you know about Ted Abadi."

I nodded.

"Ted dies, then Greta dies, and I'm friends with them both. I can't afford to be involved. I'm almost fucked as it is—this Greta thing could fuck me for good. I have to keep my name out of it until the cops catch the killer. It's the only chance I have to save my career, the *only* chance."

I said, "How can I help?"

There was a noise on the cement walk outside the vestibule. Phillips froze. I stuck my head out, thinking I'd see Doug. It was a mailman. I pulled my head back. The mailman came in and stuffed two mailboxes. Phillips and I waited until the noise stopped and the footsteps were gone.

I whispered, "How can I help?"

Phillips leaned forward to peek out the alcove. I saw sweat on his face. He wasn't as calm as he acted.

He leaned back. "A few days before Greta died, there was an argument. Scott Dolgin, Barry Melling, Greta, me. Scott and Barry wanted our script for their production company—Greta and I thought they were a farce. She'd already pitched the story to Len Ziskind. We wanted PPA to represent us."

I said, "I heard you and Greta hadn't been writing partners for years. How did you get back together?"

I wanted to know. I also wanted to stretch the conversation. Something big must have broken at Lynnda-Ellen's, or else Doug would've come by now.

Phillips said, "We'd been in contact about a year. She'd read my ads about *Last Real Man* and called to support me. I was taking a lot of heat for the ads—Ted hated them—it was nice to have someone agree with me. I regret the ads now, I don't regret the impulse. Studio movies are bad—the Industry needs to be honest with itself and stand up for artistic quality."

I said, "Ashburn says you care too much about movies."

Phillips shrugged. "Fuck Ham—Ham's a company man. For him it's the Industry first—for Greta and me, movies are first. Is it so fucking radical to say that the star system is killing us? I know stars sell movies, stars have *always* sold movies. But someone has to say no to them. Did Joan Crawford or Clark Gable write the great Crawford and Gable pictures? That's what happens today. Movie stars and their agents want control, and studios kowtow because they're geared for the global market and your international audience pays for stars. *Last Real Man* made a profit, you know. It tanked here and grossed two hundred million worldwide."

I smiled. "Will you see any of it?"

Phillips shook his head. "Fuck those dickheads—I spent my fee trying to stop production. My point is, since most of what we make is kiss-kiss-bang-bang for the global market, why not make *good* kiss-kiss-bang-bang instead of bad? The popcorn crowd in Slobovia doesn't know the difference."

"You could always write non-Hollywood movies."

Phillips just laughed.

I reached and patted the alcove wall. Apartment number six was on the other side. "Did you think the Georgette Bauerdorf story would make good kiss-kiss-bang-bang?"

Phillips nodded. "Not good—great. Six or so months ago I was desperate for work. Greta had a super subject and a first draft but her typical problems with structure. I beefed up the male role and rewrote the story into a straight homicide investigation."

"Who kills Georgette Bauerdorf?"

Phillips laughed. "You should've heard the fights we had on that subject! It was the hairiest time in our entire collaboration. Greta thought she knew who'd actually done it. If I told you the name, you'd think she was insane."

"How would Greta know who the killer was?"

"She didn't, she had no facts. Oh yes, sorry, she talked to one old lady who couldn't remember what happened yesterday much less in 1944. I kidded Greta about it — Gloria Steinem meets Sherlock Holmes. She wanted to solve an obscure woman-killing sixty years later. We might get a feature in *Ms.*"

Phillips twirled his finger like, whoopee. I sat stumped. Doug had said one-tenth: I couldn't introduce Jules Silverman or the Casa de Amor without revealing too much. *Where was Doug?*

I said, "I want to read the script."

Phillips leaned toward me. "Then *you* have to find it. I can't look myself right now, I'm out of circulation."

"You must have another copy."

Phillips shook his head. "Greta and I were too broke to pay for extra xeroxing."

"What about the disk?"

"There's no disk, nothing on hard drive, no copies anywhere except that one." Phillips clenched a fist.

"Something happened to it, and I think I know what. Greta was supposed to take the script to PPA the week she died. If Len hasn't seen it, it means it never arrived. Scott must have stolen it somehow, it and the disk. That's what our argument was about. Scott and Barry wanted the script for In-Casa Productions, Greta and I wanted PPA to legitimize us with the Industry."

I said, "But Dolgin called PPA last week looking for it."

Phillips frowned. "Then it's Barry. If it isn't Scott, it's Barry. My name's not officially on the script, now Barry's trying to fuck me out of credit and a fee. He has his own producing ambitions — I wouldn't be surprised if he fucked Scott, too."

Phillips stood up. "You have to talk to Barry."

I thought of Barry and Dolgin's mutual alibi. I whispered, "Do you think they could have murdered Greta for it?"

Phillips did a weird thing with his head. He turned it away, then turned it back as if his neck was stiff. He sat down on the bench closer to me.

He whispered, "Listen, Ann, you have to understand—and this is going to sound callous and fucked up—but I *can't* care who murdered Greta. Ted Abadi and Greta Stenholm were my best friends in the world—*real friends*, in a town where you have working relationships at most. But I can't get involved in the murders at *any* level for *any* reason. I try not to even think about them. I want the cops to catch whoever did it, but *I want my fucking career back!* I have to save it and get it back on track—I fucking *have* to!"

He stood up. "Talk to Barry, find my script. I'll call you later."

He walked out of the vestibule. He adjusted his baseball cap, checking right and left before he crossed the lawn. I jumped up and followed him. "Can I buy you lunch?"

Phillips shook his head and kept going. There was no way to stop him without muscle.

I ran to my car, grabbed the phone, and dialed Doug's pager. I hung up and watched Phillips drive off down Fountain. I gave Doug three minutes to call back. When he didn't, I tried Northeast Station because I didn't know Lynnda-Ellen's last name. The cop at the switchboard put me through to Smith. Smith said that Doug was in conference with two DA's Bureau cops. They'd showed up without warning; it was about Doug's grand-jury appearance. I told Smith what had just happened with Neil John Phillips. Smith agreed it was important. He couldn't get away, but he'd have Doug call me the minute he was free.

I walked back to apartment number six and knocked on the door. It was late morning—no one answered. I walked outside and tried the front window but the curtains were closed against the sun. I couldn't find a cut-through, so I walked around the building to the alley. The hill in back was steep; it had been dug out for access to a half basement. The caretaker's apartment under number six was boarded up. I climbed the fire escape to the landing outside Georgette's kitchen.

I pressed my face to the window.

The kitchen had been remodeled since the '40s. I imagined what it would've looked like with old appliances and cupboards. I pictured Georgette. She was exhausted after a long day entertaining the troops—a tea party at Pickfair and five hours at the Hollywood Canteen. I pictured her in pink satin pajamas and running the kitchen tap. I saw her drop a tray because she was tired, or nervous about the phone call from her fiancé in El Paso. Or maybe she dropped the tray when the doorbell rang after midnight.

Georgette had known her killer. A stranger couldn't have forced his way into the apartment. The neighbors would have heard something; the caretakers would have heard something. Jules Silverman talked his way in. He pleaded homesickness, or the war, or love. He appealed to Georgette's sympathy. But what he wanted was sex—

A man yelled from the foot of the fire escape. I looked over the railing. He identified himself as the manager. He ordered me off the premises immediately or else he'd call the Sheriff's. I climbed down the fire escape and left the premises.

CHAPTER
TWENTY-TWO

BARRY WAS in his office reading the *Wall Street Journal*. He had the front section spread out flat on his desk. He glanced up to see who'd shut his door. He turned a page.

"There you are, Ann — we need to talk. Let me finish this."

I read the headline upside down; it was a piece about international media conglomerates acquiring small production companies. I smiled. At one time Barry had wanted the *Millennium* to lead a Hollywood trust-busting crusade. I researched antitrust law, and Mark researched Viacom, AOL Time Warner, and the other studio owners. We were ready to write, when Barry pulled the plug on us and never mentioned trust-busting or media cartels again.

I took a chair and shut my eyes.

I was in a strategic fix. Last night Doug had said there were too many suspects and too many motives. I was feeling that difficulty now. I couldn't just barge in and demand answers from Barry. Almost every question I wanted to ask tied him to murder, or tied him to people maybe tied to murder. I couldn't accuse him bald-facedly. I wasn't authorized to reveal the state of Doug's case, which certain questions would. I thought my brain would melt trying to figure the right approach —

"*Ann!*"

I jerked up in my seat. Barry was staring at me. He said, "You were asleep." He closed his newspaper.

"Who are those reporters I'm supposed to talk to? I want your Lockwood piece in the can for two issues from now."

I said, "I'm still looking for a script called GB Dreams Big—I asked you about it the other night. I have to read it for the piece on Greta Stenholm."

Barry waved his hand. "Don't worry about that, I've postponed it indefinitely. I've got too much material backlogged."

"Greta is going to need a series—I want to call it 'A Bright Young Woman.'"

Barry rolled his chair forward and rested both elbows on the desktop. He said, "I received a disturbing phone call this morning."

"From?"

"I was told you were with Lockwood while he interviewed a certain person."

Easy to trace that phone call to its source. Lynnda-Ellen had called Hannah Silverman; Hannah Silverman called Barry.

I clucked my tongue. "I was surprised and saddened to learn about Jules Silverman's tastes—a man of his age and prominence."

Barry was not amused. "You can't use it. You can't repeat it to anyone."

"I also know Greta Stenholm asked you to print allegations that Silverman was a murder suspect in 1944. I can't use that either. I'm not interested in slandering Jules Silverman, or why you lied to me about knowing Greta. I'm only interested in her script, GB Dreams Big. Do you know where it is?"

"Did you tell Lockwood I lied?"

I shook my head. "Lockwood and I are not close. I was at Lynnda-Ellen's because I crashed her party last night and had information Lockwood could use. Do you know where the script is?"

"Have I made myself clear about Jules Silverman?"

"You have. Does that mean the Greta Stenholm piece is not postponed indefinitely?"

Barry rolled his chair back. He had relaxed. "Check with me later."

"What about GB Dreams Big?"

Barry shrugged. "I only know what I've heard. Greta sold it for six figures and Len Ziskind was the agent."

I said, "PPA never saw it."

Barry shrugged again. "Then I don't know."

"PPA thinks Scott Dolgin had it in development. But since I can't find Dolgin to ask him, I'll ask you. Where is *GB Dreams Big*?"

Barry started to open his newspaper. I stuck my hand out and held it closed.

Barry made a face and looked up. He said, "Greta was hanging around Arnie Tolback before she died. My money's on him for the killer. Ask *him* about the script."

The official Silverman line: Tolback did it.

I said, "You know what I think? I think you're shielding each other to protect your Hollywood interests. You and Dolgin want to protect the Silvermans because they're your ticket into the movie business. *You* want to protect Dolgin because he's In-Casa Productions, and Dolgin's taken a powder to protect himself. I do know the cops searched his apartment—"

"Scott didn't kill her. He was with me when it happened."

I shrugged. "I didn't think he did. What I'm saying is that you make the cops' job more difficult if you cover your ass instead of help."

Barry yanked his newspaper out from under my hand. He said, "I don't give a shit if I make the pigs' job impossible."

I said, "You shouldn't protect Scott Dolgin. He took your ten grand for In-Casa and bought a Range Rover with it."

Barry had tuned me out. He unfolded a second section and started skimming stock prices.

I said, "The murder hurts more than In-Casa. It hurts the *Millennium*'s market value. You want to sell it with Jules Silverman as broker and go into producing full-time."

Barry looked at me and spoke with emphasis. "The paper is *not* for sale. I do *not* want to go into producing full-time."

"You're toning down the film section to attract a mainstream buyer."

Barry sighed. "If you paid attention to marketing surveys, you'd know that our readers have changed. They aren't into heavy discussions of movies anymore. You've lost touch with the zeitgeist out there."

I stood up. Barry said, "Give me those reporters' names. I have time to make calls this afternoon."

I turned and walked out of his office.

"Ann! Get back here!"

I shut his door and ran. I wanted to laugh. Me, a bad liar? That was a brilliant performance—and on less than no sleep.

But Barry's performance was better.

A CALL WAS waiting for me at the switchboard downstairs. A police detective, the receptionist said; she'd paged me five times. I asked her to transfer the call to Vivian's extension and ran and took it in her office. I snatched up the receiver:

"Where were you? I had Neil Phillips trapped in Georgette Bauerdorf's vestibule!"

Doug said, "Tell me what happened."

I replayed the conversation as close to verbatim as I could. I told him I'd revised my impression of Phillips, then revised it again. Phillips was a tough-guy wiener type: all threats and profanity. I knew Doug would get the important points. I only highlighted two items. Phillips had explained the fight we'd heard about from Mrs. May and Isabelle Pavich. And Phillips had accounted for his suspicious behavior—

Doug got buzzed on another line. He put me on hold and came back in a few seconds. The Casa surveillance team needed him. They said that a black Porsche just squealed off and a commotion had broken out in the courtyard. Doug told the surveillance guys to catch the Porsche. He told me to meet him in Culver City chop-chop.

I took surface streets and beat him down to the Casa de Amor. The surveillance guys were holding Arnold Tolback in the backseat of their car. Tolback saw me and waved. I parked out front and ran into the courtyard.

Up the walkway: pandemonium. It centered around the third bungalow on the right. The entire harem was outside in robes and hair curlers. They cried; they screeched; they wailed for Mrs. May to come help. The noise was ghastly. I pushed through them and vaulted up the steps. An old woman had passed out stiff on her porch. She lay half in and half out of the front door.

I squatted down to take a look. It was some kind of seizure. Her mouth dropped open. She drooled and moaned, "He...He... He...He..."

I got a big blast of alcohol fumes.

A fat foot in a turquoise slipper bumped me. I looked up. The muumuu neighbor said, "Our Dorene's a binger, honey. She goes on a toot and forgets to eat."

I put one arm under Dorene, braced myself, and pulled her upright. The neighbors crowded in close. The muumuu neighbor shoved them back and told them to button it. The wailing faded to whimpers. Dorene looked ninety years old and weighed almost nothing; she was a husk. I walked-carried her into the living room and laid her down on the couch.

The living room smelled awful. It was littered with Frito bags and empty bourbon bottles. Judging by the pattern of garbage, Dorene ate, drank, and slept on her couch. Judging by stains, she didn't always make it to the toilet. So much for Mrs. May's mint condition Temple of Love. I covered Dorene with a ragged blanket. I was remembering why I hated drunks.

The muumuu neighbor had followed us inside. She locked the screen door and walked over. She said, "I'm Erma, honey."

I decided that Erma only boozed at night. She didn't realize she'd seen me twice before.

Dorene threw out her arms and moaned, "Nooooooo!" The old girls on the porch heard her. They wailed, "Noooooooooooo!" and pressed their faces to the screen.

Erma took Dorene's arms and pushed them down. She'd had practice at this. She found a bottle of bourbon and fed Dorene a pick-me-up. It was the same expensive small-batch stuff as Erma's. Dorene slurped the bourbon into her system. I kneeled beside the couch.

I said, "Dorene, who is 'He'? Is it Arnold Tolback? Why 'No'? What did he say to you?"

Her eyelids flickered. She was barely conscious, but her throat muscles worked. She sucked in bourbon, dribbling out of the corners of her mouth. Erma held the bottle steady.

I bent closer. "Who is 'He,' Dorene?"

Erma shook her head. "Dorie's out for the count, honey."

I said, "Does anyone have keys to the bungalows? Did Mrs. May leave a duplicate set for emergencies?"

Erma dug into the pocket of her muumuu. It bulged with candy bars. She dug around and handed me a ring of door keys.

I stood up and headed for the kitchen. Dorene was a junk saver. She didn't use her kitchen for cooking or eating: she used it to store junk. She used the oven to store junk, and the floor and counters to store more junk. I kicked a passage through overflowing sacks; I saw logos for Westside stores that dated back decades. Junk blocked the kitchen door. I moved bags and boxes to clear it and still couldn't get out; the hinges were rusty. I forced the door wide enough to squeeze through and ran up the path, around to Mrs. May's.

The fifth key was the right key. I let myself into her front room and checked around. Nothing had changed since Monday night. Her TV was still showing the Garden channel, her sandwich and tea remains were still on the table. I ran back to the bathroom; her purse was still there. I ran to the kitchen. The khaki pants and white sneakers still sat on the counter, still stained with blood and dirt. The kitchen door was the way I'd left it—chained.

I ran to the front door and let myself out. Doug was coming up the walk with Arnold Tolback. He saw me on Mrs. May's porch and stopped. He pointed at Scott Dolgin's bungalow.

"Mr. Tolback, would you wait there please?"

Tolback grinned at me. "Hey, loudmouth. You make it to Lynnda's party last night?"

Doug pointed at Dolgin's again. Tolback shrugged, went up to Dolgin's porch, and sat down. He pulled out a cell phone and dialed it. Doug took my arm and walked me under the arch. A screen of roses hid us. We heard Tolback yell at someone.

I jingled the keys. "Authorized entry for a change."

Doug said, "Where did you get them?"

I explained about Dorene, Erma, and the alcoholic seizure. I said, "The pants and sneakers are still in Mrs. May's kitchen. They haven't been touched."

Doug lowered his voice. "I need you to do something. I need you to look around inside Phillips's and Dolgin's place."

I lowered my voice. "I'm shocked."

Doug didn't smile. "It's desperation, plain and simple. We need some kind of a break—"

"*Detective Lockwood!*"

Tolback. Doug didn't turn his head. "Yes?"

"How long you think this is going to take? Ballpark it, I have people waiting."

"Not more than an hour, Mr. Tolback. Probably less."

"How much less?"

Doug whispered, "Phillips's and Dolgin's. Don't let anyone see you. Bring the keys back to Mrs. Johnson's—Dorene. I'll be there."

Tolback called, "How *much* less?"

Doug took off up the walkway. I took off around the bungalows to Scott Dolgin's kitchen door. I found the key, let myself in, and did a fast tour. The blinds were down but I could hear Tolback on the porch. I checked everywhere. I got fingerprint dust all over my hands. Greta's suitcases were gone; Isabelle Pavich's purse was gone. The picture of the Thalberg Building still hung crooked, and the blood hadn't been cleaned up. Nothing indicated that Dolgin had been there since Monday.

I snuck out, around, and down the back path to Phillips's bungalow. His kitchen door was chain locked. I ran back around to the front. Tolback was busy with a phone call—he didn't notice me go by. Up the walkway, the neighbors had disappeared. I ducked past Dorene's bungalow and saw them in the living room. They sat in a semicircle around Doug.

I tried the key in Phillips's front door. The door opened two inches: it was chained, too. Phillips had to be home. I jumped off his porch and ran next door. I ran in without knocking, and tossed the keys to Erma. Dorene was conked out on the couch. Erma had poured herself some bourbon and served the neighbors from Dorene's stash. I signaled Doug to come talk. The minute his back was turned, the women tittered. One old girl yanked the curlers out of her hair. Another one found a lipstick and passed it around.

I pulled Doug outside. I said low, "Phillips is home—both his doors are chained inside. He must have slipped by when the surveillance guys were chasing Tolback. What did Tolback say to Dorene?"

"He didn't speak to her. None of the tenants would let him in."

"*She's* Silverman's alibi for that night, isn't she? Her name is in the Bauerdorf file."

Doug nodded. "I'll take care of Phillips—you talk to Tolback. I told him to tell you everything."

He walked back into Dorene's; I heard more girlish titters. I walked down the path to Scott Dolgin's. Tolback was still on the phone.

"...they go ahead without me. I might make it for coffee.... That cheapskate should pick up the tab.... Yeah, I'll call you when the cops cut me loose."

Tolback flipped the phone shut. "This is blowing my schedule. I have business."

I sat down beside him. I said, "Nice suit."

Tolback opened his jacket and showed me the label. He said, "Armani, what else?"

I said, "The Silvermans have spread it around that you murdered Greta Stenholm."

Tolback just laughed. "Jules and Hannah are trying to shaft me. Deals are falling through for no reason, people aren't taking my calls—I got bad breath all of a sudden."

"What does that have to do with the Casa de Amor?"

Tolback's cell phone rang. He flipped it open. "Yeah? . . . So screw him and the horse he rode in on. . . . Yeah, call those guys, then call me back."

Tolback flipped the phone shut. "More people not taking my calls. How's this for a lead, loudmouth? 'Jules Silverman—the Conscience of Hollywood—has a conscience for shit.' He's a sex pervert and a killer. Don't you want to take notes?"

Tolback's cell phone rang again. He flipped it open. "Yeah? . . . Yeah . . . Yeah, I'll know by the end of the day."

He flipped the cell phone shut. I said, "Could you turn that off?"

Tolback shook his head. He flipped the lid open and shut for a joke. I said, "I want to hear about Greta."

"She came to work for me last November, after I started dating Hannah. I recognized her name because Hannah's nutso about her and Ted Abadi. I shouldn't have hired her, yeah—but she looked good answering phones and my partners wanted to bang her."

"Did you and she have an affair?"

Tolback laughed. "I don't bang losers. Besides, she didn't sleep around—she still loved Ted."

"I heard she did sleep around."

"You heard wrong, loud. She would've had more luck if she put out. I told her so but she didn't listen."

I said, "Then you fired her."

Tolback said, "Yeah, Hannah made me do it in March. But I didn't know the whole story until two weeks ago—I just thought somebody finked on me. I couldn't do anything for Greta in the Industry so I—"

"Couldn't, or wouldn't?"

The cell phone rang. Tolback flipped it open. "Yeah? . . . You're bullshitting me? That meeting's been set up for months! . . . They *said* that? . . . Yeah, call her people and call me back."

Tolback flipped his phone shut. "Jules, that old cocksucker. I'll strangle him myself."

I said, "You couldn't, or wouldn't, do anything for Greta?"

Tolback laughed. "Greta had a bad rep and I don't promote lost causes. Hey, I made Lynnda give her a job—I get points for that. Sure I was messing with Hannah and Jules, but not the way they think. They think I'm in on the blackmail. Why would I bother? Because Jules hates my guts and Hannah turns out to be a lousy connection? Please, the Silvermans aren't the only game in town. They just think they are."

I said, "What is 'the whole story'?"

"The *whole* story is a riot. Greta tried blackmailing Jules a total of, check this out, *three* times. You gotta admire her balls. The first was in March, with the communist witch-hunts and the old murder. Communists—*peh*, who cares? That's why Hannah made me get rid of her. The second was two weeks ago. Greta caught Jules on film at Lynnda's and sent him the pictures. Hannah kicked me out of the house for that. I saw Greta the same day and she told me everything. Ask me if I laughed my ass off."

I said, "Did you lend Greta money that day?"

"Sure, yeah, probably. Since I knew her, she was always broke."

So she spent Tolback's money on her movie marathon the Friday before she was killed. A minor item for her predeath calendar.

I said, "What about the third blackmail?"

"The third was the day of your man, Barry Melling's, party. She told Jules she found a lady who'd blow his murder alibi out of the water. She told me the same thing. That's why I'm in swinging Culver City, and talking to you. If Hannah and Jules want to shaft me, I can dig up the dirt and shaft them back. The dirt on Jules is *here*."

Tolback's cell phone rang. He flipped it open. "Yeah?... What did the lawyer say?... Call me back, yeah."

Tolback flipped his cell phone closed.

I said, "Greta asked for two things in her blackmail demand— twenty thousand dollars and something else. What was the 'something else'? Did she want Ted Abadi's killer, or Silverman's confession to the Bauerdorf murder?"

"She wanted a deal."

"For her screenplay?"

Tolback laughed. "Yeah, that farkakte *GB-ya-de-ya-de-ya* she never shut up about."

"But I heard she was taking it to Leonard Ziskind."

Tolback shrugged. "Len and Jules are tight—Jules has money in PPA. Don't ask me what Greta was thinking. All I know is, Jules and Hannah are trying to shaft me, and I'm going to shaft them back double."

We heard a door slam and footsteps come down the walk. Doug appeared; he was wiping lipstick off his chin. He said to Tolback, "Do you think you can locate Miss Silverman?"

Tolback smiled. "With pleasure."

He flipped open his cell phone and punched a number. I mouthed to Doug, "What about Phillips?"

Doug shook his head. He mouthed, "Not answering the door."

Tolback said, "Yeah, hang on." He handed the cell phone to Doug. Doug walked away. I couldn't hear what he was saying.

Tolback passed me his business card. He said, "Let's do a meal. I give you the lowdown on Jules and you write a big exposé for your newspaper. 'Holocaust Revenge—Jew Kills German!'"

Tolback laughed at his own humor. Doug walked back and handed Tolback his cell phone. Doug said, "Miss Silverman is meeting me in Beverly Hills. You're welcome to join us."

Tolback checked the time. "I have people waiting at Joss." He pointed at me. "*Big* exposé."

He walked out of the courtyard, dialing his phone.

I said, "I don't believe it—Hannah would never agree to meet you."

Doug nodded. "I told her we tailed Tolback to the Casa de Amor. She'll show up here if she thinks I'm miles from Culver City—"

He was interrupted by familiar voices.

Doug and I both turned around. Sergeant McManus and Deputy Gadtke walked under the archway and crossed the path toward us. McManus was looking solemn. Gadtke had picked a rose and stuck it in his buttonhole.

Doug HAD called the Sheriff's guys on his way down to the Casa.

We stood on Dolgin's porch while he updated McManus and Gadtke. Everybody kept their voices quiet and I was allowed to listen in. I learned that they'd found Dolgin's truck a block south of the Sony lot. I also learned that if Phillips didn't want to answer his door, the cops didn't have a lever to force him. Doug checked the time as he talked. He expected Hannah Silverman inside half an hour. Nobody doubted she would come.

I asked for the background on Mrs. Dorene Johnson and McManus gave it to me.

She'd moved into the Casa de Amor in 1943. She was nineteen at the time—which made her seventy-seven now, not the ninety she looked. She was a dancer extra at MGM; her boyfriend was an MGM executive. She was among the people who placed Jules Silverman at the Casa on October 11, 1944. Everyone had been liquored up, but Dorene had special status: the Sheriff's singled her out as a "problem drinker" in their original report. She'd also claimed she spent the crucial hours after midnight alone with Silverman. She was considered the weakest witness because of her alcoholism. She was also the only witness still living.

Dorene's "Mrs." was for show—like Mrs. May's was. There'd never been a Mr. Johnson, or any jobs after she got too old for the chorus. But she did have a sugar daddy. The Casa tenants all knew it. Someone had paid Dorene's bills and supplied her bourbon for decades. No one had ever seen him; no one knew his name. The cops figured it was Jules Silverman. They figured that a blotto Dorene was Silverman's insurance against arrest. Silverman probably hoped the bourbon would kill her.

McManus didn't know why it *hadn't* killed her. Dorene's capacity for booze was incredible — even Gadtke was impressed.

He and Gadtke had seen her every day since Arnold Tolback revealed the Greta-Georgette-Dorene link. They'd tried smooth talk, and they'd tried intimidation; they had never engaged Dorene in a coherent conversation. She'd been drinking hard for two weeks and her toot coincided with a man's visit. Various neighbors described the guy: he sounded like Jules Silverman in a dark wig and sunglasses. The cops guessed he received Greta's third blackmail threat and ran straight to the Casa. What happened then, the cops didn't know. But it had a drastic effect on Dorene.

Doug checked his watch again. He said we should set up for Hannah Silverman.

Gadtke was sent to hide on Mrs. May's porch. He would beep Doug when Hannah showed — and stop her if she tried to run. They wanted me to stay outside with Gadtke. I balked and there was no time to argue; I would hide inside Dorene's place with Doug and McManus. As Mrs. May's proxy, Erma had given the cops free access.

We walked into Dorene's front room. Dorene was alone. She'd come to and was sitting up rigid on the couch. Someone had wrapped a blanket around her shoulders. Her eyes were bloodshot but she looked semirational.

Doug bent down to talk to her. McManus said they'd seen Dorene in that condition before. She could hear and understand, but she couldn't respond. Doug might get a facial twitch if he was lucky.

Doug took Dorene's hand and explained very slowly what he wanted. Dorene batted what was left of her eyelashes. She loved the male attention; it was sort of pitiful. Doug told her they were there to protect her from Jules Silverman. Silverman's daughter was due any minute. All Dorene had to do was let Hannah talk. That was all: let Hannah talk. Did Dorene understand?

Dorene moved her lower lip. Doug looked at McManus for a reading. McManus shrugged and crossed his fingers.

Doug's beeper beeped. He stood up and pointed me to a love seat in the corner. There was so much junk piled around, we could've hidden almost anywhere. McManus ducked into the kitchen. He knew the terrain; he didn't kick any paper sacks. Doug crouched behind the love seat with me.

Ten seconds went by... twenty...

The screen door creaked. Hannah Silverman's voice: "Mrs. Johnson?... We've never met but you know Daddy, my father, Jules Silverman."

Hannah was putting on saccharine sweet. The screen banged shut, footsteps approached the couch. I smelled expensive perfume and heard bracelets clink.

Hannah said, "A friend of mine came to see you this morning. Daddy needs to know what you told him."

Silence. A small swish and a thud. I guessed that Hannah sat down on the coffee table.

She said, "What did you tell my friend, Mrs. Johnson?" Her tone was wheedly and singsong.

More silence.

Hannah said, "What is it?"

More silence. Hannah said, "I don't understand. What's in the kitchen?"

I peeked over the back of the love seat. Dorene was pointing out where McManus was hiding. She had her arm lifted; she had enough energy for that.

Hannah said, "Is there something in your kitchen?"

Dorene nodded. She had energy for that, too. I signaled to Doug: Dorene's blowing our cover.

Doug stood up right away. I stood up with him. Dorene made a whimper sound. Hannah swiveled around and saw us. Standing up, she said, "This is entrapment."

McManus appeared from the kitchen. Hannah looked down at Dorene. Dorene closed her eyes.

Hannah said to Doug, "You haven't proven anything."

What had happened to the screaming princess? She was being superrestrained—not like her normal self.

Doug said, "We'd like to speak to your father."

Hannah dug out her car keys. "Daddy had a heart attack last night. It was a mild one, but he thinks it's time to clear the air before you people kill him."

At "heart attack" McManus and Doug exchanged a look. Hannah said, "I appreciate your loyalty, Mrs. Johnson. I'll tell Daddy."

Dorene sat there with her eyes closed. Hannah walked outside; Doug followed her. I watched them through the front window.

Gadtke stepped out from the bushes and caught Hannah. He handed her his cell phone. I heard him say, "Call Daddy-poo. Tell him he can have a lawyer present."

McManus leaned down and poked Dorene. "You're faking it, lady. Now we know."

Dorene did not twitch, did not move. She looked mummified.

JULES SILVERMAN was convalescing at home. I reviewed what I knew about him as Hannah walked us through the house. Producer and philanthropist; liberal, recluse, perennial Hollywood cheese. The public saw Silverman as the conscience of the Industry. Movies buffs saw him as a spiritual heir to Louis Mayer: a producer of wholesome high-budget entertainment. He'd made mountains of money in the business, but never a great movie. His films were almost never revived except for Cinemascope festivals or festivals of kitsch. I'd only seen one Jules Silverman Presentation. It was a '50s Bible epic—and one was enough.

Hannah led us into a huge den in a far wing. The den was slate and glass, the furniture was contemporary, and the art belonged in a national gallery. Jules collected the French Impressionists. An oil portrait of him and Hannah hung above the fireplace. The mantel showcased a single Oscar—his Irving Thalberg Award for producing. Awards, plaques, and tokens of presidential esteem filled the shelves. A model stood on a stand by the door; he'd built a cancer ward for a local hospital.

Hannah said, "Daddy?"

A big fire was burning in the fireplace. Jules Silverman sat in a wheelchair in front of it. He wore pajamas and a cashmere robe. He was hooked up to an intravenous drip and an oxygen cylinder; a plastic tube fed into one nostril. There was a table at his elbow. It held water, pills, a jug of carrot juice, and that card from Hannah I'd seen: "Daddy—love, love, love, forever and ever and ever." A uniformed nurse sat behind him on a couch. She was reading *Variety* and fanning herself. The den was baking hot.

Hannah said, "Daddy, the police are here." She had a wispy little-girl voice just for him.

Jules wheeled around and gave us a cold look up and down. Hannah bent over him whispering. The nurse took *Variety* and walked out of the room. We watched as Hannah fussed with Jules. Except for age and sex, the Silvermans were identical. And they had the same imperious edge. In Hannah it was snottiness; in Jules it was condescension. Hannah got down on the floor to adjust Jules's pajama cuff. The cops exchanged a glance. I remembered what Steve Lampley had said about the demented father-daughter act.

Hannah stopped fussing and introduced us. Jules indicated the couch. Doug and I sat down. Jules wheeled himself to face Doug. Hannah pulled up an ottoman so she could sit by her father's knee. McManus and Gadtke sat in chairs out of Jules's line of sight.

Doug cleared his throat. Jules said, "You're the detective who was involved in the Burger King incident." His voice was strong.

Doug nodded.

"Then we find ourselves in a similar situation. Like you, I'm the victim of attempts to destroy my character and reputation with no basis in fact."

I saw Gadtke nudge McManus and make the jerk-off sign—very discreet. The heat in the den was getting me drowsy; I almost smiled.

Doug opened his notebook. Jules said, "Yes, write this down. I did *not* murder Georgette Bauerdorf on the morning of October 12, 1944."

Hannah stroked her father's thigh. Jules said, "*Write that down.*"

Doug didn't write it down. He said, "What is your relationship with Mrs. Dorene Johnson?"

"Dorene never told the Stenholm girl anything, because there is nothing to tell. The Stenholm girl came to me pretending that Dorene—"

Doug cut him off. "Please answer the question, Mr. Silverman."

Hannah said, "You must stay calm, Daddy." She squeezed his thigh and frowned at Doug.

Jules patted her. He said, "I met Dorene during the war. We socialized when she worked at Metro, but weren't close. I haven't seen her in forty years or more."

Doug checked his notebook. "You did not visit Mrs. Johnson at the Casa de Amor in Culver City on Monday, August twenty-seventh?"

"No."

"How long have you supported her financially?"

Jules nodded. "I was told you were a clever man."

Gadtke made the jerk-off sign again. Only I saw it; McManus was watching the Silvermans.

Jules said, "It's true, I pay Dorene's bills. That sounds suspicious given what I just said about our relationship, but Dorene was the girlfriend of a very good friend. He left her with nothing, and it's not as if Dorene could go out and work. You've met her—she's been drinking heavily since I've known her. Some years ago she asked for help, and I'm fortunate to be able to make that kind of gesture."

Silverman lifted a hand to indicate our fabulous surroundings. Doug checked his notebook. He said, "Miss Stenholm contacted you on Monday, August twenty-seventh. She claimed to have new information that implicated you in the death of Georgette Bauerdorf."

Hannah said, "Arnie is such dreck."

Jules said, "I don't remember the precise date. She made several attempts to blackmail me."

Doug said, "Mr. Tolback has provided a chronology for us."

Hannah leaned up and whispered in her father's ear. Doug said, "Miss Silverman?"

Hannah said, "I haven't told Daddy what happened at Lynnda's last night. I wanted to wait until he was feeling better."

Doug said, "We've impounded your twenty thousand dollars, Mr. Silverman. It will be returned to you after we make our case."

"You have the negatives also, I trust."

Hannah said, "It isn't *our* twenty thousand dollars — it's Lynnda's. All this is *her* fault. Why should *we* pay for her negligence?"

Jules said, "And I'm not convinced she wasn't involved in the blackmail herself."

Hannah stroked his thigh. "Daddy, Lynnda called today. The police threatened her with a tax audit. She practically threatened me if you didn't help her."

Jules spread his hands to include all the cops. "You see how it is, gentlemen? When you reach my position, everyone wants something from you. I retired from public life because of the constant demands."

Gadtke smirked. But I gave Jules credit. The cops had seen him naked and getting spanked, and he turned it from an embarrassment into a persecution conspiracy.

Doug said, "You were scheduled to attend a party given by Barry Melling for Scott Dolgin on the night of August twenty-seventh."

Jules shook his head. "Melling told you that, no doubt. He called me from the party a number of times and begged me to come. He thinks he's a friend of mine. He thinks he can use me to break into the film business."

Hannah stroked her father's thigh. She said, "Barry's a bug."

Jules nodded. "You must understand something. The Stenholm girl didn't actually think I murdered the other one. She wanted a movie deal. She couldn't obtain it by valid means so she tried to extort it from me. But I don't extort easily, and I don't believe in free rides. My father repaired shoes in Boyle Heights. Everything I have, I earned the hard way."

Jules coughed. It was a miniscule cough, but Hannah leaped up. She pressed a button on the wheelchair.

"I'm calling the nurse, Daddy! These people are leaving!"

Doug stood up. McManus and Gadtke followed his lead. Doug said, "Thank you for your time, Mr. Silverman."

The nurse burst in on the run. Hannah gave Jules a glass of water and a pill. Doug, McManus, and Gadtke walked out. I was slow to follow them; the heat had me half asleep and sweating.

Hannah caught up from behind and shoved my shoulder. She said, "Get out of this house!"

I stopped dead. We were alone in the hallway. I said, "If Barry's a bug, why do you sleep with him?"

Hannah gasped.

"Or does he just lick your Gestapo boots?"

"You little *nobody*! I'll have you *fired*—!"

I counted on my fingers. "Edward Abadi, Arnold Tolback, Barry Melling. You're lucky your father is Jules Silverman. You'd never get laid otherwise."

Hannah swung her arm back and tried to slap me. I ducked, she missed. I caught her off balance and pushed her into the wall. She fell over a Degas bronze and started to scream at me.

I ran outside and joined the cops on the front terrace. We crossed the circle drive to the fountain. The cops took off their sport coats and loosened their ties; everyone was sweating from the den. The spray from the fountain felt good. I thought about all the questions they *should* have asked Jules Silverman.

Gadtke pulled a dangly orange thing out of his jacket. It was a rubber chicken. He went, "Weeeeee! Ker-splash!" He tossed it into the fountain and let it bob around in the water.

Hannah stormed onto the terrace. She screamed, *"Get that bitch off this property now!"*

She stormed back into the house.

Doug raised his eyebrows at me. I said, "What about Ted Abadi, or the MGM transcripts stolen from Greta's apartment? What about Silverman's thumbprint on the lightbulb?"

Gadtke scooped the chicken out of the water. He squeezed its beak and did a chicken squawk. "I'm a self-made rooster! My pappy boffed little red hens in East L.A.! Now I have a big old coop in Malibu!"

Doug said, "Sergeant McManus checked the evidence locker. The lightbulb was discarded years ago."

McManus nodded. "The note said that the glass broke."

I said, "There's still the lab report."

Gadtke shook the chicken's head. McManus said, "That isn't sufficient. We need a confession or a sober Dorene—*if* she'll retract her original testimony, and even then . . ."

Doug said, "It was a first interview. We were feeling Silverman out to gauge our shot at a confession."

McManus nodded. I said, "Maybe the heart attack will help."

Gadtke pointed the chicken at Doug. The chicken squawked, "We both averted tragedy at Burger King! They tried to deep-fry my rubber ass for a sandwich!"

I laughed. Doug smiled and shook his head.

McManus said, "He'll never confess. He's had fifty-eight years to rationalize his conduct and convince himself he's innocent."

The chicken squawked. "It was an accident! I didn't mean to choke her! It was an accident!"

Gadtke grabbed the chicken's neck. "He's choking the chicken! Aagghh!"

Everybody had to laugh; even McManus laughed. I said, "But the heart attack could help. Silverman might be afraid of God."

McManus said, "If he really did have a heart attack."

Doug nodded. "If he did."

CHAPTER
TWENTY-FOUR

WE LEFT McManus and Gadtke parked on the road above Jules Silverman's compound. Gadtke had his cell phone out: he was checking medical sources for confirmation on the state of Silverman's health. They told me that Jules pulled a sick number after Ted Abadi was murdered. He was suddenly diagnosed with kidney stones, pancreatitis, eczema, and a smorgasbord of other complaints. It restricted the Sheriff's access for months.

I rode back to town with Doug. He took the coast highway east and turned inland at Sunset. I asked if that was the scenic route to Culver City. He said he didn't want to drop me at the Casa de Amor just yet. He wanted to see the Bauerdorf apartments and the place where Neil Phillips and I had talked. I said fine, I didn't have any better ideas.

Doug wasn't in a discussing mood. I asked why he was anxious for a break in the case. He shook his head. Did someone give him a deadline? He shook his head. Why hadn't he told me about the blackmail attempts plural? He'd heard it from Tolback a week ago? He shook his head again. He said he wanted to think and I could figure out the *why*s myself.

So he drove and I stared out the window at the plush real estate. By the time we hit Brentwood I was falling asleep. I dug out my herbal pep pills and swallowed four dry. Doug saw me make a face. He tapped my leg and pointed to the backseat. I looked behind, saw a bottle of water, reached for it, and drank down half in one breath. Doug didn't comment. He checked his watch, then the clock on the dashboard. It was 6 P.M., and the going on Sunset was slow.

I couldn't guess why he needed a break in the case. I *could* guess why he didn't tell me about the blackmail attempts: he didn't trust Greta. He'd decided early on she was mentally unstable. He'd known that her address and appointment books were fiction; he'd known that her revived career was fiction. Nothing she said in the last months of her life was reliable. Without corroboration, Doug wouldn't believe she'd told Arnold Tolback the true facts.

Now we had partial corroboration. But I couldn't see that it helped us much. When I laid out the whole scheme, it didn't make sense.

Greta said she tried to blackmail Jules Silverman three times. The first try was in March. The last try was August 27, the day of the night she was murdered.

She used a different lever each time. The first time it was Steve Lampley's library find—the transcripts for the abandoned book on the blacklist at MGM. The second time it was the picture of Silverman getting spanked. The third time it was Mrs. Dorene Johnson.

The second and third attempts happened for sure. Lynnda-Ellen and the Silvermans confirmed the second, the Silvermans confirmed the third. The first attempt was less sure. Jules had finessed it in the interview. He only mentioned Georgette Bauerdorf; he never mentioned the HUAC stool-pigeon stuff or selling out his Jewish colleagues. But two items said the first attempt happened. One: Hannah made Tolback fire Greta in March. Two: the transcripts were stolen from Greta's apartment sometime last winter. Technically they might be called a coincidence. Add them to Greta's claim and Steve Lampley's suspicion and they were good enough for me.

What I didn't get were the demands. Three blackmail attempts, three different levers—but the *same* demands all along?

Tolback said she'd asked for money and a movie deal. Jules Silverman said the same thing. So did Dale Denney's misdelivered message: "My client says to forget the second part. It isn't doable."

But—

GB Dreams Big was barely conceived by last March. Why would Greta be thinking movie deal at that stage? More: why would she think her only chance for a deal was blackmail? I tended to believe Steve Lampley's guess. Greta went after Jules the first time to dislodge Hannah's alibi. She wanted a confession on Ted Abadi; she thought Hannah had killed him.

Then—

Greta wrote *GB Dreams Big*. She wrote it in the months between the first and second blackmails. Neil Phillips reworked it. He talked her out of naming Silverman the killer. They agreed to show the script to PPA when they were finished. But right before she was due to take *GB Dreams Big* to Len Ziskind, she tried to blackmail Jules again.

I lost the logic there.

I looked over at Doug; he was focused on traffic. Doug would say the logic stopped because she'd become mentally unstable. I had to factor that in. Did she forget about Ted Abadi? Why would she strong-arm Jules for a movie deal when they hadn't gotten PPA's response to *GB Dreams Big*? When PPA hadn't *seen* it yet?

I snapped—

It was something Tolback said. "Len and Jules are tight—Jules has money in PPA."

I sat up. That was *it*. At some point Greta must have learned that Jules Silverman and Len Ziskind were friends. She knew then there was no hope at PPA. Ziskind and Nevenson hadn't lied: they never saw *GB Dreams Big*. But Greta couldn't tell Phillips they were screwed—Phillips didn't believe Silverman was the bad guy. She tried to go around PPA by putting pressure on Jules with the spanking picture. Jules agreed to pay twenty grand but no more. So she tried a third blackmail with what she'd heard from Dorene Johnson.

I sat back. The nuttiness was pretty stark: Greta tried to force Jules Silverman to get her a deal for a script that resurrected an old murder involving him. It wasn't even clear that she wanted justice for Georgette Bauerdorf. It looked like *GB Dreams Big* was more important. It looked like Georgette was just Greta's ticket back into the movie business.

If that were true, I'd be very sorry.

Doug turned off Sunset down a side street and circled around to Fountain Avenue. I pointed up ahead on our right. He slowed the car.

He must have rethought his position on *GB Dreams Big*. My talk with Neil Phillips must have convinced him the script did exist. I was tempted to joke about winning our nine-hundred-dollar bet. But he was looking for parking, and I decided not to speak until I was spoken to.

He found a place and we walked up to Georgette's old apartment. Doug had his hand on my waist. I pointed at her front windows as we cut across the lawn.

He said, "We need a break because this is taking too long, and because I can't keep putting off the grand jury. While the case is hot, I can plead for time."

I said, "Oh."

We walked into the vestibule. It was dusk and the light was on. Doug stopped, stretched up, and touched the fixture. He was tall enough to reach the bulb with a few inches to spare.

I walked back to the alcove under the stairs. I hadn't noticed the color of the velour bench before; it was the sandy salmon of the walls. I started to tell Doug where Phillips had sat. Something caught my eye —

I dropped to the floor.

It was low on one bench leg, stuck to the velour in green tufts. Doug bent down beside me. I scraped off the fuzz and rolled it in my fingers. I opened my hand and poked the fuzz to show him. It was heavy and stiff like carpet fiber . . .

Doug was staring.

. . . but the Thalberg screening rooms didn't have green carpets. And the emergency exits had bare cement floors.

Doug looked at me.

The Casa de Amor and the Thalberg Building — both built in 1937. Louis Mayer's secret elevator. Movie executives buying extracurricular sex. The emergency alarms that didn't work. Footsteps inside Neil John Phillips's bungalow when no one saw him enter the Casa. The people who'd disappeared. Mrs. May's "They found it." *The drawing of the floor plan in Phillips's garage.*

I had thought it was a fantasy home/movie studio. It wasn't.

It was a tunnel.

CHAPTER
TWENTY-FIVE

The assembled men crowded for a view. Doug said, "I can't tell you what or who we're going to find down there. Officially, this tunnel has been closed and nonoperational since the 1960s."

We were standing in the side street by the Casa de Amor. There were ten of us: me, Doug, Smith, McManus, Gadtke, the two Casa surveillance guys, and three guards from the Sony lot, all ex-cops. Doug laid my sketch of the tunnel on the hood of his car. I'd drawn it on the back of a search warrant form, and he'd had Sony security make copies. The proportions were off, I knew. My lines weren't straight, and I couldn't remember all the labels on all the underground rooms. But it was good enough for a plan of attack.

Doug moved his finger along the sketch. "The north end of the tunnel starts at the rear of these apartments...runs under the street...and circles the foundation of that structure there."

He pointed across Washington Boulevard to the wall the Thalberg sat behind.

The men all looked up. The building was floodlit at night and the light was visible over the trees. An LAPD patrol car drove by on Washington. Smith gave them the high sign.

He said to Doug, "One unit from West L.A."

Doug nodded. West L.A. station had said it was shorthanded; one car was a victory. But he and Smith had mustered lots of non-LAPD help. The head of Sony's security was a retired Culver City

PD captain. At Doug's call, he'd come from home to organize his night-shift crew and do liaison with Culver City police. What Doug had really wanted, and didn't get, was SWAT. He'd requested a full SWAT contingent with fear-sniffing search dogs. But SWAT only moved when a suspect's presence could be confirmed.

Doug went on. "The tunnel has a number of rooms attached, you will notice, and covers a substantial area. There might be nobody down there, or as many as four people. With assist aboveground from studio security and Culver City PD, we have the lot perimeter sealed and watched as best it can be."

I studied the cops' faces: even *I* knew the lot was a sieve. It was too big. Guarding the gates and patrolling the streets around it was no guarantee of anything.

Doug laid four DMV head shots next to the tunnel drawing. He pointed out Neil John Phillips, Scott Dolgin, Isabelle Pavich, and Mrs. Florence May.

"Consider these individuals potentially dangerous. We may be looking at a conspiracy or a hostage situation—we don't know."

Smith said under his breath, "We ask for SWAT and get squat." McManus glanced at him; they both looked tense.

Doug had picked the most experienced guys for the tunnel. Before he started on specifics, he'd gone over the shooting rules with them. He'd turned the review into a sort of motivational talk. The talk had helped but the tension was still there. I could feel it in the cops. I could feel it in *me*—and all I'd been asked to do was hold a flashlight on the drawing.

Everyone studied the DMV photographs. Gadtke was serious for once. He hadn't produced a single joke prop since he arrived.

Doug indicated the head Sony security man. He was a potbellied guy with a bland face. Doug said, "Captain Yamada grew up in this area."

Yamada nodded. "My parents worked for the old MGM. My father was a gardener and I played in the tunnel as a kid."

Doug said, "He also knows our guy Phillips. Between his information and Miss Whitehead's, I think we're good on logistics."

He forgot to credit Erma and Neil Phillips's projectionist buddy. Once we'd guessed tunnel, it was amazing how many people knew about it or had heard rumors about it.

The men huddled over the sketch; they were concentrating. Doug pointed to the north entrance.

"This is located in a walkway between two garages. It's sealed permanently—no one can get in or out. The restaurants—called 'commissary' here—are locked for the night. That leaves the south entrance, the west entrance, this spur off the north entrance that comes out in Phillips's bedroom—and two ground-level exits from the building's basement."

Yamada said, "We've searched and secured the upper floors of the Thalberg. The elevators and interior stairwells are locked."

Smith jabbed a pen at the exits I'd labeled. He said, "So, five possible escape points."

Doug said, "There is also the secret elevator. Although the door appeared to be sealed, we assume that the abandoned shaft functions as access from the tunnel. We can block escape by covering the two ground-level exits."

He let that sink in. "I'm taking the north spur. My partner wants the south entrance."

Smith nodded. "We found Dolgin's truck on Madison south of Culver Boulevard. Captain Yamada tells us the entrance is inside a shed behind the house where the truck was found."

Yamada said, "The shed is marked 'DWP' but Water & Power doesn't own it."

Gadtke spoke up. "They did a half-assed job of closing this death trap."

I looked at Gadtke. Everybody was thinking it; someone had finally said it. A few of the cops laughed. It was a nervous sound.

Yamada didn't smile. "The studio was in trouble at the time and wouldn't spend the money to do it right."

Doug folded up the tunnel drawing. He gave it to me and started pairing people off. He asked one of the Sony guards to go with Smith. He asked McManus and Gadtke to take the west entrance. He asked Yamada and the third Sony guard to cover the ramp to the Thalberg basement. He asked the surveillance guys to cover the emergency exit at the back of the Thalberg.

McManus and Gadtke and the surveillance team headed for their cars. I watched them pull out shotguns and bulletproof vests. Smith opened the trunk of his car. He had a shotgun inside, two bulletproof vests, walkie-talkies, flashlights, and a stack of LAPD windbreakers. He handed three windbreakers to Yamada and asked him how the Sony guys were fixed for vests. Yamada had borrowed some from Culver City.

Doug walked to the back of his car. Opening his trunk, he pulled out a bulletproof vest, dumped his jacket, and slipped the vest over his head.

Smith passed out walkie-talkies; he tossed one to Doug. Doug pressed a button and coughed into the mouthpiece. I heard the amplified noise come out all the walkie-talkies.

Doug called, "Listen up."

The men crowded close again; they stood in sets of two. Doug pointed to each pair. He said, "These guys have five choices—only four are smart. If they're smart, and they're down there, they're coming at one of you."

He pointed at Smith, and McManus and Gadtke. "Secure the junctions, like we discussed, then signal me and we'll decide our next move. I'll make as much noise as I can. I'd like to squeeze them out your direction. Partner, you'll be opposite the secret elevator—you might catch somebody there."

Smith nodded. Doug pointed at Yamada, and the surveillance pair. "If they resist at ground level, force them back into the basement if you can. We don't want them loose outside if we can prevent it."

Doug checked the time. "I have 9:05. We go in ten."

Heads nodded. Everybody checked their watches. McManus said, "Good luck," to no one in particular, and Gadtke made his chicken face. Smith took off at a jog. The men followed him across Washington Boulevard, jogging. A Culver City patrol car braked to let them pass. They jogged along the wall and turned the corner toward the lot entrance.

Doug leaned into the trunk and got his shotgun. He checked to make sure it was loaded. I'd never seen a police model .12 gauge. It was a sinister object, with its flat black finish and rubber stock.

I said, "What about me?"

He looked up. "You're going to gather the tenants and stay with them until this is over."

I reached into the trunk and pulled out a vest. My Colt revolver and a new box of shells were sitting underneath. I didn't hesitate—I leaned in to get them. Doug saw what I was doing. He stopped my arm and held on.

I said, "But I have to help you."

He shook his head.

"Are you speaking in your official capacity? It's way too late for that."

He shook his head. "If anything happened, I'm responsible."

"I know I'd be a danger to you in the tunnel. But I can cover the entrance once you're down."

"You can't manage a weapon with your injured hand."

"I shoot with my left okay."

He thought a second, then let me go. "Will you obey orders?"

I nodded.

"All right." He talked fast. "Put the vest on while I load your gun. Round up the tenants and assemble them in one place. If Mrs. Johnson is still out of it, put the ladies with her. I'm going to check the garages again. You join me at Phillips's place."

I climbed into the vest; it was big enough for two of me. Doug took the Colt and turned his back. I heard the chamber click as he loaded the shells.

He passed me the Colt, a flashlight, and a walkie-talkie. I tucked the walkie-talkie and the flashlight inside the vest. It was true: my right hand wasn't good for much. Doug dropped extra shells into my pocket. I held the Colt barrel down next to my leg.

Doug grabbed a pair of wire cutters, slammed the trunk, and took off. I ran around to Dorene's bungalow. She'd passed out again on the couch. I ran to Erma's and explained what Doug wanted, and how fast. Erma wolfed her candy bar and came to

help. There were only three bungalows to clear. We went door-to-
door and pried the old girls away from their bottles and TV sets. I
let Erma be the bully. She herded everyone across to Dorene's. I
told her to lock Dorene's door, then ran to make sure the other
bungalows were locked. I ran back to Phillips's place. I saw Erma
pouring drinks as I passed. I knocked on the window and told her
to shut the blinds.

I waited for Doug beside Phillips's porch. The door was open
on its chain. Doug ran up the path and jumped onto the porch.
One snip with the wire cutters: the chain broke. He walked into
the bungalow, me close behind. Doug flipped the lights and
headed for the bedroom. It was like the other Casa bedrooms—
matching bed and vanity from the '30s. Doug went to the closet
and opened it. Erma had told us where to look.

The hanging clothes were all pushed to one end of the rod. It
revealed a door in the back wall: we saw the rectangle outline.
Doug stepped into the closet. He bent down and found a lever on
a built-in shoe rack.

He tripped the lever. There was a metallic snap. The door in
the wall cracked open. Doug reached and pushed it in. The hinges
made no noise.

I moved closer. The light was low but good enough to see by.

I saw a landing and a wooden staircase leading down. Wall
sconces provided the light. The landing was furnished with a love
seat and a standing ashtray. Moths and mold had eaten the upholstery. The walls were two-tone cream. The carpet runner was
green, mildewed, and worn to the nap in spots. Empty brass urns
flanked the love seat.

Cool air blew up from the tunnel. I breathed in the underground smells—dirt, old cement, damp wood, and damp paint.

Doug pulled me back into the bedroom. He pointed to a gap
between the bed and the wall. "Sit there—the bed will be some
protection. You can cover the tunnel and the bedroom door. Give
me your radio."

I got it out. Doug flipped a switch. "We're all on the same tac-
tical frequency. You listen in and holler if something happens."

I sat down, braced my back into the wall, and rested the Colt on my knee. I had a clear view of the closet.

Doug said, "Please don't do anything stupid."

I just smiled at him. He gripped his shotgun, stepped into the closet, and started down the stairs. The stairs creaked like crazy. I heard it in stereo—once from the tunnel and once from the walkie-talkie.

His footsteps stopped; he had paused at the bottom of the staircase. He was waiting for the signal from Smith and the two Sheriff's guys.

I wiped my hands on my jeans. I was suddenly dripping sweat. Smith's whisper came over the walkie-talkie: "The south exit is covered."

McManus's voice came—almost on top of Smith's: "West exit covered."

Gadtke whispered, "This is no tunnel. It's a whole fucking *town*."

Doug said low, "Roger. Do you have lights?"

Smith whispered, "It's bright as day." McManus said, "We have lights."

Doug said, "Same here. Wait for me."

I heard the hiss of static, and pictured Doug entering the tunnel. Then there was silence.

I strained to listen. The silence lengthened . . . and lengthened. I pulled the radio closer and strained for any sound. Nothing: silence.

I felt my body seize up. My mouth went dry. My stomach got tight; my legs and arms got heavy. I had to make a deliberate effort to grip the Colt and keep it aimed at the closet. It took me a minute to identify the problem. Then I realized: it was rank fear.

Jesus!

I jumped. A gunshot from the tunnel! Small calibre—I heard it in stereo. I struggled to stand; I grabbed the edge of the bed. I could barely breathe.

"Police! Stop or I'll shoot!" Doug's voice from the walkie-talkie.

More gunshots—pounding feet—a groan and a crash. The walkie-talkie fritzed out and went dead.

I didn't even think. I forced myself, I propelled myself, forward. I fell into the closet, caught my balance, straightened out, found my legs, and started running down the stairs. I bounced off the end wall, changed direction, and hit the tunnel going flat out. Water had leaked and the old carpet was slick. I slid and slipped, and found my footing again. The tunnel stretched long in a straight line ahead of me; it *was* bright as day with the wall lights. There was nobody anywhere in sight.

I booted it and ran, slowing down once to listen. The only sound was my own panting breath.

Up ahead, I saw a broken walkie-talkie on the floor. It was outside the door to a bedroom suite.

I heard a noise and ran inside.

Scott Dolgin lay on the floor. There was blood all over, on the floor, on him. The blood was pumping fresh from a wound in his neck.

He was unconscious. I looked around for something to staunch the blood. I saw a sleeping bag, a pillow, and a pile of take-out cartons. I grabbed the pillow and wadded it against Dolgin's neck. I needed something to hold it there. I started to unbuckle my belt—

All the lights went out.

I froze. Everything was pitch-black.

Oh, shit!

A shotgun blast—somewhere in the distance. A man yelled. The sounds echoed and re-echoed down the tunnel. I couldn't tell what direction they came from.

The walkie-talkie: *"Suspect in west corridor headed north!"* A response; voices shouting and garbled.

More shots. The pistol twice. A shotgun back.

I heard a woman scream, and a second woman scream. They sounded close.

I pulled out my flashlight and ran into the tunnel. *Scream your heads off*, I thought. *Scream them off!*

I ran to the T-junction and stopped. The tunnel forked right and left. The women screamed again. The sound came from the left fork.

I turned left and ran. I pictured the east side of the tunnel: a kitchen, a conference room, a string of offices.

The screams were coming from an office.

The tunnel took a right. I took the right and kept running. I kicked open the first office door. The screams stopped suddenly.

I sprayed my light over the walls and furniture. I didn't see any women.

The office was equipped and functioning. Desk, filing cabinets, ancient Dictaphone, ancient typewriter. The desk was covered with papers. An in-out tray was full of memos. A large graph tracked "Pictures in Production — 1939." A framed photograph of Irving Thalberg stood propped on the blotter.

A woman screamed. *"Help!"*

It was loud; it was right *there*. I whirled around. It came from a wall of cardboard boxes. I recognized the boxes — they contained Neil Phillips's MGM memos. The boxes were being pushed outward from behind. An office adjoined: someone was trying to escape.

I grabbed a high box and toppled the stack. Loose paper poured out in piles. A body fell over the boxes and tried to tackle me. Fingernails clawed at my throat. My light beam caught a face.

I yelled, *"Mrs. May!"*

She kept clawing my throat; she was blind and deaf, crazed. I whacked her with the flashlight. She screamed and let go of me. I shoved her over the loose paper, back into the inner room, following her.

I slammed the door and put the light on my face. *"Ann White-head!"*

Mrs. May's eyes went wide; she realized who I was. She wore her gardening clothes from Monday. She looked completely terrorized.

She fumbled at something inside her shirt. I started to duck. She pulled out her necklace, snapped the chain, and shoved it at me. I caught her flailing hand and grabbed the necklace.

Someone whimpered. I stuck the necklace in my jeans, turned and shined the light around the room. It was a doctor's office. It was small and narrow, and the floor and walls were white tile. I saw a porcelain sink, glass-front cabinets, an examining table with stirrups, and a plastic model of the female reproductive system.

My light hit Isabelle Pavich. She was huddled in a ball under the sink. The light caught her and she huddled back, whimpering. I was actually glad to see her.

Mrs. May stumbled over and knelt down with Pavich. They put their arms around each other.

"Police!"

Male voices. They were close.

I heard running feet in the outer office. Someone was sprinting straight for us. I heard him trip and skid on the loose paper. He slammed into the door full force.

Pavich screamed. I dived for a corner. I aimed my gun and flashlight at the door.

"Police! Stop!"

The door crashed open. Neil John Phillips staggered toward us. He was waving an automatic.

I yelled, "No!"

I heard Doug yell, "Hold your fire!"

Phillips fired wild at the cops. I screamed and pulled the trigger. Gunfire drowned out my shot.

Bullets and buckshot shattered the door. White light dazzled the room. I tried to cover up. Phillips flew forward and hit the floor facedown. The women shrieked. Mrs. May panicked and stood up. She flung out her arms to deflect bullets. The sink exploded. Her chest erupted. I screamed and curled up tight. She collapsed on top of me. Blood gushed over me.

The roaring stopped.

I LAY VERY still. I was pinned to the floor. The air was filled with smoke that burned my nose. My ears were ringing. I couldn't move my chest to breathe. Warm blood glued my eyes shut.

Someone lifted Mrs. May off of me. I was rolled onto my back.

Blood seeped into my mouth. I tasted it and wondered whose it was.

Someone wiped my face. Someone pressed their head over my heart, and found the pulse in my wrist.

The Colt was pried out of my hand. I felt lips on my cheek and lips at my ear. I felt the lips move — someone was trying to talk to me. Someone wanted me to say something.

What was I supposed to say? Clearly it was the end of the world.

CHAPTER
TWENTY-SIX

I woke up on the couch in Doug's living room. The hospital had given me an injection for the pain. It knocked me right out.

. . .

I could just turn my eyes. The clock said 1:54 A.M. I would've believed anything. I'd lost all track of time.

. . .

My head ached. I craved a drink of water.

. . .

I saw a pitcher and a glass on the coffee table. I tried to lift my arm and say, "Water." The effort was too much for me.

. . .

I closed my eyes.

. . .

The last thing I remembered was the emergency room. The doctor had said I must have a lucky angel. I'd been hurt worse than I realized: bulletproof vests are useless for arms and legs.

I was full of wood and tile splinters, bone fragments, and shotgun pellets. The doctor tweezed, dug, probed, and stitched up multiple holes. I also had a cracked rib and three fractures in my right hand and wrist. The impact of Mrs. May's body had done the rib; beating on Dale Denney had done the hand; the pry bar at the pool house had done the wrist. A ricochet had grazed my left leg and missed a big artery by inches. That, and no head wound, were the lucky parts.

The doctor had understood that I couldn't talk. She'd called it shock. She gave me some pills and said they'd help with the shaking.

. . .

Doug had carried me out of the tunnel. He'd laid me on the Thalberg lawn and tucked his windbreaker around me. I remembered shivering; I was wet to the skin. I'd lain on my side, facing the Casa de Amor. My nose and throat burned. My ears rang for a long time.

The cops had carried the other bodies out of the tunnel. Neil John Phillips, Isabelle Pavich, Mrs. May. They were laid on the lawn near me. Doug tried to block my view—but I saw. Shotgun rounds had ripped out Phillips's back. The exploding sink mangled Pavich above the neck. Mrs. May had no chest. I saw Smith push her intestines back into her belly. I saw Gadtke close the flaps of Pavich's face. The cops were covered with blood. I threw up on the grass. I threw up and threw up until there was nothing left. I lay there looking at my own vomit.

A whole parade of new cops had arrived. Cops in plain clothes; cops from the Sheriff's and the LAPD. Lawyers from the district attorney's office. Everybody was asking questions. They'd tried to question me.

Scott Dolgin was still alive—I heard a paramedic say so. An ambulance had taken him to UCLA.

Doug drove me to the closest hospital. He'd carried me into the emergency room, jumped the line, flashed his badge, and demanded a doctor. He wouldn't fill out any forms, or even wait for the nurse's answer. Walking straight through to the examining rooms, he grabbed the first doctor he found and coerced immediate treatment. The doctor cut off my clothes and washed me clean. I was stitched, taped, and gauze-wrapped all up my left side. I got a plastic cast for my right hand and she gave me a shot for the pain. I had refused to be checked into the hospital. I had refused to let go of Doug.

. . .

...outh was so *dry*.

. . .

Someone came into the living room. I opened my eyes. It was Doug. He looked grim and drawn; he still wore his bloody clothes. He saw I was awake and said, "How do you feel?"

I started to cry.

He came and sat beside me on the couch.

I couldn't control myself; I was helpless and crying hard. The tears streamed down my face.

He wiped the tears with his hands.

The tears kept coming. I didn't gulp or sob—I wasn't making noise. It was just tears.

He had fixed me a bed on the couch. He took the sheet and pressed it against my face. He wiped my cheeks and eyes, found a new dry spot, and wiped my cheeks and eyes. He did it again and again until I'd soaked the edges of the sheet.

The tears stopped finally. Doug folded the sheet and smoothed the blanket over it. His expression was unreadable. He reached for the water, poured a glass, and helped me sit up. I swallowed two mouthfuls and lay back on the pillow.

Doug said, "Can you nod your head?"

I nodded.

"You're going to be asked to make a statement, several statements, as to what happened this evening."

I nodded.

"No one considers you in any way culpable, but you'll be entitled to legal counsel if you wish."

I nodded.

"I want you to nod if I'm correct. You heard gunshots and made the decision to enter the tunnel."

To see if you were hurt, I thought. I nodded.

"You discovered Dolgin, and you heard the women call for help. Your intention was to rescue the women."

His tone was so impersonal: *he was mad at me.* I shut my eyes. I prayed I wouldn't cry again.

Doug said, "Was that your intention?"

I nodded.

Doug said, "You didn't signal your whereabouts by radio because you didn't think of it in the heat of the moment."

I shook my head. I *forgot* the walkie-talkie in Phillips's bedroom in my panic to find *you*. I felt tears start to ooze, and kept my eyes shut.

Doug was silent.

He said, "However it happened, in the last analysis, you almost prevented the deaths. We heard you call out to warn us that you were inside with Phillips."

Doug was silent for a time.

"The guy was prepared to take everyone down with him — Dolgin, Mrs. May, Miss Pavich, us. He could have evaded us easily once he cut the electricity. Instead he led us back to the office."

His voice was tired; I'd never heard him so tired.

"You saw the boxes of memos. We also found the stolen transcripts, but we don't know yet if they're relevant to the crimes. It appears that Phillips was leading a make-believe life down there."

As a protégé of Irving Thalberg, I thought. As the greatest screenwriter who ever lived.

"We have to assume he murdered Stenholm and Abadi, and that he's the one who attempted to murder you. Until we can talk to Dolgin, however, all we have are assumptions."

Doug paused. "They've operated on him — the bullet was lodged in his neck. He's in critical condition, but the doctors think he'll make it. He's the only witness left."

Doug paused. Then: "We need a motive."

He was silent again.

"I've got to get back to Culver City — I never should've left. I have to do a walk-through with the shooting teams. This is a very big mess."

I opened my eyes and tears just gushed out.

Doug lost his formal tone. He said, "Please, baby, don't."

My vision blurred. Doug leaned over and picked something off the floor. I felt a bath towel on my face. He pressed it there, and ~~~~ my cheeks and eyes.

~~~~ no control; I tried. The tears wouldn't stop. They stopped

gushing after a while, but they didn't stop. They slowed down to a steady drip. Doug dried them as they came. My nose was running. He wiped it, too.

He said, "I couldn't reach your sister and I don't want to leave you alone. Is there anyone else I can call?"

My sister. I had to adjust to remember her. She'd gone to the desert with Father today. I thought of Vivian or Mark: I couldn't picture it. There wasn't anyone who could possibly help.

Doug said, "Yes? No?"

I shook my head. My eyes were wet—Doug was a blur. He said, "Then I'll get someone to check on you. I'll leave provisions on the table, and I'll leave this. We found it in Phillips's office."

I felt him set an object in my lap. I could see a white square, but I couldn't tell what it was. Doug leaned forward and lay the back of his hand on my cheek. His voice was quiet.

He said, "Ever since I met you, I've wondered how far you would go. Now I know."

He stood up. I watched him walk into the kitchen to get his things, and I heard the front door open and close. His car engine started; I heard him drive away. The tears dripped, dripped. I dried them on the pillow and lay there, listening to nothing. I forgot about the object on my lap until I tried to move my legs.

I lifted my head to see what it was.

It was a bound screenplay with a white cover. The cover said *GB DREAMS BIG*.

I COULDN'T SIT up, but I freed my arms from under the blanket. They moved—I wasn't sure they would. My left arm was taped stiff. My right arm was okay except for the cast on my hand. Doug had dressed me in a pair of his pajamas and rolled up the sleeves. I flexed my fingers to see if they worked. Only one knee would bend very far. I propped the script against it and opened the cover.

I read the title page.

Someone had Xed out *GB DREAMS BIG* in pencil. The same pencil retitled the script: *GEORGIE AND NANCE*.

A second name was penciled in on the writing credit. It read: "by Greta Stenholm & Neil John Phillips."

I turned the page. The script began:

EXT. OZEE'S AUTO COURT AND DESOLATE LANDSCAPE. EARLY EVENING.

A cheap motel on State Road 121 near Grapevine. Oil derricks litter the bald, churned-up, treeless land. In the background, isolated figures move around the derricks, silhouetted by the setting sun. There is the muted sound of machinery and men's voices. The sounds are carried away by the wind. Closer in, bedsheets billow on a clothesline, spattered with windblown oil.

A title appears over the landscape and motel: EAST TEXAS. SPRING 1934.

INT. OZEE'S AUTO COURT. CABIN NUMBER 2. LIVING ROOM. EARLY EVENING.

A cheap, underfurnished motel room—pure poverty. This and the following scene should be shot in black-and-white, or washed-out color, the way we imagine the Depression years.

Present are GEORGE BAUERDORF, *a struggling wildcatter two wells away from the strike of his life, his worn-out first wife,* MOTHER, *and his two dark-haired daughters—*CONNIE, *14, and* GEORGETTE, *10. These aren't trashy people. They're a middle-class family turned into nomads as the father gambles on oil.*

MOTHER *is cooking supper at a primitive gas burner in a curtained-off area. She looks pale, even sick.* GEORGE *sits at a table in his shirtsleeves, reading the Dallas newspaper.* CONNIE *and* GEORGETTE *sit near him, playing with toys.* GEORGETTE'S *toy is a* STUFFED

GEORGETTE
(to her rabbit)
When we grow up, Bunny, we're going
to roam the world looking for oil. We'll
start in Texas, and then ride a mule to
Venezuela, and after we find all the oil in
Venezuela, we'll fly an airplane to the Dutch
East Indies and find more.

GEORGE
Georgette, for Christ's sake, stop your
yammering! Tell her, Mother!

MOTHER
Your father's had a long day, Georgie.

CONNIE
I miss New York. When can we go
home?

GEORGE
(warningly)
Mother...!

MOTHER
Will you get out the plates for me, sweetheart?

CONNIE *pulls a sulky face and* GEORGE *raises a threatening hand.*
CONNIE *jumps up and runs to her* MOTHER.

GEORGETTE
(whispering)
The Dutch East Indies are really close to
Russia, so we'll go there next in a sampan
and a dogsled—

With a swift, violent gesture, GEORGE grabs GEORGETTE'S
STUFFED RABBIT and throws it out the open window.

EXT. REAR OF OZEE'S AUTO COURT. EARLY EVENING.

In extreme close-up we see the STUFFED RABBIT lying in the mud.
It should look like an injured body. A gust of wind spatters it with oil.

INT. OZEE'S AUTO COURT. CABIN NUMBER 2. BEDROOM.
NIGHT.

GEORGETTE has been sent to bed without her supper. There is a
Murphy bed for the parents and two folding cots for the girls. GEOR-
GETTE sits on her cot with her STUFFED RABBIT, which is damp
from being washed. She is sewing a red velvet garment for the
STUFFED RABBIT. The garment is trimmed in yellow fur, like the
robe of a medieval queen. The garment should stand out from the bleak
surroundings. The color can be enhanced in postproduction.

> GEORGETTE
> Baku, Bunny—just think, Baku. It will
> be cold in Russia, not like Texas. The rigs
> get ice on them and the roughnecks slip
> and hurt themselves. We'll have to dress
> for the elements.

GEORGETTE'S voice caresses "Baku" as it caressed "Dutch East Indies"—magical and mysterious names to the little girl. She holds up the
odd garment she's working on for the STUFFED RABBIT to see. From
the next room we hear the raised voice of GEORGE.

> GEORGE (O.S.)
> When I come home at night, I expect three
> things, Mother. I expect clean clothes, I
> expect my dinner on the table, and I expect
> the girls to keep their damn mouths shut!

The rest of the speech is unintelligible, although we hear the angry tone of his voice. We hear MOTHER'S *apologetic tone in response. With that fading on the soundtrack,* GEORGETTE *hugs her precious* STUFFED RABBIT *and smiles to herself.*

SLOW FADE TO:

EXT. THE HOLLYWOOD CANTEEN. HOLLYWOOD, CALIFORNIA. NIGHT.

A master shot of an old barn on Cahuenga Boulevard. A sign painted above the doors says HOLLYWOOD CANTEEN. *There are stars-and-stripes banners, and arc lights shining crisscross beams into the night sky. Soldiers and sailors, all sorts of servicemen, mill out front. There are only men, no women, and there's a long line at the door to get in. If a hostess is checking the servicemen in, we can't see her. Cars pass, honking. Male motorists shout patriotic sentiment and bloodthirsty encouragement. The servicemen shout back.*

A title appears: OCTOBER 11, 1944.

There are young men in civilian clothes lurking in the street. They are 4-Fs and dishonorable discharges. Two men in uniform get into a shoving match with two men in civvies. We hear "Coward" and "Bug case" from the soldiers. Other servicemen spectate as the civilians are chased away from the Canteen. A big-band dance tune hops on the soundtrack. It's coming from inside the Canteen.

INT. HOLLYWOOD CANTEEN. NIGHT.

A high-angle shot of a cavernous hall with a cafeteria, a stage, and tables and chairs arranged around a large dance floor. It looks like a saloon, with murals of the Old West on the walls and wagon-wheel chandeliers. The main attraction of the Canteen is the movie stars and name musical acts. Maybe Harry James and his orchestra are playing tonight, and Betty Grable is the chief hostess. The dance floor and cafeteria are packed. The hall is jumping with servicemen, and young women in bright dresses. Men outnumber women ten to one.

The place is loud, but the gaiety has a desperate, almost violent, edge. On the peripheries of the frame, in isolated knots, servicemen shove each other because they want food and women. But the camera doesn't focus specific attention on the violence, it's just part of the atmosphere, like the men fighting outside. The camera swoops in and picks a gold-and-diamond RABBIT PIN *out of the crowd of dancers.*

INT. HOLLYWOOD CANTEEN. NIGHT.

Extreme close-up of this obviously expensive piece of jewelry.

INT. HOLLYWOOD CANTEEN. NIGHT.

The camera pulls back from the RABBIT PIN *to a medium shot of two people dancing. The pin is on the dress of a young, dark-haired woman, twenty years old. The pin identifies the grown-up* GEOR- GETTE BAUERDORF *for the audience. Her* PARTNER *is wearing an Air Force uniform.*

> GEORGETTE
> (pointing to her partner's wings)
> I'm learning to fly an airplane.

> PARTNER
> (laughs)
> Fly an airplane? What for?

I turned the page.

Someone had stuck a loose piece of paper into the script. The paper was covered with penciled notes in the same handwriting as the title page. Neil John Phillips's handwriting.

Phillips had a list of comments:

"—lose Texas prologue—too depressing—creates mood audience won't shake—

"—story opens at H'wood Canteen—lose desperate atmospherics and rabbit pin. GEORGIE beautiful brunet—dancing in arms of handsome pilot her age—pilot names battles fought and Pacific islands seen (check historical accuracy)—Georgie fascinated—

"—she passes friend, NANCE, on dance floor—Nance star, beautiful blond (think ditzy and ballsy, think Diaz or Zellweger)—Georgie whispers she has pilot while Nance has lower form of enlisted man—a running contest between the two girls—Georgie keeps count of flyers she meets—

"—Navy pilot taps Georgie's partner on shoulder. Georgie sees his wings—happy he cuts in—

"—pilot's name JEFF STONE—second male lead—major suspect in Georgie's death until real killer caught—had good job at Metro before war—offers Georgie screen test when war over—Georgie flattered—"

Phillips's comments ended there.

I turned to the next page of the script.

The typing stopped and there was handwriting instead. The handwriting didn't belong to Phillips: it belonged to Greta. She'd printed one word over and over on the blank page. The same word, with no spaces, on line after line.

I turned the page.

She'd done the same thing again. The same word, line after line, no spaces and no margins.

I turned the page. It was the same: the same word.

I started flipping pages.

She had filled every page of the rest of the script with one word. The word was block-printed, in capital letters, in red ink, in tight lines, covering the entire page from top to bottom.

There were at least one hundred blank pages in the script, and she'd written the same word at least three hundred times on each page.

"MOVIESMOVIESMOVIESMOVIESMOVIESMOVIES
MOVIESMOVIESMOVIESMOVIESMOVIESMOVIES
MOVIESMOVIESMOVIESMOVIESMOVIESMOVIES
MOVIESMOVIESMOVIESMOVIESMOVIESMOVIES
MOVIESMOVIESMOVIESMOVIESMOVIES"

Line after line, page after page, over and over, one single word from Greta Stenholm.

The word was: *Movies.*

CHAPTER
TWENTY-SEVEN

I CRIED FOR the rest of the night. I cried when I was awake, and I cried in my sleep. I cried so hard in my sleep that I woke myself up again.

I hurt my rib crying. I soaked the sheets and blankets crying, and soaked my pajamas crying. At one point I crawled off the couch to find a dry place to lie down. I thought I headed for the bedroom. Doug's neighbor came in the morning and found me on the kitchen floor. I was naked and shivering from the cold. He carried me to the bedroom, tucked me into bed, and made me swallow some pills.

After he left, my voice came back. That's when I started to howl.

I didn't know how long the howling lasted. It felt like hours—it could've been one continuous scream. I howled until my throat got raw and my voice got hoarse. I stopped making any sound, and I still howled. I fell asleep exhausted, sweating, and almost delirious. When I woke up, the sun was on me and it was afternoon. I ached everywhere. I crawled into the front room for my painkillers and took double the dose. I passed out on my way back to bed. The phone might've rung; I thought I heard it ringing. The neighbor might've come in. I woke up on the living-room floor; someone had put a pillow under my head. Someone had turned on a lamp. The sky outside the windows was dark. It was night again.

I rolled over and flinched: the lamplight hurt my eyes. I needed to go to the bathroom. The hospital had given me a cane; I could see it propped against the coffee table. I reached with my foot, tipped the cane toward me, caught it, and used it to stand up. I limped to the bathroom and went. Feeling sticky and gross, I sponged off with a wet washcloth and rinsed my hair. I found a robe of Doug's to put on and limped back to the couch.

He had left fruit and crackers for me. I picked out a pear and ate it. It was hard to swallow but I was starving. I ate another pear, and a soft banana, and lay back.

I put my feet up on the table. What a view Doug had—city lights to the horizon. I felt profoundly calm inside. I felt peaceful and calm and clear in my mind.

Sometime during that awful day, I had dreamed about John Alton.

JOHN ALTON was a legendary cinematographer. He was best-known for *An American in Paris*; he'd photographed the climactic fantasy sequence and won an Oscar for it. But movie buffs liked his black-and-white work better. He was considered one of the great stylists of film noir—classic film noir of the '40s and '50s. I revered John Alton; everybody I knew who knew about movies revered John Alton. And it was one of the thrills of my life to actually meet him and talk to him before he died.

It had happened in Vienna in 1993.

I'd gone to the Viennale with my director boyfriend, who was invited to the festival with his latest film. That year they were paying tribute to the emigré filmmakers of the former Austro-Hungarian Empire. Billy Wilder was the biggest name, but he hadn't come. Among the people who did show up were Robert Siodmak's brother; Francis Lederer, Louise Brooks's costar in *Pandora's Box*; and John Alton.

I first spotted him in the lobby of the Hilton. He was ninety-two or ninety-three years old—a very old man. He was short and built like a peasant. He dressed in bohemian black and still wore his cap backwards for the camera viewfinder. I was too awed to go up and introduce myself, so I just sat in the lobby and watched him. He still had his marbles, his legs, and his eyes. He also hadn't lost his zest: he was flirting with every woman in the place. The festival provided guides for the participants; he flirted with his guides. There were women directing traffic and running the hospitality suite; he flirted with them.

It was hilarious, and I'd realized there was every chance he'd talk to me. I waited until he was alone, walked over, and asked if I could buy him a drink. He didn't hesitate. He put his arm through mine and I got, "With pleasure, my dear. What is your name?" in a deep, thick German accent.

We'd gone to the bar in the hotel. I had a moment of worry when he took my arm: if he turned out to be a lech, his movies would never be the same for me. But he never crossed any lines. He was a subtle and old-fashioned sexist, he didn't know how to take women seriously but they continued to delight him.

And he delighted me. He was an ugly man up close, with tremendous personal magnetism. He ordered wine and started talking and I was riveted. The problem was: he didn't want to talk about movies or himself. He wanted to talk about the Rembrandts he'd seen on a museum trip that day. It was a rare experience to hear John Alton analyze Rembrandt's lighting effects. But when I tried to bring the conversation around to Alton's treatment of light, he would get bored. If I pressed he'd say, "You fascinate me, go on," and I'd feel like an idiot. Here was a guy, I thought, who'd worked for MGM in the 1920s; he'd grown up with the movies, he was as *old* as the movies almost. But he couldn't have cared less about them. I pointed this out, and he agreed. He'd left Hollywood in the early '60s because he was finished with pictures. I asked why. He said it was because pictures were bad. Why bad, I'd asked — in what way, bad?

We were sitting together at a small table. Alton had put both his hands on my forearm and he'd said, "There was no longer any Art."

I LAY DOWN sideways and pulled the blanket over me.

People had announced The End of Cinema since practically the beginning of cinema. The world wars started and ended movie eras in dozens of countries. Lillian Gish always maintained that movie art ended with silent film. In the States people dated the end from the breakup of the studios and their star contracts. Or dated it from the invention of television. Or dated it from the '70s, from *Jaws* and *Star Wars* and the blockbuster mentality—the mind-set Michael Powell criticized in his book. And now people marked the corporate era in Hollywood as a *new* end to movies. The editor of *Variety* was vehement on the subject. Global entertainment was a growth industry, and we lived in a time of "movies-as-merchandise." Studios didn't produce movies, or story or character or art: studios produced "product" aimed at mega box-office returns and feeding other divisions of the international conglomerates that owned them.

My dream was short and simple. It took place in a fin de siècle coffeehouse where I'd hung out during the Viennale. I was sitting opposite John Alton at a window booth. We weren't talking, but his hands rested on my bare arm exactly the way they'd done when he said, "There was no longer any Art." The sensation was vivid; only a dream could've conjured it from the past like that. Alton had had big, callused hands. They weren't the sensitive artist hands you'd expect: they were peasant farmer hands. Those were the exact hands on my arm in the dream.

I knew what the hands were telling me.

It wasn't that movies were bad. Would Alton argue that no one made an artful movie between 1963 and 1993? I'd asked him that question—not in the dream, in real life. I'd mentioned David Lean and Martin Scorsese, Wim Wenders and Akira Kurosawa, my favorite screenwriters and cinematographers. I threw in Jane Campion and Kathryn Bigelow to see how he'd react. Louis Mayer said that no woman would ever direct on his lot; and no woman ever did.

Alton's only reply was, "You fascinate me, go on." He just didn't give a damn anymore.

I didn't give a damn anymore either. Movies in general were bad, unless you liked computer-generated special effects; they were thin and so male, and full of fear and despair. It had worn me down for sure. But somebody somewhere was always making a good one. There was hope from the independents and digital technology—hope maybe even from the resurgence of powerful women in Hollywood. Bad or good, though, hope or no hope, misogyny or no misogyny, the point was I'd stopped caring. It had happened between last night and tonight. The love affair was over. I was finished with the movies.

But I wasn't finished with Greta Stenholm.

She said at the party, "You're ready to give up. But *I* didn't give up, and I won't let *you.*"

How did she know? I'd thought I just needed a break. She understood things I hadn't understood—and dragged me along for the ride.

I will beat the System, she'd said.

She hadn't beaten it in the end. But she saw into its guts.

She gave Georgette Bauerdorf her stuffed rabbit. She'd carried the rabbit around with her in an Air Force duffel bag; it was with her when she was murdered. I'd described the rabbit in my crime-scene notes. A threadbare toy in a strange homemade dress—a crimson velvet gown trimmed with gold fur that resembled a lion's mane. Georgette had sewed the dress, and she'd told the rabbit all her plans and dreams.

Five people were dead. Six, including Georgette. I had to find out why; the carnage had to have a purpose. I owed Greta that much. I owed them both.

CHAPTER

TWENTY-EIGHT

CAMERA TRUCKS lined the street in front of the mansion. They were mostly from local TV stations, with a couple from national news channels. It was a sign of my shell-shocked state that I couldn't imagine what they'd be doing at the house.

It was Friday morning. The day was already sunny and hot.

Physically, I was managing to function. I felt stiff and sore; my head ached and my stitches pinched. But I'd had a good night's sleep, woken up early, and driven to Los Feliz without much problem. It hurt the first time I used my left leg for the clutch. After that it got easier.

Emotionally and mentally, I wasn't functioning right. I knew it. But I didn't know how bad it was until I turned into the driveway and reporters rushed my car shouting questions. I hit the brakes and froze. I couldn't make sense of what the reporters were saying. I just sat in the front seat — I couldn't speak or move. I was saved by a Metro guy I recognized; they were still keeping watch inside the mansion. He ran onto the lawn, ordered the reporters back to the sidewalk, and came and almost lifted me out of the car. I pointed to the passenger seat. He grabbed my cane and bag.

He escorted me into the mansion, up to my temporary room on the second floor. I asked him what was going on. My throat hurt and I had to cough out the words. He said the media had labeled it "the Tunnel Massacre." The cops involved had been seques-tered; one witness was in the hospital, and I, Ann Whitehead, had been missing since Wednesday night. I was the only person out running around who knew what had happened in Culver City.

Why was the mansion still being watched, I asked; were the cops waiting for me to show up? He shook his head. He said Detective Lockwood had requested their continued presence: Dale Denney had been released from custody the previous night.

None of this information really registered. None of it made me feel anything. I was numb.

The Metro cop said I should go to bed and rest. I realized I was still wearing Doug's pajamas; I'd worn them from his place. I sent the cop out of the room. He thought I was going to bed. What I did was change into fresh clothes. He caught me in the hall as I was leaving the house. He tried to stop me: he didn't succeed. He helped me out to my car instead, and kept the reporters off. As I drove down the street, they chased the car, shouting questions. I drove fast in case they decided to follow with their trucks.

I BOUGHT THROAT lozenges on my way in to the office. Sucking a lozenge, I skimmed the radio dial; the talk shows were taking calls about the Tunnel Massacre. And the press had staked out the *Millennium*. I saw the camera trucks, and cameras, and reporters, when I turned the corner off Franklin. I could see Barry. He stood outside in front of the building. Reporters surrounded him two deep; they'd stuck microphones in his face and he was talking.

I pulled into the curb down from them. Barry was deflecting questions about me. I got out of the car and headed for the front doors. Barry saw me coming. The reporters spotted me and rushed my direction. They shouted over top of each other. It was deafening, but I handled it better this time. I kept walking, and waved the cane to keep people at a distance. Barry held the door open; he told the reporters he'd have more to say later. I walked into the newspaper and led the way to his office.

He told his assistant to hold his calls, slammed the door, and locked it behind him. I sat down. All his TVs were going, sound off. One channel showed pictures taken an hour before. I was limping into the mansion on the Metro cop's arm.

Barry sat on his desk close to me. He was fired up. "*Where have you been?!*"

"I—"

"It doesn't matter, you're here! Tell me everything! This is the definitive end to that pig's career! What a coup for us—what a lucky fucking *coup!*"

He reached behind him for a pen and a notepad. "I'm going to write the piece myself for next week. Start at the beginning."

He waited with his pen ready.

I cleared my throat. I said, "Who murdered Greta Stenholm? Was it Scott Dolgin? If so, why? Was it Neil Phillips? If so, why?"

"Who murdered Neil Phillips? That's what I need from you."

I didn't say anything.

Barry frowned at me. I still didn't say anything. He said, "*Ann.*"

I said, "There was a fight over her screenplay *GB Dreams Big* before she died. You were there."

"I don't have time for this now. Tell me what happened Wednesday night!"

I said, "Who killed her and why?"

I had the cane in my left hand. I swung it up and whapped it on the edge of his desk.

Barry jumped. "For Christ's sake, I don't *know* anything! Scott was with me when she was murdered. Past that, I don't know *anything!*"

"Who killed her and why?"

"I don't know!"

"Who killed her and why?"

"I don't *know!*"

"Who killed her and why?"

My voice sounded dead; I sounded like a robot. It was horrible even to me. But there was nothing I could do about it.

Barry sat looking me over. He seemed to notice my injuries for the first time. I looked back at him, and for a minute we had stalemate.

He spoke first. He said, "You should know that—"

"Who killed her and why?"

He snapped. *"Will you let me talk?"*

I didn't say anything. He set his notepad down and leaned forward. "I'll tell you what I haven't told the staff yet. I've signed the deal with Entertainment Media Group—the newspaper is sold."

He waited for a reaction. I didn't have one. He said, "The new owners are on the line about keeping you for film. They'll take my recommendation."

I didn't say anything. I didn't feel anything.

Barry said, "I'd like to leave the paper with a bang, and Lockwood's forced retirement would be a nice legacy. You know what happened in Culver City. Did you actually see the tunnel? Were you inside of it?"

Barry realized he wasn't getting through to me. He took a fatherly tone. "Don't be stubborn, Ann—this isn't a good time to get fired. There are no jobs out there for you."

I said, "Who killed Greta Stenholm and why?"

Barry started to stand up. I braced my cane against the desk and blocked him. He sat back down.

"You're sick. Go home, get some rest—we'll discuss this when you feel better."

"Who killed her and why?"

Barry shrugged. He reached around and picked up his notepad and pen. He said, "All right, you tell me what you know, and I'll tell you what I know. How's that?"

I said, "You first."

Barry said, "I don't *know* who killed her, and I never gave a flying fuck. I only wanted the Lockwood piece, if you recall. You threatened to go to the *Times* with it."

I was silent.

Barry said, "I have a producing deal in the works with Jules Silverman. I'll be in a position soon to offer you a job. You'd be perfect in development with what you know about story."

"Who killed her and why?"

Barry said, softer, "Or I can fire you right now."

He waited for my answer.

I stood up and tapped his notepad with my cane. I said, "Neil

Phillips shot first. He is responsible for the deaths of Mrs. Florence May and Isabelle Pavich, and for his own. I don't know who put the bullet in Scott Dolgin's neck. Douglas Lockwood acted with integrity and intelligence, and the cops who went down into that tunnel are very brave men."

I unlocked Barry's door and walked out of his office.

My only thought was: Entertainment Media Group. They turned good weeklies into film industry pap. They always added "Entertainment" to the name of the newspapers they bought. *The Entertainment Millennium.*

I ESCAPED FROM the building by the parking lot door. I thought I'd avoid the reporters that way, but my car was surrounded. Someone had spotted the Colt and the box of shells in the backseat. A roar went up when I appeared. I heard "gun," and "Doug Lockwood," and "Rampart links," and "grand jury probe," and "official investigation," and other phrases I now recognized as pertinent.

I didn't have the strength to force through the crowd. I stuck my cane out like a wedge and cut a path to the driver's door. Someone jostled me; it sent pain all through my left side. I stopped, feeling faint. A stitch popped in my arm. Someone saw the blood on my bandage and said to back off, give me room.

I climbed into my car and drove. I made sure I wasn't followed before I parked on a side street.

Scott Dolgin was next.

I called UCLA to see if he was awake. I couldn't get past a nurse at the intensive care unit. She wouldn't answer questions or take a message.

I needed gas. I got my wallet and checked how much money I had. I was close to broke. I dug around in my bag for loose bills. I found a couple of ones—and I found a chain necklace. I didn't wear necklaces. I held it up: there was a key on it. The key was stamped with the name MAILBOX BOUTIQUE and the number 65.

I tried to think . . .

The necklace was important. Someone important gave it to

me. My mind would not remember how or where I acquired it. But I knew it was important.

Mailbox Boutique was a local company that rented private mail drops. I started the car and drove to the nearest gas station. I bought gas, then checked the public phone booth for a directory. It had one intact. I flipped to the yellow pages for Mailbox Boutique locations. I ran down the list. I got to "Culver City" and started to shake. I leaned against the booth. Culver City. The Casa de Amor.

Mrs. May.

Mrs. May had given me the necklace. The hospital dumped my tunnel clothes: Doug must have emptied my pockets. Mental images oozed up. Of a dark room, of white tiles, of whimpering—

I thumped my forehead on the glass. I tensed my muscles and willed the images to go away. If I started to remember I would be paralyzed. I'd start to scream and never stop.

I took deep breaths and kept reading.

There were six Mailbox Boutiques in West L.A. and Culver City—five more in Venice and the Marina. I wrote down the ones closest to the Casa de Amor. I felt my mind click on. I had a plan; I focused on it.

I got back in the car and drove to the freeway. Dots of blood seeped through my shirtsleeve; I'd popped more than one stitch. It didn't help the driving, which was already a strain. The freeway was a strain.

I tried the Mailbox Boutiques in geographical order east to west. The key didn't work in the first three. The fourth Mailbox Boutique was in a strip mall at the corner of Robertson and Culver. I parked and walked in. All the stores were arranged the same: numbered mailboxes covered the back and side walls. I walked along until I found sixty-five and tried the key.

The key worked; the door opened.

I saw folded sheets of paper inside. I didn't stop to worry about fingerprints. I grabbed the papers, relocked the mailbox, and hurried back to the car to read.

It was a handwritten note dated August 30, 2001. Last Thursday—eight days ago.

The note was addressed to "Mommy May," and it looked like it was scribbled in a rush.

Dear Mommy May—

If youre reading this it means you think something happened to me and you used the key like I asked. Take this info to the cops in case of my disappearance or death I swear its all <u>true</u> and Im sorry if it hurts you because you've been sogood to me

Bens real name is Neil Phillips. Ive known him since Bev Hills High but we havent been friends for a long time He found the tunnel under the Casa when he worked at the Columbia mailroom which is why he pressured you to rent to him and why he wanted the last bungalow because its the only one with direct access tothe tunnel (Remember you told me history of Casa and how MGM had a secret underground city You saidthey closed the tunnel 30 years ago and it was hard not to tell you N found it again. He moved into the suite inthe corner where the examining room is where you told me that the studio had their own MD perform abortions on actresses)

I paused, but I would not let myself picture that room.

On July 12 last year N shot his agent Ted Abadi (Im sorry I know its terrible) He was blackballedby the Industry and Teds agency fired N as a client. It was a spur of the moment act because N knew no other agency would take him and his career was over. I didnt realize N did it at first He asked me to be his alibi becaus he didn't have one and he told me he was home alone. I helped him out because I was alone that night too and the cops were going to be on me I was sure But a few monthslater I realized from something N did that he killed Ted himself. I stupidly asked N about it instead of going to the cops N threatened to kill <u>me</u> if I told the cops and hes made my life <u>hell</u> ever since. He made you rent to mebecause he wanted to keep me close. Hes latched onto InCasa Prods and my friends and *business associates He almost never leaves me alone (Hes gone tonight thats how I can write this and get away to hide it) He thinks hecan use me as his ticket back into Holly wood and I can't do anything becaus of Ted because Im an accessory and because N says he'll hurt <u>you</u>*

Last Thursday night. It was Phillips who jumped me at the pool house. I knew why now: I'd seen the tunnel diagram that morning.

N murdered my frien Greta. He came to Bary Ms party and killed her for a screenplay she wrote (Tell the cops he snuck in the back so nobody saw him, I didnt) You remembe that fight in my apartment It was over the same script. G sold it for big bucks and N wanted his name on it because they were partners once and he thought she owed him. I was mad too because I thought the script could launch InCasa if she'd attach me as producer I lent her money and helped her when she wasnt working But she wouldnt help me or N and N killed her because he was desperate (He's not crazy he just wants what he wants. Hes always been that way)

But N cant find a copy of the script. He broke into Gs car before he killed her and couldnt find one And she only had a partial draftwith her when he killed her He thought she left it where he killed her and searched there attacked one of Barrys writers whos doing a feature on InCasa. Ns plan was to tell Gs agent that hes the ghost cowriter. But how can he say that when if he hasnt even seen the whole script? He made me call Gs agent for a copy buttheysaid they didnt have one N is really getting crazy and he doesnt trust me He thinks I have the scriptand holding out on him

Greta fooled everyone with her story about a six-figure movie deal. I'd seen Phillips two days ago. He was still looking for a copy of *GB Dreams Big* and playing the injured cowriter. And Hamilton Ashburn told PPA he'd seen the script. He hadn't; he was trying to screw Phillips with Len Ziskind by saying it was bad.

When I gaveyou the maibox key Mommy I said I leaving town for the weekend to get away but it isn't true but tell Isab it is. N wants me inthe tunnel with him I say its better if Im availabl and not suspicious. I dont know how long that will be but I know youll do the right thing if Im gone too long Goto the cops and tell themabout tunnel Im sure thats where I am. Show them this statement N said if I accuse him he'll say Im the killer and its his word against mine But it wont be becaus I was with Barry M when N killed G

N says he'll frame me with evidence but dont believe it I didn't do anything really wrong <u>I swear</u> and what I did do was under duress. big hug . . .

Scott Dolgin signed his name at the bottom. The signature, like the writing, was herky-jerky.

I stared out the window.

I believed it. It was the only explanation that fit all the facts.

I wondered why Dolgin didn't grab Mrs. May and run to the cops if he'd had time to write a note and stash it blocks away. One guess: he wasn't thinking straight. Another guess: he hoped to avoid a scandal and save himself somehow by some non-police-involved miracle.

Doug must have suspected Phillips. He must have suspected him the minute they received the anonymous tip accusing Dolgin. Who else would have phoned it in? Not Mrs. May, the surrogate mother who removed damaging evidence from Dolgin's bungalow. Not Isabelle Pavich, who wanted to marry him. And Dolgin and Phillips covered each other for Ted Abadi's death.

Two people had called In-Casa Productions a "farce": Greta, and Neil Phillips. It was Phillips in the back office at Barry's party.

Doug had guessed a lot of things. He would never have guessed she was murdered for *GB Dreams Big*.

I folded up Dolgin's confession, put it in the glove compartment, and started the car.

If Barry hadn't been protecting his movie interests, we would've known about the fight the day I found her.

If only I'd hung on to Phillips when I had him at Georgette Bauerdorf's. If only Doug had come.

I saw the fateful *ifs*. I saw the big sweep of Neil Phillips's crime and his ambition. I saw every last detail, every decision, every minute of every day since the day last year he shot Ted Abadi in a rage of frustration.

I knew I was suffering a kind of insanity. I could see everything and feel nothing.

I DROVE TO the Casa de Amor. As I pulled up, I didn't even look toward the Thalberg Building. More camera trucks were parked at the curb; more reporters milled on the sidewalk. A cameraman was panning the Casa's facade. Crime-scene tape had been strung across the entrance to the courtyard, and across the back gates. Two Culver City cops stood guard, watching.

I cut over the lawn before the press people noticed. I was prepared to use Doug's name as a password. I didn't need it; the cops knew my face and waved me forward. They lifted the tape so I could bend under it, then stood together to screen me from the reporters.

There was tape across Mrs. May's porch and Scott Dolgin's porch. A triple string of tape cordoned off Phillips's bungalow and front path. I walked up to Erma's and knocked on her door. Loud sobbing broke out in Dorene's bungalow. It echoed through the courtyard until Erma's voice cut it off:

"We all know Flo's wishes! She wanted to be near her Harry!"

A woman wailed. *"Home of Peace is so far! Flo will want fresh roses every week!"*

Erma's voice was impatient. "We're old, Shirl, we're not crippled! It's just a short hop on the freeway!"

I walked next door, knocked, and went in. The Casa tenants were holding a wake. They sat around in black dresses, without their makeup. Erma wore a black muumuu. The living room had been straightened—the Frito bags and empty booze bottles were gone. Dorene sat on the couch, propped up by pillows. Only Erma recognized me.

She said, "Honey! What happened to *you?*"

"I need to talk to Mrs. Johnson."

"Were you in the tunnel, honey? Is that what happened?"

A tenant sniffled. Erma said, "Quiet!"

It was no good: the tenants heard "tunnel" and started to cry. Crying led to sobbing. They sobbed into their Kleenex and clutched each other's hands. Dorene's eyes filled with tears. Erma shook her head at me. Then she gave in and cried, too.

I sat down between Erma and Dorene. Dorene's crying was silent. I said, "I need to talk to you about Jules Silverman and Georgette Bauerdorf."

Dorene didn't answer and didn't look at me. I didn't know if she could hear, or if she was crying because she saw everyone else crying. Her black dress had moth holes.

I tried again. "Mrs. Johnson, I need to talk—"

Dorene opened her lips. She whispered, "Fix me a drink."

I stood up and walked to the bar. I poured her a bourbon over ice, and the same for the other tenants. I handed glasses around; that stopped the crying. Erma turned hers down. Too early in the day, she said.

Dorene guzzled her drink and seemed to perk up. I'd poured her the stiffest one. I said, "What did you tell Greta about Jules—?"

"*Ben!*"

Dorene blurted out the name. I said, "What about Ben?"

A tenant wailed, "*It's all his fault! The policemen said—!*"

Erma broke in. "Button it, Shirley—we know what happened. You're upsetting everyone."

Shirley bit her knuckles; she was past sixty and jaundice yellow. Another tenant put an arm around her.

Erma leaned close and spoke low to me. "Ben threatened Dorie, you know, before she collapsed outside. He said not to talk about your Silverman person."

I spoke low, too. "How do you know?"

"Dorie said."

"What else did she say?"

Erma shook her head. "Dorie will never tell you what you want to know. None of us knows."

"She told Greta Stenholm."

Erma shrugged. "Greta was a beautiful girl."

I looked at Dorene. A lie came to me. I raised my voice and addressed the tenants.

"Mrs. May died because of a man named Jules Silverman. He is a murderer. Mrs. Johnson has information that will help the police catch Silverman, but she won't give it to them."

Shirley let loose. *"Floooooooooooo!"*

The other tenants joined in. *"Poor Flo!" "Dorene!" "Tell the police!" "Flo is dead!" "Dorieeeeeee!"*

Shirley wailed and the tenants sobbed. The noise built but Dorene didn't move or speak. The noise built more. It made my head ache. It didn't affect Dorene.

Erma finally got mad. She reached around me and slapped Dorene in the face. Dorene fell against my shoulder. The tenants gasped and shut up. Dorene lay there and still didn't speak.

Erma heaved herself off the couch, went to the bar, and started pulling out the bourbon bottles. I looked at Dorene: she was watching the process.

Erma said, "You're on the wagon as of now, Dorie. No more joy juice until you tell her what she wants to know."

Erma set the bottles by the front door and went back for a second load. Dorene's arm shot up. She was pointing into the kitchen.

Erma nodded. "Drunks only understand one language, honey. There's something in the kitchen. I pulled Dorie out of a cupboard this morning."

I leaned Dorene off me and stood up. "Which cupboard?"

"Under the sink—you'll see where."

I walked into the kitchen, using the cane to push junk out of my way. The doors under the sink were open. I got down on one knee and stuck my head inside. It was dark. I took the cane, reached for the light switch, and pushed it up. The ceiling light went on. I opened the doors wider.

The cupboard, like the kitchen, was crammed with sacks.

The sacks were paper, plastic, and cloth. I hauled them out and opened them one by one. They held empty liqueur bottles, old restaurant menus, old lingerie, used cosmetic containers, *TV Guides* from ten years ago, Las Vegas souvenirs, obscene corkscrews, joke cocktail napkins, fancy swizzle sticks, and matchbooks from bars all over North America.

My hands got covered with dust. I dumped sack after sack and shoved the contents into a pile. It was nothing but cheap, useless junk.

Erma called from the living room. "Find anything, honey?"

I stood up and searched the sacks on the kitchen counter. I searched the sacks in the sink. I searched the sacks in the cupboards over the sink. I searched the sacks that blocked the kitchen door. I searched all the drawers. I searched the broom closet. Dust rose and stuck to my clothes. I brushed it off and sneezed and sneezed.

I pulled sacks out of a corner cupboard. There was a lazy Susan for pots and pans. I twirled it and pulled sacks off. I searched the sacks one by one. I reached behind the lazy Susan and felt around the back edges. My fingers touched something. I pulled it out. It was just another sack—a crinkled paper sack from a defunct local grocery store. The top was twisted shut.

I untwisted it.

The sack wasn't full like the rest of them: I had to reach way down in. I found a bent-up license plate. I pulled it out and unbent it. Enamel flaked off at the crease. It was an old gold-on-black California plate. The number: 59 B 875.

I set the license plate to one side. I was suddenly moving in slow motion.

I pulled a woman's ring out of the sack. It had a violet quartz stone in a filigreed setting.

Amethyst.

I set the ring beside the license plate.

One last thing at the bottom of the sack. I pulled it out.

A roll of light brown, stretchy material. Thin red borders and a frayed end—like someone had torn a section off it.

No labels or identifying trademarks. I took a guess: a Tetra Brand, ten-inch, nonrubber elastic bandage. Obsolete in America by 1944. Impossible for the cops to trace, because any soldier could have brought it home from a foreign hospital. Impossible to find because it was hidden on a back shelf in a private whorehouse in Culver City.

I sat down on the floor and pressed the bandage against my mouth.

CHAPTER
TWENTY-NINE

I WAS CLOSE now. I had one idea and one goal.

I borrowed twenty dollars from Erma and headed out to Malibu. It was Friday afternoon — the coast highway was jammed with traffic leaving town. I sat in the car and sweated because my jacket hid the bloodstains on my shirt. I inched along in first gear. I was in pain but I didn't want to take any pills. I didn't want to mess up my clarity.

I turned inland at Ramirez Canyon and drove up to the Silverman estate. Silverman's gates were standing open. I didn't stop to wonder why — I drove straight in. There was nobody on the road. I drove almost to the house, veered off, and hid the car in the trees.

I'd brought my smallest tape recorder from home. I loaded a tape and wedged the recorder into my jeans. I threaded the microphone wire under my shirt and clipped the minimicrophone to my collar. I checked the mirror. The round black dot looked like a button.

I turned on the recorder and cranked the volume. I closed my jacket over the bulge in my jeans.

I left the cane in the car and limped to the edge of the tree line. A helicopter was parked in a clearing on the land side of the house. The propellers were spinning. I saw a man in the cockpit and a man crouched beside the landing gear. Hannah Silverman was bent over talking to the guy outside. She held her hair to protect it from propeller wash.

The Silvermans were making a getaway.

I stayed in the trees and circled the drive on the ocean side. Stacks of Vuitton luggage sat on the terrace of the house: it was too much for just the weekend. Three Latin maids walked out the front door. One had a picnic basket, one had carry-on bags. One was pushing a dolly. They piled some of the luggage on the dolly, then argued over how to get the dolly down the steps. I ducked, left the trees, and limped across to the terrace. I hid behind the stone balustrade and waited.

An excellent time to run for it, I thought. Doug in trouble, the cops sequestered: when the smoke cleared the Silvermans would not be available for questioning. Jules wasn't taking chances.

I watched the maids wrestle the dolly down the terrace steps. Luggage fell off. They piled it back on and headed to the clearing. I lost sight of them around a corner of the house.

I climbed the balustrade and dashed for the front door. I hopped on my good foot for speed.

The front door was open and the foyer was empty. The whole big place was quiet—I couldn't hear any maids or medical help. I started down the hall toward Silverman's den. Silverman was coming up the hall toward me. He wore street clothes and bombed along in his motorized wheelchair. A blanket covered his lap and legs. On the blanket was his Oscar statuette. He looked fine.

Silverman saw me and stopped the chair. He said, "How did you get in?"

I kept walking. For technical reasons I had to be closer to him. I said, "Your gates are open."

Silverman tried to go around me. He called, "Hannah!"

I stepped in front of his chair. He dodged the other direction. I stepped in front of him. His rubber tires squeaked on the marble floor. I smelled menthol rub.

I said, "59 B 875."

Silverman tried to go around me again. I grabbed the wheelchair and wedged one foot against the tire. He hit the green button on his chair arm. I put my finger on the red button. The wheelchair stalled out.

I said, "An amethyst ring. A license plate. A bandage roll."

"*Hannah!*"

I said, "You stole her car and the contents of her purse to throw the cops off. You wanted them to think it was a burglary gone bad and they were looking for a thief. You drove east instead of west to throw them off. You picked a black neighborhood to dump the car to throw them off more. When you ran out of gas, you removed the license plate and hitchhiked back to the Casa de Amor, where you knew a drunken brawl was in progress. You needed an alibi because you knew you were seen talking to her in the Canteen parking lot. You picked the worst drunk for your alibi—"

Silverman's face had gotten hard. He said, "You want money, of course."

"I found the sack in Dorene Johnson's kitchen. The cops don't have anything else on you. The lightbulb with your thumbprint was tossed, and Dorene's too alcoholic to make a retraction stick. But the cops may or may not care about Georgette Bauerdorf now that they have a confession on Abadi and Stenholm. They were looking at you for Greta because she was found in a bathtub, too."

Silverman grabbed his wheels and tried to back the chair up. I held on. "Are you interested in who killed Ted Abadi?"

Silverman stopped fighting me. He let go of the wheels and shook his head. He said, "Not in the least."

I stood back. "How is it that Dorene still had the sack? Why didn't you get rid of the evidence?"

Silverman glanced down the hall. There was nobody around—nobody to come save him. A leather pouch hung off the wheelchair arm. Silverman reached in and pulled out a glasses case. He got out his glasses and put them on. He said, "Remind me what your name is, I've forgotten."

"Why didn't you get rid of the evidence?"

Silverman tilted his head and studied me. "Ann, if memory serves, and I'm told you're some sort of anti-Industry critic for Barry Melling."

"Why didn't you throw everything down a sewer? Why carry it all the way back to the Casa de Amor?"

Silverman crossed his hands over the Oscar in his lap. He had relaxed. "You're offering me a trade. You have the sack but you don't want money. Like every reviewer in the world you want a job in pictures, and you'd like me to arrange it for you."

"I want what Greta Stenholm wanted."

Silverman smiled. "Good, because I don't believe anyone who claims altruistic motives. The first time the Stenholm girl blackmailed me, she wanted the name of Ted's killer. I didn't believe her. But I believed her when she asked for money and a deal to write and direct. You want me to satisfy your curiosity on a few matters and provide you an entrée to the picture business."

I said, "Yes on both counts."

Silverman nodded. "I will help you on one count. I'll pick up a telephone and find you a job by next week at the latest."

He reached for his wheels. I wedged my foot against one tire.

"You were in a panic, maybe even a blackout. You arrived at the Casa and realized you still had the license, ring, and bandage roll. You also had a time crunch because your ship left Long Beach at six in the morning, and it was already, say, three. Everybody at the Casa was drunk or passed out. Dorene was a famous pack rat and your best alibi, so you buried the evidence in her kitchen. You meant to come back and get rid of it, and you tried to, say, after the war. You couldn't find it, but Dorene suspected something because you searched her kitchen. To be on the safe side, you've supplied her with booze all these decades. No need to kill her outright — not with her thirst. Besides, you're not a killer. You just had a thing for Georgette that got out of hand. She told you she was engaged to the soldier in El Paso, and you forced your way into her apartment to convince her of your feelings. You were young and in love."

Silverman took off his glasses and put them back in the case. He said, "You tell a good story."

"It was an accident — you didn't mean to kill her."

"You'll hear from someone next week. I'll have them call you at your newspaper."

"But rape isn't an accident. You stuffed the bandage in her mouth to keep her quiet. That's how she died — suffocation."

Silverman looked at me. "You're an imaginative girl. You have a great many story ideas, I'm sure."

"Only one. It's about the murder of a Hollywood Canteen hostess and her best friend's search for the killer."

I unbuttoned my jacket and showed him the tape recorder.

Silverman went pale. "*I admit nothing!*"

I turned to leave. He grabbed the Oscar and swung it at me. I blocked his arm, ripped the statue out of his hand, and chucked it away. It went clanging and skidding along the marble floor. Silverman stood up to retrieve it. He got his legs caught in the lap blanket. He flailed and fell forward and hit his head on the floor. The wheelchair shimmied and tipped over on top of him.

He moaned once. I saw him convulse, then he lay there, silent. I stepped around him and walked out of the house.

CHAPTER
THIRTY

I DROVE straight to the Malibu Sheriff's substation. It wasn't far from Silverman's. The coast highway was clear going that direction.

I parked in the parking lot. I pulled Scott Dolgin's confession out of the glove compartment and put it in the sack with the Georgette Bauerdorf evidence.

Grabbing the cane, I limped into the reception area of the station. I was spotted with blood. I'd taken off my jacket, and the effort with Silverman had popped more stitches on my left side. The deputy at the desk took one look at me and asked if I was the lady from the Tunnel Massacre. I said I was, and said I had something to report. He ran around the desk, showed me into an empty office, made me sit down, and asked me to wait.

He came back in a minute, followed by what appeared to be every cop on shift. One guy identified himself as the watch commander. I didn't get his name; he was a sergeant. He started to tell me the situation with the tunnel, how the Sheriff's and LAPD viewed it, what the district attorney was saying, how the media was acting. I only heard words; I couldn't absorb what they meant. I knew the cops were waiting for a firsthand account from me. But I was in no way capable of that.

When the sergeant finished, I told him we had to locate Doug Lockwood. I held up the sack. I said it contained physical evidence pertaining to our three murders.

Three, the sergeant said. He'd heard there were two murders. I told him to tell his Unsolved guys McManus and Gadtke that I got what amounted to a confession on Georgette Bauerdorf. An audiotape and other proof were in the sack. And they should hurry, because Georgette's killer was trying to leave L.A. as we spoke.

The sergeant took the sack and took off. The other cops filed out behind him. The desk deputy asked if I felt all right, if I'd like water or a Coke. I said, water, thanks, and aspirin if he had some. He brought me water and two aspirin, and left me alone again. I wanted the painkillers now, but they were in the car.

I sat there.

I was in a strange state. My brain registered that everything was over. But my thoughts were racing down a very strange track. I couldn't control them.

I didn't want to talk to Doug. I didn't want to talk to the authorities. I didn't want to go home. I didn't want to go to the paper. I didn't want to go any place where I'd be mobbed by reporters. I didn't want to rest. I didn't want to see a doctor. I didn't want to think about the future.

I was thinking about my sister.

Father flew back to Texas today. Sis would be a wreck. She always was after their visits. I had to try again with her. I had to get her away from Father. Not everything was finished: I had to get her away. He was killing her. He'd kill her. I had to prevent it.

Part of me knew this was craziness.

Part of me thought it was stone-cold reason. Saving Sis was absolutely the only thing left for me to do now. I had to do it without delay. I had to do it right this exact very minute.

I reached for the telephone on the desk and dialed her number.

A woman's voice answered the phone. I said who I was, and the voice said she was Sis's neighbor. She'd been trying to get ahold of me. Come to Venice as soon as possible, she said. Something had happened to Sis.

A DOZEN PEOPLE stood in the hall outside my sister's apartment. They turned and looked as I stepped out of the elevator. I knew from their faces it was bad.

A woman walked toward me. It was a neighbor I'd met, a friend of Sis's from AA. Her eyes were red from crying.

She said, "I only found her an hour ago. Nobody heard anything—we were all at work. I've called the ambulance."

I lifted my cane and pushed people aside. The neighbor followed me into Sis's apartment.

She whispered, "We had a date for coffee. I called but her phone rang and she didn't answer, so I came down..."

I stopped still.

"Ann, I'm sorry—"

I put my finger to my lips. I had seen.

Sis did it in front of her shrine. She'd called it that when she put it together. She'd taken family photographs and mementos of her past and made an altar on an old table that was a Whitehead heirloom. She burned candles there, she'd told me. She talked to Mother's picture and prayed for Father's enlightenment.

She lay twisted sideways in a chair facing the shrine. Her eyes were open and she was staring at the ceiling. She'd shot herself through the heart. Blood was crusted around the wound. It had soaked her clothes and the chair upholstery. Both of her hands were clenched around the Colt. She'd laid the muzzle right on her chest and pulled the trigger with her thumbs.

I could not move. I could only stare at the body.

The phone started to ring. I didn't move. The neighbor waited for me to answer. I didn't move. I had no power to move.

The neighbor answered it herself. "Hello?...One moment, please." She tapped me. "It's your father."

I just stood there. She put the receiver up to my ear and tapped me again. I said, "Yes?"

Father said, "I'll be damned—Elizabeth Ann."

"Yes."

"Where the hell's your sister? She's supposed to take me to the airport. On second thought, since you're there, how about you drive? I had plenty of your sister on Wednesday."

"Yes."

"Then get over to the hotel and I mean pronto. I like to be there early, you girls know that."

He hung up. I just stood there. The neighbor hung up the telephone. She took my arm and tried to lead me to a chair. I pulled away from her. I raised my cane and smashed it down on Sis's shrine. Photographs and mementos flew. I raised my cane again and smashed it down on the shrine. The neighbor tried to catch my arm. I raised my cane again and smashed it down on the shrine. Glass shattered and wood cracked. I raised my cane again and smashed it down on the shrine.

I TOOK THE off-ramp at La Cienega and turned south.

A primer-gray van curved down the ramp behind me. We were being followed. I knew now it wasn't coincidence. There was a van like it parked in Sis's alley. I'd seen it again outside Father's hotel. It had followed me from Venice; now it was following me to the airport. I couldn't see who the driver was. I had my suspicions.

Father looked around. "Why're we going this way, missy? I believe the 405 takes us directly to the airport."

I said, "I want to show you the pumpjacks in Baldwin Hills. It's kind of great in the middle of a city."

Father shook his head. "They're just old producing fields."

I shrugged. He said, "You better not make me late."

I'd picked him up at his hotel downtown. He was waiting out front with a drink in his hand—he had a buzz on. Night was falling; I stayed in the car. He didn't notice my injuries. He hadn't heard about the tunnel. He only watched two things on TV: sports and weather. The Colt was wedged under my seat.

Father turned on the radio.

"There is sad news for Los Angeles tonight. Retired film producer and prominent philanthropist Jules Silverman died this afternoon at his Malibu estate. He was eighty-five. Silverman won an Academy Award for—"

I turned the radio off. Father said, "What is wrong with you?"

He turned the radio back on. I turned it off. I said, "Didn't Grandpap make his first bundle in the East Texas oil boom in the thirties?"

Father looked at me. I said, "Did he know a wildcatter named George Bauerdorf?"

Father reached for the radio. "I don't recall the name. Why?"

I swerved and bumped two tires over the median. Father grabbed the dashboard. "Watch out, for Christ's sake!"

I swerved back into the lane. Father tried to grab the steering wheel. I shoved his arm away.

"What in the jumped-up hell is going on, Ann?"

I checked the mirrors and slammed on the brakes. Father caught himself on the dashboard. *"Goddamn it to hell!"*

The van almost rear-ended us. It cut into the left lane and speeded up. I checked over my shoulder. The driver was Dale Denney.

He pulled up beside me and rolled down his window. His nose was still taped; his face was puffy and bruised. I floored the gas. It flung Father against his seat. The van cut into my lane and accelerated ahead of me.

Father shouted, *"Who's that now, Christ?!"*

The land was dark on both sides of the street. We were in Baldwin Hills. There were no houses; just the oil fields fenced with chain-link.

I saw an opening in traffic and cranked a U-turn. The car jolted over the median; there were loud thumps. I headed back north.

Father yelled, *"Stop the damn car!"*

I checked my mirrors. The van kept going south. Denney hadn't noticed I was gone yet.

Father lunged for the steering wheel. I elbowed him off. I stood on the brakes, skidded across the gravel shoulder, and plowed into the chain-link in the dark. I hit the steering wheel. Father's head hit the windshield and snapped back.

I went cold. I could see everything very clearly. I reached under the seat, found the Colt, cocked the hammer, and aimed it at him. He was a foot away. I pulled the trigger. The gun kicked, the muzzle flashed. Father slammed sideways. I pulled the trigger again. Father's arms went up. I pulled the trigger again. Father's shirt caught fire. He yelled and thrashed for his door handle. The door flew open and he fell onto the shoulder. I aimed down. I pulled the trigger again. I emptied the chamber. The noise numbed my ears.

But something was wrong.

I lowered the Colt.

Father was rolling on the gravel. He was trying to put out the flames on his shirt. He yelled, *"Jesus H. Christ!"* and cursed me by name. But he wasn't bleeding. He wasn't shot. He wasn't dead.

I jerked open the cylinder of the Colt, dumped out the spent shells, and picked one up.

Blanks. Doug had given me blanks —

I was rammed from behind. My neck whiplashed; I dropped the shell. I jammed the car into first, twirled the wheel, and punched the gas. I fishtailed back onto the pavement going north.

Denney pulled up on my right. He was pointing a gun through his window. I ducked and covered up. My passenger window exploded. The bullet grazed my hip. The impact burned — my thigh burned and went numb. I stood on the gas and booted it for the closest freeway. Denney stayed on my right bumper. I saw the freeway entrance and waited. At the last second, I yanked the wheel right. Denney swerved to avoid me. He scraped a cement pylon broadside. I cranked a hard right and floored it up the ramp. The engine strained.

I checked my mirrors and cut over to the fast lane. I took the box of shells and dumped it on the seat.

Brass .41 shell casings. The base looked normal. The other end was crimped shut. Blanks. That's why he kept loading the Colt for me.

There was a piece of paper in with the shells. He'd left a note. I opened it and read by the light of the dashboard:

"I didn't want you to do something that couldn't be undone. I love you."

I heard a horn and checked my mirror. Denney came barreling up the freeway behind me. One of his headlights was gone.

I hit the gas. I whispered, "Doug."